GRAVE CREEK CONNECTIONS

GRAVE CREEK CONNECTIONS

A novel by

Daniel Isaac Morris

ISBN-10 0-9828250-0-5

ISBN-13 9780982825006

ACKNOWLEGEMENTS

Lin Fowler and Fred Schroyer helped put this book into final form. Lin is a steadfast friend, as is Fred…but—well—Fred is Fred.

Thanks to Kelley and Dan, for their forbearance and love. Special thanks to my extended family and the friends who give meaning to life.

FOR BARBARA

This book is a work of fiction, and any similarities to places or persons, living or dead, is coincidental. While I refer to certain historical facts, be aware that these may at times be fictionalized and intentionally inconsistent with true historical accounts. The book, *Who Really Wrote the Book of Mormon?* authored by Wayne L. Cowdery, Donald R. Scales, and Howard A. Davis gives an account of the controversy concerning the founding of Mormonism and the Church of Jesus Christ of Latter Day Saints. The controversy is well documented, and this work neither supports nor disputes the authors' findings, since any controversy of a religious nature is settled as matter of belief and faith. I have the deepest respect for the beliefs, and particularly the family values, of the Church of Jesus Christ of Latter Day Saints.

The unfortunate scandals that involved a few individuals and took place at the New Vrindavan community in West Virginia are matters of historical and court record. There is no intention here to assign blame or judgment. I respect the Hare Krishna beliefs and the International Society for Krishna Consciousness (ISKCON).

The facts concerning the history of Moundsville, West Virginia and its state prison are authentic, except there is no evidence that Nazis or Russians ever were present at the prison or in Moundsville—this is pure fiction. I invite readers to visit the penitentiary (tours available) to experience the vibes for themselves.

There is a lovely county in the southwestern corner of Pennsylvania, but it is not George County, the people and places of which are entirely fictitious.

GRAVE CREEK CONNECTIONS

*Now Gentle Reader the writer who wishes well
to thy present and thy future existence entreats thee
to peruse this volume with a clear head a pure heart
and a candid mind. If thou shalt that thy head and
thy heart are both improved it will afford him more
satisfaction than the approbation of ten thousand who
have received no benefit.* —Solomon Spaulding

CHAPTER ONE

WETLAND

Peepers, new frogs of spring, threw their voices into the otherwise soundless gloom as the loping drone of an engine imposed itself on the wetland night. A black van pulled to a stop on a remote back road in the western end of George County, Pennsylvania.

In the nondescript van, with its mud-spattered license plate, two people sat in the dark for some time to make sure no one followed or approached. The sound of the engine was replaced by a bullfrog croaking in the distance, as the driver killed the ignition.

"I've been here before," said the driver in a hushed voice. "This is really the middle of nowhere. Let's get this over with." The driver pushed a button on the dash and a solenoid releasing the tailgate clicked from the rear.

The driver's partner gave a quick nod and reached for the door handle. They got out and quietly closed the front doors, then went to the back and raised the tailgate. Inside, under a blanket, was a form — undeniably a human body, in black plastic. In fact, the body had been placed feet-first into a large garbage bag, while another bag had been pulled over the head to the waist, where the two were joined with duct tape.

The eerie blue glow from a spelunker's flashlight cast over the body. Its special luminance gave off enough light to see, but was not bright enough to attract attention from a distance.

They carried the body to the breast of a dam that held back a small pond. They laid it out to remove the wrapping. "Make sure you don't leave anything," said the driver.

"If you want to be sure about everything, why don't you do it yourself?" said the other.

After some difficulty with the tape, they removed the two bags, revealing a young woman barely out of her teens. She was dressed in slacks and a blouse and wore an oversized pullover sweater. In the night air, wisps of white vapor rose from the figure under the sweater.

"Put her face down with her head over the dam, away from the water, and push her hair up above her neck," said the passenger, who stood at her outstretched feet, fumbling for something in a jacket pocket.

The passenger took out a revolver, retrieved a silencer from the other pocket, and threaded it onto the muzzle of the gun. Then the passenger pushed a small switch under the barrel, causing a fiery red dot to form on the girl's sweater. The gun was adjusted until the dot, which seemed much brighter in the dark, was centered at the base of her skull. There was a brief thud as the silencer muffled the blast, loud enough to end the peepers' song, but not to carry any distance.

The two then unceremoniously pushed the body over the breast of the dry side of the dam, where it fell to the bottom. They picked up the plastic shrouds and strips of tape, made a last sweep of the scene, and returned to the van. After a few moments, the vehicle eased from its original position, then stopped. The passenger got out and turned on a bright flashlight that flooded the former parking spot. After a few seconds, satisfied, the passenger got back into the van. "Not a track, nothing from which anyone could get an impression. The dirt was packed hard where we pulled off, so it's cool." The van snapped into drive and slowly faded into the night.

Minutes later, a gentle spring rain began to form faint circles on the surface of the pond. It was a rain that would cause crushed grass to rise anew and cleanse the scene as if the van were never there. Unaware of the new addition to their wetland, the peepers found their voices once again and the cool, damp night settled in.

CHAPTER TWO

THE SEARCH BEGINS

The farm pond wasn't much of a pond anymore, overgrown with cattails and lily pads and green scum floating over its surface. Over the years, much of it had filled with silt. In the shallow end, the water had been overtaken by a colony of frogs. In the deep end, where children used to swim, they would now have to wade, but the water was so filled with algae and duckweed that wading was unlikely. Whitetail deer tracks and raccoon prints dotted the mud where a trickle from a spring sometimes flowed, adding to the ooze that the shore had become. Mosquitoes, dragonflies, and an occasional bee dipped and dived about the green-colored muck.

The pond rippled and refracted the April sunlight in a way that belied its stagnant condition. From the rise above it, the water looked healthy and inviting, as it lay stretched out in the spring sunshine. The first leaves of the summer to come were showing promise in small buds on the trees surrounding the pond.

"Morning, Eden," said Sheriff Buckey.

"Morning, Buckey," Eden replied.

Eden Whitloe had been a Deputy longer than he liked to think about. When the Sheriff appointed him ten years ago— unbeknownst to him, at his father's request—he was fresh out of college and ambitious only to follow the path of least resistance. Employment opportunities for philosophy majors weren't—well, let's say no one was beating down his door with offers. He wasn't detectably ambitious, a major reason Buckey swore him in as Deputy. Buckey didn't need some kid with political aspirations snapping at his heels when reelection time rolled around. Whitloe was the perfect Barney Fife for the Sheriff of what could have been Mayberry, had it been farther south of the Mason-Dixon line.

The Mason-Dixon Line formed the southern border of George County, which was "the north" as far as southerners were concerned. And Eden Whitloe was no Barney Fife—close, but neither as dim-witted nor mild-mannered. Eden was taller, but not lanky, with not an ounce of fat. He didn't work out, yet had that appearance. Had Buckey been tasked to describe his Deputy, he would have called him unambitious and nondescript—pretty accurate, since Whitloe always wore a uniform and military hairstyle.

No one called the Sheriff by his first name. "Just call me Buckey," he told folks. He once admitted to his Deputy that he never liked his first name, "Oliver." It sounded too formal and "Oliver Buckey" was not an electable name for a Sheriff. He told Eden it sounded like a funeral parlor owner, or someone who sold farm equipment.

But Oliver Buckey looked the part of Sheriff. He wore those reflector shades and had a 44 waist, although he bragged that his belt was a 38, just like his pocket gun. When anyone referred to the overhang above his belt, he just smiled. "That's my tool shed. Every man needs a shed for his tool." Buckey was big on clichés; county Sheriffs get a lot of practice.

Sheriff Buckey had the name and look of a one-horse-town Sheriff. He affected it and used it for all it was worth. Eden Whitloe, nicknamed "Eeed," was no competition, lacking an electable name, Sheriff's gut, or affected redneck accent. Eden worried about Buckey surviving the next election, since Buckey would have to reappoint him. Eden made sure Oliver Buckey remained the Sheriff of George County, since that was how Eden would keep his job and more importantly, his pension.

Buckey and Eden got along just fine, both down-home good old boys. The Deputy was about fifty watts brighter than the Sheriff and wasn't nearly the country-boy Sheriff that Buckey was, but perhaps time and circumstance would take care of that.

"Don't feel like rain," offered Buckey.

"Nope," the Deputy said, looking into the clear April sky. "Not a trace of a cloud. It'll be a fine day if all of this stuff Amara McClure claims she can do will do any good, whatever it is that Amara McClure does."

"Don't start now," Buckey warned. "You know full well what Miss McClure does. You know as much about it as I do. We've been over it enough this past week. You gotta git with thuh program, boy." Even though the Deputy was nearly his own age, Buckey often called him "boy." Just to make sure his Deputy knew his place in the pecking order.

Amara McClure could have been called any number of things, particularly in these parts. Out in California or up in New York City, they would have called her a psychic. But down here in southwestern Pennsylvania, we might call her a conjurer or even a witch. In some remote parts of the county, she would be shunned or maybe even burned at the stake.

CHAPTER THREE

A SHORT HISTORY OF GEORGE CO. CRIME

Myra Kinchloe had been gone for over a month. The 21-year-old coed had been missing since the annual St. Patrick's Day party at Dunlow's Restaurant and Bar. The young college coed had apparently just up and vanished.

This wasn't a big city case of a drunken university student going to a scroungy bar and falling into the hands of some pervert. She attended Rainelle College, an upper-class, church-related liberal arts college, not one of those hard-drinking state universities. It took its name from the county seat and its religion from the Presbyterian Church.

The town of Rainelle is so small that it doesn't even have a slum. There is no spray-painted graffiti, except one message that lasted about a month. It was out of reach on the railroad overpass, and was painted over as soon as the railroad people got around to it. When graffiti or trash appear, articles in the *Georgian Observer* soon follow with angry citizens demanding that the police "do something." It was during those times that Eden Whitloe felt it was much better to be a Deputy Sheriff than a Rainelle police officer.

George County has its share of crime, mostly of the stolen-bicycle variety. There is a dope bust nearly every year, and most assuredly just before any election. Buckey liked to have the newspaper reporters come up to the courthouse while he unloaded a truckload of weed onto the sidewalk. Every election year, the *Georgian Observer* featured a picture of Sheriff Buckey standing on the courthouse lawn, in front of the statue of George Washington, holding a marijuana plant—that is, Buckey holds the plant, not George. Deputy Whitloe told him that some day there would be a statue of him right beside the one of our first president. He would be holding a branch of pot, just like the heroes of old held an olive or palm branch.

Up until 1996, no one living could remember a murder. But, in '96 Fred Schroder up and offed Don Skomish over a bimbo they were both seeing. After an all-night bout with Jim Beam, Don picked her up at Kelley's Saloon. She wasn't very pretty, resembling Charles Laughton, complete with a mole sprouting hair. No one had any idea that Fred was all that attached to her, but they found out soon enough.

No one thought old Fred meant to stick Don as bad as he did. Fred may have thought he'd give Don a little poke and Don would go away and lick his wounds. But after the little poke, Don rushed Fred and the knife got in the way. Most reasonable folks would say it was an accident, but since it was a full-fledged barroom brawl, everyone in Rainelle was out for Fred's well-weathered hide.

Aside from some poor thief who was hung on the courthouse lawn in the mid-1800s, no one in the county gave a thought to the death penalty... until Fred came to trial. Rednecks from southern George County wanted the D.A. to stick IVs in Fred's arm, but good sense prevailed and he got by with a little manslaughter time up at the Lewisburg Pen.

Until Myra Kinchloe came up missing, crime was business-as-usual in George County: stolen bicycles and gas station drive-offs. No drive-by shootings, never a true stickup, no violent crime since Buckey took office, and Buckey took full credit for it.

Of course, we don't count the "Sean Ryan murder." No one knows for sure if it was a murder. No one could prove anything, and there never was enough evidence for trial, but that didn't keep people from talking. You can't say someone was murdered just because his wife went to Carl Dulaney's Hardware and bought some rat poison.

There was never an autopsy because no one in George County could perform one until the County got a real coroner. You would suppose that, if someone were shot, the authorities would have to check them out, but no one was ever shot. They did autopsy old Don Skomish, though. They paid the coroner to find out if he was drunk and what killed him. Of course, they could have asked anyone in the bar about the drunk part, and with a six-inch knife sticking out of his chest where his heart was, the cause of death was pretty obvious. More tax money well spent.

Sean Ryan was cremated two days after he died, so they couldn't dig him up and prove it was rat poison that killed him. Joey Dulaney—that's Carl's kid—did say Kathleen bought the rat baits, but there wasn't a thing they could do about it. The "Sean Ryan murder" was just one of those everybody-says things. Kate Ryan left town, and no one heard from her again until folks read her obituary in the Wheeling, West Virginia papers.

CHAPTER FOUR

MISSING PERSON

When Myra Kinchloe came up missing, it was a shocker to the community. If she had been a skank who frequented Lin Kelley's Saloon, folks might have felt differently. She might have been just another runaway. In a few days, a missing-person report would have been filed, and posters would have appeared at the Interstate truck stop. A few months would have passed, and that would have been the end of it.

But Myra wasn't a loose woman, and she had disappeared on her way back from Dunlow's, a nice, respectable place. She was a student at Rainelle College. Her dad, Bradford T. Kinchloe III, was on the college's Board of Trustees and was a muckety-muck in the Presbyterian Church. He wasn't about to let Myra be forgotten, which he made clear to Buckey on no uncertain terms. "Your reelection," Brad Kinchloe told Buckey, "depends on whether my daughter is found in one piece."

Brad got news crews from the area TV stations in Pittsburgh and Wheeling to interview him, although it never did turn into a media circus. "Small-town coed missing" doesn't cut it in big city news outlets unless there's a politician or a celebrity involved.

On top of Brad Kinchloe's attempts to get news coverage, Ted Dunlow, the restaurant owner, offered a reward for information leading to the arrest of anyone involved in Myra's disappearance. Dunlow's wasn't a dive. It was a well-respected establishment, frequented by the town's attorneys and businesspeople. The D.A. was a frequent visitor at Dunlow's bar. Ted said that he didn't want people to think Myra's disappearance was related to his restaurant and bar. "I don't run that kind of place," he said. "We don't allow no trash to hang around."

"What makes you think trash was involved?" Eden Whitloe asked Ted, just to get his goat.

"Nobody from the right part of town would do anything like that," Ted replied indignantly. It occurred to the Deputy to ask what he meant by "doing anything like that," but he let it go.

The reward wasn't helpful. It's not that George Countians couldn't use the money. It's that no one in these parts messes where they have no business. If it was one of theirs, it might have been different. But it was a big shot's daughter, so everyone tended to their own affairs.

Attention focused awhile on Myra's boyfriend, if you wanted to call him that. Myra was quiet and bookish, and her boyfriend was a geek. Hiram J. Tarpley's friends would have known him as "Hi," if he'd had any. A stereotypical nerd, a self-caricature, Hiram wore horn-rimmed glasses, and though Eden half-expected it, they weren't held together with adhesive tape. Hiram had an honest-to-God pocket protector crammed with every color of pen and pencil. He always buttoned his top shirt button, and his Adam's apple darted above and below the collar as he talked or swallowed. He blended Ichabod Crane with Ray Bolger, his high-water pants hitched high and a long surplus of belt hanging after he used the last notch. "Nervous, twitchy, dork," Eden Whitloe noted in the margin of his note pad.

The interview started with Eden saying, "Hi." Hiram Tarpley said, "Who, me?" and it went downhill from there.

As it turned out, Hi had the perfect alibi. He was at a youth counselors' meeting in nearby Morgantown, West Virginia the night Myra came up missing. He had been there two days prior to her disappearance and returned to Rainelle when he heard about her. Witnesses verified that he attended class and accounted for all of his time in Morgantown.

Street talk in Rainelle helped little. Townsfolk hummed with speculation about Myra's disappearance, but the frequency of the hum was like the 60-hertz variety; it contained little information and was mostly annoying.

"Bet she'll be back and showing off a big wedding ring. Probably flew out to Las Vegas and got married in one of them wedding chapels," speculated Carl Dulaney, as he sat for a haircut. "Bet they had one of them weddings with Elvis impersonators," he said.

"Nope, I don't think she'd ever do that," said the barber. "She'd be afraid her daddy would write her out of his will."

"Might be pregnant," suggested Carl's boy, Joey, who was next in line for a haircut. "Some girls leave town to have their kid, you know."

"How do you know so much about that?" asked the barber, punching Carl in the shoulder so that Joey couldn't see him. Carl didn't seem to take notice.

Everyone in town knew Myra's daddy had inherited oil and gas money and invested in real estate. Just about everybody sucked up to him, to his face, but he was known not to part with his money easily. If Myra had gotten into boy trouble, she would have known how to deal with it, even if she didn't tell her father. Eden Whitloe had the feeling that something really bad had happened to her. He knew it would be fortunate indeed if she returned unharmed.

It wasn't that Myra was a spoiled brat or trouble or anything like that. That's what you would expect from talking to her daddy, but she wasn't the least bit wild and not nearly the nerd her boyfriend seemed to be. She was attractive in the way that a chorus girl who fades into the scenery is attractive. Not bad, she just didn't stand out.

Lord only knew what she saw in Hiram Tarpley. But the Deputy

made a mental note: if any future daughter of his came home dragging a Tarpley, he would be cleaning his gun at the time.

CHAPTER FIVE

HEEDING THE PSYCHIC

"Buckey, the voters are going to see you're using Miss McClure, and her hocus-pocus or witchcraft or whatever it is, as the last-gasp effort of a desperate man," Eden Whitloe said.

"Ain't got nothing to lose," Buckey replied. "Hell, we've tried everything else I know of to find Myra. The FBI hasn't been much help since there's no real evidence of a kidnapping. If we only had a ransom note or something to go on…"

"I s'pose you're right," the Deputy said. "Well, most folks nowadays have a better opinion of psychics. Now they're on TV shows, all respectable, you know."

Standing on the low rise above the pond, the Sheriff of George County and his Deputy could see some of the volunteer fire department boys from down at Bravesville dragging an aluminum Jon boat to the water's edge. Some deputies, wearing hip-waders, were searching the muck and cattails with long clawed poles at the shallow end of the pond. Yellow plastic tape had been strung from tree to tree to bar the curious from the pond. It gave the VanBurean place the appearance of a real crime scene investigation, like in the movies.

"You know," Eden mused, "we probably should have checked out this pond to begin with. It's a great place to dump a body."

"Yeah," Buckey scowled. "This and three dozen other farm ponds in the county. Amara McClure's drawing looked like this one. But why would you pick it? You some kinda psychic too?"

"I dunno," the Deputy said. "It just feels like it could be right…"

"Horseshit," muttered Buckey. "Hey!" he shouted to the men below. "You turnin' up anything?"

"Lotsa garbage and muck." A volunteer fireman held up a forkful of nasty, dripping trash. "Ain't no body though."

The scene was reminiscent of the cops bringing up Marion Crane's car in *Psycho*. Except here there was no car; the pond wasn't deep enough to conceal one. The lawmen were beginning to wonder if it was deep enough to conceal a body.

"Who knows if this is even the right pond," Buckey said irritably, indicating the first signs of doubt about the talents of Miss McClure.

"I'm gonna go and see if Amara's home. She should be out here telling us if this is the place. Hell, the pond looks like her drawing, but then, what pond doesn't? I'm going back to town... shoulda had her out here in the first place... come along if you want to, we won't be gone long." Buckey muttered as he headed toward his car.

Buckey and Whitloe arrived in Rainelle around noon and went directly to Amara McClure's house. She was feeding her nine black cats.

Amara never had too much to do with her neighbors, but they knew a great deal about her anyway. She was a retired college professor from somewhere up in New York State. John Hanratty thought she taught at Cornell but someone else said Wells College. When the Deputy interviewed her, it turned out she attended Cornell and later taught at Wells.

It wasn't a part of the investigation, but out of curiosity, Eden Whitloe looked her up online. Her undergraduate degree was in psychology, master's in English, doctorate in medieval literature. A quick look at the courses she taught revealed nothing unusual. But he did note that she had directed a seminar on extrasensory phenomena.

Amara wasn't bad looking for an older lady. Age is a tricky thing for women of her years, which he figured as late 50s. She fit what a psychic might look like—a bit plump but not fat—sort of attractive in an older-woman sort of way, not what you'd call pretty. She had long graying hair and had an ever-present shawl over her shoulders. All part of the image, perhaps. She never dated nor married. A few years back, anyone like that would have been talked about, but now it was just another life-style. No one assumed she was a lesbian, but she did seem to dislike men. Perhaps males were too down-to-earth practical for what she offered.

Amara just seemed to be one of those people who preferred life by herself. She never hung out a sign proclaiming her mystical powers; laws about that sort of thing are tricky in Pennsylvania. But word got around about her. She developed quite a trade in what we once called fortunetelling.

Her clients ran from college coeds to bridge club ladies. She dabbled in Tarot, but her main thing was to meet an individual in her parlor and talk. She wouldn't do readings by phone, fearing that people would think her to be a TV telepsychic rip-off. She had amazing skills in reading people's faces, body language, and asking leading questions.

The Deputy checked her out when Myra Kinchloe disappeared. He wanted to know if Myra had visited her in the past few days. Amara said she didn't remember Myra, so that was the end of that. Eden had completely forgotten about Amara until the Sheriff felt his first twinges of desperation about their unsolved missing person.

Eden Whitloe stood on the lawn and watched as Sheriff Buckey walked up to Amara's back door. Buckey spotted her on the small back porch busily feeding and talking to her cats. She paid particular attention to Milagro, a sleek black tom. Eden had teased Buckey, telling him that Milagro was the reason the Sheriff suspected Amara might be a conjurer or witch.

"Hello," began Buckey. "How you doing today?"

"Fine." She turned toward the Deputy, waved, and smiled. "Hi!"

Then she dropped the smile and turned her attention to Buckey. "What's up?"

She knew the Sheriff had been out to the VanBurean place. He suspected that she knew he had found nothing. So there was no sense in dancing around.

"Ah... we've been out at the VanBurean pond all morning, and..." Buckey cleared his throat. "... we haven't turned up anything yet."

"That so?" she said without concern, devoting her attention to the cats around her feet.

"I'd like for you to go out there with me. Maybe you could give us some pointers, take a new look at things..."

"Sheriff Buckey," she said abruptly, "I told you when we got into this thing—I'm not a scientist."

"I know, I know," he said, almost with a whine in his voice. "I just wondered if you could give us a little more help. I think we might be on the right track, but we need... ah... a bit more direction. That's it, you know, just a few pointers."

Amara sighed. "I'll go out there, if that's what you want, but I don't think it'll do any good. That's just one of the places I felt strongly about, that's all. I can't come up with a mental picture of the place unless it's strong. Remember, I told you that three other ponds are strong possibilities."

"If you don't think there's any point in going out..."

"I really don't. I could recommend something, though."

"I'm all ears."

"I've been thinking about this. I think we need a new direction. From what you're saying, and what I'm feeling right now, I think we should move toward the western end of the county. I have a feeling that there is a place across the border in West Virginia that's involved, somehow. The body isn't there... but there is a... a Victorian brownstone... ah, hell, I lost it. That's what I get for standing here, trying to come up with something."

"You want to talk about it now?" asked Buckey, hopefully.

"I think you should bring your Deputy with you, and we should work together. I say we include Mr. Whitloe, because he seems to be the one who has done a lot of the legwork on the case. And, he seems... more sensitive."

"What do I do with the crew out at the VanBurean place?" Buckey asked, hopelessly. The poor bastards had been out there since sunrise, searching around the dam and probing through the muck. Now he was faced with telling them all their work wasn't worth beans. He could only hope no one would tell them Buckey sent them out there because some old wizard-woman thought they might turn up something.

"You might want to give up on that one. It has some of the characteristics of the site, and a similar look, but it doesn't feel right," Amara said.

"How about we come back by around 7:00?" he asked. "We'll have more time then."

"Anytime this evening is fine with me. I'll be here."

As they moved out of earshot, heading for the car, Eden Whitloe burst out. "Bullshit! You know damned well where all of this is going to lead—absolutely nowhere."

"Well, Sherlock, have you developed new leads on your own? If you've got something better, let's have it right now." the Sheriff snapped angrily.

This wasn't like the even-tempered Buckey at all. He had made a political career out of being an unflappable Mr. Nice Guy. But a real crime, with potential political implications, was something he had never faced. Eden realized that now wasn't the time to push his buttons.

"Come on now, Buckey, lighten up. You know I don't have anything new," Eden admitted. "But I don't think going to that old house for a—some sort of séance—is going to solve anything."

"First," Buckey began calmly, "I didn't mean to snap at you like that. But you have to understand: We've had no leads in this case, and I've had Bradford T. Kinchloe III up my ass since St. Patrick's Day. Now, if you and I can get something—anything—out of a meeting with McClure, we are going to give it a shot. If you don't want to go back with me tonight, that's fine. I'll put someone else on this."

Deputy Whitloe knew this was an ultimatum. If Buckey took him off this case, that was the end of the line—and his pension. "You're serious, aren't you?" the Deputy asked.

"You'd better believe it," Buckey said quickly. "You know more about this case than anyone else. I don't want to replace you. And you don't want to go job-hunting, now do ya?" He smiled to let Eden know he would rather his Deputy would stick it out with him.

"I'm not asking you to believe what Amara tells us. I know you think it's horse puckey. Just come along to humor me, okay?"

"Tell you what," Eden offered. "I'll go and add whatever I can to the Ouija session, or whatever it turns into. But I'm going to ask for one thing."

"What's that?"

"Since you seem to have all of your"—he almost said balls—"career tied up in this case, let me work it full-time. If I don't develop leads within a couple of weeks, I'll go back to keeping the drunks from pissing behind the ticket booth at the Grande Palace."

Buckey didn't blink or hesitate. "You got a deal. We have to be at her place at 7:00. Now: you hafta realize you'll be pretty much on your own. You don't have much more authority in this than a private investigator, you know that, don'tcha?"

Eden fleetingly wondered what else he might have extracted from the Sheriff. He didn't want to let down an old friend—and above all, he didn't want to be forced out of his job.

"Deal!" Eden exclaimed happily. He had not the least inkling of what he had let himself in for.

"I'll pick you up around 6:40. Be ready for anything," Buckey said gleefully.

"What do you mean by that?" the Deputy asked.

"Amara thinks you're... how shall I put this... sen-si-tive," the Sheriff grinned. "Personally, I believe she thinks you're cute." He chuckled his way to his car.

CHAPTER SIX

SUNSET BOULEVARD

At 7:00, the two lawmen stood on Amara's back porch, ankle-deep in cats. Milagro had adopted Buckey and rubbed against his leg. Deputy Whitloe knew that under other circumstances, Buckey would have sent Milagro sailing. But he patiently waited for Amara to answer the knock.

When she came to the door, she—honest to God—wore a Norma Desmond turban like something from *Sunset Boulevard*.

"Hello, Mr. Whitloe," she said softly. Her sultry voice made Eden's stomach churn as he thought of poor old unsuspecting William Holden. She looked just like a plumper version of Norma and he began to wonder if Erich Von Stroheim—Norma's chauffeur Max—was lurking somewhere.

"Hello, Miss McClure," Eden said.

"Oh, Sheriff Buckey, I'm so glad you brought Mr. Whitloe along. Come right on in, gentlemen," she cooed, opening the screen door.

Queen Anne, Victorian, film noir—this was the setting as they walked toward her formal parlor. The whole thing was decorated for effect. Pictures of psychics from the 1930s and 1940s adorned antique tables, covered with retro linen covers. There were potted palms and large vases filled with peacock feathers. The parlor's effect on them was… spooky.

The head spook spoke. "Welcome to my home," Amara began. "We can sit in the parlor, or at the dining room table—your pleasure."

"I brought a notepad, so could we sit where I can write?"

Eden said.

"The table it is then."

Buckey and his Deputy sat on one side of the rectangular table and Amara sat on the other. Eden imagined that the lights soon would dim and there would be trumpets sounding, bells ringing, and ectoplasm everywhere.

Suddenly, Amara stood. "Oh, I almost forgot—will you have some coffee or tea?"

"Coffee, black," both lawmen said in unison.

She soon returned from the kitchen, carrying a serving tray with a carafe of coffee, cream pitcher, sugar bowl, and three cups.

She served the coffee. "Now isn't this cozy," she smiled and snuggled into her armchair. "Where shall we begin?"

Eden had a brief flash of Josephine Hull and Jean Adair. He resisted the impulse to sniff his coffee for the telltale whiff of bitter almonds.

Eden looked at Buckey, who looked back at his Deputy and shrugged, turned an open palm toward him to say something.

Amara spoke. "Mr. Whitloe, why don't you just start? I've heard most of what is known about this case, but it might help if you could trace the narrative from the beginning. As you go, I may get a... well, I don't know how to explain, but some might call it an impression. Anyway, as you go through it, I'll get these sort-of flashes. I'll write them down and see what develops."

"Okay," the Deputy said.

"And if you have any impressions, write them down as well," she continued. "Give Sheriff Buckey paper so he can write, too. But don't try to make any sense of it, just record your impressions. And above all, don't ignore something just because it seems irrelevant. When it comes to this sort of thing, there is no such thing as irrelevance. Make drawings or doodles if you like."

The Deputy wrote down the first thing that popped into his

mind: "Bullshit."

"See," she said, "you have something already. That's marvelous! Don't worry about showing it to us now. We'll try to consolidate everything later."

Eden felt that her voice was sounding more and more like his patronizing English teacher, and it was becoming more and more annoying. Working discreetly, he scratched out what he had written, making sure it couldn't be read later.

Eden began, "Myra Kinchloe went to a St. Patrick's Day party at Dunlow's on the evening of March 17." Amara wrote something on a yellow legal pad.

"Her father, Bradford Kinchloe, reported her missing to the State Police at 8:00 a.m. the following morning. We learned that her roommate, Elizabeth Mayow, had called Mr. Kinchloe at 7:00 a.m. that morning when Myra hadn't returned from Dunlow's. Ms. Mayow said it wasn't unusual for Myra to return late. But when she didn't show up by 7:00, she suspected something might be wrong and called Myra's father.

"The police couldn't do much at that point. When someone is missing only a few hours, there isn't much we can do. But around 1:00 that afternoon, Mr. Kinchloe began raising Cain with the State Police. So Dan Brackenridge, over at the police barracks, called Buckey to let him know that Kinchloe was upset and to see if he could help."

Buckey wrote something.

"Why don't you tell about that part," Eden suggested to the Sheriff, who returned a frown.

"Yeah, Kinchloe was pretty upset," Buckey said. "I knew there wasn't much anyone could do until some time had passed. Most law officials will treat this sort of thing as a runaway for a couple of days. And in this case, we have an adult who is off somewhere, so no one is going to get too concerned for quite a while, except her father. Old Brad was havin' himself a fit."

Now Eden was writing on his notepad.

Buckey sighed. "So I told him I would put someone on it right away. I called Eden here, and asked him to go out and look around for her."

At this point, Buckey waved his hand toward Eden, handing off the story to him, as Amara wrote something down.

Eden Whitloe blackened out what he had written and resumed his narrative. "I went out to Dunlow's and poked around, asked some questions."

"Mr. Whitloe," Amara said.

"Yes."

"It would be a lot more helpful if you provided more detail. Names, who you talked with, what they said, that sort of thing."

"Oh, yes, yes ma'am, sorry," he replied. "Like I said, I went out to Dunlow's and talked with Ted. That's the owner, Ted Dunlow. He said he remembered seeing her come in, but that was the last he remembered of her that night. He told me there was a pretty big crowd." he paused for a response. Buckey wrote something, but no one spoke.

"Then I talked to a..." the Deputy flipped up a couple of pages to a list of names he had stuck in his pad. "... a Miles Noran. He's a student at Rainelle College, and had been seen dancing with Myra earlier in the evening. He said Myra and her girlfriend, June Talbot, came to the party late because they had been shopping over at the Ohio Valley Mall. They said something about coming back on Route 250 by way of Moundsville. People in Rainelle call that 'the back way.'"

"Did he think there was anything significant in coming back that way?" Amara asked.

Eden replied, "As you know, folks usually come back on the Interstate. He remembered them coming the back way because they mentioned stopping at New Vrindavan to see the Hare Krishna community and their Palace of Gold. Why? Do you think that might have some bearing on the case?"

"Probably not," she replied, and went back to her pad. Eden noticed that she wasn't writing, but was drawing or doodling. She drew a chain of square waves—like a string of ocean waves with square corners, like architectural dentils.

Eden averted his eyes from her drawing and resumed. "Next I looked up the girlfriend who was with her. June Talbot is the same age as Myra, and the story we got from Miles Noran checked out. She said they came back by way of Moundsville. Other than that, there was nothing remarkable about their trip. They hadn't met, or spoken to, anyone other than some shopkeepers there, nor had they been followed by anyone she knew of."

Buckey noticed activity at Amara's tablet when Eden mentioned the name "Moundsville" again.

He continued, "I suspected that the women might have attracted the attention of someone at the mall, and that someone could have followed them to the bar that night. However, no one at Dunlow's could recall seeing anyone who seemed unfamiliar, or out of place."

"Did you ask if they stopped anywhere between the time they left the mall and when they arrived at Dunlow's that evening?" asked Amara.

"They said they traveled directly from the mall to the party. June Talbot mentioned that Kinchloe had talked about stopping at the bathroom after they left Moundsville, but she wouldn't stop at the gas stations on the way back. Most businesses between here and there aren't franchised, and there are no fast food places."

"And they definitely didn't stop at New Vrindavan?" Amara asked. "There are some pretty bizarre stories that have come out of there."

"No, that crossed my mind as well. She said they had mentioned it, but it was getting late and they wanted to get to the party. It's been pretty quiet over at the palace since the troubles," he added.

"I heard a bit about that, but I'm not quite sure what went on," Amara said.

"You, or anyone else," said Buckey. "Almost all I know about it is from the papers. There was at least one murder of a Hare Krishna devotee, and another one disappeared in the '80s. Since their Guru, Kirtanananda, began serving a 12-year prison sentence for racketeering in 1996, the commune has been running under tight-fisted leadership, and it's been quiet ever since.

"By the way, his real name was Keith Ham. He also went by a devotee name of Swami Bhaktipada, if you ever need to keep them straight."

"So, you think New Vrindavan doesn't have anything to do with Myra's disappearance?" she said.

"I didn't say that," said Buckey. "Anything is possible. We want to keep an open mind here. We just don't have any reason to suspect anything."

"Anything suspicious happen on their trip between the New Vrindavan area and Rainelle?" Amara asked, turning to the Deputy. She had been drawing domes that were unmistakably like those around the Hare Krishna temple.

"You been there?" Eden asked.

"Been where?"

"New Vrindavan," he said.

"Oh, you shouldn't be looking at what I'm writing," she cautioned him. "No, I've always wanted to go, but I've been sort of afraid since… you know… the problems they had."

"The only thing suspicious between New Vrindavan and Rainelle is Rock Lick," Buckey said with a grin. Rock Lick was a small village on the West Virginia side of the state line and was the closest place you could get alcohol legally in the western end of

George County, since the western end was dry.

"Okay," she said, "we all know about Rock Lick. They didn't stop there either, did they?"

"No," Eden continued. "They went right on down the road past Crimson Maples Park and wound up in Dunlow's parking lot. I went through that lot with a fine-toothed comb. Didn't come up with a thing."

The Deputy couldn't help but notice Amara was doodling what looked to be figure eights.

"I questioned Brad Kinchloe for about three hours on the 19th and he couldn't tell me a thing, except how his daughter's character was right up there with the saints. And, from what I've found out so far, I think he's right. I also spoke with her roommate, Elizabeth Mayow, and received a similar report. No dope, sex, or rock 'n roll. She must be a real nonconformist kid.

"In the big city when something like this happens, you just round up the usual suspects and go from there. But in George County, we'd just wind up with Joe Bill Tusten. We'd have to keep him for a week with the county paying his room and board and he'd probably enjoy the stay. And that's all I have. You want to add anything, Buckey?"

Buckey frowned. "We did go through her apartment. We took some papers and stored them over at the office. I impounded her computer, and we have been going through the hard drive and CDs for anything suspicious. I hired a computer geek who teaches at Rainelle College to see if he could find anything. So far, no luck. And we had the same luck, or lack of it, with her email account at the college and her computer there. You know the first thing you think of in this sort of case is the Internet, but we've pretty much given up on that aspect. We checked the major dating services and it doesn't seem likely she would be looking for anything in the way of excitement that way," said Sheriff Buckey.

"Eden," he said, putting his hand on his Deputy's shoulder, "is going to take a new look at all of those files beginning tomorrow. He's volunteered to take on this investigation full-time. In fact, he's going to give Mr. Kinchloe a full report and answer any questions he has. Aren't you, Eden?"

Eden Whitloe answered with a smirk directed at Buckey. It began to dawn on him why Buckey was so eager for him to take on the investigation. The Sheriff could claim later that it was an underling's screw-up if things didn't turn out well. He might not get off the hook entirely, but it would dilute the responsibility considerably.

"Is there anything else either of you can add?" asked Amara.

"Not unless you have some sort of question. That's it," Eden replied.

Amara looked thoughtful. "What happened to Myra's friend? Why didn't she say something when Myra came up missing?"

"Oh," Eden said, "she left long before Myra did. Said she had to get back to campus to work on a term paper."

"Well," Amara said, "perhaps we'll think of something else if we start putting our notes together. More coffee, anyone?"

"We're fine," Buckey replied for both of them.

"All I have are these two black blobs," the Deputy said pointing to the two places where he had written and scratched out.

"What do they mean to you?" she asked.

Let the bullshit flow, he thought. This would be like telling a shrink what your dreams mean. "What do they mean to you?" the shrink would ask.

"I can see a couple of ponds," he improvised. "It may be... uh, like those tunnels that go under the railroad tracks. A couple of places they have those metal culvert things, one for each lane of traffic." He was feeling more creative now. He was getting into it.

"Sheriff, do you have anything?" Amara said, straining to look over to our side of the table.

"I'm not much of an artist, so I didn't draw anything. I did write down a couple of things though. This seems so…"

"Now, don't start that," she cautioned, sounding like a third-grade teacher. "None of our impressions is stupid."

Eden was thinking how relieved he was that she didn't know about the actual origin of his black blobs.

"Rough road."

"What was that?" she asked.

"That's what I wrote," replied Buckey. "Rough road. Up above it, I wrote start, but that was just to remind me where we started."

"Anything else?"

"This is embarrassing…" he began.

"Don't hold back now, this could be important. If not for you, it may be for me later."

"Hare Rama… Rama… Rama…" Buckey mumbled, sheepishly.

"What?" Eden asked.

Buckey looked at his Deputy with a frown, followed by a look that could kill.

"Hareramaramarama…" he mumbled quickly, between partially clenched teeth.

"Anything else, Sheriff?" she asked.

"Right about Rock Lick, I wrote Bud," he said.

"Very good," she replied, still with that third-grade teacher inflection. "Anything after that?"

"Somewhere between there and Crimson Maples, I wrote the word keyhole. I don't have any idea why, I just wrote keyhole, for no reason at all."

Amara looked a bit surprised, but turned and asked Eden if the word "keyhole" had any meaning for him.

"The only time I ever imagine a keyhole is if it has to do with one of those old skeleton key locks," he said. "With all of the deadbolts and entrance locks today, you don't see much of those anymore. There isn't one time I ever thought of a keyhole during this entire case. And..."

"And... ?" Amara asked.

"I always think of the kind with a circle at the top and a triangle thingy at the bottom. A typical keyhole-lock symbol, I guess. Aw... I just think of Alice in Wonderland," he admitted.

"Take a look at this," she said, turning her pad so they could see it. At the top, she had written something he couldn't read, then there was a square with vertical stripes, but directly under that she had drawn the square wave thing. Next came the temple domes, and right below that she had drawn a sign that said 'Beer To Go.' The O's in To Go had been filled in so they looked like his black blobs.

Where Eden had thought she had been making figure eights, there were several carefully drawn old-fashioned keyhole symbols.

Eden could make sense out of the temple domes, and the 'Beer To Go' sign was a milestone for Rock Lick, but the rest was... well, spooky. The filled-in O's had to be a coincidence. Lots of people do that when they doodle. The square wave and square thing, who knows, but those keyholes sure had him spooked. Later, when he looked at one of the notes he had referred to under his pad, the number eight listing had a flat-bottomed "8" beside it that made it look just like a—keyhole. Maybe that one was due to fatigue and thinking about all of this entirely too much.

Eden was jolted back to reality when Amara said she wanted their papers. The men handed them to her and she put them in a metal cabinet. With a dramatic gesture, she produced a farmer's match and set them on fire. She must have had some flash paper in there too, because the whole thing went sort of "whoosh" and up into flames.

That's when she lost Eden. He could imagine sitting around and using whatever mental abilities they might have to brainstorm new ideas or directions, but now it was hocus-pocus time for the rubes. Mumbo-jumbo, hanky-panky. To his thinking, the old gal was about three kitties shy of a litter.

"That's about all we can do for this evening, gentlemen," she said. "I will meditate on it before I go to bed and I should awaken with some fresh ideas. I shall call you on the morrow if I come up with anything," she said dramatically. "Since you'll be handling the case full-time now, Deputy Whitloe, please leave me your phone number, and I'll place my calls directly to you."

He thought of poor old Bill Holden—trying to escape the clutches of Norma—and ending up lying facedown in that trashy, murky swimming pool.

Much to Buckey's pleasure, they managed to avoid Milagro on the way out. When they were seated in the county car, Eden and Buckey looked at one another. Together they shrugged as Buckey drove away toward the office. His big smile revealed that he was enjoying his Deputy's discomfort all too much.

"Don't say it," he cautioned Eden. "I know, I know what you're going to say. She's bat shit, guano, gonzo—full of crap, right?"

"Never crossed my mind." Eden looked at the Sheriff, trying unsuccessfully to keep a straight face.

He burst out laughing. "I thought I'd shit, watching you while she burned those papers."

"I'll have to meditate and sleep on it," Eden said in his best Amara McClure voice, which he did a bit too well. "I'll get back to you on the morrow."

"Aw, hell, Buckey," he said, "we've come this far, we might as well go with the flow. When she calls, I'll listen, and who knows, maybe she'll come up with something."

"What was it with those two blobs, anyway?" Buckey asked.

"I'll tell you some day," Eden Whitloe promised, "but you

know what?"

"What's that?"

"I still think the old gal is looney-tunes. If she's a psychic, I'm The Amazing Kreskin. I don't think she's crazy. But I think she's got herself and some of those teenyboppers at the college convinced she has some sort of mystical powers, and I don't think she's going to be one teensy bit of help.

"All that said, it's… it's…"

"It's what?" Buckey asked.

"Those damned keyholes," he replied. "I'm gonna be dreaming about those keyholes."

CHAPTER SEVEN

RANDOM CREEK

At the office, Eden Whitloe picked up the boxes and milk crates of stuff from Myra Kinchloe's apartment, then drove the 15 miles to his Random Creek home. Not much of a house, but home. Sarge, Annie's big orange "Morris" cat, was waiting in the driveway. As Eden got out of the car, Sarge came over, took one sniff, and ran. He just sort of hung out with Eden since Annie died. They had never gotten around to having kids, so Sarge was a stand-in. They always figured there would be time later for babies, not knowing that her earthly time would be very limited.

Sarge always came running when Eden set his dish out back, but first Eden checked the mailbox. He tossed the bills on the kitchen table, the rest in the trashcan, and kicked off his shoes by the back door.

Deputy Whitloe went to the bedroom and took off his gun belt, stripped to his T-shirt and boxers, and flopped onto the bed with the room light still on. Too tired, or lazy, to get up and turn off the light, within seconds he was zooming through one of Amara McClure's keyholes.

After what seemed like only a few minutes, he was wide-awake. It was one of those I'm-too-tired-to-sleep situations. If anything would make him sleepy it was reading, but he didn't have an unread book in the place. The Bible was out, as there had been enough spiritualism for one day. So he found an old magazine.

It featured an article titled "The Nation's Attic," about the Smithsonian Museum in Washington. As he flipped through the pages, a photo of the old building caught his eye. It showed a flower garden in the foreground. The caption read:

Completed in 1855, the original Smithsonian Institution Building, popularly known as the Castle, was designed by architect James Renwick Jr., whose other works include St. Patrick's Cathedral in New York City and the Smithsonian's Renwick Gallery.

As he studied the picture of the building, a square wave went through his head and superimposed itself on the photo. Along the edge—the part they call the cornice of the building—and along the skyline of the central part where the main entrance was, the line was broken by a square wave, or what the *American Architectural Handbook* called a crenellation.

It struck him that nearby Moundsville had a similar medieval style building: the Old Moundsville Penitentiary had been built about 12 years after the Smithsonian building, and it had the same crenellated battlements. This seemed far too much a coincidence—the Moundsville square wave connection.

According to the architectural handbook, the Moundsville prison was smaller than its prototype, the Joliet Correctional Center in Illinois, but it was built in the same castellated Gothic style with turrets and battlements, much like a castle. Moundsville prison was known as a hellhole, hard-time prison because of miserable conditions and crowding. It had been built for 840 men, but eventually housed more than three times that number.

Because of the poor conditions, it was closed in 1995. After that, it became a tourist attraction and prison riot-training center. Just about every law enforcement person within a hundred-mile radius has toured the prison at least once.

When the prison first opened, Eden took the tour. He had a former guard for a guide, who took great delight in locking up several of the tourists he lured into the cells. Moundsville isn't the country club image most people have of prisons, and a few minutes locked in one of those cells is an experience to last a lifetime. It doesn't take much imagination to see yourself doing hard time with hard-assed Warden Bordenkircher and his infamous dogs.

He thought maybe all of those keyholes in the cells were an answer to the other part of Amara's puzzle. Could Moundsville hold the answer—the key—to the disappearance of Myra Kinchloe? Well, probably not. It likely was no more useful to the investigation than the Palace of Gold up on Hare Krishna Ridge, a short distance away.

Suddenly Amara's square with vertical stripes hit home. A cell, a prison cell, in Moundsville State Penitentiary. Now he was really getting spooked. Maybe thinking about this in the middle of the night wasn't his best activity.

Suddenly, Eden remembered something else far removed from Moundsville and the Palace of Gold; he had forgotten to feed Sarge.

He jumped out of bed and went down to the kitchen, fixed a big bowl of dry cat food, and opened the back door. "Here, Sarge, come and get it!" A large sleek black cat blurred past him in the dark, and he immediately thought of Milagro, who was supposed to be fifteen miles away in Rainelle.

Seconds later, a furry touch against his leg made him nearly jump out of his skin. But it was just Sarge, letting Eden know that he was standing there like a simpleton, holding Sarge's dinner in his hands. Sarge was happy for his late-night snack and Eden scratched his head apologetically, then returned to his bedroom, this time quenching the light off before falling into bed and to sleep. And soundly he slept... except for a stray dream about a keyhole, a prison cell, a turret, a Budweiser sign, and a seated, life-like statue of Srila Prabhupada, the founder of New Vrindavan.

Saturdays were always tough for Eden; since Annie died, they always felt... empty. He got out of bed, showered and shaved, and opened the fridge so see what wasn't curdled or moldy. He found an unopened container of peach yogurt, two weeks past its expiration date, but who could tell when yogurt is spoiled anyway? It tasted like yogurt always tastes—spoiled. He stirred up the fruit on the bottom and gobbled it down. The orange juice didn't seem to have that funky taste it gets when it's old, so he drank a full glass of that.

Random Creek was a great place to get away from everything, and he always looked forward to getting home from the office. It was quiet and the nearest neighbors were a half-mile down the road. Eden's house was five miles from the nearest village big enough to have a small store, so he usually made do with what was at hand. He bought groceries in Rainelle from time to time and tried to avoid convenience stores, whose prices kept him away from their convenience, or Sculley's General Store and Gas Station in Whitesville, where a bunch hung out that he liked to avoid— particularly on Saturday morning.

They weren't bad folk. Mostly they were the same sort of retirees that hang out at a typical McDonald's, except there are no McDonalds in Whitesville. In the summer, they'd sit on the store's porch and spit tobacco juice into the road out front. Sometimes it reached the road. In the winter, they sat around the coal-fired stove inside and spit toward its open door. Some had a better aim than others. The bullshit was so thick around the place it would defy a bulldozer. So Eden avoided Sculley's whenever possible.

Weekend radio was useless unless he wanted to hear some never-was talk about what his ball team could-have-been. Sundays were worse, church services for shut-ins in the morning and Bible-thumpers in the afternoon. *National Public Radio* was a good fill-in, except when they ran opera. And TV was TV. So Eden usually brought home some simple work from the office. After finishing the yard work or puttering, he would read a while or catch up on what was going on at work.

Being Saturday, Eden slept late, with one ear cocked to the phone—if Amara was going to call, he figured it would be before noon. When the call didn't come, he made sure the answering machine was on to take her call if he dozed off or went outside.

Still wearing boxer shorts, he went out to the car and brought in Myra Kinchloe's stuff. He was spreading it around the living room when the phone rang. He wasn't anxious to hear from Miss McClure, but he was kind-of intrigued about what she might have to say after her "meditation."

"Hello," Eden said, fully expecting to hear Amara on the other end.

"This is Buckey. I just wondered if you had heard anything from McClure yet?"

"Not a peep," Eden replied. "Maybe she's busy feeding her kitties."

"Man, how would you like to have to put up with a bunch like that?"

"I think that big black one kind of likes you," Eden said, as a thought of the big cat outside his door last night flashed through his mind.

"Well, let me know if you find out anything."

"You'll be the first," Eden said, and hung up. He went to the mailbox. The *Georgian Observer* had arrived, so he took it to the back porch, pushed Sarge off his chair, and looked over the news. Sarge stalked off, miffed.

There was a picture of the VanBurean Pond on the front page with a headline that read, "Sheriff's search comes up empty." Everyone knew what Jim Morris would write about the debacle, so he didn't bother to read the non-story under the picture. Jim Morris and Buckey never did hit it off.

He turned to the entertainment section and found there was a movie he wanted to see playing. Since Annie died, he felt funny about going to the movies alone, something he hadn't done since he was a kid. Whenever he sat in a theater alone, he felt people around him were thinking, there's a pervert who goes to theaters to do whatever those guys do when they sit alone in the dark.

"Hey, Sarge," Eden yelled at the big orange fur ball that had taken up a perch on the newel at the bottom of the stairs, "you can have your chair back now. You'd better watch out for that big black guy though, he'll whip your ass." He got up and went in to check the answering machine.

The movie was okay, but like most these days, there were too many car chases, too many explosions, and it was far too long. It was filled with long walks down long hallways, long drives down long wet roads, and lots of moaning music. He knew the number of shots fired in that one movie exceeded all the rounds fired by all the police in Pennsylvania for an entire year—including Philadelphia. The police had never fired that many shots—ever.

Except for the teenaged acne case who sold him a ticket, no one spoke to him at the theater, including the usher who handed him his stub and nodded to the right toward theater three. It may be, he thought, folks are afraid to speak to anyone who goes to the movies alone. Serial killers must come to mind. What must it be like for a woman to have to deal with a similar circumstance? He thought of Myra Kinchloe for the first time since leaving Random Creek for the movie.

When Eden got home, the answering machine light was blinking. Amara had finally called, he thought. On the way home from the theater, he had thought about what he might say to her. The more he thought about Miss McClure, the more he became convinced she was a kook. The powerful feelings he had last night had faded into the sunlight of the afternoon, and this evening, after a day's relaxation, it all seemed so, so silly.

Keyholes, barred cells, and Hindu temples turned back into doodles on some goofy old lady's legal pad. They are now where they should have been in the first place—up in smoke.

He played the message. "This is Buckey. I was just curious to hear if you'd heard anything. If you have, give me a call, if you haven't, never mind." There was a beep that indicated the end of the message. The next message started with just a dial tone, but nothing else.

All day and not a word—he was a bit perturbed as he punched Amara's number into the keypad, looking at his watch. It was after 11:00 p.m., but surely she wouldn't be in bed yet. But her voice mail answered. "I can't come to the phone right now, but you may leave me a message at the tone. I am sorry, I don't accept voice mail appointments or give readings over the phone. Thank you... beep."

He didn't leave a message. He thought if she was off doing God knows what, and didn't have the courtesy to call, the hell with her. Maybe she thinks she had reached him already through mental telepathy or some psychic spirit-line.

On Sunday morning, Eden Whitloe breakfasted on a bagel and salami he found in the bottom of the fridge. It didn't seem reasonable that something that tastes like salami could spoil. He slathered the bagel with cream cheese. There was a bit of greenish stuff on the cheese but if you scrape that off, it's like new, isn't it? Anyway, he'd had no ill effects from Saturday's breakfast and the orange juice still tasted fine.

Deputy Whitloe set about the task of looking over Myra's stuff. It hadn't been catalogued, so he took out a legal pad and started to list it. School papers, term papers, letters, notebooks, greeting cards, and more stuff than anyone could sift through in months. If someone had the inclination, they could read through all of it, and they might even find a clue to Myra's fate. But if it were left to him, that wasn't going to happen.

There were dozens of programs and ticket stubs from concerts, plays, and poetry readings. He wondered how she ever had time for classes. She must have been one of the world's worst pack rats.

Eden looked down at the legal pad, and it occurred to him to try to recreate the notes he and Buckey had made at the "séance." He started by redrawing his two black blobs. Although he knew they weren't really mystical insights, they were a part of the thing and he felt they had to be there. Next, he wrote Buckey's contributions, "rough road" and "Hare Rama, Rama, Rama." Then, just for the hell of it, he wrote Buckey's "hareramaramarama," the way he had said it. He couldn't help noticing that after the "harer" part, it turned into amara, and by going back to the last "a" and using it again, it became amara over and over. Just one more unrelated coincidence—perhaps.

Amara's part was a little tougher. He massaged his temples, trying to remember. At the meeting, he couldn't read what she had written at the top, so he wrote "illegible." Then, under that, he remembered there was the square with vertical stripes and under that, the square wave thing. The temple domes were harder because he couldn't draw them the way she had. The sign that said "Beer To Go" with the O's in To Go filled in was easier. Then there were those damned keyholes. He couldn't recall how many there were, so he made a note to that effect. After that, two red maple trees with a right-facing arrow flashed through his mind. He couldn't even imagine anything like that on the tablet she'd shown him. What the hell, he figured, write that down anyway... no, make a drawing.

Maybe the exercise didn't accomplish anything but at least he would have something to refer to later, something more than smoke. And, as he was thinking about Miss McClure and her hocus-pocus, he thought again that she still hadn't called. Maybe she considered Sunday a day of rest.

Back to Myra's crap. He poked through some of it, but it went nowhere in providing insight into where she might have gone. He lackadaisically thumbed through a scrapbook of concert programs. Ticket stubs for rock concerts from Aerosmith to ZZ Top were arranged in alphabetical order in one section. In another, he found a ticket for the Delf Norona Museum and burial mound, and another ticket for a tour of the Moundsville Penitentiary.

Given his experience with McClure's square waves and crenellations, he gave these more than passing interest. It was evidence that Myra probably had been there, but that was something anyone could expect, even without the ticket stub. Many students in the Ohio–West Virginia–Pennsylvania region had visited the popular attraction, the Moundsville Prison.

Suddenly the phone flashed into his consciousness again. He checked the answering machine. And he went to the back porch to finish reading the *Georgian Observer*.

Sarge was in his favorite chair, so rather than disturb him, Eden perched on the end of the porch swing, where his position gradually evolved from sitting to reclining to a fitful afternoon nap. Buzzing flies are one reason he disliked sleeping out-of-doors, but he spent part of the afternoon dreaming of winged keyholes buzzing around his head. The keyholes were joined by skeleton keys that swarmed together as they flew into prison cells that were locked, but had only barred doors without walls.

Eden believed phones should still have bells that ring. At the office, he had found an old phone with a real bell ringer and immediately made it his. When it rang, he knew it wasn't a radio or television commercial. The phones at his house were booper phones that announced themselves with the *boopboopboopboop* electronic sound that he didn't immediately recognize as a real telephone. When he was half-asleep, it took a while to figure out whether it was the phone, a commercial, or just a figment of his imagination.

By the time he figured out what was ringing, the answering machine had picked it up. "When you get back or wake your dead ass up, give me a call." It was Buckey's voice.

Eden figured he wanted a report about what he had learned from Amara, so there was no hurry to call him back. Eden considered telling Buckey some fantastic story about how Amara had revealed all of the missing information on Myra and that she had been kidnapped by Hare Krishnas and they had flown to Los Angeles to solicit funds in the airport. The keyholes and the striped box represented the imprisoned Kirtanananda Swami and the two blobs were the barrels of a shotgun that—*boopboopboopboop!*

"Hello," he mumbled into the mouthpiece of the phone.

CHAPTER EIGHT

SUICIDE?

"This is Buckey—"

"O, Buckey—sorry, I was just getting ready to call you. I was out getting ready to mow the lawn," Eden lied. "Hey, I still haven't heard a thing from McClure."

"Well, I have. She's dead," Buckey said flatly.

"Myra Kinchloe's dead?"

"No, no!" Buckey said. "Amara McClure's dead. A neighbor reported hearing a gunshot near her place sometime around noon. They reported it to the state police at about 12:15. When they didn't get an answer on her phone, and she didn't answer the door, the police forced a window. Eden, they found her in her bed with one gunshot in the right temple. They're saying it's a suicide."

"No shit!" Deputy Eden Whitloe, now chief murder investigator, was stunned and couldn't think of anything else to say.

"Goddamn it," said the Sheriff, "my term's nearly up, and what do I get? A prominent citizen's daughter missing, and now a suicide—I hope. With my luck, the criminal investigators will call it murder; then my ass will really be grass."

"Do you have any details yet?"

"Only some preliminary stuff," he said. "The weapon is a .38-caliber revolver she kept in her nightstand. Had it registered in her own name—all legal. They found it in the bed next to her. It looks like she just lay down and shot herself. She was fully clothed—still had that damned turban on she wore the other night. I think she dressed up just for the occasion.

51

"No sign of forced entry, doors locked, no sign of a struggle, nothing missing, only the neighbor heard the shot, no strangers seen around the place, no... well, they're still checking it out. One of the investigators seemed to be impressed with some black dust he found—probably can't tell the difference between powder residue and fingerprint dust. Give these kids an hour of crime scene investigation class and they're experts—too damned much television. All them CSI shows... looks open-and-shut. I really don't see it turning into a homicide."

"Everybody in the county knows she was helping us out on the Kinchloe case..."

"Hey Eeed, tell me something I don't know. Shit, when Morris gets through with this, he'll make everyone believe I had something to do with it," Buckey said angrily.

Eden protested, "I don't see how. I know we'll probably take some heat because of the publicity, but there is no way anyone can make any more out of it. It'll blow over."

"It'd blow over a hell of a lot faster if Myra Kinchloe turns up alive and well," Buckey said.

Eden replied, "Yeah, but that won't happen anytime soon. And when we do find her, daddy's not going to be thrilled with what we turn up."

"I think you are absolutely right-on," Buckey said dejectedly. "Well, there's nothing we can do right now, so sit tight until morning. We'll go over how to handle all of this tomorrow. We should have more information then."

Eden slept fitfully, dreaming of keyholes and a ghostly Amara. Buckey slept fitfully, dreaming of losing the next election. Came the dawn, and the men met over coffee in the Sheriff's office.

"Did you turn up anything in Myra's stuff?" Buckey began.

"All I learned was that she never threw anything away. Maybe she thought everything turns into a collector's item. She probably figured on making a fortune on eBay in a few years," said Eden.

"You got that right," the Sheriff replied. "My old lady's been after them stuffed toy animals all along. Says we'll retire as millionaires pretty soon. The way things are goin' with Power Ball, the game shows, and lawsuits and all, everybody'll be a millionaire by then anyway."

"Buckey, there's one other thing. Myra had been over to Moundsville to the Delf Norona Museum and the penitentiary. She had the ticket stubs in her scrapbook."

Buckey sighed. "Yeah, her and every other college kid around here. We made a big deal about her coming back to Rainelle the back way the other night. But ya know, I don't think that has a damned thing to do with anything."

Eden asked, "Anyway, did you find out any more about Amara McClure?"

"Not much. They're doing an autopsy later today, but that won't help. They're just doing it so the coroner's office can send a big bill to the county. The old gal shot herself, plain and simple. Either that, or it's a real slick murder, but there's no reason to think that. No close relatives, no estate, no insurance policies, or other motives so far."

"Did she leave a note or letter?"

"No suicide note, no letter," the Sheriff said. "Did leave a pad with some of her notes. I can't get the originals until the coroner is done. But I asked Phil Braddock to send over some photocopies if you'd like to take a look." Buckey handed Eden three pages of notes.

"Buckey, did you take a close look at the notes she burned the other night?"

"Nope. I just got a quick glance when she showed them to you. Why?"

"I think this one page is her notes, this one is yours, and this other one is mine," Eden replied, turning the pages so Buckey could see.

"I thought she burned them."

"Me too. But she must have used sleight-of-hand and switched them. Or, she could have traced them from the impression on the next page of the pad. But this looks like the original to me. It's hard to tell from a photocopy."

"Well, why in hell did she pretend to burn them?" Buckey asked.

"As best I can figure, it was part of her act," Eden offered. "She looked at us like any other couple of suckers who came along for one of her 'readings,' and gave us the same treatment everyone else gets. I figure she was putting on an act from the start. Don't ask me why she kept the notes. I don't have a clue."

"So I guess we're at a dead end then," the Sheriff sighed.

"If that was a pun, I'll try to ignore it," Eden said, trying to lift the Sheriff's spirits. Buckey did not react.

Eden said, "There's a couple of things I want to check out before I give up." The Deputy had little to work with, but he wasn't telling the Sheriff that. He now had two immediate goals. One was to keep Buckey's hopes alive and the other was to delay having to work the Grande Palace ticket booth anytime soon.

"I'll check in with you this evening around quitting time," Eden promised.

CHAPTER NINE

LATE BLOOMING FLOWER CHILD

While reading over stuff on Amara McClure, Eden kept coming across references to another local psychic or seer of some sort. There were newspaper clippings with those Sunday feature pieces about a furniture maker and sometime psychic by the name of David Quinn.

As he searched the newspaper files, Eden ran across an article about Quinn's involvement with the Krishnas in the early '80s: "Krishna Dropout, Drops Out." Seems that Quinn had been a Krishna devotee, but left New Vrindavan after becoming disenchanted. He undoubtedly agreed to the article as a means of promoting his business. He looked to find an out-of-the-way area, and not surprisingly moved to the west end of George County near the small village of Brightbrook, not too far from Eden's Random Creek estate.

At first rumors circulated about Quinn. But he didn't seem to have been involved in any of the New Vrindavan scandals, so he was eventually accepted—as much as anyone ever is—into the broad and diverse community of Brightbrook. Eden also learned from the articles that Quinn made a pretty decent living designing and building one-of-a-kind furniture for Pittsburgh interior designers. He set up a shop in his home in an empty gas station and marketed his work over the Internet.

But the Deputy's interest piqued when he learned that Quinn had a reputation as a psychic. From the papers, Eden gathered that Quinn worked in a manner similar to Amara's, and everyone called him "one of those fortunetellers." According to the locals, his psychic enterprise was more of a diversion than a business, and Dave was perceived as a sort of latter-day Dennis Hopper or a present-day Woody Harrelson. It was widely believed he was a flower child who had dropped out during the '70s, then dropped out of the counter-culture to become, more or less, a hermit.

There was only one David Quinn in the white pages, and no one by that name in the Yellow Pages under "furniture." Eden jotted down Quinn's phone number and called.

"Hello, this is the David Quinn residence."

"This is Deputy Sheriff Eden Whitloe…"

"Already gave to the Sheriff's anti-drug campaign." Quinn interrupted.

"This isn't about the campaign. I'm calling concerning an investigation into the disappearance of a Rainelle College student. And I would like to talk to you briefly. I promise I won't take up much of your time."

"I can't imagine how I might be able to help," Quinn said. "But I'll be glad to answer any questions. Always willing to help the law, if I can." He seemed to be sincere and not the least bit sarcastic.

"Mr. Quinn…"

"Dave. Please call me Dave. I feel old enough the way it is."

"Ok, Dave. I would like to meet with you to discuss some things I've found during this investigation, to see if you can shed some light on what they might mean."

"What sort of things are we talking about here?"

"Well, uh… they're uh… symbols of some kind," the Deputy fumbled.

"Oh, you want me to use my omniscient mystical and psychic powers to help you probe the infinite. Why didn't you say so?" He laughed heartily.

"Come on now, Dave," Eden said, "I need help here. I know you know something about this stuff and... well, I suppose I'm grasping at straws, but could you try? I promise not to take much of your time..."

"Come right now," Dave said. "I have a glued-up piece in the clamps, and I can't do anything for a few hours. So, if you come right now, I'll try to help. Um, by the way... is there any way you could work out a consulting fee for me?"

"I really don't think so," Eden said, "but I'll check into it if you like."

"All right. Go out by Crimson Maples. I'm in what was the old gas station on the right as you come into the village on the main road. I'll look for you within the hour," he said, and hung up.

When Eden arrived, Dave was sitting out front. He obviously was not your run-of-the-mill George Countian. His beard was fairly well groomed, but two braids of it looped from where his moustache should have been, down to somewhere below his chin. His hair was shoulder length, graying, but washed and combed. He wore a tan pocket T-shirt under what looked to be a handmade leather vest. And, instead of trousers, he wore long cargo shorts. Although no one wore earth shoes anymore, Dave was wearing what looked to be a new pair of Kelsos.

He flashed a smile with teeth any celebrity would have killed for, stood up, and stuck out a calloused hand as Eden approached. "Pleased to meetcha. I'm Dave Quinn. Call me Dave."

It was hard to determine Dave's age. Maybe late 50s or early 60s; if his graying hair were touched up, he could pass for late 40s. His blue eyes complemented his smile, and definite smile lines and crinkles around his eyes were the only lines on his face. Those blue eyes, flecked with green, looked as if they could penetrate steel. Measured using the doorway for comparison, the Deputy estimated the furniture-maker at a little under six feet and 175 pounds—no doubt about it, an aging flower child. Eden took an instant liking to him.

"Eden Whitloe," said the Deputy, as he shook hands. "Call me Eden."

"I'll do that. Come on in, Eden," he held the screen door open. Inside was a meticulous woodworking shop. They passed a small kitchenette just off the front of the room, and Eden paused to look over the layout.

"Ain't much, but it's home," Dave said, as the Deputy looked around. "Let's go back to the dinette there, and sit down. I'll pour us some coffee; it's no bother, already made some."

"Black," Eden said.

"You got it," Dave replied, pouring a cup and setting it on the table in a retro red-and-chrome dining booth. He sat down on the other side of the built-in booth, settling in as if for the day, wrapping both well-worn hands around the coffee cup.

Deputy Whitloe pulled out the photocopies Buckey had given him of Amara's drawings and put them on the table before them.

"So what can I do for you?" Dave asked.

"As you may have heard, Sheriff Buckey and I have been working on the disappearance of Myra Kinchloe…"

"Read about that in the papers. Uh, Friday, I think it was. Yeah, Friday. Mara McClure's been helping you guys, right?"

"Amara McClure," Eden corrected him.

"Yeah, I know Mara," he went on as if he hadn't heard. "We're good friends. She used to come out once in a while and we'd talk business together."

"Not furniture business," Eden ventured.

"Oh no, psychic business." He drew out "psychic" in a whisper as one would about a secret affair. Eden couldn't tell if there was sarcasm in it.

"She'd come out and I'd share some of the techniques of the business with her. What we'd do is pretty much discover what people want to hear, and then tell them that in some obscure way that they can interpret as they like. It's mostly technique," he said. "You know, like in the *Wizard of Oz*."

"Huh," grunted the Deputy.

"Frank Morgan—he got Auntie Em's picture out of Dorothy's basket and started to bullshit her. You know, take what he knew and could discern from it, then embroidered on it. That's the kind of thing we'd do. It's pretty simple, really."

"Do you think she had any sort of extrasensory ability?" Eden asked, feeling stupid for asking.

Dave chuckled loudly. "I doubt it, but you never know about that sort of thing. I'd say she's 99.9 percent quack, but who knows? This stuff is really strange. I surprise myself sometimes.

"I don't think she's a nut, but what tipped me was her interest in the showmanship part of the business. Seems like she had a greater interest in how she was coming off, rather than actually doing something worthwhile," he said.

"I suppose you haven't heard about her then?" Eden said.

"Heard what? Is she in some kinda trouble? You're not arresting her for psychic bullshitting are you?" he asked, amused, but concerned. "You can tell me. We are tight, but not real friendly—intimate, if you know what I mean."

"Dave, she's dead. Killed herself with a handgun."

"Aw, shit! I'm real sorry to hear that, real sorry," he said. "She mighta been a quack, but she was fine people. That news sure ruins my day; I'll really miss the old gal. You know, you never think about that sort of shit happening to someone like that. You expect them to go to bed one night in the far, far future and not wake up, but nothing like that."

"I'm really sorry you lost a friend, Dave," Eden said, consoling him.

They sat silently and drank their coffee, and after a while, Dave went over and checked his glue-up.

"Really makes you wonder," Dave Quinn said, to no one in particular, as he stroked the wood he had recently formed into a coffee table.

"So, you really think this psychic stuff is just so much trickery then?" Eden asked, avoiding using his word, 'technique.'

"If you remember, I said mostly technique, *mostly* technique."

"What's out there beyond... mostly?"

"Ah... that's the other part—that's the part that's infinitely infinite," Dave grinned.

"And... ?"

"I hope you've got some time," Dave said slowly. "Look, this is like talking about... well, first, let me say that none of this is new. Hell, it goes back to the beginning of time, at least back to the beginning of Man. Take any subject you like—religion, mysticism, paranormal events, extrasensory perception—anything you can't explain in ordinary terms.

"This thing—see, if you start putting verbal descriptions around it—the word thing indicates it has form or limits. But there ain't no limits for what I'm talking about. Okay, Eden—Mr. Whitloe—I'm about to use a word that I don't use real often. I'm going to use it here because it conveys more than any other word I can think of. Fucking is the word." He fairly shouted it, and Eden noticed he seemed more like Dennis Hopper's "Billy" from *Easy Rider* than before.

"When folks start diddling around with this shit, they don't know what they're fucking with. You get me?" He didn't wait for an answer. "Christ, there's kids out there fucking with this stuff like it was Playdough. They don't know—they don't have any idea. Their relatives, their families and friends find out about it though, when someone, or everyone, around them dies. You screw around with this shit and you wind up with it biting you in the ass. A kid starts pissing around with pentagrams and the first thing you know, he's offing mommy and daddy and all the kiddies at school.

"Is it real? Shit, what's real? Is this table real? It doesn't matter if it is or not, does it?" Again, he didn't wait for an answer. "The last question in your mind when you are out there making a body count is, Is this stuff real?" He was pounding real into the table, using both hands like meat cleavers.

Eden interjected: "Hey, I didn't mean to... you said it was technique she was interested in..." but Billy the Quinn didn't let him continue.

"That's what we would use to make a little money on the side. A few readings for the teenyboppers and gillies, a few tea leaves for the blue-hair ladies—it puts cash in the cookie jar and I get my cookies from it, that's all I meant by that. The other thing... I think I prefer infinite a lot better—*in-fy-nite*—without limits, that says it best. It's up here." He jabbed his temple with two fingers. "That's where it is man. Maybe the physicists would call it another dimension—hell, maybe it is.

"Look at it this way: imagine one of those Chinese puzzle boxes that has a series of buttons, levers, and slides. If you push all the right ones in the right sequence, a drawer pops open and reveals the prize. Does any of this make any sense, or am I rambling? I know it's simplistic, but I was never a philosopher, and I have a real hard time describing what I mean. I get too emotional and turn people off."

The Deputy raised his brows. "Like the thing in the Clive Barker movies? Sounds pretty basic to me."

"Yeah, maybe like that. But in this puzzle, the buttons, levers, whatever, are infinite—the combinations for pushing, pulling, turning, sliding them are likewise infinite. The real kicker is that the drawers slide open—and what is in those drawers is infinite as well—infinitely good or infinitely evil."

"Yeah," Eden said, trying to indicate that he knew what the hell Quinn was talking about, "that's life."

"The puzzle is also an analogue for those who are dissatisfied with the flow of life, or maybe just pissed off at the world. The puzzle is for those who want to fuck with the current, swim against the tide. They want to get there faster, mess with the system, create some excitement, take shortcuts... shit, is any of this making sense?" he asked desperately.

"I, uh... I think so," Eden replied.

"Are those voices real, are your hallucinations really hallucinations, or have you entered another... another, uh... part of the—and I don't like the analogy much—the puzzle?"

"Are you talking about mental illness?" Eden asked.

"Hell, I don't know. I think mental illness—whatever that is—may be a key to the puzzle. Drugs, hallucinogens, chanting, prayer, meditation, mania, and depression, all are altered states; all may be keys to the kingdom. But, there may be an infinite number of keyholes and keys."

"Like these?" Eden asked, turning the paper so Dave could see the keyholes that Amara McClure had drawn.

"I suppose so," Dave said, noncommittally. "We talked about this when she was out here once. My guard was down and she got me talking about it... kind of like now."

"What do you mean, your guard was down?"

"It's part of the reason I had to get out of New Vrindavan. I felt myself being drawn deeper into—" he jabbed two fingers of each hand into the air, forming quote marks—the puzzle."

"Are you a recovering alcoholic?" Eden asked. "You needn't answer if you don't want to."

"Don't worry, I won't tell you a damned thing that I don't want to tell you. I've never touched alcohol except for a beer at a frat party once. I wanted to be able to say to my kids that I never did drugs. So I never had any kids." He gave Eden a big toothy grin. "It wouldn't make any difference if I told you. I don't give a shit if you believe me or not. I wouldn't believe some old hippie fart if he told me this shit either."

Eden believed him. There was no reason for him to lie.

"So when you start fucking with the infinite… that's what Professor Marvel called it anyway—you do know Professor Marvel, don't you?"

"You mean Captain Marvel, Billy Batson…"

"No, I mean Frank Morgan, *Wizard of Oz*," he said disgustedly, exasperated at Eden's ignorance of trivia. "You probably read too many comic books. Didn't I tell you about the Wizard?

Eden didn't say a word.

"You came out here to see if we could make some sense out of what happened to Myra and Mara, right?" he continued without waiting for an answer.

"Deputy: Did you ever wake up in the middle of the night, terrified beyond all reason? If you can divide the infinite into regions, there must be a fairly large one dedicated to mayhem, suicide, and murder. I think most suicides are a result of someone breaking through and finding something over there in a drawer that should have remained closed."

"You think that's what happened to Amara?"

"You betcha! I figure Mara was meditating, cogitating, ruminating, or whatever, on this stuff," he shoved the papers slightly, "and had some sort of breakthrough she couldn't deal with. Popped open one of those drawers that's supposed to stay shut. Unless some Lazarus thing happens and she comes back to life, we'll never know what it was that got her. All I know is, it's something no one should be messing around with."

"Can you make anything of it?" Eden asked hopefully.

"Oh, so you got one person missing, and I just told you this stuff may have contributed to Mara's suicide, and now you're asking me to go mucking about in it. You really love me a whole bunch, don't you?" he flashed that toothy smile again.

Eden answered meekly, "I just hoped... I just hoped you could help out, a little."

"What the hell. It's been a while since I took an upstream swim, so let me have a look at those." Dave pulled the papers toward him. "Nobody lives forever. I think Jim Morrison had something to say about that. He didn't drop out until it was too late; then he took the permanent trip."

Eden pointed to the photocopy of his notes. "That one there with the two black blobs. They don't mean anything. That's just where I scratched out what I wrote down."

"No," Dave said. "Everything means something. Nothing gets thrown out."

"I remember writing and later scratching out Bullshit, but for the life of me, I can't remember what the second blob was about," said Eden. Now he could already smell the piss behind the ticket booth at the Grande Palace.

"Tell me how you all happened to come up with this stuff," Quinn said.

So the Deputy laid out the whole story about Myra Kinchloe and how she happened to come back from the Ohio Valley Mall past the turnoff to New Vrindavan.

"First of all, these keyhole things, you already have an idea what they are about. You agree with that?" Quinn asked.

"The only thing that bothers me is, Buckey—Sheriff Buckey— wrote the word keyhole," Eden said, pointing it out on his photocopy.

Dave grinned. "Kinda gets your attention when you see both of them together, don't it? I don't know if it means anything more or not. Let's make a note of it. Now, these canopy-looking things—is that what you see as the Palace of Gold connection?"

"That's what Amara drew when I explained to her that Myra Kinchloe came back from her shopping trip and passed by New Vrindavan."

"You think the Krishnas had anything to do with any of this?" Dave asked, incredulously.

"Well…"

"After all they've been through, I can pretty much assure you that if there is any connection, it isn't a physical one. They're back in tight with the International Society of Krishna Consciousness, and the tourists are bringing money again. They sure as hell don't want to screw anything up. They are sensitive as hell to adverse publicity," he said, without making it sound defensive at all.

"I would put Buckey's Hare Rama and rough road in about the same category. The road over to the Palace could qualify as rough and—well, it's probably just stuff he recalled when he was stimulated by a reference to the place.

"Buckey's Bud as a reference to Rock Lick could be different. Bud has a different meaning for beer drinkers than pot smokers, so we can't just write it off, for now. I'm not writing anything off. I'm just trying to assign each thing some measure of importance.

"'The Beer To Go' with the filled in O's may be just doodling, but it might be something. I'll have to think about that one. It's kind of hard to say if she was really picking up anything or if she was just trying to keep you guys hooked on her mumbo-jumbo shtick. That's why I don't know how much importance to give this square wave and block with the stripes. Do you?" he asked.

"I think it looks like the battlements on the top of the old Moundsville Penitentiary, and the block represents a jail cell," Eden replied.

"Hmm, could be," he said. "Tell you what… it's getting late, and I have things I really must do before I can get to bed. Why don't you leave this with me, and I'll take a look at it later? I'll sleep on it."

"That's the same thing Amara told me," Eden said, and smiled at him.

"Yeah," he said, "but I'm a hell of a lot tougher than she was."

"Ever ride a Harley?"

"No, but I had some pretty hairy experiences in a VW bus one time," he grinned.

It was late, so the Deputy didn't go back to the office. By the time he could have driven to Rainelle, Buckey would have left for the day. So the Deputy took a cross-country route home to Random Creek. The back-road drive was a lot better for his state of mind anyway. He kept thinking about his conversation with Dave as he passed through the State Gamelands, ever alert for deer straying onto the roadway. Man, that Dave seems to be a nice guy. But boy, what a bullshitter!

The wetlands always seemed wetter this time of year. A small flock of Canada geese had made their home on one of the shallow ponds created by the State of Pennsylvania for just that purpose. The State bought up the land back in the early '60s and had reserved it for use by hunters. It was dotted here and there with foundations of homes that had been bought out and razed when the Game Commission took over.

Eden Whitloe came out at the top of the ridge behind his place, dropped over, and found his way home, where Sarge was waiting in the driveway for his evening meal.

Inside, the answering machine light blinked a greeting. "This is Buckey. Give me a call when you get in," said the machine. Eden dialed his number.

"Buckey. This is Eden."

"Anything to report?"

"I met with Dave Quinn—don't know if you've heard the name

or not?" He paused so Buckey could answer. When he didn't, Eden continued.

"Dave's an ex-Krishna. He knew Amara McClure, so I was over there picking his brain this afternoon."

"Oh, yeah, I heard of him. Made the newspapers back in the '80s when the Palace boys were being charged with all sorts of nasty shit. Did they leave him with any brain worth picking?"

Eden whistled. "Whew, old Dave's really out there!"

"I heard he and Amara were both waiting for the return of the mothership," the Sheriff said. "They were both doing the fortunetelling thing, weren't they?"

"Yeah, but I got the idea that Dave knows more about what he's doing. I don't know how much I buy into this psychic, other-world crapola, but what he says makes a lot of sense—if you boil out the bullshit."

"Is he willing to work with you?" Buckey asked.

"We kind of hit it off. I think he likes me and he'll help as much as he can."

"If that's it, I've got some news for you," Buckey said.

Shit, what now? Eden thought. "Go ahead, I'm sitting down."

"Amara has a niece. Her sister, who died many years ago, had a daughter, Shele Ocevan. Kind of an unusual name, I thought, but it turns out it's Irish—or at least it was when they came over on the boat," he said. "So far it's been just Miss Ocevan. Get it Eden, MISS Ocevan."

"You're as subtle as a sledgehammer, Buckey. You got anything else to tell me before I prepare my bath for the evening?" Eden asked.

"Use lots of bubble bath and deodorant, you're gonna meet Miss Ocevan tomorrow," he said, as he hung up.

The phone rang immediately.

"House," said a male voice on the other end of the line.

"What?"

"House," said Dave. "Keyhole house. Does that mean anything to you?"

"No. Where did you come up with that?"

"A good mystic never reveals his sources," he said.

"Sounds like we're back to Moundsville Prison. That's a keyhole house if I ever saw one."

"Thought it might be important, so that's why I called," Dave said.

"Thanks. Let me know if anything else comes up," Eden said. He hung up, discouraged. Now he wondered how tightly wrapped Dave Quinn really was.

A dream about Shele Ocevan followed him into sleep. She was a librarian, and like all librarians, had sprung, fully formed, from the librarian mold that God keeps somewhere in his basement. Every time the need arises, someone goes to the librarian mold and pops one out.

The dream revealed that Shele Ocevan looked exactly like all other librarians. Long, stringy hair, part of which was tucked up into some attempt at a bun. Except for a hint of rouge to touch up the pallor from working in dim-lit, dusty shelving, she wore no makeup. She had a hint of breasts, well concealed by a Mother Hubbard denim dress and a cardigan sweater with tissues stuck in the pockets, so she wouldn't be mistaken for another breed apart—male librarians. Male librarians look just like their female counterpart, if you replace the Mother Hubbard with corduroy khakis and keep the cardigan. Horn-rimmed glasses are optional for each gender, but more often than not are part of the uniform.

Eden Whitloe awoke, convinced he was having a psychic experience. Somehow he knew Shele Ocevan would be a librarian who would make a stop at Andy Walbridge's funeral home and pick up the ashes of Amara McClure. Leaving the home with Amara's urn cradled in both arms, unencumbered by breasts, she would tuck it into her car. She would take it off to a place she had reserved in the medieval history stacks in a library in upstate New York where Amara would sit in her jar for all eternity. It seems like anyone who died under unusual circumstances in George County left word that they wanted to be cremated. Eden made a mental note to look into a prearranged burial plan soon.

Chapter Ten

Shele the Librarian

The Deputy stopped at the convenience store, the one he never visits, and picked up coffee and doughnuts to munch as he went over the day's reports of stolen bicycles, folks who departed the BP without paying, and the bums caught pissing behind the ticket booth at the Grande Palace.

As he entered the office and passed by the front desk, Eden noticed quite a large group of people in the waiting area. One looked exactly like the librarian—female variety—of his dreams. Another woman, with long, dark-reddish hair, was sitting a bit farther toward the end of the bench. She was turned away and was talking with an older man who was dressed like a chauffeur. Eden immediately thought of Max, Norma Desmond's *Sunset Boulevard* chauffeur. The librarian could have been Norma, if she had worn a turban and something other than her Mother Hubbard.

On the other side of the room sat a sullen-looking, pimply faced teenage boy with the reddest hair Eden had ever seen. Its bright orange really set off his pimples. His skateboarder-flop, combed over to one side, had a tinge of green sprayed through it. He wore large safety pins for earrings, and a tattoo of a skull and pentagram adorned his right shoulder.

The Deputy immediately went to his office, shut the door, put his feet on the desk, and began eating his doughnut, washing it down with coffee that was too hot. Somewhere between doughnut, coffee, and paper juggling, Sheriff Buckey walked in.

"Get rid of that shit," he said, "I got folks waiting out there to talk with you."

"With me?" Eden asked, puzzled.

"Yes. I told them that you were appointed to head up the Myra Kinchloe investigation. And you are the one to see if anyone has questions about Amara McClure," he said.

"Where does that leave you in all of this? I'm just a curious flunky!" Eden angrily dumped his coffee and doughnut into the trashcan.

Buckey scowled. "I'll make the introductions. Then I'm going back out there and get that little red-headed geek and take him down to juvenile hall, if I don't kick his ass first. He spray-painted Mrs. Welchner's rose trellis day-glo orange and she's having a hissy fit. Or, you can take him, and then spend this evening watching for bums at the Grande—Mr. Flunky."

"That's okay, Buckey," Eden said. "You bring whoever it is that wants to see me right in here and I'll take it from there."

"Did you see Shele on the way in?" Buckey cocked an eyebrow at the Deputy and treated him to a lascivious grin.

"Let me guess, she's—uh—librarian, right?"

"Now, how did you know that?" Buckey asked, seemingly amazed. "Somebody had to tell you. She's not just a librarian though. She's an Assistant Professor of Library Science. You read about her in the files somewheres, right?"

"No, Buckey. Hell, she's got librarian written all over her! Anyone could have told that."

"Well, I couldn't. She sure had me fooled."

Eden postured. "I suppose some of us are more sensitive about these things. Some lawmen have an uncanny ability to—"

"Oh, shut up," the Sheriff broke in, "I'll go get her."

He left and returned a few minutes later, opening the door for Shele Ocevan. He followed her to the desk, where they stopped.

"This here is Miss Shele Ocevan." Buckey sounded like he was introducing the Queen of England. "That's Eden Whitloe—Deputy Whitloe."

Eden just about fell off the chair as he tried to stand to take her hand, which she extended over the desk.

"I'm very pleased to make your acquaintance," she said.

He heard himself saying, "Abba, abba, abba, duh... the ple—pleasure is all mine. Please take—have a chair."

Deputy Whitloe directed her to a chair that would give him a better view of her legs as she sat down. Wise move. All that stuff about librarians—strike that. This was most definitely not the librarian of his dreams. He had dreams that were of the Shele-induced type before, but they ran to those of the wetter variety. Oh God, she crossed her legs.

Green eyes. Not bluish-green or greenish-brown, but absolute emerald green. He couldn't help thinking about how difficult it must have been for her to carry Amara's urn wrapped in her arms, "encumbered" as she was. She wasn't tall, but tall enough. She wasn't thin, but thin enough. And she wasn't pretty. She was absolutely drop-dead gorgeous.

His mind raced. Assistant Professor... she should be mid-thirtyish, about the right age. Of course she could be engaged... or a lesbian... or—

"Abba, abba, duh," Eden stammered again, just for starters.

She smiled. "I'll bet you say that to all the girls."

"I mean, I—uh, how long have you been in town?"

"I got in Monday. I've been making arrangements so I can return to New York, back to work. I never dreamed there were so many details to handle."

Eden sympathized, "I know, it will take a while. I'm hoping you can make some time available to answer some questions—"

"What sort of questions?" she interrupted. "I thought this was pretty open-and-shut."

"Oh, it is, it is," he fumbled. "Open-and-shut." Not wanting to seem anxious to spend time with this beautiful, green-eyed, auburn-haired woman—was her hair brownish-red, or reddish-brown?—he continued, "Um, it's just routine. It won't take long. If you have things to do over at her house, I can follow along and ask questions while you work there." He managed this without a stutter or stammer. Did I sound too hurried, too anxious?

"Can you handle a dust cloth?" she smiled a perfect, pearl-white smile.

"Abba, abba, duh, I suppose so."

"Good," she said, "then stop by this afternoon, and you can ask your questions while I go through her papers."

"Is the older couple out there with you?" he asked.

"Oh, that's Norma and Eric Strohman," she said. "They were friends of Aunt Amara's. They can drop me off at the house on their way back to the motel. They're going to check out and return to New York this afternoon. I'm staying at the house until I can make other arrangements, so I can meet you over there. Around 1:00, okay?"

"See you then," he said. As she got up his eyes followed her flowing curves out the door.

Almost immediately, Buckey's face appeared in the doorway.

"Well?" he grinned.

"Holy shit!" Eden exclaimed, "I really love this job."

CHAPTER ELEVEN

BODIES

The morning was young and Buckey's Deputy still had reports to go over. But his mind raced ahead, most assuredly not on the papers in his In basket.

Around 11:30, the phone rang. Buckey was out, so Eden took the call.

"Hello, this is Dan Brackenridge, over at the State Police barracks. Is Buckey there?"

"He's out right now. Can I take a message?"

"Eden, is that you?"

"Yeah, Dan, what's up?" he asked.

"You sitting down?" he didn't wait for an answer. "Got another one for you."

"Missing or dead?" Eden was surprised at how matter-of-fact he sounded. Was this getting to be routine?

"This one's dead. June Talbot, Myra Kinchloe's girlfriend, the one that was with her the night she disappeared," he said. "Shot in the head, just like that McClure woman; only this time, it ain't no suicide."

"How can you be so sure?"

"She's shot in the back of the head—most of the occipital blown out—and they can't find a weapon," was the reply.

"Are you going to be around for a while? Fax the report over and I'll stop by to see you."

"I don't plan on going anywhere. Come on over," Dan said.

He found Amara McClure's phone number and called Shele.

"I may be late. Something came up and I have to go over to the State Police barracks for a while. If I don't get there by 2:00, I'll have to call and set up another time to see you, if that's all right?"

She sounded disappointed, saying she had lunch planned when he arrived. He told her to save it for a late afternoon snack instead. Eden was looking forward to seeing her far more than he wanted to see Dan Brackenridge, but duty called.

Not thrilled by the prospect of missing lunch with Shele, Eden got his stuff together and headed out to the Interstate. The State Police barracks was just off the main road that ran from the Interstate exit to the Rainelle business district.

Dan filled the Deputy in on the details of the case. They both had the uneasy feeling that the June Talbot case, the Kinchloe case, and Amara's death were all somehow intertwined. It occurred to him that the suicide could be what Buckey had called a "real slick murder." Two people in the same town who knew each other, being shot a few days apart, was too much of a coincidence. Even if there was no motive, the house was locked from the inside, and she was killed with her own gun.

"Two kids found her out at the state gamelands," Dan began as soon as the Deputy arrived. "They were fishing in one of the ponds out that way—"

"Which gamelands?" Eden interrupted. There were several throughout he county. The one he had driven through on his way home yesterday was the largest.

"The one out by Brightbrook."

The kids had found June lying right out in the open, below an earthen dam that held back the water of a small stream that formed a pond.

Dan said, "No one but kids would try fishing there. The ponds out that way are seldom stocked this time of year, and I don't think that one ever is. The dam had hidden the body from view and it was pure chance that the boys found it. If they hadn't happened along, she might have laid there until hunting season next fall."

Dan said the boys were questioned, but couldn't add much to what the crime-scene investigators turned up. The investigators, efficient as ever, turned up very little.

"Single gunshot wound to the back of the head," he recited matter-of-factly, "instantaneous death, no gun found at the scene, body didn't appear to have been moved. No footprints, no tire marks, no dropped papers, shell casings. No apparent motive, so far—no one with anything to gain from her death. No signs of a struggle and no evidence of assault or rape. Looks like someone just took her out there and dropped her like a bad habit. From the looks of the top of the dam, she was shot there—might have been kneeling with her head forward or lying on her stomach. Then, somebody just kicked her over the edge. One of the state cops who had been working homicide up in Homewood said it had all the earmarks of a gangland-style execution."

"Not what you'd expect for George County," Eden said. "But then, we don't expect any sort of murder in George County, do we?"

When Eden asked if they had connected Amara's handgun to her suicide, he got a surprising answer. Since everyone had thought of her death as an open-and-shut suicide, the coroner either hadn't gone after the bullet, or assumed it was in such bad shape it would be useless for ballistics. It depended on who was telling the story and which story you wanted to believe. Small-town ineptitude was explanation enough.

Whatever the case, the bullet was now history. The Deputy's gut told him both women were killed by the same weapon, but there was no point in telling anyone now.

"Can I use your phone?" Eden asked. Dan handed it to him and rose to leave.

"Hello, this is Eden—Eden Whitloe, the Deputy."

"Oh, hello," said Shele. "Are you going to make it today?"

"I'm on my way over, if that's all right."

"Come on over," she said. "I'll have something ready for you to eat when you get here."

Ah, yes, something to eat, he thought, remembering how she had crossed her legs in his office, as he hung up the phone.

He asked Dan, "I suppose you have someone dragging the pond for a gun?"

"Oh yeah, dragging the pond," Dan replied. "We don't have enough men right now, but we'll get to it tomorrow or the next day. Hmm... you know..." Dan began.

"What?"

"Wouldn't surprise me none if we find that other girl—uh, Kinchloe—the same way." Eden felt that Dan was watching for a reaction. He wasn't about to give the state cop the satisfaction.

He left the office shaking his head. Probably get around to dragging the pond in a day or two. Only two people dead so far, and one still missing. No good reason to rush—shit!

CHAPTER TWELVE

BACK AT AMARA'S PLACE

Eden went up the short driveway to the rear entrance of Amara's musty old Victorian, which now smelled of cinnamon. He noted that no cats rushed to meet him when he knocked. Shele came to the screen door, juggling two open boxes of letters and papers while trying to flip the latchhook on the door.

"Here, take this," she said, handing him a box as he entered. "You can set it over there," she pointed to the kitchen table. "Sorry for the mess."

There were boxes, folders, and newspaper clippings everywhere. It looked as if she were looking for something in particular. She was nearly as disheveled as the kitchen. She had attempted to tie her hair back, but strands hung into her face and eyes. Her blouse had spots of dust from the boxes, and her Bermuda shorts were wrinkled from where she had evidently been sitting on the floor. Her clothing was immaculately laundered and ironed; she was just what folks used to call "mussed." On Shele, mussed looked great.

"What happened to all the cats?" Eden asked, as he put the box on the table.

"All eight of them went to the animal shelter when they first found Aunt Amara," she said. "Can you imagine living here with eight cats? There's not much I could do with them. They'll probably be put to sleep if they can't find them homes," she said a bit coolly.

"When I was over here with the Sheriff, I counted nine. They must have missed one." He had the feeling Milagro was the missing kitty.

"No hungry cats have shown up, so any missing probably found a new home." She paused. "Anyway, go ahead," she said.

"Abba, duh, go ahead what?" He had been distracted, looking over an expanse of creamy thigh and wondering what it might be like to—

"What you came over here for was to ask me about Aunt Amara's suicide," she said, with a hint of exasperation.

"Oh, yes, Aunt Amara." Moving rapidly from lechery to suicide was no easy task. "Have you found anything? I was hoping you might turn up something in her papers—bank statements, late payments, debts, that sort of thing?"

"I met with her attorney over the financials. There was a term life insurance policy that will cover most of the funeral expenses, and most of her pension will revert to her professional association. She left a sort of will that essentially gives everything else, which is pretty much nothing, to the humane society." she said.

Shele sighed. "I thought maybe there was a financial motive for her taking her own life, but I turned up absolutely nothing. She rented the furnished house and didn't have any other real estate. I wondered about a terminal illness, maybe one of those things she didn't want to suffer to the end, so I checked her doctor, but nothing there either. It's pretty useless trying to figure out why anyone kills oneself."

"Are there any other living relatives?" Eden asked.

"Maybe some distant cousins, but so far as I know, I'm it. Her sister—my mom—died long ago, when I was little. Believe me, if Aunt Amara had anything, I'd be the one digging for it, because I'd be first in line."

"You know, Shele, we're both examples of those sad cases of people who have no living family. I'm really sorry—" He saw no advantage to mentioning his in-laws in Arizona, at this point.

"Well, that isn't to say that we formed a family when she was

living. I called her once in a great while, but that was the extent of
our relationship. We were never close."

Eden wanted to suggest that this would be an excellent time to
establish a close friendship with someone who knew her last family
link, namely him. But so far, this was feeling only like a professional
relationship.

"I suppose we can't get this over with soon enough," he said.

"I guess that's the way I feel," she said. "I just want it go away.
But if I leave it like that, I'll never have any peace—you know?"
she said, as if she wanted him to convince her to do something else.

"You mean you need closure?"

"If I—we—decide it was a simple suicide, I'd like to know if it's
symptomatic of something genetic—you know, something I might
have inherited. Is it something I should watch out for? Does that
make any sense?" She didn't wait for him to answer.

"Okay, I'll come right out with it. I know you'll think I'm nutty,
and I don't have anything to go on, but here it is anyway. I have
a feeling you are going to poke around in this thing until you
convince yourself it was a murder."

Eden was taken aback. "You sound awfully certain about that.
Did you find something I need to know about?"

"You want to know what I found? Nothing. There is absolutely
nothing to make me think anything other than suicide, and that
bothers me. And, I know if it bothers me—it bothers you."

"Well, it does bother the heck out of me," Eden acknowledged.
"But I don't see any evidence that suggests anything but suicide, at
this point."

"She didn't use alcohol or other drugs," Shele said. "She appears
to have been mentally stable, although who could ever tell about
Aunt Amara. She was healthy as a horse, had a good life, and
steady income. She had visitors constantly in and out of here, and
she was working with you guys. Well, who would just up and kill

themselves in the middle of solving a crime?"

"Yeah, I know. We're still at square one," he said.

"Eden," she began. He liked the fact that she used his first name. "It's all over town that they found the friend of that missing Kinchloe woman out at the state gamelands. They found her shot in the head, just like my Aunt Amara. And that—that Kinchloe girl is still missing—and God knows what else," she tried to stifle a sob, and tears welled over onto her cheeks. "Two women dead, and someone may have murdered both, and one missing. Who knows who may be next?" She hung her head and began to sob, her shoulders shaking.

Eden had been through dicey moments as a Deputy, but he preferred any of them to dealing with a sobbing female. If a gorgeous, redheaded, green-eyed woman was enough to turn him into a tongue-tied doofus, then imagine when she started to cry. What to do? If he reached out to her, would she lash out and tell him to keep his harassing hands to himself? He decided to risk it.

Wordlessly, he simply put his hand on hers. To his surprise, she put her hand on top of his and gently squeezed it.

"I'm sorry," she said, "I hardly know you, and here I sit, blubbering. You must think I'm a big baby."

"No, I don't think that. And I think you may be right about your aunt. All indications are suicide at this point. We may not know each other very well, but I think we are on the same wavelength."

He hoped that left an opening for their relationship to develop into something more personal.

"Thanks," she said, slipping her hand further up his arm. "I thought you might agree with me. I'm a pretty good judge of people, and I felt I could trust you from the very beginning."

There was the opening he hoped for. He put his hand on hers that was squeezing his upper arm, and she pulled it to her breast. Deputy Whitloe felt his knees turn to jelly. For the first time, he noticed the fragrant perfume of her hair.

"Well! I'll bet you're hungry," she announced, and stood. "I promised you lunch." She strode to the refrigerator. Shele set out potato salad, baked beans, and made sandwiches.

"Aunt Amara didn't have much food on hand. I guess she ate out a lot. Do you eat out a lot?"

He wanted to tell her he was a starving bachelor and would appreciate any help he could get, but didn't. "You know how it is to live alone," he said. "I eat too much junk and fast food. I do it to avoid cooking."

"Yeah. We single people need someone around to remind us to take care of ourselves! Do you have anyone—I mean, are there any other people in your life?" she asked.

"Um—since you brought it up, how about you? You go first," he smiled.

"Oh," she blushed, "I didn't mean anything by that. I was just curious—concerned, you know."

"Well, if you are looking for someone to take care of—" he teased.

"You never know," she said. "Let's see how much care you need."

She shoved a plate his way. "Here, clean up your plate like a good boy."

Clearly, Shele Ocevan knew what she was doing.

They ate in silence. As they ate, she looked through Amara's papers, tossing keepers into a cardboard box on the floor and the rest into a trash can.

She took their plates to the sink, rinsing them, while Eden enjoyed the view.

"So, where do we go from here?" she asked, still facing the sink.

Eden bit his tongue. To bed, to bed, he said in his head. But aloud he said, "Oh—uh—I've been assigned to the Kinchloe case, at least until she turns up. That case includes June Talbot—and for now, I'm including your aunt. Remember, I'm a deputy, so I don't have a lot of legal standing, but I do have more access than ordinary citizens or private eyes."

Shele looked thoughtful. "At my campus, classes are out in a couple of weeks. Then finals and commencement. I'll get my student assistant to give and score the exams, and she can fax me the class roster. I'll do the grades and get them back in, and not have to go back up there for a while.

"Actually, if you think I can be of any help, I'll phone the dean and arrange not to return until fall matriculation," she said.

Normally, he wouldn't want to have some amateur hanging around and dabbling in an investigation. But it was time for an exception.

"Well... Shele, it's great that you want to be involved... but I don't think it's a good idea for you to—well, I don't want to feel responsible if anything might happen... and I don't think Buckey— that's the Sheriff—I don't think he would approve... you know what I mean?" He paused for the objection that would be followed by her insistence that she be included.

"I suppose you're right," she began, as his heart sank. "I guess I would just be in your way."

"Well, but do you have any special skills?" he asked hopefully. "The Sheriff was all for getting your aunt involved, because he thought she had some sort of psychic powers."

"Oh, I've got some very special skills," she looked at him, grinning suggestively. "I'm good at organizing and document research—a good paper sleuth. Also, you should know that I was pre-law as an undergrad, so I have some useful knowledge. I don't know about psychic abilities, but I have great intuition—I'm a woman, in case you didn't notice. Plus, I make good company."

Eden's heart beat a little faster. Atta girl, leave me an opening.

You have some very definite assets, and yeah, I noticed that you are a woman. "Um, I think that would impress Buckey. Abba, duh—uh, I could ask him about it. No, I'll write a proposal—duh, abba, after I ask him." Eden was struggling to get his "abba" under control.

She seemed as excited as he was, hopefully for the same reason.

"Okay," she began, "let's assume Buckey agrees to us working on this together—then what?"

"Then we really dig in," he said. "This will take a lot of research and legwork. I hope you are tenacious and don't discourage easily. We may be at this all summer."

"Oh, don't make it sound so grueling," she said. "I'm sure we'll have time for fun."

Ding. It began to dawn on the Deputy that she was looking for some excitement in her life. And maybe that could include jumping his bones.

"I'm sure we will," he said, "find time for some fun."

They spent the rest of the afternoon looking through Amara McClure's lifelong accumulation of papers and junk.

"Did your Aunt have a computer?" he asked.

"No," replied Shele, "I think she used one over at the Senior Center for e-mail. I have her address in my wallet. Just a second— I'll look for it."

In a few minutes, Shele handed him a scrap of paper: amac55@ adsalesnet.com. It would be useful only if he could trace her account. That might take a court order, and that required a reason. For now, it was pure speculation.

Eden found one interesting thing and pocketed it, without mentioning it to Shele—no need to bother her with it, yet. It was a ticket stub for the Delf Norona Museum and the Moundsville Penitentiary Tour. A lot of people in the tri-state had visited the Moundsville tourist sites, and he was sure there was no connection between her visit and Myra's—but then, who really knew? At this point, if a straw came up, he would grasp it.

When he turned the prison tour stub over, there was one of Amara's signature drawings—a keyhole! Was the prison the "Keyhole House" Dave Quinn had mentioned?

"I need to get back to the office before 5:00," he said to Shele, who was busily going through a box of costume jewelry.

"Okay," she said, "give me a call when you want to get together—actually, give me a call tomorrow."

"You bet," he said, as he headed toward his pickup in the driveway.

CHAPTER THIRTEEN

SEARCHING FOR SYMBOLS

The Keyhole House, 129 Gunnison, private, was built in 1889. It has the box window where railroad telegraphers would sit and watch for coming trains. They would take the telegraph message and attach it to a pole with a loop and hold it out to the coming train. The engineer would put his arm through the loop, grab the message, drop the stick, and never stop the train.

That's what came up when, on a whim, Eden searched "keyhole house" on Google. Aside from all the porno hits, the one in Gunnison, Colorado, was about the best he could come up with and that wasn't looking very hopeful.

He searched "Who-is" for "adsalesnet.com" and found it was a service that was used by sex toy merchants and others who want to remain anonymous. They made a business out of keeping their clients' names private and away from law enforcement. He felt there was no point in pursuing the e-mail thing any further, but he would ask them for access to Amara's e-mail files nonetheless. The rest of the evening was devoted to surfing around the net looking for information on the three women. The next morning Eden spent poking around the usual databases for leads but didn't come up with much more. He found that Amara—as with a lot of people her age—had encountered some credit card trouble in the past, but she had only missed a couple of payments.

Just for the hell of it, he got in the pickup and drove out to the gamelands where the boys had found the body of June Talbot. He drove by three different ponds until he came to one that still had some tell-tale, yellow crime scene tape clinging to a few of the bushes near the dirt road that led up to the shallow end. He got out and walked up a slight incline so he could get an overview of the dam. From that short rise, it looked very much like the VanBurean pond. Eden could imagine Marion Crane's car being pulled from the depths by a tow truck. It looked somewhat like Amara's drawing that Buckey had shown him earlier. Must be a dozen ponds in the county that look exactly like that, he thought.

Turning to where he had just begun walking, he looked at his truck parked at the side of the road. In his mind's eye, he could imagine someone getting out of a car, dragging a young woman along by the hand, and leading her to the breast of the dam, all the while holding a gun on her. He could see her standing there looking down to the embankment as the person raised the gun and—Eden jumped. He was startled by a crash in the brush off to his right as a huge whitetail buck bounded down a maintenance road leading off from the pond.

Deputy Eden Whitloe got back to the office around 10:30. Buckey came in shortly after. Eden could hear him out in the front office, batting the breeze with someone at the receptionist's desk, so he stuck his head through the door to catch Buckey's attention, and waved him toward his open door. The Sheriff spent several minutes finishing his conversation before heading his way.

"If you have a moment, there's something I want to ask you about," Eden said, as Buckey came into the office, took a seat, and put one leg over the arm of the chair. Eden supposed this was to let him know that he belonged to Buckey, and Buckey was perfectly relaxed in his Deputy's presence. At least this body language was preferable to a bite on the neck by an alpha wolf asserting his dominance. "Anything from the master sleuth on the Kinchloe affair?" Buckey asked.

"I think the Kinchloe disappearance, the Talbot murder, and

the McClure suicide are linked. We should refer to them all as one case."

"No shit, Sherlock," Buckey scowled. "Did it take you two whole days to figure that out?"

Eden winced. "You know how few leads there are on this mess, so why don't you give it a break? The Grande Palace ticket booth is looking like prime duty compared to this shit, so maybe you want to take over the investigation?"

Eden had learned that when he wanted something from Buckey, he had to begin by making it look as if he was the one being greatly put upon. Then the Sheriff would be more agreeable, so he could keep Buckey's good will. Like most lifetime elected officials, Buckey desperately wanted everyone to like him.

"I'm sorry, Eden, I just got off the phone from talking with Myra's daddy," he said. "I feel like I just got reamed, and I couldn't say shit to him about it. You got anything new?"

"I wanted to ask you if I could use Miss Ocevan as a consultant," Eden said hopefully. "It wouldn't cost the county or anything. It would be like an extension of the arrangement you had with her aunt."

"Is she a psychic too?" Buckey sounded sarcastic.

"No, I don't think so. She was in pre-law and has a lot of research experience. And, because of her aunt, she has an interest in the case, and she's really, really bright."

"The only reason I would even consider it," Buckey began, "is because I got her aunt involved in the first place—I guess I sort of owe her. So, okay. But you're responsible for her, you got that straight?"

"Yes, sir!" the Deputy snapped back at him. "You want me to put the request in writing?"

"That might be real advisable. If any questions come up later, I can refer to it and claim you're the one who screwed up. And Eden.

Keep the pecker tracks off the county's pickup truck seat."

"Absolutely sir, I'll keep that pickup seat as clean and as neat as it was after you took Kathy Robinson out to the state park a couple of years ago."

Buckey grimaced. "I didn't hear that. Get the hell out of here!"

At noon, Eden called Shele to check in. He was looking for more help from her in the investigation than he was likely to get from Buckey.

"I have something over here I want you to see," she said mysteriously. "Don't get all excited; it's just a notebook. It's probably nothing, but I want your take before I tossed it."

"Hold on to it, I'll be over right after work," Eden said. "I have some good news for you. Buckey approved your working with me on this. Nothing official, of course. It will just be a matter of you helping out in a clerical way."

"That's great!" she exclaimed. "I'll see if I can get the landlady to let me rent until the end of September. It would be nice if I could stay right here."

"That would be great," he said, "I'll be over sometime after 5:00." He called Dave Quinn's number and there was no answer, no voice mail, and no answering machine. What a way to run a business. He supposed Dave could pick up psychic vibrations and didn't need any of the hi-tech conveniences the rest of us require.

About 15 minutes later, Dave called. "I was just wondering if there was anything new on the investigation," he said. "Did you turn up anything on the keyhole house?"

"That's funny," Eden said, "I just called your place. There was no answer."

"I had a psychic vibration that let me know you were trying to reach me," he said. As the Deputy was rolling his eyes, Dave added quickly, "I have caller I.D."

Dave's abilities as a seer suddenly dropped several points.

"Nothing new on this end," Eden reported.

"I think if we could get together, I could come up with that keyhole connection. I've had some pretty strong feelings about it since you were out here. There are some things I didn't think of before."

Dave's wanting to "get together" gave Eden a moment when he wondered about old Dave's gender preferences. He didn't seem interested in Amara from that standpoint, and it flashed through his mind he might have more than an investigator's interested in meeting with a deputy sheriff. A vision of the cop in the Village People flashed by briefly.

"I've got Amara's niece helping me on the case now. She's a paralegal, you know," Eden lied. "She may be able to provide some insights. I'll bring her out with me, if you don't mind."

"Sounds good to me. Give me a call before you come. I'll look forward to meeting her. You know, I don't think Amara ever mentioned her niece," he said.

Eden noted that Dave didn't seem the least disappointed upon hearing that Eden was bringing a woman along.

CHAPTER FOURTEEN

LEY LINES AND ANCIENT FORCES

When Eden Whitloe arrived at Amara McClure's house—now it could be called Shele Ocevan's house—he found her in the back yard relaxing in a lawn chair with a magazine. "Looking for clues?" he grinned.

"Oh, Eden, I didn't hear you drive up! I guess I was absorbed in reading this crap." She turned the magazine so he could see it: the Metaphysical Journal.

"I'll bet the old gal had a lot of stuff like that," Eden said.

"The cover story is *The Old Straight Track* by Alfred Watkins," she said. "I thought it might be about railroading. Was I wrong! Turns out it's a book about some sort of lines that run between ancient sites—ley lines, the author calls them."

"I remember seeing a program on *Discovery* or *A&E* about straight lines, or roads that connected up Anasazi sites in the southwest. Is it anything like that?"

"I think so," she said, "it's all pretty esoteric—about energy rays, magnetics, and psychic forces. You know how aunty was. She should have been British. If there was a paranormal or extrasensory phenomenon, she was into it. The guy who wrote this stuff was a Brit too. Seems like all the flat-world, flying saucer, extraterrestrial types are over there. Aunt Amara was never one for logical explanations for much of anything."

Eden smiled. "Now, don't go knocking Miss McClure too much—she is responsible for my beautiful, new assistant, you know." He laid it on thick.

"Well, now, aren't you the smoothie." She blushed slightly. "Anyway, check out this paragraph—"

Alfred Watkins originated the term "ley line" in the 1920s to describe alignments of ancient structures, paths, and natural sacred sites in England. Watkins believed these "straight tracks" to have been used by ancient traders. He said "leys" determined that people from the Neolithic Era, through the Bronze and Iron Ages, and well into the Christian era in Britain, located their holy sites on straight alignments with other holy sites. Since his death in 1935, others have theorized that leys were built for ritual or funerary purposes. Some leys have been found to demonstrate definite astronomical alignments. Since the 1960s, the term "ley lines" has come to be associated with belief in dowsing, geomantic lines of force—geomancy, the Chinese occult system of feng shui, and other supernatural phenomena. More recently, authors like Paul Devereux contend that such alignments manifest a metaphysical component. See Paul Devereux: *Shamanism and the Mystery Lines.*"

"Isn't feng shui about putting your surroundings in harmony so you can live and work better?" Eden asked.

"I think that's it. I remember seeing a *60 Minutes* or *20/20* about how some Asians are cleaning up by designing offices and homes so they have the right qi, I think they called it—the right energy forces to make your surroundings whole," she explained.

"Isn't it pronounced chee, instead of key?" he said. "I always have a problem pronouncing foreign words. When I went to school, we learned phonics. That's why I can't spell worth a darn."

"Depends on whom you talk to and who's doing the translating," Shele replied. "The Americanized key seems to be most used, though. There are some feng shui freaks who believe pets can determine where you should sleep in your home. Dogs like to sleep in the best places."

"I usually get to sleep where my cat sleeps. Seems like I have to kick his butt off the sofa every time I want to take a nap. You think Amara was into feng shui design?"

"Probably that, and anything else she could use to pry a buck from some sucker's wallet," she said. "If she wasn't a con artist, she had all the makings to become an excellent one. She was something else."

"Shit!" Eden exclaimed, as if he were alone. He was alone in his thoughts.

"What?" she said.

"Oh, I just thought of something funny, that's all. Well, not funny ha-ha, but curious. Here's another insight into the keyhole thing..."

"You mean the keyhole-shaped doodles Amara made?"

"Yeah. Dave Quinn—that's a guy your aunt knew, a sort of colleague, you might say—he's an ex-Krishna you'll meet soon. Anyway, he called the other night and said, I quote, house. That didn't mean much until he said, keyhole house. At least that's what I thought he said at the time. Now I'm thinking—go ahead, call me nutty—this is another straw I'm grasping at. Suppose instead of keyhole house he was saying qi whole house? What do you think?"

"Some pretty far-out shit, that's what I think," Shele laughed. "Suppose he did say qi whole house. What does that do for us? I think the whole feng shui thing is just a scheme to loosen some yuppies from their gelt."

Eden ran with it. "Amara, June, and probably Myra were killed by Chinese mafia hit men who were doing freelance house cleaning in George County—cleaning up the excess qi. Hell, how should I know? I'm just a country-bumpkin Deputy-assed Sheriff. But, you know what? I know one thing: all of this stuff may not be paranormal, extrasensory or psychic, but its all sure-as-hell tied together somehow. The more we understand what's going on, the more we'll be able to deal with whatever comes down."

"Eden, let's make sure we are on the same page here. I don't have time for any of Aunty Amara's mystical, psychic bullshit. Knowing her and her shenanigans, I don't believe she did either. If you buy into the 'dark powers' or other mystical stuff, that's fine, but don't look to me for support. If you're okay with that, we can work together, if not, I'll get my hat." She was serious.

"No, I'm with you on the metaphysical stuff," he quickly assured her. "But I have to keep an open mind. There are too many things out there to be explained entirely by chance or coincidence. Maybe it's just crap we don't have a rational explanation for yet, but I have a tough time explaining some things with scientific or rational processes. But I promise I won't look to you for anything other than a scientific approach to this case."

"Feng shui has made a big splash with Generation X-ers. Some of them are really into it. There's a lot of money in it," she said.

"Yeah, and just about anything else that isn't rational or smacks of recognized religion. All the New Age stuff—crystals, channeling, mandalas, runes, you name it. I always thought that was what Amara was into. I believed she was some kind of New Age guru, the Edgar Cayce of George County," he said.

"Oh, she was probably the guru of George County all right, but she was a lot more charlatan than guru," Shele grinned. "I think the New Age stuff passed her by, though. If she'd been on top of it, I would probably be sitting in a Philadelphia lawyer's office and we'd be splitting up her fortune right now.

"Aunty needed an agent and some direction. On her own, she wasn't much more than a carny with a mitt camp. If she'd gotten into the crystals, channeling, and feng shui routine, Lord knows where she would have gone with it."

"Are you an atheist?" Eden asked abruptly. He really didn't mean for it to sound that direct, but after the anti-supernatural diatribe, he was curious.

"I suppose I should be put off with that kind of question. Normally, I'd tell you it's none of your damned business. But given the circumstances—no, I'm not an atheist," she answered. "I suppose on one level I'm the same as anyone who was indoctrinated into Christianity as a kid. Religion doesn't hold up very well under a rational microscope, but I'll agree with you on one thing. We are left with some things that only religion, or the metaphysical, can explain. After all, what does it cost to claim you are a Christian? Given the prospect of heaven or hell after all this is over, I might as well invest a bit in Christianity—maybe I'll slip into heaven by the back door. If I were an atheist, I would never even get a chance," she laughed.

She added, "I try to do what my Christian upbringing says is right. Let me put it this way: I don't belong to any organized Bible-thumping bunch. I'll go to whatever church you want to drag me to, but don't expect me to join up, or swallow a lot of their dogma."

Eden smiled. "You don't have to worry about me dragging you to tent revivals. I'm not much of a churchgoer myself. When my wife was living, she made me go to the Presbyterian Church across from the courthouse, but I never really got into it. I don't think some of the heavy-duty Christians were into it either, except for the business contacts. They probably had a lot in common with your aunt."

"Well," she said with relief, "I'm glad that's out of the way. I'll try to keep an open mind, but you know where I stand, and now I know where you are coming from—I think."

Eden looked her in the eyes. "Well, now that part of truth-or-dare is out of the way, maybe you can tell me what you think of me some time."

She smiled and averted her eyes. "Oh, I'll reserve that one for a future date. Sometime a lot later—Dudley."

Eden grinned. "Look, I'm a Deputy Sheriff, not a Mountie. And

I don't have a horse named Shep." He watched Saturday morning cartoons, too. "So that's what you think of me, huh?"

"Down boy," she soothed. "We'll get into that some other time."

"There's just one thing—"

"What's that?"

"I'm going to introduce you to David Quinn..."

"And?"

"David Quinn may actually be the guru of George County. Don't get me wrong, he knows a lot about the New Age stuff, or whatever you want to call it. He's not getting rich with it, so I don't think he has the same approach your aunt did." Eden hoped to ease the introducing of Miss Rational to Mr. Mystic.

CHAPTER FIFTEEN

GETTING TO KNOW ALL ABOUT YOU

Eden had a problem with drooping eyes as he talked with Shele; his eyes kept drooping to her chest. But his professionalism triumphed, and he continued preparing her to meet the mighty Quinn. "Old Dave is really—uh—out there. Probably did too many peyote buttons or shrooms back in the '70s—Carlos Castanada city. I couldn't place him at first, but he reminds me a lot of Billy, you know, Billy the Kid, the Dennis Hopper character in *Easy Rider*. Only he doesn't say 'man' a lot. I guess he got over that part of being cool."

"I'll be glad to meet him," Shele said. "Believe me, I won't mention my doubts on what we just talked about. I'd really like to meet someone who actually believes all that stuff. That is, if he's sane."

Eden chuckled. "Well, Dave talks a good game. He seems like a nice enough guy. I sensed his fondness for your aunt. You know, I never thought of it until now, but he never even mentioned anything New Age. He kept referring to the infinite. Come to think of it, he never mentioned karma either. That was big with the hippies back in the '60s and '70s."

"A bit strange for a guru."

"Old Dave's kinda strange for a furniture maker, too." Eden said. "And I don't think he'd like the term guru. He seemed to like Amara, but he also recognized her shallowness on spiritual things. He told me that he would share techniques of the business with her. That part of it is finding out what people want to hear, and then telling them in ways that were open to interpretation. According to him, Amara wasn't so much a psychic as a... well, you shouldn't be offended by this, because from what you're telling me, you'd agree with him... a quack."

"Oh, that's exactly what I think. She walked like a duck, so—" Shele said, a bit defiantly.

"I just don't want to make Quinn out as the bad guy. I don't want you to think he was being harsh," Eden assured her. "He doesn't have a harsh bone in his body. He does the same sort of fortunetelling that Amara did for pocket change, and I think he gets his jollies doing it. Who knows, maybe that's how he meets chicks!"

Shele rolled her eyes.

Eden pressed on. "Dave got involved with the Krishnas over near Moundsville. Evidently, he was a devotee until just before the Krishna murders and Swami Kirtanananda's racketeering conviction. There was a big power squabble or something. Guru Prabhupada founded the Moundsville bunch. He died in, I think, 1977. Kirtanananda was one of the New Vrindavan founders who took over the commune's leadership about when Prabhupada died. Anyway, to make this windy story short, after Kirtanananda became the head cheese, Quinn left the movement and started his furniture business out in Brightbrook.

"I don't know why he lost faith, or dropped out, but his perception was that New Vrindavan had lost its spiritual initiative and turned toward materialism. I don't know if Kirtanananda's taking over had anything to do with that."

Shele smiled. "You know, I'm beginning to like this Dave Quinn. A devotee who becomes a rebel and goes off on his own—that interests me."

"I just think he's a mellow guy who dropped out and tuned in to his own views," Eden said. "Anyway, he dropped into the right place. Several flower children took up residence near Brightbrook in the '70s. Folks just left them to themselves, and over the years they have blended into whatever social structure there is in that end of the county."

"Well, let me know when you want to meet with him. Outside of putting this crap mountain into some kind of order, my time is free. Bring on old Mandrake," Shele said.

"Oh," said Eden. "I almost forgot. You said something about a notebook."

"Oh, yes, that. It's probably just Aunt Amara's pseudo-metaphysical stuff. Here it is." She handed Eden a small loose-leaf notebook.

The first few wrinkled pages offered little, just some anonymous phone numbers.

Then came a page with a mess of doodles... and keyholes, or the figure Amara had drawn that resembled a keyhole.

Eden pointed to the figure. "Does that mean anything to you?"

"I don't believe... uh... you know, I'll bet she drew those around the time she was having all the locks changed in her house. I remember her saying that. The doors all had those old skeleton-key locks, and someone told her to change them for security. I'll bet that's it. I remember seeing some of the old skeleton keys."

The next page farther bore three scrawled references:

- GN Dulnev—*Parapsychology and Psychophysics*
- VP Zolokazov & VA Zagriadsky, *Experiments on Levitation & Telekinesis*
- LM Porvin & SV Speransky—*Study of the Man-Animal Bond*

Eden remarked, "Hmm, all Russkies. Evidently, Amara was interested in Russian studies of the paranormal. These must be notes she took in a library."

"Yeah, the old Soviet Union was really into that stuff during the Cold War," Shele agreed. She looked over Eden's shoulder as he thumbed through the notebook. "I wonder what they've been up to since their funding collapsed?"

"They all work for ad agencies now," he quipped. "Isn't that where you would go if you knew all about mind control and predicting what people might do?"

Shele snorted. "Oh look," she said, pointing a bit farther down the page to an address:

Vasily Zagarev
1118 Eighth Street
Moundsville, WV 26041

"Yeah, another reference to Moundsville," Eden observed. "Seems like everybody involved in this had some affinity for the place. Folks from this end of the county go over there to shop. It's a dangerous curvy-hilly road, but it beats traveling back through to Rainelle."

"There's something in Rainelle?" Shele winked. "Did I miss something?"

Eden laughed. "There's not a heck of a lot in all of George County! Folks in the center or eastern part never go west unless it's to work in the coal mines."

They looked for Vasily Zagarev in the phone book, but no luck. Directory Assistance said he wasn't listed.

Eden frowned. "We'll keep this of course, but for now the notebook seems to be a dead end."

"Okay," she said. "Do you have any other leads?"

"Nothing solid. But I do have an idea. Why don't we take a break from this and get dinner? And maybe a movie?"

"Okay," she agreed. "On one condition."

"What?"

"That we don't discuss any of this while we're out. Enough for awhile!"

"Deal. When shall I pick you up?'"

That evening they headed to Morgantown, and soon were dining in Eden's favorite little Italian restaurant.

He quickly discovered to his dismay that, aside from Amara's death and the investigation, they had little to talk about—at first. But they soon found a common interest in offbeat movies. They watched a *Moonstruck* rip-off, a chick flick, which Shele found wonderful. Eden pretended to be moonstruck too, and got through the evening with some hand touching, which developed into handholding, which advanced to a hand that found its way into his lap. By the time they left the theater, he held his jacket in front of him as a shield against curious eyes. All in all, quite a successful evening.

When he pulled up to the house, Eden walked her to the back door to say goodnight. Spring peepers sang away, and a near-full moon shone upon them. Eden's thoughts were headed exactly where you think they were. He took her hand and they looked at one another. In the distance, a train horn sounded faintly. And that was when Shele suddenly began to act very strangely. Her soft, dry hand in his suddenly began to perspire, and her eyes grew distracted. "I've got to go in," she said quickly. The train horn sounded again, a bit louder, as the train approached, and Shele shuddered. "I'm sorry, I have to go!" she squeezed his hand, gave him a quick peck on the cheek.

"Shele, what's wrong?" Eden said, disconcerted.

"It's not you! I like you, a lot. Call when we can meet with Dave Quinn." The train horn sounded much louder, and Shele looked like a frightened doe, ready to bolt. She squeezed his hands, hard. "Call me!" She abruptly turned, entered the house, and quickly closed the door.

Eden drove toward his house on Random Creek, bewildered. Great evening, all going well, and suddenly at the end, Shele fell apart. Afraid of men? Not likely. She said it wasn't me—and she likes me—and to call her. What the hell was that all about?

Sarge was waiting in the driveway when Eden arrived at the creek. It was midnight, but he decided to call Dave Quinn anyway.

"Yeah?" said a sleepy voice on the other end of the phone.

"Oh—I didn't get you out of bed, did I?" Eden asked innocently.

"Who the f—... who is this?"

"It's me, Eden Whitloe, the Deputy Sheriff."

"Umph. It's real good to know you law officers are watching over us around the clock. But ya know, some folks sleep after midnight."

"Sorry, guess I lost track of the time," the Deputy fibbed. "If this isn't a good time, I'll call back later."

"Well, now that you got me up, I'll be awake the next couple of hours, so you might as well go ahead. Did you learn something new?"

"Not really," Eden said, "Reason I called... would it be okay for me to stop by tomorrow? I want to bring over the other person who's helping me on the case—the one I told you about."

"Oh, yeah. Amara's niece is helping you. Yeah, go ahead and bring her over. I'd like to meet her."

"Any particular time good for you?"

"In my line of work, there's no good time and no bad either," he said. "You come on over whenever the mood strikes you. If you come in the afternoon, there may be someone here you can meet. I'll be here all day."

"Who is it that we might meet, Dave?"

"Oh, I'll introduce you when you get here."

"Afternoon it will be, then," Eden said as he hung up.

CHAPTER SIXTEEN

THE MYSTIC AND THE MORMON HERESY

At 11:00, Eden called Shele.

"Hey Shele, it's Eden. First—are you okay? You seemed upset when I left the other night."

"Oh, I'm sorry. If I told you why, you would think I'm silly. It was nothing—just a personal hang-up—absolutely nothing to do with you. You're fine. We're fine."

"But," he pressed, "if we're going to work together, I need to understand you. Was it something I said?"

"No, no. Eden... look... it's just a silly phobia I have."

"Of me?"

"No, silly! Of... of... well, trains. Every time I hear a train horn. Please don't laugh. There's a reason for it, not your concern. I'm fine. Now, what else did you call for?"

"Oh... well... I called to say that we're on to meet Dave this afternoon. He also said he wants us to meet someone. He didn't say who... "

"Pick me up anytime after noon. I'll be here."

They arrived at Dave Quinn's furniture shop at 1:30. No one answered so he went around to the side door with its unlatched screen. "Hello, inside," he shouted.

"Hello, yourself," said a female voice. "Dave'll be out in a minute."

"Is it okay if I just wait here?" he asked.

"Oh, I'm sorry," she said, "You must be Deputy Whitloe. Come on in."

She gripped his hand with a firm shake. "I'm Colleen McKay."

"Hi, I left my—uh—partner—in the truck. I'll get her."

Eden walked around the front of the shop and waved for Shele to join him. They entered the shop just as Dave came from a back room. The scent of turpentine took over the horsy smell of oak shavings as he entered the room.

"Just finished cleaning some brushes," he said, extending his hand to Shele. "Hi, I'm Dave Quinn. And this is Colleen McKay," he motioned toward Colleen. "I heard you introduce yourself to the Deputy Sheriff."

Shele freely explored the place with her eyes, "Real nice place. You make some beautiful furniture. Do you sell to individuals?"

"It's all made to order for designers," Dave said. "All one-of-a kind. If there's something you'd like me to make let me know. Expect some sticker shock, plus you'll have to wait for—I think the backlog is caught up now—about 9 months. I put the best material in it and each piece is an individual work of art—at least to me."

"Oh, I was just curious," Shele said. "When I make my first million, I'll give you a call."

What kind of work do you do?" Dave asked her.

"I'm a teacher. Library Science. Up in New York state."

"I heard you were helping Eden with his investigation," Dave said. "You going to be in George County very long?"

"For the summer. I hope we can wrap it up before I go back for fall term."

"Colleen, here, is from Amity, up the road. She has a craft shop—it's real work by real artisans."

Colleen smiled, "Why thanks, Dave. That's a real compliment, coming from you."

Shele and Eden expected Colleen to be an earth-mother, and they weren't disappointed. She looked to be Dave's age, but with more facial lines and gray streaks through her fading auburn hair.

She had an aged Janice Joplin look, no makeup on a round face. Her Mother Hubbard dress gathered at the waist with voluminous folds of a skirt. Her legs were strangers to depilatories. And she wore the vest of the aging counter-culture uniform, in her case denim. But for all their flower-elder appearance, Colleen and Dave were fastidiously clean.

"You're from Amity... that sounds awfully familiar," said Shele.

"*Jaws*. Amity was the village where Peter Benchley's shark story took place. Then there's *The Amityville Horror*. Oh, we hear a lot from thriller writers. Then there is the Solomon Spaulding thing—"

"That's who I was thinking about—Spaulding," Shele interrupted. "Didn't some Spaulding have something to do with the controversy about the origins of Mormonism? And didn't Amity play some role in it?"

"Oh, you bet," said Colleen. "It was a big flap back in the 1800s. Then some guys stirred it up again in the '70s with their book, *Who Really Wrote the Book of Mormon?* It rekindled a controversy that's still smoking."

"How does Amity figure into it?" Eden asked.

"Hold on," said Dave. "I'll get us some coffee."

Colleen, warming to her subject, forged ahead. "Solomon Spaulding wrote this novel, *The Manuscript Found*. But in the '70s book, the authors claim his manuscript was really a novel that was ripped off by some guy named Sidney Rigdon. The story goes that Rigdon and Joseph Smith later passed off the manuscript as the Book of Mormon. And, that's the heretical version—so far as the LDS is concerned—of how The Book of Mormon came into being."

"LDS?" Eden inquired.

"Latter Day Saints," whispered Shele.

"Oh, I remember now," Eden said. "Didn't the church's founder say the Book was translated from some gold plates?"

"The official LDS version," said Dave, "is that an angel appeared to Mormon founder Joseph Smith, Jr. and told him about gold plates that would reveal God's plans for America. This angel, named Moroni, told Smith to dig up the plates and from them learn the history of the Americas. So Smith and some others came up with The Book of Mormon, which they say was translated from those plates. Some say Smith made up the whole thing. Others, including the authors of the '70s book, say The Book of Mormon was just the Spaulding novel, stolen by Rigdon from a printing shop in Pittsburgh, and it became The Book of Mormon."

"Okay, Dave, but what does Amity have to do with Spaulding?" Eden asked, growing exasperated.

"Well, Spaulding left his novel at this printer's in the early 1800s, and then moved to Amity in 1814. It was around that time that Rigdon supposedly got hold of the manuscript," Colleen answered. "Spaulding is buried in the Presbyterian cemetery out in Amity."

This historical-literary chitchat is nice relationship-building, Eden thought, but it's not doing much for the investigation. It's time to cut to the chase.

Eden interjected, "That's very interesting. Now Dave, you've had some time to mull over the facts about Amara, Myra, and June. What do you make of it so far?"

"Well, I thought about it awhile. Then I called in Colleen. See, Colleen is more into the paranormal than I am. She hasn't had the same loss-of-faith experience I had. So I think she's better equipped to deal with what you need."

Eden's exasperation was beginning to surface. "So what do you think we need?"

"You need someone skilled in the way you believe Mara was. I know Colleen actually can deliver the results that Mara only pretended to produce."

"So we're back to séances and Ouija boards?" Eden sighed.

Colleen ignored his sarcasm. "I've never had much use for

Ouija," she said. "But we might get insights through the exercises that Amara was trying. I think you might have tuned into something when you and the Sheriff met with her."

Oh boy, here we go, Eden thought.

Perhaps true to her talents, Colleen read his mind. "I know you're convinced it was just smoke and mirrors. But underneath the bullshit, I believe Amara was getting at something. Let's put the mystical stuff aside for a while—I know you're uncomfortable with it—and put our heads together."

Shele interrupted. "I know it's irrelevant to the case we're working on, but... I am very curious... back to the Mormons for a second... Colleen, what do you think is the real story about The Book of Mormon?"

Colleen was pleased to return to a favorite topic. "I think it doesn't matter. In the spiritual realm, reality doesn't count for much. Belief has the force of reality to people. Do you know of any religion that isn't real as far its devotees are concerned? Ask the faithful if their religion is real."

"This sounds like the barracks discussions we had in the Air Force," Eden scowled, now openly impatient and exasperated.

Colleen said, "Forget about a logical, scientific basis. I can call it real, or you can say its coincidence. If it doesn't work, I can say it's because you didn't believe strongly enough," she grinned. "Isn't that the mystic's cop-out?"

"Dave, you're awfully quiet over there," Eden interjected. "What do you think?"

"I'm just listening," he said. "This is Colleen's thing. I'm here if you need me."

CHAPTER SEVENTEEN

THE WV/PA TRIANGLE

There was a long pause in the conversation. Colleen got up and refilled her coffee cup. Dave leaned back, putting his hands behind his head as if to remove himself from the group. Eden stewed and Shele pretended to sip from her cup. Eden felt it was up to him as the authority figure present to start things off once more.

Eden said, "All right. You know, it just struck me—here we are in some Bermuda Triangle thing. We have the Grave Creek Mound over on the Ohio River, and Prabhupada's Palace of Gold in the hills between here and there, and up in Amity we have the grave of old Solomon Spaulding. Three pretty mysterious places, I'd say. And we can throw in the Moundsville prison."

"Yes," Colleen said. "Grave Creek Mound is just one of numerous earthworks built throughout the area. And the others... did you ever hear of ley lines?"

Shele laughed. "How about within the past couple of days? You ever hear of Alfred Watkins?"

"You bet," said Colleen. "*The Old Straight Track*. I read that one years ago. Watkins was the one who originated the term ley line. Did you know there's a road that leads from Kutz Canyon in New Mexico to Pueblo Bonito in Chaco Canyon, over thirty miles away? That road is completely straight, not conforming to the landscape. It's been interpreted as a spiritual line, like Watkins' ley lines or the spiritual lines of feng shui."

Shele said, "I've heard of the Chaco Road—"

Colleen interrupted. "Listen, here's another: just west of here is another spiritual line, the Hopewell Road over in Ohio. Twice as long, lined by walls up to three feet high, and about 200 feet wide. There are such roads worldwide, and no good scientific explanation. And I'll bet you never heard of Lukas Mieder or Wolfgang Brunner..."

Here we go again, Eden almost said out loud. Right off the track and back to more paranormal mumbo jumbo. *Maybe I should remind everyone that I'm investigating the disappearance of a coed who may be dead by now?*

Dave picked up the thread. "Nazi mysticism in the 1930s may have influenced the whole master-race idea. *The Raiders of the Lost Ark* movie revolves around the Nazi interest in the occult. The Nazis actually had agents searching worldwide for keys—hey, Eden, there's that word again."

Colleen chimed in. "The Germans wanted to replace the Church with a German National Church founded on pseudo-scientific theories, mysticism, and the cult of Aryan racism. And some other-worlders, who are really out there waiting on the Mother Ship, claim the German rocket program resulted from an alien connection, and that Germans developed flying saucers from alien technology."

Shele broke in, "Some Christian fundamentalists believe the West won the war because it was actually a war between the occult and God."

"If we could get back down to earth for a minute—what about Mieder and Brunner?" Chief Investigator Whitloe asked, realizing that this river of baloney would have to run itself dry before they would ever return to the disappearance of Myra Kinchloe.

"Ach, ya, Mieder und Brunner—ferry interestink," Colleen grinned in an affected German accent. "Lukas Mieder and Wolfgang Brunner lived in Moundsville in the 1930s. They worked for the Nazis, trying to discover a connection between the Adena

Indian culture, with its shamanistic beliefs, and the mystical origins of life and occult power. One scholar thinks they sought a Tibetan–Aryan–North American connection."

"Lost tribes of the Aryan Nation?" Eden suggested with a straight face.

"If you believe the LDS story," Colleen responded. "The Mormons—or Solomon—whoever came up with it first. They believe that Jaredites came to America and were destroyed. They were followed by the Mound Builders—who they say were the Lamanites and Nephites—the lost tribes. The Lamanites became red-skinned to mark them for their sins. Warfare eventually broke out, with the Lamanites eventually winning."

"Sounds like there's a lot of room in this for some space aliens," Eden suggested, still poker-faced.

Ignoring his remark, Colleen went on. "So Meider and Brunner come along, looking for ways to harness the unleashed powers of the never-never world. Follow along here: Middle East, Egypt, Tibet, Siberian Straits, North America, and bingo, Moundsville. Only yesterday, the Asian-American land bridge theory was considered nutty. But these guys may have found the first association with the lost tribes coming over from Asia. But then they gave up before World War II broke out."

"So the Russians took up where the Nazis left off?" Eden suggested. His head was beginning to ache.

"Sort of," she said. "The Nazis pursued pure mysticism. But the Russians believed they could tap mystical forces scientifically—pure rationalism. During the Cold War, the Soviets dabbled in telekinesis and mind control. At one point they had Americans so concerned that we were sucked into conducting experiments ourselves."

"The theory is that the Russians discovered the Nazi expeditions when they moved into Berlin, and continued from there," explained

Dave. "They sought military applications for telepathy, telekinesis, animal communication—anything paranormal."

Eden said, "You know, there was an address for a Russian in Amara McClure's notebook."

"Vasily Zagarev," said Shele excitedly. "His name was Vasily Zagarev."

"He was there in the late '60s or '70s," Colleen recalled.

"So we have a Russian and a German living across the street from each other," Eden scowled. "But is that really significant? Many immigrants came to West Virginia to mine coal. Moundsville prison even had its own coal mine—"

Dave interrupted, "Eden, this isn't about immigrants. The Russkies were in Moundsville because of the Nazi connection. They had connections that gave them access to prisoners, who were allowed out to take part in psychic experiments."

"Are you serious?" Eden was incredulous.

"Yes. The prisoners talked about it openly; they thought it was bullshit. But it was an easy way to make cigarette money without risking their health in medical experiments. I figure the Russians were drawn to Moundsville by the Nazi records, and perhaps Grave Creek Mound, but then they stayed out of convenience."

Eden said, "While we're at it, how does the Krishna community—New Vrindavan—fit into this?"

"Ah," Dave said, "I could tell you more about New Vrindavan than you want to know. Nori Muster's *Betrayal of the Spirit* might give you a clue. Colleen?"

Colleen beamed. "I think the Grave Creek forces—whatever they are—were responsible for locating the Palace of Gold up on Hare Krishna ridge, whether the Krishnas know that or not. You don't have to know about an earthquake fault line to build a house over it—look at the San Andreas fault in California. I have convincing evidence of a strong line running from the Grave Creek

Mound out the ridge, and over to—guess where? Amity. Call it a ley line, a road, whatever, but it's there."

"A whole lot of coincidence—" began Shele.

"That's the point," replied Colleen. "But if you think all of that's just coincidental, think about this: run the line in reverse. Begin at Amity, then go to Grave Creek, and extend the line about 1500 miles. Guess where you are?"

"Bumfuck, Mexico?" Eden said, trying to lighten things a bit.

"That's right above Nogales," said Dave. "Spent the night there with a senorita back in '78—great weed, but she was awful."

"Okay, that's it!" said Colleen angrily. "You're not serious about any of this, so forget it!"

"I just don't see what all of this has to do with anything, that's all," Eden said in an unintended whine, feeling like a party pooper. "So far, we have a ton of history on the mysticism of the region, but nothing at all about what happened to Myra Kinchloe."

"Chaco Canyon," spat Colleen.

"She's in Chaco Canyon? How do you know that?"

"That's where the 1500-mile line ends," she said with a hopeless upthrust of both palms.

At this point, Eden stood up and stretched for effect. "Guys, it's getting late, and we're all getting too intense. Let's sleep on it and meet again soon. I still have an investigation to do."

Thanking Dave and Colleen for their hospitality and contribution, Shele and Eden found their way to his truck. Shele turned to Eden, "You're the one that suggested there was some sort of Bermuda Triangle/Grave Creek connection."

CHAPTER EIGHTEEN

FEAR OF DERAILING

Halfway out the driveway, Eden suggested they drive by his place on Random Creek, since it was only a couple of miles out of the way. He needed to feed Sarge anyway. And of course, his plan included being alone with Shele for a few hours.

When they reached the house, Sarge was waiting in the driveway, attitude showing. Ignoring the person who provided his sustenance, Sarge rushed past Eden to take up a position at Shele's ankle and curled his tail around her leg to indicate he had taken possession.

She spoke to him in some feline gibberish they both seemed to understand, and leaned down to scratch him behind the ears. Sarge immediately rolled over and exposed his tummy for similar treatment. Oblivious to Eden, or anything else, she obliged.

"I do that too, when a beautiful woman scratches me behind the ears," he said.

"If you were as cute as Sarge, you might find someone who would do just that."

"Meeowr..." Eden made a kitty sound.

The cool evening breeze ruffled the drapes on Eden's bedroom window, gently cooling the couple's bodies. Neither of them was in a hurry. It had taken a lot of time to build to this point, and as far as Eden was concerned, they could spend months enjoying the payoff.

Eden was enjoying her—encumberances—and Shele was moaning softly, when she suddenly froze.

"Oh, no," she said softly, and he felt her body become tense.

"What's wrong?" he asked.

"I'll be fine in a minute," she replied. "Just hold me tight for a little while. It will pass. Then we'll continue."

Eden did as told, bewildered but holding her tightly, waiting, as the crickets and peepers outside their window joined the horn of a distant coal train in the valley, as it approached a rural crossing in the darkness.

Shele raised her hands to her ears and covered them, trembling and clenching her teeth. The train grew louder, then passed in the distance, its deep rumble fading back into the sounds of the night creatures.

Shele relaxed and exhaled as though she had held her breath for several minutes, her smooth skin now damp. "Okay, it's passed," she said assuringly. "Where were we?"

Much later, as they lay relaxing, Shele murmured, "Eden?"

"Mmm?"

"Eden, I need to tell you what that was all about."

"But—"

"No buts! You know whenever I hear a train, even a faint horn in the distance, I get really edgy and anxious. I have to tell you why it happens."

"You don't have to."

"Yes Eden, I do, so you'll understand. For me, being around a train is like waking from a nightmare and being unable to shake its grip. Have you ever felt that? Did you ever wake up in the middle of the night, terrified beyond all reason?"

"Um, yeah, when I was a kid."

"Eden, I was treated for PTSD when I was much younger."

"PT who?"

"PTSD—post-traumatic stress disorder. I had suppressed an early childhood experience, and it was bubbling up in nightmares. That was the reason I went to a therapist.

"My nightmares always involved trains. In every dream, I stood in the middle of railroad tracks that stretched to infinity. It was always in the middle of a very dark night. Then, suddenly, the blinding headlight of a locomotive would appear out of nowhere. The engine belched steam and smoke like a demon sent from hell to kill me. And I would be paralyzed. Couldn't move, just stand and watch as the engine approached. Then I'd hear the locomotive's brakes screech, its horns scream, and... and just before it would take me, I would wake up.

"Wow, that's some bad shit," said Eden. "So that's why you react the way you do when you hear a train horn?"

"You can imagine how that sort of dream would be for a little girl. It's no wonder I surpressed it.

"I still feel unreasonable fear when I'm near a train, or hear its horn, or even drive over railroad tracks. The therapist was eventually able to determine the reason for my fear. After months of therapy, she allowed me to learn that my parents both died in an automobile accident. It happened when I was four. No one ever gave me details, and I was so young, I suppressed it. But the therapist brought it all out into the light, and after that I went back and read old newspaper accounts of what happened.

"My parents went to a party, and took me with them. There was a babysitter who took care of us little kids, while the adults partied. Later, we were driving home from the party. It was real late when we started home. My mom and dad were in the front seat and I was in the back. It was before anyone thought much of seat belts and car seats, so I was just sitting on the seat with my stuffed dog. You know, I used to sit in the front seat on my mother's lap? Pretty careless parenting by today's standards, don't you think?

"It was very dark. My dad was taking a back road home through the country that I didn't know, so I was a little scared. He had been drinking, so I think he took the route to avoid being stopped.

"Well, along this back road was one of those rural railroad

crossings that has no barrier or lights, just an unlit sign. You know, I get that anxious feeling just thinking about it. Anyway, a train plowed into us. It practically tore the car in two and it killed my mom and dad."

"Oh Jesus," Eden said softly, hugging her gently.

"I had no memory of it, until the therapist pulled it out of me. To this day, I can't recall it in any detail. I'm not sure if I remember it, or remember what the therapist told me. All I can recall is the brilliant headlight of the train, filling the car with white light and blinding me—then nothing.

"The newspaper said the police thought my dad had been drinking and driving. Some people said they thought the train engineer was negligent for not sounding the horn before the crossing. Well, you know how these things happen, my parents were dead, the engineer was taken at his word, they wrote a report, my grandparents took me in, and that was that.

"So if we ever stop at a railroad crossing, be prepared for a basket case. When that locomotive comes, it looks to me like one of those evil, fiery-eyed horses in a Henry Fuseli painting. And you've seen how phobic I am about train horns. I've learned to live with it, but I've never dealt with it very well.

"Living in Rainelle has been a trip. There are those damned huge coal trains that rumble through every hour and blow their horns at eight crossings near town—I've counted them. Being here isn't easy for me, but maybe it's theraputic. Exposure to the stimulus over and over—."

Eden held her. "My God. I'm glad you told me."

Then Shele tried to lighten the heavy conversation. "I'm glad that's off my chest. Hey, did you know they have a name for fear of trains?"

Eden took his cue. "Locomotiphobia?" His eyes twinkled in the darkness as he tried to help ease the situation.

"No," she laughed. "Siderodromophobia. It's from two Greek words—sideros means iron, and dromos means running. Fear of running iron. Railroad people call locomotives iron."

"Seems like any phobia or illness has a name these days, I guess if you call it something, you can begin to deal with it." Eden said. "Don't worry about me using it though, I can't even pronounce, let alone remember it."

The phone rang. Eden glanced at the clock—5:15 a.m. What moron would call at this hour? The answering machine caught it as they listened. "Hey, if you're there Eden, pick up. It's Buckey."

"To hell with him. Let him leave a message," Eden grumbled. But after a few seconds, Buckey slammed down the receiver, leaving no message. Eden realized that when they got home, he was too busy meowing to check for messages. So he stumbled from bed out into the dining room to check.

The message-alert light blinked. Eden grabbed pen and paper and pushed the button.

"Hello Eden, if you're there, pick up," said Buckey's voice, and hung up. And again, a few minutes later. And again, an hour later. Then a fourth call: "Hey, Eden. I suppose you're out somewhere with that red-head of yours—but whenever you get your sorry ass back home, call me right away. New developments in the Kinchloe case—and no, it won't wait until tomorrow."

Well, it already was tomorrow.

Eden returned to the bedroom. "Buckey says he's onto something important in the case, and he sounds like he's been there all night. So I gotta get into the office."

On their way to Rainelle, Shele asked what Eden thought of their meeting with Dave and Colleen.

"At one point, I almost got into the idea of a psychic helping us find Myra. But after all that, I'm thinking, what a pants-load. I sat there and listened to that shit for most of the afternoon just to be polite, and now I know exactly as much about what happened to Myra Kinchloe as I did when she first disappeared.

"Now I've got a head full of Nazis, Russians, Krishnas, Mormons, and aliens. My mind is ringing with ley lines, feng shui, telekinesis, and other paranormal bullshit. I know more about the history of all that crap than I ever wanted. Right now, I'd settle for some good old-fashioned evidence of any kind: bullets, fingerprints, tire tracks, shell casings, motives, suspects—that's what I need to work with. I have a tough enough time dealing with a here-and-now world I can touch!"

He sighed hard. "Okay, now what did you think?"

"Well, I didn't think much of it at first. But now, I'm getting creeped out," she said. "None of the pieces mean much, but when you put them together—well, I don't know what you get, but to me, it's... creepy. That Moundsville-Amity ley line just north of us—ooh," she shuddered.

They said little after that, riding back to Rainelle into the early morning twilight. The trip was uneventful until Tim Rutherford's stupid sheep wandered into the middle of the road. Eden saw him just in time to make a quick Kyle Petty to the sheep's right, dodging up onto the shoulder and back down again, without breaking the tires loose from the pavement. A move executed like that— particularly in a pickup truck—was a thing of beauty, and it almost put Shele into his lap, even better.

"I'll bet you meant to do that," she said, as she stayed tightly pressed against him for the rest of the trip.

CHAPTER NINETEEN

MYRA KINCHLOE AT THE KEYHOLE HOUSE

When the Deputy arrived at the Sheriff's office. Buckey's patrol car was in the lot beside the building, and Eden could see light from his office window. Eden hadn't called him because he had an uneasy feeling about the messages on the answering machine. He sensed it was the end of the line for Myra Kinchloe, and there would be hell to pay for Buckey. And if Buckey caught hell from Brad Kinchloe, the Sheriff's Deputy was sure to get a double dose from the Sheriff of George County.

Eden made deliberate noise opening the front door and walking down the hall, to alert the Sheriff of his presence. When he opened Buckey's office door, the Sheriff sat at his desk with his back to the door. The dim lamp in the window provided the only illumination, and Buckey formed an ominous silhouette against the light. The film buff in Eden couldn't help but think of Sydney Greenstreet, a thinner Sydney. He remembered thinking, if I'm going to stay in the sleuthing business, I've got to lay off the film noir.

Buckey mumbled, "That you, Eeed?"

Buckey never called him Eeed unless he had been drinking. Which was uncommon—Buckey seldom drank, and no one could recall him being really drunk.

"Sit down over there," he said, brushing the air toward a nearby chair.

"Buckey," Eden said gently. "She's dead, isn't she?"

"Man, I'm really getting my money's worth, ain't I? The boy's a real fucking psychic. You guessed it, Sherlock. The game commission boys found her around 2:00 yesterday afternoon, out beyond Brightbrook."

"How'd it happen?"

"Back o' the head, just like that—uh—other one—uh—Talbot girl."

All Eden could say was, "Damn."

"It was out there in the gamelands. You go out to Brightbrook and hang a left on the other side. There's those—those two tubes that go under the railroad—the tunnels—"

Two black blobs flashed through the Deputy's mind. "To Go" with the O's filled in. "I know the place."

"—over the next ridge, you drop down on the other side to the gamelands. There's an old foundation out there with a pond beside it. Shit, Eden, it looked just like the pond Amara drew. I remember the tree standing in front and everything. Shit."

Eden thought he heard a sob. "Well, there's a dozen ponds out that way—"

"Don't give me that shit," Sheriff Buckey said suddenly. "It was the place. The exact same fuckin' place." He swiveled his desk chair toward Eden, looking directly at him with bloodshot, rheumy eyes and repeated, "exact... same... fuckin'... place!"

"Well, Buckey," Eden said, "that's pretty far-out—"

"Far-out! Far-out! Hell, psychic boy, you don't even know the half of it. There's more."

"More?"

"Oh yeah, the best is yet to come. I told that old janitor—you know—Seif Largent, out at the police barracks? I told him about where we found her. You know what he said?"

"No, but I expect you're going to tell me," Eden replied.

The Sheriff sort of giggled grimly and said, "Get this: he told me that the foundation was all that was left of a place folks out there called—you ready?" he went on without waiting for a reply. "They called it the Keyhole House. Seems the doors and windows were shaped like keyholes. It was really unusual, and if the state had been on their preservation shit like they are now, it would still be there—probably on the National Register. Hell, I can't even locate a picture of it."

Eden sighed. My God. This can't be real. Then he asked, "Well, Buckey, where do we go from here?"

"I got a funny feeling it's going to be a long time before we get back to busting drunks and chasing bike thieves. I may just have to hang it up if Brad Kinchloe delivers on his promise to find someone to run against me. He said he'd fund a campaign for Barney Fife before he'd see me elected again."

"Aw hell, Barney—uh—Buckey," Eden quickly corrected himself. "Brad's out of his mind with grief. He'll come to his senses. It'll blow over." Eden tried to cheer his boss.

"Yeah," the Sheriff mumbled, "it'll all blow over, right after Hell freezes over. So we're going down to the morgue and give those girls' bodies a good going over. And this afternoon we are both going to talk with Elizabeth Mayow, Myra's roommate."

"Okay." Eden quietly closed Buckey's office door behind him and went to his office. Two down: The Keyhole House and the two black blobs.

Eden was eating lunch in the diner when his cell phone rang. "Whitloe."

It was Buckey, who sounded like he'd been weeping. "Ah, shit, Eden," he sniffed.

Now what? Eden thought. "Buckey, what's the matter?"

Buckey began, "Don't worry about interviewing Elizabeth Mayow today—"

No one ever accused the Sheriff's Deputy of being faint-hearted, but now he felt his heart sliding rapidly into his stomach. "Why?"

"Found her this morning."

"Dead?"

"Hey Eeed, you got that psychic shit really nailed. I'm gonna have to get you a fuckin' turban. We're going after the mother of all *Guinness Book of World Records* on this one. Hell, the uptown media boys are going to be in here with bells on. And by the time they're done with us, we'll be the ones who killed JonBenet Ramsey and dropped the glove and planted the blood in the O.J. case.

"Eeed: after three murders and a suicide in one week, all on my watch, they'll be using me—and you—as examples of hick-town Keystone Cops. We'll replace the Boulder police as the all-time schmucks of law enforcement."

Oh, boy. Gotta get him off that scared-about-our-image track. Let's try a little graveyard humor. "Buckey. You've been making fun of my psychic ability. Let me tell you just how Mayow died." There was no response, so he pressed on. "She was shot in the back of the head, just like the other two. Right?"

"Holy shit, Eden!" the Sheriff yelled. "Don't you know Pee-Wee Herman could have come up with that?"

Well, I achieved my goal; Buckey's not thinking about the P.R. problem anymore.

"Get your ass back in here, and don't talk to any media types. Above all, don't mention any of that psychic bullshit. Now repeat after me: No comment! You got that? No comment!"

CHAPTER TWENTY

A NEW DEPUTY INITIATED

Eden's call interrupted Shele at lunch.

"There's more breaking news," he said in a rush. "I'll get back to you as soon as I can. I'd take you with me, but Buckey's got a bug up his ass—"

"I understand," she said. Eden didn't believe her.

When he got back to the office, three satellite trucks blocked the alley beside the building, and he could barely squeeze past. When he got out of his truck, four reporters pounced, microphones stabbing at his face. "Are you Sheriff Oliver Buckey?"

"No comment," Eden blurted.

"Sheriff Buckey, do you believe there is a serial killer lurking in your county, stalking his next victim?"

"No comment."

He worked his way toward the door.

"It's your community, Sheriff. Does that mean you don't know if it's a serial killer?"

"No comment." He reached the entrance, wiggled inside, and locked the door. He looked up to see Shele standing near the reception desk. She was dressed in a dark blue suit with a laminated card clipped to her lapel—one of those temporary Sheriff's Deputy IDs cards that Buckey hands out when he swears someone in quickly.

"I thought I made it clear that you weren't to be here," the Deputy said, trying to sound annoyed.

"I don't think you made it clear at all. All you said was Buckey

123

had a bug—" her voice tapered off as the Sheriff stepped out of his office.

"'Bout time you got here! Your assistant over there seems more anxious about working on this case than you do. I deputized her so she could work her way around the reporters. We're gonna need someone who has the smarts to work public relations on this mess," said Buckey.

Eden got the message that he didn't have the smarts Buckey needed, so he didn't say a word. He just went to his office. Buckey followed.

"Hey Eden, I don't care if you're pissed off and mad at me. We—both of us—got our ass in a sling on this, and we need all the help we can get. Besides, I think that gal has more talent than the part you are interested in," he said as good-naturedly as he could muster. The Deputy knew there was no use protesting.

"We're due over at the hospital morgue at 2:00 with Dr. Vinnie," Buckey said.

The morgue was yet another film noir flashback. The hospital was built in the '40s, so the morgue was just the right shade of institutional green and there were chrome doors on the refrigerator where the cadavers rested in their pullout drawers. The door to the place had an honest-to-God frosted window with a peeling, hand-lettered announcement that it was the place we were looking for.

True to the genre, Dr. Vinnie was inside, having a sandwich and smoking a cigarette at the same time. His paper coffee cup sat on one of the examination tables. It could have been better only if he were drinking from a beaker—a beaker warming over a Bunsen burner.

Algernon Vincent was known to all as Dr. Vinnie. Today, no one could imagine anyone naming their kid Algernon, but then, Vinnie wasn't from Generation X. He looked as if he had stepped out of the '40s or '50s. Come to think of it, he looked just like Hank

Quinlan—Orson Welles, in *Touch of Evil*—in a white coat. He might even have exceeded Hank in seediness.

Dr. Vinnie looked up and mumbled through his sandwich, "Be with you guys in a sec." He laid the remains of his sandwich right down on the table. No plate, no napkin, right on the stainless steel. Maybe over the years he had become used to alcohol and formaldehyde flavoring in his snacks.

He went over to the foreboding refrigerator and dragged out three drawers, one after another, then picked up his sandwich and resumed munching. Were it not such a grim scene, Eden would have laughed out loud. Dr. Vinnie washed down the last bite with coffee and said, "Well, there they are. You can look 'em over to your heart's content. If there's anything you need, let me know. If you want to take 'em out and put 'em up on a table, I'll call for a couple of guys."

"Not necessary," said Buckey. "We're not going to do the pathologist's job for him. We just wanted a quick look. Maybe we'll see something helpful."

"Now, that'n there," he waved his coffee cup toward June Talbot's lifeless form, "got a prelim report on her. Sez an indication of a trace amount of Extascy in her. Not enough to kill her though. That one, over there," he nodded toward Myra Kinchloe, "had some mescaline, we think."

`"They all look the same, Eden said. "Not much difference in height, weight, or anything else. Hell, they could have been sisters—triplets even."

"I guess you're right," said Buckey as he leaned over to examine Myra more closely. "I'm sure as hell glad they're not all Kinchloes, though."

"I'm guessing they were shot by the same person," Eden ventured.

"You got that Sherlock shit workin' again? Let's hear it," he said, looking up through bushy brows at his Deputy.

"Well, the entry wounds are all in exactly the same place, and the exit wounds are high, almost at the top of the head. The guy had to have the gun at the base of the skull and pointed up at a very sharp angle."

"Think he was a midget?" Buckey asked grinning and raising his eyebrows.

"Go ahead, make fun," Eden replied. "I'll bet the sucker was short, shorter than normal, I'd say not much more than five feet."

"Caliber and type of gun?" Buckey questioned.

"I'd put my money on a snub-nosed .38 revolver. It's easy to carry and more dependable than a smaller gun. It doesn't leave shell casings laying around the murder scene either. That state cop said it looked like a hit. Sloppy hit men like automatics, but the methodical ones who don't like getting caught use revolvers. They usually use a .22, but that's out because a .22 wouldn't do that much damage."

"Hey, I'm impressed. So you don't think it was a serial killer, huh?" he said.

"Nope. I do not, and here's why. Serial killings are random, done by a kook who's looking to get his rocks off. These girls aren't randomly selected victims—unless—" he stopped and was thinking.

"Unless the killer happened across two of them at the mall or somewhere, offed the one, and then killed the other one in case she knew something. Maybe he did the same for Amara McClure," Buckey said, finishing the Deputy's thought.

Neither of them had noticed, but Vinnie had left the room. When the door opened, he announced that someone wanted to see them.

"What's the name?" asked Buckey.

"She said to tell you that Miss Ocevan wants to see you," Dr. Vinnie said.

"Well, show her in—" Buckey said broadly with a sweep of

his hand.

"I don't think that's a real good idea," Eden interrupted, motioning to the cadavers stretched out in front of them.

"Hell, it'll give us a chance to see what she's made of." Then to Dr. Vinnie, "She's my Deputy. Bring her on in."

Normally, pale white skin and red hair were attractive to Eden, but a redhead losing her breakfast in the hallway was anything but.

After he led her outside to fresh air and she finished wiping her mouth, Shele began, "I should have known what I would see, going into a morgue, but I would have thought—"

"—that the Sheriff would have looked out for the delicate nature of his rough and tough Deputy?" Eden finished for her—with some satisfaction.

"Fuck you," she said angrily.

Eden never dreamed the F-word was in Shele's vocabulary.

"Hey, you wear the badge, you gotta walk the walk," he goaded.

"I'd tell you to kiss my ass but you'd think it was a romantic invitation, you dumb shit!" she raged back at him with tear-filled eyes.

That did it; he could tell she had had enough. When he put an arm around her, she tried to jerk away, but he held on and walked her toward his truck. "I've got a car," she complained, still trying to pull away, "one of the Deputy's cars."

He bit his tongue to keep from saying, those are for real deputies who can keep their lunch down when they see a dead body, but he knew when to shut up. He was up to his chin in it by now anyway.

"I'll send Junior Slaughter over for it. The walk will do him good," he said, pushing her onto the seat of the truck. She sat, choking back sobs she didn't want him to hear.

"Wait," she choked, "wait, I came over here to tell you guys they have a suspect. He's down at the Sheriff's office."

The Deputy was already halfway to his door on the driver's side when he stopped in his tracks. He continued around, opened the door, and got in.

"Before you go any farther, did this guy have dark brown hair?" Eden asked.

"I—uh—I think so," she said.

"He have some gray around the edges and a scruffy looking-beard? Was he about five-eight and 165 pounds?

"That's about right," she replied. "Why, is it someone you know?"

CHAPTER TWENTY-ONE

A SUSPECT

"Aw, shit, its Joe Bill Tusten," Eden said, reaching for the ignition and putting the transmission in drive. "Hell, he's always hanging around trying to get arrested. He'd confess to shooting the Kennedys and Lennon if he thought he'd get a free night in the slammer. He's always on the prowl for a free meal and a place to flop. We quit arresting him years ago."

Shele was puzzled. "If the guys at the office know that, why did they send me—" she stopped as she realized she had been sent on a fool's errand. The good old boys at the office knew what Buckey would do when she got there, so had a little fun at her expense.

Neither of them said anything. Conversation would only make things worse, so they sat in silence as they drove to the office. The new Deputy was angry at the way Buckey had made her a Deputy and then set her up, and Eden was even angrier at the way the buttholes were treating his new partner.

When they parked, Eden opened the door for Shele. Leaving her behind, he marched up the walk to the door in a pissed-off strut. He jerked the door open and slammed it behind him.

"Okay, where the hell is Tusten?" demanded the Sheriff's Deputy.

"Who?" asked a startled Junior Slaughter, who seemed taken aback by Eden's attitude.

"Joe Bill—your fucking suspect, that's who."

"Joe Bill, that ain't the name he gave. The only Joe Bill I know is—" he stopped abruptly. "Joe Bill Tusten," he finished quietly, "and that—that—uh—ain't him."

"Oh," Eden said, his anger instantly diluted. "I thought it—uh—might have been—uh—oh, forget it. Where is the suspect?"

"You know the way back to the tank. We've been keeping him back there away from people until you and Buckey could get here," he explained. "Says he wants a lawyer."

"Okay, okay, when Buckey gets here, send him on back." Eden picked up the key to the holding cells and walked toward the rear of the building.

The Sheriff's Office was built fifteen years ago with Federal grant money, so the county commissioners insisted on two holding cells, male and female. The cells were inside a larger room that locked from the outside. Everyone called the door to the larger room the tank. The cells locked electronically, but the door to the tank required a big skeleton-type key. Inside, the walls were painted pink. A few years ago, someone suggested that pink holding cells calmed the prisoners. Then last year some local gay rights wackos from up toward Pittsburgh complained that it was insensitive to gay prisoners. Eden wanted to repaint it baby blue, but cooler heads prevailed. The pink more than likely made them nauseous—that was the effect it had on Eden.

Flickering fluorescent lights were sickening too, and the lights in the tank had been flickering on-and-off for as long as he could remember. No one bothered to fix them, because no prisoner was held more than a day or two. They never had more than a dozen real prisoners in any given year anyway. That dozen was in addition to the usual drunks who came and went, but Buckey said they could never really put drunks in the prisoner category. It was commonly believed the Sheriff liked the lights flickering because it annoyed the people in holding, and it kept the drunks awake after they sobered up.

Eden supposed he should give up renting movies and watching

The Movie Channel. But honest to God, the suspect looked just like Dennis Weaver with a week's growth of beard. Not the "Chester" Dennis Weaver like on Gun *Smoke*, but the one in—you guessed it—*Touch of Evil*. The only difference was that this character was even geekier than the motel night attendant Weaver had played.

"I want a lawyer," said 'Dennis' from the back of his cell.

"What's your name?" the Deputy asked.

"Can you do something about the lights? They're giving me a headache."

"They've been that way for years. You're not going to be here that long anyway, and we're not going to change them just for you. If you are charged, you'll be moved over to the county jail after you are arraigned," he told him.

"I have my rights," the suspect began. "I get to make a call and I get a lawyer. And no one has read me my rights yet."

"I don't think you've been charged with anything yet," the Deputy said. "You are being held here for your own protection. You've heard of protective custody, haven't you?"

The suspect didn't respond, so Eden asked again: "What's your name?"

"Herman McMurchy."

"Middle name?"

"Harold. I know all about protective custody. That's what they said they were holding me for when I was down in Weston."

The state mental hospital in West Virginia, Eden thought. Then Mr. McMurchy began to get—well—sort of twitchy. He glanced at his hands, his feet, around the room, then at Eden. His eyes danced and gleamed. Suddenly, he sat down on the cot in his cell, still twitching, and just sat there staring at his hands.

"Is there anything you would like to tell me?" Eden asked.

McMurchy sat in silence as the Deputy repeated the question. Eden was about to leave the tank, when the door opened and

Buckey poked his head inside.

"Deputy Whitloe, could I speak with you for a second?" he asked, as Eden moved toward the door. Eden suspected the Sheriff was being more formal than usual in case someone would overhear them or we were being recorded.

Once outside, Buckey whispered, "Bug's on," meaning there was an open microphone in the tank. Eden tried to recall if he had said anything he should not have.

"Okay," Eden said in a low voice. "Now, what's this nut bar all about?"

"Dan Brackenridge found him out on the Interstate," Buckey said. "He was walking along trying to get a ride, I think. There didn't seem to be much to it at first, but Dan found a gun on him and it sort of went from there."

"What kind of gun?"

"One of those little .32 caliber autos—cheapo—made in Taiwan or someplace."

"That's not our gun. A .32 won't make the kind of mess those girls' heads were in."

"I know, I know, but maybe there's another gun. Maybe— oh—hell, Eden, he's all we got. It'll probably turn out he's more of a Forrest Gump than a Jeffrey Dahmer, but it will divert the reporters for a while. This'll make it look like we're doing something."

"Buckey, you're the boss. You do what you think we must and I'll back you up, but I don't like it. Here we got some schizo who's not taking his lithium. He says he's been in the State Hospital down in West Virginia—"

"You think the kind of guy who would do something like this isn't a nut case? You think Gacy, Ramirez, and Dahmer were choir boys?" the Sheriff asked.

"Buckey—Buckey, you know what I'm saying. Sure, we can hold

this guy. Sure, we can work him over and make him crack. From the looks of it, that would take about five minutes. He's pretty fucked up right now. We keep him under those lights and he'll probably have a seizure. I can get a signed confession out of him tonight if that's what you want. We might even save our jobs. Is that what you want? You tell me, I'll do it, but it isn't what I want to live with for the rest of my life."

"Hell, I suppose if we did get a confession, the D.A. would laugh us all the way back from the courthouse and—aw hell, Eden—" Buckey looked down at the key he was holding.

Eden was thoughtful. "Okay, let's keep him here for the night. We'll tell the media he's in protective custody pending interrogation. We give him supper, breakfast, and a ride to the state line in the morning. It will keep the reporters off our ass for a while and buy us time."

"You don't think there's any chance that he did it?" Sheriff Buckey asked hopelessly.

"Not one chance in a million. We'll call the hospital down there and see when he was released. I'll bet it was yesterday. He just doesn't fit. Even if he did, there would be hell to pay getting a conviction."

The next morning, Junior drove Herman Harold McMurchy back from whence he came. Fortunately, it turned out that he wasn't considered violent and wasn't in criminal custody. He had just wandered away from Sharpe Hospital, where he was admitted for observation. Eden supposed he picked up the gun somewhere along the way. Who knew why? If he was a killer, he was someone else's, not theirs.

Eventually, the reporters and the satellite trucks left. They grew bored, filed their reports, and when they saw nothing breaking, moved on to their next human tragedy, a family shootout in the next county.

The only non-event for the next few days was Joe Bill Tusten's clumsy attempt to break into the Sheriff's office. He said he was going to sue the county because the Sheriff wouldn't arrest him.

CHAPTER TWENTY-TWO

CLUELESS

Then the investigation sort of—well—just tapered off. There was distressingly little progress. The investigation of the deaths of Amara McClure and the girls dead-ended in a few weeks. Folks were startled when Myra's dad, Brad Kinchloe III, abruptly put the house up for sale and moved to Utah. Just left. Moved up around Moab, folks say. No one thinks Buckey will miss him much.

Shele decided to stay in Rainelle for the summer. Eden offered his place, but she refused. He told her it was "the little old lady in her" that wouldn't let her do it, but she said it wouldn't "look right" and they both had reputations to keep. He did get her to visit his place on weekends. They became inseparable that summer.

The couple certainly tried to advance the investigation. They went over the route the girls reportedly traveled the night Myra disappeared. Together, Eden and Shele walked the access roads of the gamelands and spent more than one interlude on a blanket spread out in beds that deer had made in the tall meadow grasses, grasses planted especially for the use of game. It was during those times that Eden felt Shele was somehow distant—detached. He thought maybe she was fantasizing about someone else, but wrote it off to his lack of experience and his inclination to compare her with Annie.

Alone, he searched the gnawed-off concrete of the foundation of the Keyhole house. He didn't know what he expected to find, but he didn't find it. No one could even locate a photograph of the old house, so he tried to imagine what it might have looked like.

135

One old-timer, Cord Smith, said its windows were an entire circle on top with a rectangular window cut into it at the bottom. The entrance door and the interior doors were the same. It was singularly strange for this part of the country, a strangely Moorish design, but now it was as if the house had never been.

Cord was a spinner of tall tales and you could never be sure if he was jerking you around, but he seemed dead serious when he told Eden the house had been haunted.

"I wouldn't shit ya," he assured him, as he reached into a can of Copenhagen and took a pinch. "Tell ya, the truth is, I'm glad to see the place gone. It was pure spooky, it was. I know whatchure thinkin', but it was haunted for sure. And finding that body out there by the pond proves it. Chickens come home to roost, ya know," he added cryptically.

Maybe there was some truth in what he told the Deputy. According to him, newlyweds had built the house and were its first residents. After a couple of years, the young wife apparently developed some kind of mental problem. Cord claimed to have known them and was sure the wife was "as crazy as a bedbug."

"They smoked a lot of dope back then," Cord said. "Grew their own—lots of people grew it right out in the open before the drug laws. Lots of folks had stills, too. I never knew too many dope smokers or boozers that warn't depressed, but with her, it was really bad. I think the husband just gave up on them ever being happy together.

"Well, one day she was sittin' in a chair out by the dam. Don't know if she was fishin' or just lookin', but word is he snuck up behind her and blew her brains out. Then he goes up in the attic and hung hisself from a rafter. Nobody knows what really happened, but that's how they found 'em. Anyway, that's how folks tell it. From then on, the husband became a haint and roamed the house, moanin' over his dead wife. Now you got this murder. Them chickens done came home to roost, I'm a-tellin' ya."

Eden searched the dam embankment of the pond below the remaining foundation walls. He imagined a young, frail woman sitting in a Victorian straight-backed chair looking out over the water with a shadowy figure behind her. He imagined he could see both of them reflected in the rippling surface of the pond. At that moment, a hunter fired his gun some distance away and a flock of startled doves took wing over his head. Cord was right about one thing—the place surely was spooky.—

The pond had shrunk in the summer sun and a new growth of green cattails was springing well beyond its surface. The spot where Myra Kinchloe had been dropped by an executioner's bullet was grown over already with milkweed and sumac. It was as if she, like the Keyhole House and the young couple, had never been there. Only the quiet wetland endured.

State investigators had gone over every square foot with metal detectors, but Eden and Shele spent an entire day on their hands and knees combing the area with their fingers. The deputies assembled an ammunition case full of "artifacts." They called them that because out of all of the junk they found, none of it seemed to be evidence of anything or even relevant to the case.

"Proves what I thought all along," he said to no one in particular.

"What, did you find something?" asked Shele, from the other side of the pond.

"I found nothing. Like all of our other searches, I turned up absolutely nothing," he said to her.

"Well, what does that prove?" she asked.

"A hit man leaves exactly this sort of evidence. Nothing! A serial killer might leave evidence. They nearly always leave a clue or two. At least they do in the movies. Some serial killers leave a veritable road map to their house. Some of the shrinks say they want to be caught. This had to be a hit. Nothing else makes any sense."

The tubes that allowed traffic to pass under the railroad weren't particularly significant and an examination of them provided nothing—the house, the tubes, all coincidence. It was now hard to imagine that Amara's vision was accidental, or coincidental for that matter. Was there some transmission that happened—images carried to Amara by some radiation caused by violent death? Neither Shele nor her partner would deny it, neither would they confirm or admit to it.

"If it was a hit, as you say, what was the motive?" Shele asked. "We ruled out kidnapping a long time ago. Brad Kinchloe had money, but not the kind kidnappers look for. I think the guy killed Myra by accident, then the others by necessity—the necessity to cover up the first murder," Shele proclaimed.

"Plausible," he said, "but how do you kill someone by accident by shooting them in the back of the head? I'll grant you he could have assaulted her, killed her, and tried to make it look like an execution-style murder to cover it up. But the pathologist found no evidence to suggest that was the case," he reasoned.

"That doesn't mean it didn't happen," Shele argued. "The assault could have taken place with her lying face down. The angle of the bullet would be exactly as you describe it."

"There was no evidence of that where they found her," he reminded her.

"The guy killed her somewhere else and brought her here and set up the scene to look like it was an execution. Then, when he killed the other two, he arranged it the same way so it would look like—you know—"

"You're guessing," he challenged her.

"You too," she came back.

"But my guess is more consistent with the evidence and more in keeping with what might have happened," Eden said. "You don't have to work in a lot of conniving and cover-up to get to where you want your theory to lead."

"Okay, Sherlock, we've had this argument in different forms before. If it's a hit man, what's his motive?" she asked.

"It's pure speculation. Both theories are. But if it is an execution, at least some of the victims had to have been involved in something, or to have known something that had to be kept secret. Maybe they were about to reveal a deep dark secret—"

"Yeah, like Joe Bill Tusten is the kingpin of the Rainelle mafia and McMurchy is his caporegime from Chicago," she chided.

Eden sighed and walked away aimlessly toward the breast of the dam. "Whoa—what's this?" he cried. "It looks like a rusted-out frame of a gun—" He squatted, staring at the ground.

Shele ran to the edge of the embankment, where she was balanced precariously beside him. Suddenly, Eden grabbed her ankles, and together they rolled down the slope, holding each other tightly, giggling their way to the bottom, where they came to rest with Shele on top of him.

"Hey," he said, "get up for a minute."

"What's the matter, you got a problem with me being on top?" she teased.

"There's something poking me in the back."

"Don't tell me it's that gun frame," she held his wrists to the ground.

"No, really," he replied, "there's something under me in the grass."

She climbed off of him, and he fumbled behind his back until he grasped a plastic film canister. "Hmm," he said, shaking it end-for-end. "Probably dropped by some hiker. It's plastic, so the metal detector missed it."

"Sounds like something's in there," Shele said.

"Yeah... maybe I better let the lab guys look at it. I've probably smeared any prints that were on it. I'll bet it just dropped out of some photographer's bag and has nothing to do with the murders anyway."

"Wouldn't it be great if it contains an undeveloped roll of film, left by the killer?" said Shele.

"Hey, while you're wishing, why don't we just wish it contains pictures of the girls, their killer, and the killer's name and address? Shele, it's probably someone's stash can."

And that's how the months slipped away—like summer smoke. Lead after lead went up into the summer haze as well. Not that they ever uncovered anything substantive to begin with. By now George County was pretty much back to normal—whatever that may be—and Buckey was getting edgy about his main Deputy spending so much time on "the case." Maybe it was because he needed help tracking down bicycle bandits and dealing with ticket booth defilers. It was a tough job for one man.

Near the middle of July, Eden the Chief Investigator got a lab report on the film canister. An entire page told him what he already knew. Inside was a roll of exposed film—no cassette—just film. Upon developing it, the lab found no images. There were no edge numbers, so whoever exposed it must have taken the film out in broad daylight, then neatly rolled it up and put it back in the canister. Moreover, there were no usable fingerprints. Junior Slaughter told anyone who would listen he thought it was a stash can.

"Dopers use those things to hold marijuana or shrooms. I'll bet he put that piece of film in there to throw off anybody if they found it."

"It was probably nothing more than a piece of trash left behind by a hiker or hunter." Eden assured him.

CHAPTER TWENTY-THREE

ROADTRIPPING TO KRISHNAVILLE

One sunny Sunday, Shele said she wanted to see Prabhupada's Palace of Gold up close. The couple had driven by the small village of Limestone and the turnoff to New Vrindavan several times, but had never taken time to visit.

They expected the visit to net absolutely nothing about the murders, but they would still tell Buckey that their little lark was part of the investigation.

The trip out the ridge was uneventful. However, for anyone who has never seen the palace, it's a shock to make the last bend in the road and see a genuine full-blown, life-size Hindu temple sitting there among the West Virginia hills. It's nothing short of bizarre.

There is also an otherworldly ambiance that must be due to the absolutely exotic and alien setting. It's as if one has left the western hemisphere altogether. The beautiful palace, built by skilled and unskilled devotees in the '70s and '80s, had fallen into disrepair after the troubles of Kirtanananda Swami.

When they were there, workmen and women were busy with the tasks of restoration. Enthusiastic but unskilled work left by the hippie-age devotees was now but fading patent gold leaf and crumbling concrete. The chatras—the canopies Amara had sketched—still marked the four corners of the structure, but were now crumbling. The proud dome that still seemed to gleam in the distance was in desperate need of regilding. Cast concrete balustrades grinned gap-toothed with missing balusters. Huge stain-glassed windows hung in decaying filigreed frames.

The '70s scions who gave the accumulated wealth of their families to escape the world of materialism and join the spiritual communal life were decades gone, their wealth depleted. But the new devotees dreamed of better days ahead and were at work once again fulfilling their dream. A dream that was now based on hard work and tourism.

The Palace seemed a microcosm of the universe. Built by exuberant flower children who claimed they sought a world of peace, love, and understanding, they instead found themselves caught up in a real world with all its temptations—money, power, and sex. The palace they built had the potential of becoming a moldering antique, like the temples at Angkor Wat, Pueblo Benito or the Grave Creek Mound.

That would not happen, in the near future at least. There was a new spirit driving those who worked on the temple. They were trying their best to restore its former grandeur, and no doubt the deprived and bereaved spirit of Srila Prabhupada along with it.

That day, Eden had more positive feelings for the new order of hard work and determination than he did for those first dreamers, who built a monument to the present without a thought for a future world of ever-changing values. Exuberance had taken a backseat to endurance, an approach that had led to decadence.

From overhead, sitar music and chanting drifted on the summer breeze from a loudspeaker. Heavy incense that would stay in their clothing long after their visit permeated the atmosphere and became part of the chanting and visual experience that was the incongruous Palace of Gold.

The interior was a phantasmagoria of stained glass, marble, mirrors, crystal, and travertine fashioned in traditional Hindu style. Its opulence, though somewhat faded, was phenomenal and belied its fading exterior.

The most striking part of the lavish interior was the altar room.

On a golden altar sits "Lord Krishna's pure devotee"—or at least a full-size likeness of him. Prabhupada is dressed in the traditional garb of an ascetic and is so realistic that he seems almost electrically alive. The charged likeness stays with you for years.

Highlighted by gold-leafed Vedic motifs, the altar was constructed from black and white onyx and enhanced by intricate enamel work. There is a dome above the altar that contains thousands of pieces of crystal and the floor is made of the same black and white onyx that was used in the altar.

"You think he knew anything about ley lines?" Eden asked Shele in an amused whisper.

"Oh, he knew. Just looking at that dude sitting there, he may not have called them ley lines, but I'll bet he knew a lot more than we'll ever discover in our entire time on this mortal coil," she said.

"If only he could talk, maybe he could tell us who we're looking for," Eden said. "He looks like he knows, but I don't think anyone else here was involved or could tell us a thing."

"How would we even begin to ask?" Shele asked.

"Dave said he still has a friend over here by the name of Krishna Katah—that's his devotee name, anyway. I think I'll ask someone if he's still around. Maybe he can turn us on to something."

As it turned out, Dave's friend had gone to California, so the couple decided to keep their investigation to themselves. The people they met were kind, congenial, and helpful. After all, they were the "tourists," bringing what the original devotees had brought their way—money now needed for restoration.

Eden was convinced that if dark secrets were buried on Hare Krishna Ridge, they had been there long before Myra and June traveled the road from Moundsville. If the Palace of Gold was on an Old Straight Track, it was purely by accident, even if the founding guru was aware of it.

They explored for an hour before walking down the hill past the

Palace to the resort or convention center part of the complex.

"Not my idea of luxury," said Shele.

The buildings were intended to be a sort of Hare Krishna Disneyland that was planned in the '80s but never took off. Interest diminished over the years but some of the facilities were still used.

Like tourists, the couple strolled along a cobbled path toward a giant statue of a cow and paused to study it.

A pale, white woman wearing a sari appeared from nowhere and said in a hushed voice, "They said you are looking for Krishna Katah—Isaac Daniels."

"Yes," Shele replied, "do you know him?

"Maybe I do, maybe I don't. Is he a friend of yours?"

"Aadishree," called a male voice from some distance.

"Can you tell me where I might find him?" Shele asked.

"I must go. They are calling for me." She looked off to where the voice came from, then furtively back toward the couple. "Isaac isn't here anymore. He went away just before Kirtanananda Swami went to prison. If you find out anything about him, please let me know. If you know any of his friends, tell them he never arrived in California."

"Aadishree," the call was more insistent now, and she turned and walked toward the voice.

"Yikes! What do you make of that?" asked Shele.

"Strange things happened in those times," Eden replied.

CHAPTER TWENTY-FOUR

FOOL'S PARADE

Departing the Palace of gold, Eden said, "It's 3:00, too early to go home. Do you want to see Moundsville?"

"Probably as exciting as Rainelle. Why not?" she replied.

Moundsville was the setting for two movies made from Davis Grubb novels, *Fools Parade* and *Night of the Hunter*. If you saw *Fool's Parade*, you know what the town looks like. The story was set in the 1930s, and one doubts that they had to do much to replicate that period. Some vintage cars were put on the street, and maybe they rolled the sidewalks out a bit farther because there were more people and more happenings in Moundsville back then. The prison that James Stewart was released from is closed now, although prisoners were still held behind its rusticated and crenellated facade back then. That was 1971 when Stewart, George Kennedy, Strother Martin, and a very young Kurt Russell were there. Today, tourists, guides, and gift shops replace the prisoners, actors, and all.

Across the street is Moundsville's attraction and namesake: looming over the whole is the Grave Creek Mound, and beside it, the Delf Norona Museum.

Knowing the prison tour would take too long, they elected the mound experience. They hurried, anxious to climb the 295-foot Grave Creek Mound. You ascend it via a walkway that wraps around it and dates to Franklin Roosevelt's Works Progress Administration days in the 1930s. Like a serpent, the stone walk-stairway winds around the structure at a shallow angle that makes for an easy climb.

They made it 45 minutes before closing time and hurried to the doorway leading to the mound. Before they could get through the passageway, a docent who was leading an excursion of some sort was blocking the way.

"Native Americans of the Adena culture were here from about 1000 B.C. to about 1 A.D. They had well-organized societies and lived in an area that encompasses much of present-day Ohio, Indiana, West Virginia, Kentucky, and even parts of Pennsylvania and New York. A later group of Mound Builders, the Hopewell, lived from about 1 A.D. to 700 A.D. and their culture appears to be more highly developed than the earlier Adena, the docent droned.

"We believe the Grave Creek Mound was built during the late Adena Period and was constructed in several stages between 250 and 150 B.C. This particular mound is only one of several built by the Adena. However, it is on a far larger scale than others in the area. Most of the others range in size from 20 to 300 feet in diameter."

The group moved toward the door. Rather than become a part of it, Eden said to Shele, "Let's just poke around. Here is an interesting item. Check it out and tell me if anything sounds familiar."

Shele studied a photo of the Grave Creek Stone, captioned "The Grave Creek Stone was discovered in 1838 during the excavation of the Grave Creek Mound."

Eden frowned. "It's long been controversial. No one knows much about it. In fact, no one even knows where the original stone is now. The Smithsonian is said to have four casts of it, but it's been cast, recast, drawn, and redrawn several times, so no one is really certain this is what the original looked like. Several scholars have translated the inscription. One claims it reads 'Bil Stumps Stone,' and another claims it says, 'The mound raised-on-high for Tasach this tile queen caused-to-be-made.' This same guy says the script is Iberian and the language is Punic. Not surprisingly, a prevalent hypothesis is that the stone is a hoax. It wouldn't be the first from that period. Far out, huh?"

"Hmm," said Shele. "I can't see anything familiar, or significant. If I use my imagination,... see, over there on the right—and—holy crap—look at this," she pointed to the engraving at the bottom of the stone.

Sure enough, there was something that resembled the skeleton key used to unlock the holding cell back at the Sheriff's office.

Shele said, "The handle part isn't just right, but it sure looks like some sort of key."

"Ah, duh, I don't think the Adenas had locks," he teased.

In her best professorial voice, Shele intoned, "What we have here is an ancient stone-age version of Joseph Smith's gold plates. We have before us, if we could decipher it, a message for the ages concerning the welfare of mankind—how to design multilevel marketing and organize a Tupperware party."

"Shele," he said to her as though she were a small child, "I think it's time we went outside and climbed the mound."

The walk to the top was easy due to the gentle grade of the spiral climb. Once on top, they could view the surrounding area. Across the street, where they had started, was the Moundsville Penitentiary. Now they could see past the high stonewall and into the prison yard. The interior was being used as an impoundment for stolen vehicles. Outside the wall, a group of tourists milled around the main entrance.

Shele said, "I'd really like a look at the inside of the prison. Do the cell blocks really look like ones in old movies?"

"Maybe even more so. I can't begin to think about being locked up in a place like that. I've tried to imagine it, being driven up there as a prisoner and put into a cell. It gives me chills to think about it. I was on one of the first tours, and it still had prison vibes. I suspect it still does. In 1997, it became a law-enforcement training site. They had a mock riot to test new high-tech gear and negotiating techniques. Turned out that the rioters gave up earlier than they thought they would, so they didn't get to test some of their equipment. I don't think it was the great negotiating, I think those guys just wanted out of the damn place in the worst way. That prison is haunted, you know," Eden said matter-of-factly.

"No way!"

"Yes way. Halloween is party time at the prison. They make a big deal out of its being haunted. Back in the early '80s, when a whole bunch of prisoners filed lawsuits against the prison, they combined them into the single case called Crain vs. Bordenkircher. Bordenkircher was known as a badass warden at that time. I don't know that he was particularly cruel, but he didn't put up with a lot of shit from either the prisoners or the state. I figure if he were still in charge today, the ACLU would call him insensitive and politically incorrect. And you know what, I don't think he would give a shit."

Shele exclaimed, "This is really fascinating! I'm glad we're working the murder case together. I'm getting to learn some neat things!"

"Well, there's more. You know, I hadn't thought of it until now, but the warden later became the county Sheriff. He was sued by one of the Krishnas who was accused of murder. The guy claimed that Bordenkircher took away his beads. In the Sheriff's typical style, Bordenkircher told the press the lawsuit was a load of horse apples.

"Anyway, the prison was shut down when Judge Recht ruled it violated the Eighth Amendment. That's the one about cruel and unusual punishment. Anyone who visited the prison in those years could tell you that simply being there was pretty cruel. And you can tell from up here, by today's standards at least, it's pretty damned unusual."

"This whole area has weird vibes about it," said Shele. "Here we are standing on what was once—no, still is—a graveyard, and God knows what else. And, over there, across the street is what was once a living grave."

"Yeah, I'm beginning to see why the Indians thought this whole region was spooky enough to avoid. And don't forget the Palace up there on the ridge." At that, a shiver ran down his spine.

Shele added, "And if you look off to your left, over there, you can see down along Eighth Street."

"You mean where those Germans and Russians hung out?"

"Pretty strange," she replied. "You can almost imagine a group of prison trustees trooping over there for a psychic experiment."

"And don't forget those ley lines, oh niece of Amara McClure," Eden reminded her.

"I wonder if anyone has been up here with a dowsing rod?" she said, as if to herself. She didn't seem to be kidding. "Can we come back next week and tour the prison?"

"Only if you don't insist on bringing a coat hanger or peach branch."

"You gotta deal," Shele exclaimed. "It'll have to be soon, because"—she stopped as if she hadn't thought of it before—"because I'll have to go back to work in New York soon."

Like two kids who thought summer vacation would never end, they suddenly faced a fast-approaching September. It was like the end of summer for Eden when he was twelve. School seemed in the far future—until the school bus stopped at the house.

"Then it will have to be this week or next weekend," he said. "Wednesday?"

"Works for me."

They had grown really close over the summer, and it would

be tough when she left. Eden needed to think about his future…
and if he wanted to make room for her. Since Annie's death, he
had grown to like living alone, especially the freedom. But Shele
was special, one-of-a-kind, once-in-a-lifetime. Did she want a
permanent relationship? They had not discussed it. It was as if the
summer would never end. It had seemed they could just continue
forever and never have to confront the question.

Came Wednesday, and they drove back to Moundsville, parking
in the prison lot. The tour began at the side of the prison. Most
prisoners, including the ones in *Fools Parade*, left through the cage,
or "the wheel." It was a revolving barred gate designed so only a
few prisoners could leave at once. The irony of a revolving door
exiting a prison wasn't lost on Eden, who was well aware of the
recidivism rate in modern prisons.

Tours entered through the Wagon Gate, where it was assumed
new prisoners were admitted. The Wagon Gate is a sort of two-
story garage affair built into the stone wall with some sort of trailer-
like thing on top of it, so you could call it a three-story building.

The tour guide explained this is where they held the first
executions. That announcement was followed by a demonstration
of the gallows, complete with a dummy unexpectedly and noisily
dropping through a trapdoor from above. Evidently, executions
back then were a sort of party time with the public invited to
enjoy the show. On one occasion, according to the guide, they ran
out of scheduled executions, so they ran in another one that was
unscheduled, just to make sure there was enough entertainment for
the day.

The prison is about half the size of its prototype, Joliet in Illinois.
No plans exist, so any understanding of the design must be acquired
by examining the 1867 Board of Directors report. The prison
encloses about seven acres with a wall five feet thick at the base.
Each corner of the wall had a large turret for the guards who gained

access by inside staircases.

As they passed through the door, into the prison yard, the tour guide said, "In 1986 the West Virginia Supreme Court handed down the decision that the penitentiary was to be closed by July of 1992. The prison didn't officially close until 1995, when a new and more modern prison was built in Mt. Olive, downstate.

"After the prison closed, all sorts of ideas were suggested for its use—a shopping center, an old folks home, a small business center—but none seemed workable. At one point, a casino was proposed. About the only thing that wasn't suggested at that time was making it into what it is today.

"But the prison became a tourist attraction, and that's why we are here today. You should come back when we have our 'Dungeon of Horrors' around Halloween. People pay to spend the night and experience the ghosts of the prison. The place is haunted, you know," the guide said with no trace of jest.

"Who would have guessed?" Eden mumbled to no one in particular.

"We are going across the yard and into that door across the way."

Once inside, the group saw the cellblock stretching out before them. Shele seemed particularly interested in the convict artwork that adorned the cell walls. It ranged from childish, to accomplished, to psychotic.

They stood in front of one cell that was painted stark black and white. Symbols and figures seemed to emerge from the floor and float across the cell, spreading across the walls and ceiling. In one corner, the images converged into what appeared to be Christ presenting the keys of the Kingdom to St. Peter. "See," she said, "there's your key again. I'll bet the guy who lived here would have made a deal with the devil to get a key to his cell."

The guide asked if anyone would like to experience the prison as the prisoners had, by stepping into a cell. Most stepped in, so Shele and Eden joined them. When everyone was in, he slammed the doors shut remotely with a huge lever at the end of the block. Now there's a sound you don't soon forget. One could imagine that former inmates never forget that reverberating sound and its finality.

The guide said, "Now I'll show you how the guard could operate each cell individually, from up here where I am." He began letting the 'prisoners' out, one cell at a time. He left a couple locked in their cells.

"We'll all meet at the end of this cell block and go through that door on the far end to the cafeteria," he said, ignoring shouts from those still imprisoned. He pretended not to notice until he sensed panic in one woman's voice, but even then he pressed it a bit. "I can't get this thing to move," he said. "It seems to be stuck." His voice strained as he attempted to move the immovable lever. "I suppose we can pick you up on the way back through."

The group was laughing, but the guide acted genuinely concerned. The 'prisoners' were even more anxious. "Oh, oh, I see," he said, "I forgot to turn this latch," as he set them free.

Over an hour later, we were turned loose to view the area where prisoners received visitors.

"I'll bet they didn't have conjugal visits back then," Eden said to Shele. She smiled.

Outside the visitor's area were exhibits of devices prisoners had made. There was an assortment of crude and well-made shanks — the knives prisoners fashioned from anything at hand, including a toothbrush. Of particular interest was an ingenious tattoo needle made of a ballpoint pen and what looked like a doorbell coil.

In one corner was a grim reminder of the prison's past. In 1951, West Virginia abandoned hanging, and let nine more death-row inmates take a seat in Old Sparkey, the state's electric chair. It seems just about every state nicknames their electric chair Old Sparkey. Now the chair was on display along with its electrical control panel. The room was sealed off with a glass window, so no one could try it out for size.

"Talk about cruel and unusual. I think that should take first prize. Imagine strapping someone in that and—shit, I'll bet that hurt, ah, at least for a little while," he said to Shele.

"I think anyone that receives a lethal shock is immediately rendered unconscious, so it wouldn't be painful at all. There might be some muscular contractions, but they probably wouldn't be aware of them," she said clinically. "It might be much more humane than hanging. Alabama and Nebraska still use the gallows and in eight other states, it's optional. You think that's bad? Idaho, Oklahoma, and Utah still have firing squads. For all its redneck, hillbilly reputation, West Virginia may be one of the more civilized states. They have no death penalty at all," Shele explained.

"You've been reading up in preparation for our visit over here, haven't you?" Eden said.

"Hey, you're just jealous because you don't have all this shit right on top of your head," she smiled. "I'll take Prisons for $500, Alex."

"I think I'd go for the IV rather than spend the rest of my life in a place like this. There might be some that are more modern, or even like country clubs, but they are still prisons," he said.

Eden found a clerk who was an ex-prison employee, and asked if she knew of prisoners taking part in medical or psychiatric studies. She expected they had, but didn't know, and doubted anyone could say. He pressed her on how he might find out. She said the prison kept few if any records of that sort of thing. "Records of that sort could become lost," she said quietly.

Eden bought a T-shirt with a picture of the prison, and Shele bought one of those stupid-looking prisoner hats. They hadn't learned a thing about Nazis or Russkies, but they knew a lot more about the old prison than they would ever need.

Driving back to Rainelle, Eden asked if she wanted to see Amity. She eagerly agreed, knowing this would be their last investigative trip of the summer.

Aside from the churches, a fire hall, and a few stores and shops, there's little to see in Amity. Colleen McKay's shop was right on the main road, with a "Closed" sign in the window, not that they had intended to visit her. Eden wasn't up for any more of the region's mystical history. Her shop was quaint, but seemed to have a reserved pall hanging over it.

The Presbyterian Church dominated the village. Eden parked in a gravel drive leading to the cemetery. They strolled through the cemetery, which surrounded the church. They looked for Solomon Spaulding's grave, but Eden didn't want anyone to know they were looking for it. People living near the church probably were pestered by curiosity seekers, and Eden didn't want to be counted among them. Nor did he want the world to know he was looking for a Spaulding link to a recent murder. It all seemed so ridiculous, and if anyone found out, they might send him to be Herman McMurchy's roommate.

"Here we are, walking over the dead—again," he said to Shele, who was examining one of several table tombs, with their huge stone slabs laid flat instead of upright. The slab is supported by legs underneath, like a table.

"I've not seen gravestones like this before," she said.

"They're more common in the British Isles. I think they are Celtic. Anyway, they seem to be used by the Presbyterians— Scotch-Irish, mostly. And older—I don't know of any recent ones. Great tabletop for a picnic," he added.

"Maybe for Hannibal Lecter," Shele said. "You think old Solomon is here somewhere?"

"According to the cemetery records, he's here. Born in 1761

and died 20 October 1816. A couple of days of a wake at most, and then planted out here around October 22nd, I'd say. I checked a calendar at the library. He died on a Sunday."

"Well, this is a needle in a haystack. I doubt that we'll find him," Shele said.

"Wait just a minute. Over there, across the drive from the table tombs. There it is."

"There what is?"

"Solomon Spaulding's tombstone."

They had missed it because they were looking for a very old headstone. Spaulding's had been replaced with a newer, large monument. Sure enough, there it was, complete with its epitaph:

IN MEMORY OF
SOLOMON SPAULDING
WHO DEPARTED THIS LIFE
OCTOBER 28, A.D. 1816,
AGED 55 YEARS.
Kind cherubs, guard the sleeping clay
Until the great decision day,
And saints complete in glory rise
To share the triumphs of the skies

They turned and walked the crunching gravel drive back to Eden's truck. The air had cooled quickly, and a few golden leaves dropped and skittered before them.

"We could tour downtown Amity," Eden joked, "if there were a downtown to tour. I suppose we had better set sail for Rainelle."

He didn't mention the date discrepancy. It was just one of those records-versus-the-tombstone things, he reckoned. And he could have sworn he saw someone duck behind the side of the church as they studied Solomon's gravestone... but given the setting... well, it probably was just his mind playing tricks. The whole place was beginning to get on his nerves...

CHAPTER TWENTY-FIVE

SUMMER ENDS

What was left of summer slipped by quickly and Shele packed to return to New York for the fall term. Eden busied himself with the final report of their investigation. Buckey insisted on a lengthy, detailed document, a CYA for anyone who might question their effort and how they spent the county's money. Eden understood that some eyebrows in Rainelle might rise about how the Sheriff's Deputy spent the summer roving hill and dale with that strikingly beautiful Irish lass, what's-her-name.

Eden felt like he was documenting a failure. Four violent deaths. Three murdered and the fourth at best a suicide. June Talbot, Myra Kinchloe, and Elizabeth Mayow had been shot, execution style, by a person or persons still unknown. Which was another way of saying that Eden and Shele didn't have a clue. They had spent over two months digging through the records and debris of four lives and had next to nothing to show for it. Not one hair, fiber, semen stain, or shell casing. Maybe you could count a few bits of lead they recovered from the girls' skulls, but they proved to be from bullets that could have been bought anywhere and were too damaged for ballistics.

The lives of the four were everything they appeared to be. Not a surprise in any of them. Aside from Amara McClure being a bit of a charlatan, none of them had more than a speeding ticket. No enemies, and except for small credit card bills, no outstanding debts, so no one owed huge amounts to the mob for gambling or dope. All checks run on their personal lives came back clean.

Amara even had a permit to carry her .38. Buckey, himself, had signed it.

It was as if someone had visited "Normalville" and randomly selected four mutual acquaintances, then snuffed them for no reason at all. If it hadn't smelled like a mob hit, the Sheriff would have jumped on the serial killer theory immediately. In either event, the chance of turning up a suspect or even a hopeful lead was right up there with winning the Power Ball. The thing that kept the idea of a hit man alive was the cleanliness of it all. No serial killer, or anyone else, would have been that careful, that antiseptic.

After arguing the hit-man theory for weeks, Shele finally admitted that she subscribed to the serial killer theory. In their periodic arguments, she tried again and again to convince Eden or sway his reasoning, but he remained convinced there was someone out there who wanted all three girls dead for some particular reason.

Shele and her summer lover briefly said goodbye. They promised to write, but both knew that unless something brought her back this way, their summer affair would be no more than just that. It was hard to imagine a woman like Shele Ocevan spending the rest of her days with a country boy Deputy Sheriff who had all of the ambition of an old tomcat looking for a place to nap.

So, they made promises both knew neither would keep and said their goodbyes. Eden would miss her, but now had the capacity to get over her. They would exchange e-mails from time to time, a phone call now and again, but Eden never expected her to return to George County to take up with "her Dudley."

CHAPTER TWENTY-SIX

A CONFRONTATION

For all intents and purposes, the Deputy Sheriff of George County had given up. The investigation was running off in all directions and had become mired in dead-end leads and scant, disjointed evidence.

Of course, there was endless speculation about what happened to the women. Everyone had a pet theory, and to Eden and Buckey's constant annoyance, everyone was more than willing to share. But nothing stood out. No one saw a common thread to connect the killings.

Although the women knew each other, it almost seemed as if they had been chosen at random, perhaps by some serial killer who happened to be passing through George County, or worse yet, a serial killer who still stalked the county's byways. Worst of all was the thought that the killer was just a random fiend, who murdered young women for thrills.

The idea for a meeting between the investigating law officers and the women's families began innocently enough, when Buckey ran onto Beth Mayow's dad, Herb.

Herb asked how the investigation was going. Whether Buckey intended to be vague or was just being honest, they got into an argument about how ineffective the investigation had been.

"If the Mayows or the Talbots had a lot of money like the Kinchloes, I'm sure we'd get more information about what happened to Beth," Herb said sarcastically. "I'd know a lot more if I was some big wig in the Presbyterian Church. I'd get a lot more direct information.

"Since Brad Kinchloe went to Utah, the rest of us ain't heard shit, and Buckey, you know it too. We're treated like a bunch of mushrooms—we're kept in the dark and fed horseshit."

Buckey agreed the parents were overdue for an update, so he decided then and there to meet with them, and that's how the Sheriff and his Deputy wound up in the meeting room at the Sheriff's Office. Eden later said it might have gone better if the room had been arranged living-room style, but State Police Officer Dan Brackenridge insisted on having a table between the parents and the law enforcement people. Worst of all, Dan insisted on sitting at the head of the table.

The State Police always get their way, so Buckey and his Deputy sat side-by-side on the right side of the table while Dan ceremoniously took his chair at the head. Maybe he didn't intend to appear as the honcho in charge, but that's how it must have looked to the families. And to the Sheriff and his Deputy.

Herb Mayow and his wife Mabel sat directly across from Buckey and Eden. Blain and Margaret Talbot sat beside them. They had none of the country-club airs of a Bradford Kinchloe III, and undoubtedly nothing near his six-figure income. The Talbots and Mayows looked like what they were, plain white bread and hard-working.

Not deferring to Dan in the least, Buckey proceeded to introduce everyone. Then he asked his Deputy—lest anyone needed a reminder of the pecking order—to turn down the lights. He began a thorough, meticulous, detailed explanation of how the investigation had progressed since Myra's disappearance. He used a PowerPoint presentation that included what Eden thought was gratuitous stuff Buckey had found on the Internet.

Buckey not only brought the parents up to date, but emphasized that everything possible had been done to give each woman's case equal attention. It was more of a PR conference. Eden though it was a campaign to assure everyone Buckey was reelectable.

"—and that's about all I can tell you up to this point," Buckey concluded.

"That's it?!" Blain Talbot fairly screamed as he rose, fiery-eyed. "Listen, Buckey. They may call me Plain Blain, but I ain't stupid. You mean, after all this time, all you have is—is—that—that— shit? Hell, Buckey, you ain't told me a damned thing I didn't already know.

Then he turned his wrath on Dan Brackenridge "And what the hell have the State Police been doing all this time?"

Dan began spouting PR jargon the police reserve for news conferences. It was a mistake because Blain recognized it instantly.

"Oh, bullshit!" Blain shouted. "This whole thing stinks. First we've got two hick-town Sheriffs stumbling over each other. And then sittin' here all high and mighty at the head of the table you got a Gawd-a-mighty know-it-all bureaucrat that can't find his ass with both hands!"

Tears of anger pooled in his eyes. It turned to anguish as he slumped to his chair, elbows on the table, holding his head in his hands. He brushed aside his wife's attempts to console him as he sobbed, "Hick-town lawmen, what can they do? We live in freakin' Mayberry."

Herb Mayow tried to bring the meeting back under control. "Chief Brackenridge, is there anything you can tell us? Do you have any theories on who might have done this?"

"Harrumph. Well, I'm very, very reluctant to spec—" he began.

Mable Mayow was the sort of a small, thin woman, you expect to see passing out crayons and paste in Sunday school, one of those church ladies who wears a hat and gloves to meetings on Sunday. She hadn't uttered a word so far, and no one imagined that she would. But Mable jumped right in when self-assured Brackenridge said "speculate."

"Aw, shit, chief, there you go again!" she said helplessly. "Try to be a human being for just once! We're all adults here, so don't feed us a bunch of crap. Herb just wants to know if you have any ideas, that's all."

"Turn the lights up, Eden!" Brackenridge commanded, annoyed that anyone would question his competence. "You want to know what I think? I'll tell you, but it's only what I believe from what I know this far."

Brackenridge began by reassuring the parents they had every right to be concerned and skeptical, and he congratulated them on their parenting. No one was buying it, so he began to level. "From what we've learned—and believe me, we've gone through their lives with a fine-toothed comb—these women were model citizens. We don't often encounter people of their caliber in this line of work," he assured them. "That's what has made these cases so tough."

When he told them he would share some things he hadn't even revealed to Buckey, Eden was sure he saw the Sheriff's jaw drop. Brackenridge explained that his information came through an investigator friend in Montreal, one Jean Tessier.

Tessier had worked a serial killer case involving the murder of three young girls in Canada. The girls were younger than Myra, June, and Beth, but they were all picked because they appeared to be virgins. The killer turned out to be a woman who was acquiring victims for her husband.

"Tessier got involved in that case because he was an experienced profiler," Brackenridge explained. "So, when we weren't having much success with our investigation, I called him for ideas. I kept this quiet because I didn't want to raise false hopes. And you all know the press would have a field day with it." Buckey and Eden were ticked off enough the way it was.

"Well, Mr. Tessier looked over what we had. He wouldn't give me a written report, but he told me on the phone that he was convinced the George County murders were committed by a woman."

Eden saw Buckey wince out of the corner of his eye and was conscious now that his eyes had rolled back in his head and his mouth was hanging agape. He could only hope Dan didn't notice.

"Tessier described the woman in very general terms—sort of like a psychic, I suppose," he added, glancing at his colleagues. "According to him, she was probably middle-aged, heavy set, with dyed hair, and perhaps was a lesbian."

When he added that Tessier believed she worked at some sort of service job, "like a maid, a waitress, a barmaid, or bartender," Eden about fell off his chair and immediately felt guilty for thinking of Lin Kelley.

"Oh, I checked out the women at Dunlow's bar," Brackenridge quickly assured everyone. "First of all, the only one that fits the description is the assistant bartender. She's a grandmother and everyone in town knows her. Ted Dunlow hires college students mostly, so that whole exercise was a waste of time. The only other person that came to mind was Lin Kelley down at the Wagon Wheel, but that doesn't seem likely 'cause everyone knows her too. Hell, we sure can't investigate middle-aged women for miles around."

After that, Dan sort of took over the meeting and thanked everyone, cautioning them not to share anything they had discussed. He tried some small talk as the parents left, but he was largely ignored as the Deputy ushered them out. On the way to the door, he put a hand on Eden's shoulder and asked him to keep quiet about his investigation of Ted's employees.

"I never let on to any of them that they were being checked out," he said.

"Good thinking, chief," Eden said, hoping he kept a place in the chief's good graces.

Hunting season came and went. No new bodies. And of course, no new evidence. Eden was content that he had done all he could for the four women, but he did not like coming up empty. The idea of a middle-aged woman casting a net in George County, fishing for young women for her horny husband, seemed as preposterous as ley lines and mystical forces.

He began to wonder if Dan had invented that Tessier tale on the spot, just to get the Talbots and Mayows off his ass. He reluctantly filed the "profile" away with all of the other Grave Creek connections.

Soon, even before the first snowfall, it was as if none of it had ever happened. Things in Rainelle settled back into a routine. He remembered Marion Barry's comment about his city of Washington, DC: "If you take out the killings, Washington actually has a very, very low crime rate."

Ted Dunlow was taking reservations for holiday office parties at his bar, and college students once again were making Holiday shopping trips to the Ohio Valley Mall. Someone had suggested a fall-term memorial service for the murdered students, but everyone at the college — most of all, the administration — avoided mentioning the deaths of the four women at all. Nothing is harder on enrollment numbers than word getting around about a few dead students. The college didn't cover up the incident; it just wasn't mentioned.

Time slowly passed and the seasons imperceptibly changed as the seasons do in George County, Pennsylvania.

CHAPTER TWENTY-SEVEN

A WHOLE LOT OF DIGGING

In early autumn, a nasty storm found Sarge and his Deputy partner nestled in for an evening of movies and popcorn, when both were startled by a tremendous thud. It sounded like it came from the kitchen, but when Eden checked, everything looked normal.

"Hmm, maybe a bird trying to get in out of the rain?" he suggested to Sarge, who didn't give him so much as an inquisitive look.

But the sound had been so loud that Eden checked the back porch. The porch swing hung by one chain. The free-swinging arm had been dashed into the house by the wind and had broken off at the back. He guessed the armrest had broken from old age and rot, or had come unhooked somehow. The wind finished the job of shattering that end of the swing.

Back inside, Eden grumbled to Sarge, "I can't fix it; might as well throw the damned thing away. I should have taken it down for winter." The swing was Sarge's favorite dozing place, and the cat now adopted a mournful look.

At that moment, Eden thought of Dave Quinn. Now there's a guy who could fix anything made of wood. He would ask Dave the next time he was in Brightbrook.

The weather that everyone said wasn't all that bad in George County turned particularly bad that winter. The real snow began before Christmas, and George County would see little bare ground until after Groundhog Day. A brief spell of warm weather was followed immediately by more snow and sleet until nearly St.

Patrick's Day.

Funny, but for almost a year, Eden hadn't thought of St. Patrick's Day and the party Myra Kinchloe had attended. He had often thought about the girls though—Myra, June, and Beth. He wouldn't call it an obsession, but hardly a day went by that he didn't picture them lying in the morgue, a picture that refused to fade.

In time, the Deputy was called to Brightbrook to check an abandoned car. Folks out that way would buy a clunker and drive it until it quit. Formalities of titles, VINs, licenses, and niceties like insurance were just added expense, so when a vehicle died, they just walked home and forgot about it. Someone from the Sheriff's office would go tag it and a tow truck would haul it in. Scotty McMillan, the tow-truck operator, had a whole area of his junkyard filled with carcasses from George County's western end. No one ever claimed them, and eventually records of their existence would be expunged. They were crushed and scrapped—and some would probably reappear, out near Brightbrook, a few years later.

Eden tagged the car door and decided to see if Dave Quinn was home. Dave's shop looked oddly different; perhaps he had moved stuff in for the winter. At first, Eden thought Dave wasn't at home, because the place had that unlived-in look. Maybe he had gone south for the winter. Many who retired to George County wintered like snowbirds in Florida, to return in April.

Eden banged on the front door with the palm of his hand and shouted loudly for Dave. No one came to the door, so he tried the side, knocking and shouting a few times. After a long delay, Dave opened the door.

"Oh, I thought you were out front," Dave said. "I just got to the front door, then heard you back here. Come on in."

"I didn't mean to disturb you," Eden began.

"Oh, you aren't disturbing me. I was just cleaning up in the finishing room. If I let it go, I wind up with all that dust in the varnish, and then I have to spend my time sanding stuff down to finish it again—ounce of prevention, you know."

"I was out this way tagging an abandoned car, so I thought I'd stop by," Eden explained.

"Well, thanks. I appreciate the visit," Dave said warmly. "Gets lonesome out here this time of year. There's not many visitors. Sit down and take a load off."

"It's not entirely a social call," Eden admitted. "I suppose you could call it business."

"Oh, want me to conjure up something for ya?" he asked with a wide grin. "Seems like I didn't help you much with that last case you were workin'. You never did find out any more than you knew when you were out here before, did you?"

"Not so far," Eden said, indicating that he hadn't given up. "We never did develop any good leads. All we had were bodies that didn't tell us much. No evidence of a struggle, minimal ballistics— not much of anything. I'm still on the case, though. You never know when some drunk in a bar, or a hunter, or—"

"Yeah, there's always hope," Dave said. "I figured you hadn't made much headway, or there would have been something in the paper."

"Well, one reason I'm here is to ask if you could fix a porch swing for me. I think the thing came off the hook during a windstorm and—"

"Sorry, I don't think I can help. I don't do repairs—"

"But it shouldn't take much," Eden pleaded. "Just a new piece for an arm—oak, I think. If I had the tools, I'd fix it myself, but it looks like a band saw job—and I don't expect you to do it for free."

"Look, Eden, I'm sorry, but I just don't do repair work. It's not my thing. And it doesn't have anything to do with you, it's just—if I do it for you—I'll have every hoopie in the county at my door, you know what I'm sayin'?"

167

Yes, Eden thought. I know what you're saying. You're too much la grande artiste to lower yourself to do someone a favor.

"I suppose so," Eden said, feeling as if he had just asked Cezanne to do a black velvet painting of Elvis. "I understand," he lied.

So they passed pleasantries, talked about the unusual winter weather, told some more guy lies, and then Eden left. He was still sort-of pissed at Quinn's refusal. Halfway home, he said aloud, "Damned old fart ex-hippie, what should I expect?" He pounded the steering wheel for emphasis. Eden often expressed his disappointments this way when alone.

A few days later, Dave Quinn called. "Hello, Eden," he said lightly. "It's Dave—uh—Dave Quinn."

"Oh, yeah," Eden said flatly, conveying that he was still disappointed. "Whatcha want?"

"Now, don't go gettin' all pissy on me. I know you're unhappy at me for not agreeing to fix your porch swing—"

"Oh that. I forgot all about it."

"Bullshit. Look, I'm sorry, I was in a foul mood that day. I'll make it up to you."

"Don't worry about it. I threw the thing away," Eden lied.

"Good, 'cause I wasn't going to fix it in any case—it probably was some made-in-the-Philippines piece of shit. Look, I'm going to make you a whole new swing. It'll be a genuine Quinn. You'll love it, guaranteed."

"I'm sorry, Dave, but I just can't afford it." Eden was relieved that he didn't have to tell three lies in a row. "And I'm not going to accept it as a gift—"

"I know, I know. You have your pride, so I'll tell you what I'm gonna' do, I'm going to let you help me out as a barter for it."

"I don't think so—" He wants me to turn a blind eye during his dope harvest next fall.

"Hey, hear me out," Dave insisted. "I'm only asking for some labor and sweat. All you have to do is help me dig out a big walnut stump and carry it to the road. I have a pickup with a hoist, so I can take it from there."

"I didn't think walnut was all popular any more."

"It's making a comeback. And this thing has some of the finest figures and burls you've ever seen. It will keep me in designer wood for a year. Those little gay-bob interior boys up in Pittsburgh will go nuts over what I can make from it. "So, what do you think?"

"Um, lemme think about it," Eden said. "You aren't going after the walnut now, are you? We'd freeze our asses off."

"I'll wait until it warms up a little, but I don't want to go out when it's hot either. It'll be hard work, it'll get you in shape. Take off that winter blubber. I'll make a mint. And don't worry, it's on property I own, so we won't have any problems that way."

Eden mulled it over for a few moments while looking down at his waistline. "All right, call me when you want to go—and have my swing ready by the time the daffodils bloom." He felt better about Dave, but the guy was still an old hippie fart.

After the long winter, it was good to have a swing to enjoy the warm spring sun on the back porch. Sarge avoided it for several days, disliking the oil finish, or maybe the strange art-nouveau form Dave had twisted the image of their old swing into. It was comfortable to a fault. And good it was on the back porch, for its artsy-fartsy style didn't match his interior decor.

Eden had not been sitting long when Dave called to collect his debt. He drove up in a military surplus weapons-carrier truck that looked to be from World War II. Spray-painted in a scrawl across the side was FARM USE ONLY. That was so he didn't have to pay for a license, insurance, or safety inspection. Painting that phrase on the truck was one step better than ignoring registration all together. In a few places, paint broke through a solid layer of an oxide-colored rust finish, what Dave and his designer friends would call a patina.

"I've got all the tools we need," he said, "but if you have a mattock or axe, bring them. Bring an extra pair of leather gloves. We'll probably run through a pair or two."

The "stump" was a wind-fallen tree. The trunk shattered when it fell and the stump and roots, although partially exposed, still firmly held the soil. The tree's branches were sprouting green buds, and if left alone it might have lived to grow into a whole grove of walnut trees.

When Dave had first made the offer, Eden figured they would dig the thing out in a few hours and he would have his swing paid for. Now the sun was setting on the second day, and Dave announced, "We'll probably have 'er out by the weekend. You probably don't want to work Saturday, do you?"

Hell no, I don't want to work Saturday. Thursday or Friday either, since I'm taking vacation to do this, Eden thought. But a deal was a deal, and three or four days' work was a very good price for a genuine Quinn swing. Eden figured it would sell for seven hundred to a thousand wholesale, maybe more. He convinced himself he was getting in shape for spring, but after the first day, he was sore in places he didn't know he had and he felt like he was getting older.

Late Friday, they stopped on their way to the old rustbucket of a truck and looked back to survey their work. The gnarled walnut had stood for eons on a low hill against the sky in an open meadow. Eden wondered what the old tree had seen since it sprouted from its rich Pennsylvania soil. It was big and thus quite old, but as much a passing life form as everything around it. Even the lifeless rocks were not permanent, worn as they were from some antediluvian mountain range. He wondered if Neanderthalic creatures had passed this way, and if those short-lived people thought of the world as a more permanent place than we do.

"Want to come back out and finish tomorrow?" Dave asked. Saturday morning, they finally finished digging around the base and cut free the roots that held the tree in the ground. You always hear about the taproot. If there was one, it wasn't identifiable from several other huge roots. By noon, working together, they could rock the stump in its hole and were satisfied the thing was loose enough to be hauled out.

It weighed at least a ton, so they had long abandoned hope that it could be lifted out and hauled by hand. Dave planned to rig a cable around a system of pulleys and, using the winch on the old truck, haul it out and as close to the road as possible. From that point, the hoist might help them maneuver it onto the truck.

Eden went to the hole to rig a sling of nylon straps around the stump, while Dave set to work fastening pulleys to nearby trees and a rock. When they finished, the stump resembled a dog on a very long leash. The leash went first to a very large rock outcrop, then to a tree almost as large as the walnut they were removing, then finally to the winch on the front of the truck, making a big figure Z. To make sure the truck didn't get dragged into the hole, Dave chained it to a fencepost behind the rear tire. That part seemed to Eden to be the weakest link in the scheme, and he fully expected to see the ancient weapons carrier pulled in two.

"Ready?" Dave shouted.

"Whenever you are."

"Get out of there and I'll start the truck. Yell when you're clear," he shouted. Eden heard the truck start as he scrambled out of the hole and ran to where he thought it might be safe. He could almost feel a cable whipping around his legs as he imagined it snapping from the strain.

"Clear," he yelled as loud as he could and the truck motor strained to produce the power needed for the winch as the slack on the cable was now tightened like a crossbow string.

"Don't jerk it," Eden yelled as something on the other side of the field groaned and gave way. It was the huge rock that held the first pulley. It wasn't in the ground as deep as they reckoned, so it tipped and gave way.

The truck engine whined and quit. "Shit," Dave shouted. "I got a chain—a twenty-footer. We'll hook it to that tree past the rock. It'll hold, minor set-back, no problem."

Dave figured the angles and pulleys as well as any engineer. The stump came right out of the hole as slick as if he were pulling a turnip from an autumn garden.

They snaked the thing to a few feet of the truck's front bumper. Dave jumped in the old shitbox and turned it around. More straps, more chain, and the stump was on the truck. The truck springs groaned and Eden held his breath, wondering if the whole thing would collapse.

Dave reached inside, turned off the ignition, and sat on the running board. "Let's take a breather before we start gathering stuff up."

"I hate to stop 'cause it's so damned hard to get moving again, but I'm too pooped to move," Eden panted.

After a bit they started untying nylon, taking chain clevises apart, and putting the stuff in neat piles on the truck bed. Dave studied the site, considering what could be done to restore the excavated real estate to its original condition.

"I can come out here and fill the hole," he said as we stood on the edge of the old stump's socket in the earth. I'll rake it out and re-seed it. No one will ever know we were here."

"I don't think there's much to do over there where the rock pulled free," Eden said as they walked over to examine it. "It wasn't in too deep. It just scooted three feet and stopped."

Dave arrived at the rock's original location first. He started kicking sod back into the rut that had been created by the rock's movement. "Take a look at this," he said, bending at the waist.

"What?"

"If you know anyone who needs a hearthstone, this would make a fine one." He was now on his knees, digging with gloved hands at the edge of a large, flat stone.

"Looks to be about three by four feet," he said, continuing to dig around the edge. Suddenly he said, "Hmm! That's funny—"

"What is it?" Eden asked.

"Look here." Dave stroked the edge of the stone with his hand. "It's been cut."

"What do you mean, cut?"

"It's been dressed. Not sawn, but dressed with a chisel or something. It looks like the back of those old limestone headstones you see in 1800s cemeteries. This rock didn't get here by itself. It was put here."

"Dave," Eden said, "you're saying someone cut this big-ass stone from another rock and dragged it out here. And then put that big mother rock on top of it? Bullshit."

"Umm... it gets better," Dave went on. "This stone—it isn't native. It's not limestone or even sandstone; it's granite. Eden, there ain't no granite in these parts, except for imported tombstones. So, it isn't bullshit. Maybe someone is buried here. They dragged this stone out here, and then put that big-assed rock on top of it. It might have been on the surface when they put it together, and it just sank over the years. Hey, maybe the Crypt Keeper did it," he suggested.

"I still think it's bullshit," said Eden.

"Hey, I didn't say it was a tombstone for sure, just a possibility. I don't see any writing or carving on it. A tombstone would have a—uh—epitaph or something carved on it."

"Maybe the epitaph is on the other side. Or maybe it's a Geological Survey marker," Eden suggested.

"Yeah, Eden," he said sarcastically, "the Geological Survey put the marker out here. Then to make sure no one would disturb it, they put a two-ton rock on top of it—to mark the boundary of what? Get the shovel and prybars out of the truck. Let's turn it over," he directed, like a university archeologist talking to his summer intern. "Maybe there's something on the other side,"

"Hey, Dave, I thought we were pooped out. If we start this, we'll be here all evening."

Dave ignored him and kept digging with his gloved hands. Eden dragged his feet to the truck and returned with the tools. They dug around the edges and cleared off the top of the stone. Except for some chips and marks from today's work, it was flat and unmarked. But for its perfect rectangular shape, and granite composition, it was singularly unremarkable.

"Push this rock down there along the edge. I'll use it for a fulcrum and get some leverage," Dave said.

They worked around the edge until they got the prybars between the slab and what appeared to be more stone under it. When it was partially raised, Dave jammed a piece of wood under the edge of the slab. It was now high enough to get their hands under it and pull it over.

Clumsily, they flipped the slab over. Beneath it lay a stone-lined, box-like chamber. Eden the Investigator half-expected to find the remains of a Woodland Indian or maybe even an Adena burial. He later remembered thinking that it would be a chief or someone important to have this elaborate burial site.

But there was no immediate evidence this was a burial at all. If it were, it would be filled with silt by now and would take some digging to find any remains.

Suddenly, the lawman he had set aside for the day spoke up: "Let's leave this alone until we can get someone in here to excavate. Let's put the stone back in place."

"Not so fast, Eden," said Dave. "Take a look at this side of the stone."

There appeared to be some sort of inscription. Apparently, someone put it face down to protect whatever had been cut into the stone.

"You know, Eden, this looks kinda like the writing in the middle section of the Rosetta Stone," Dave said. "That stone is in three languages. The top part is Egyptian hieroglyphics. The middle is Demotic, a language used by Arabs and modern Egyptians. The bottom is Greek. The three versions of the same message allowed some French guy to figure out Egyptian hieroglyphics. It was a big deal in the 1800s. Until then, no one could make sense of the hieroglyphics."

"You can read this thing?"

"Oh my, no! All I said was it looks like the writing on the middle of the Rosetta Stone. I saw a cast of it at the Carnegie Museum up in Pittsburgh. Hell, I'm not sure it's Demotic. It just has that look to it."

"I say we put it back and I'll go back, fill out a report, and get someone from the college out here—"

"Ah—Eden—this is my property... I've owned it for thirty years... I think I have something to say about what I want to do with this."

"Well, okay, yeah. But—this could be historically significant... who knows the value of it... this stone and what's under it?"

"That's my point, Eden. Whatever is here may be worth something. If we let some government agency in here, they may confiscate the whole site."

Eden frowned. "I'm not sure what to do here. I don't know the law about this sort of thing."

"You said it, Eden: you don't know what to do, or what the law says. So I'm not risking whatever rights I have."

They stared at the stone and the space below. They walked over to the stone that had been on top of the engraved slab, and sat on it.

They argued for some time, and then Dave suggested that Eden might get a share in whatever derived from the site. The late afternoon sun slipped into a ruddy glow on the horizon.

"All right. Dave. Come over to my place around 10:00 tomorrow—unless you're going to Sunday school," Eden grinned.

CHAPTER TWENTY-EIGHT

ARCHEOLOGY ON THE ROCKS

From the side window, Eden could see Dave Quinn with what looked like a homemade briefcase under his arm, tapping on the door.

"Come on in," Eden said. "Have a seat. I remember you take your coffee black."

They enjoyed pancakes and sausage over chitchat, and then Dave plunged in. "Well, we've both had time to think it over. Your thoughts?"

"It just seems to me we oughta get an archeologist—"

"Hold it. Before you say anything else, I have to tell you some things. When we lifted the stone on the sarcophagus, or whatever it is, I felt a strong wave of déjà vu. I thought about it so hard, I couldn't sleep. It kept going through my head again and again, like a song you can't get out of your mind. What do they call that?"

"An earworm. I had one that lasted for weeks. Also called repetunitis."

"Whatever. Anyway, it finally came roaring back—what I was trying to recall, not the song. Remember when we talked about Solomon Spaulding and his novel, Manuscript Found? Well, that's it!" he exclaimed joyfully. "In fact, it's often pointed out as a direct parallel to Joseph Smith's discovery of the golden plates that led to the Book of Mormon, and some tried to use it as proof that Smith ripped off the whole thing."

He excitedly fumbled through the makeshift briefcase, producing a sheet of scruffy-looking notepaper. He put on a pair of half-lens reading specs, and intoned:

I happened to tread on a flat Stone. This was at a small distance from the fort and it lay on the top of a small mound of Earth exactly horizontal. The face of it had a singular appearance. I discovered a number of characters, which appeared to me to be letters, but so much effaced by the ravages of time that I could not read the inscription. With the assistance of a lever, I raised the Stone—

He peered at Eden over the reading glasses. "Well, what do you think? That's old Solomon Spaulding's description of finding the manuscript. Déjà vu all over again, right? But read Joseph Smith's version of finding what he claims to be the origins of the Book of Mormon: he gives a similar description of digging up the gold plates. He says they were buried at Hill Cumorah, just a few miles south of Palmyra, New York. Uh, that's beyond Rochester, up there in the Finger Lakes region. Anyway, Smith said he used a lever to pry up a stone that covered where the plates were buried."

Eden snorted. "Seems like there were a lot of folks prying stones off burial sites back then." Both of them knew Spaulding's story was a tale he made up and intended to publish as a novel, but Joseph Smith's story became part of a well-established religion that now has over nine million members.

Eden told Dave that maybe Solomon's story wasn't just made up... maybe he found something like they found yesterday. Maybe he found something but kept it to himself. Maybe he used the tale to embellish his story. It was all guesswork. No proof of anything— except for what they had found.

"Now, if you're ready for some really weird shit," Dave resumed, "just over the hill from where we dug up that stump, there was a frontier blockhouse called the Swanson Fort, built in the late 1700s. Back then, a blockhouse was just a log cabin with a palisade fence, where settlers could go to escape the Indians. It wasn't really a fort in the military sense, but people around here just use that word.

"Remember, Spaulding said his find was a small distance from the fort. That's another parallel with Joseph Smith's story: both the Spaulding tale and Smith involve finding something under a rock near a fort. Is that spooky, or what?"

Eden was in deep thought. "Hey, maybe our find is just like Smith's. You haven't seen any angels hovering around, have you?"

Dave ignored that. He explained that one problem in researching anything in the mid-1800s was that hoaxes were so popular then. The Cardiff Giant, sea serpents, perpetual motion machines, chess-playing machines, and stories about lost tribes abounded. One guy had people convinced that Patagonia was inhabited by a race of giants. Anything exotic appealed, and few folks knew much about the world beyond their hometowns.

"Every medicine show had its Wild Man from Borneo, or some such. All this stuff was driven by the Enlightenment," Dave said. "When scientists, let alone the common folk, were presented with real discoveries like a duckbilled platypus or the remains of a mammoth, no one would believe them. No wonder they were skeptical. It seems the nineteenth century was one of hellacious good fun."

Eden mused, "Ya know, it's not hard to imagine Solomon Spaulding mulling over how he would reveal what he had found to the world. He would start with a fanciful tale, embellish it, and let it lay awhile. Then, little by little, he would slip "truth" to folks. It might have worked except for one thing—he died before the Revelation of Spaulding could be published."

If it weren't for the indisputable fact of a religion with over nine million believers, a revelation of pre-Columbian lost tribes would seem as fantastic as Eden's freshly hatched, hare-brained theory about Spaulding.

Dave said, "Meanwhile, let's get back down to earth. What do you think about our present situation?"

"Shit, Dave, I don't know what to think. As a Deputy, I know what I'd normally do, but this ain't normal."

"Well then, here's what I think… first we go back and take photos of everything at the sight. We'll rig a flash at several angles to clearly reveal the inscribed writing on the cover stone. Then we'll fish around to see if anyone knows anything about what we've found. Then we'll put everything back, cover the site with soil, reseed it, and cover any bare soil with hay. Our activity might draw attention, so we'll leave as if nothing ever happened, except we harvested that stump.

"Then sometime in the summer, after the grass has grown and everything is forgotten, we'll come back, remove the cover stone, and see what we have. If the structure beneath it is empty, we'll report the site to the folks up at the Carnegie Museum in Pittsburgh and let them take it from there. If we find something valuable— well, we'll make our plans from there." He rubbed his hands together.

Eden, ever ready with a classic film scenario, had a quick flashback of *The Treasure of the Sierra Madre* with Dave doing that little Walter Huston dance on his grave.

They agreed to silence, and to always work together when approaching anyone with the photos or questions. They began to refer to the stone and what was under it as "The Site."

The weeks dragged by. If you want to make your life seem longer, try to keep a secret, Eden thought. The tension, piled atop the recent murder investigation, was making paranoia his bedfellow. Imaginary people were watching, knowing exactly what was up. The waiting game was one Eden never played well.

A tricky part of their deception was finding someone who might know anything about the writing on the stone. Rainelle College was too tiny to have an archeology department. An eccentric professor there indulged herself by digging around the county's Indian burial grounds, but they doubted that she would be of value.

But Dave knew a history professor at Oberlin College in Ohio, an old college classmate. This was promising because of the pre-Columbian earthworks and Indian artifacts in that part of Ohio. Professor Gustav Bimelar had done archeological digs in Ohio and West Virginia, and had worked the famous Meadowcroft Rock Shelter dig just north of George County. Meadowcroft goes back 15,000 years and is one of the oldest Indian sites in the east, even predating the Clovis culture of the Southwest it's claimed.

"Gus is an expert on the Hopewell and Adena Indian cultures," Dave said. "And he's far enough from George County so no one would know him. Even if he can't decipher the inscription, he might know someone who could."

So they decided that Dave would ask Bimelar to visit, to renew old times and see something interesting. Dave's tale would be of a friend who visited a southern West Virginia site where petroglyphs had been discovered recently, and here were pictures he sent. Dave would explain that his friend was secretive about the find and thought it might be valuable.

This sounds like the guy who goes to the VD clinic to find out something about an STD for his "friend," Eden thought. Bimelar would know better, but he might play along and be helpful.

Came spring, and Gus arrived at the Brightbrook furniture shop on a sunny, breezy day that was too cool to enjoy outdoors, but too nice to stay inside.

Gustav Bimelar was early fifties, taller than either of them, and quite thin. His wispy beard combined blonde and gray, matching his hair. Perhaps he expected to go tramping around outside, for he wore hiking boots and field clothing, or maybe that was just part of the uniform.

181

Dave introduced him as Professor Gustav Bimelar, but Gus protested the title and formal name, insisting on Gus. It took a while, but Dave twisted the conversation to the petroglyph discovery, mentioned his "friend," and produced the photos.

"Hmm, interesting," he mumbled with a slight German accent. He held a reading glass to the eight-by-ten of the inscribed cover stone. "I agree with you Dave. It resembles Demotic, but it isn't. Demotic uses brush strokes—like calligraphy—so it's not easy to cut into a stone tablet, unless you use modern methods. Regardless, it isn't Demotic."

"Well, any idea what it is then?" Eden asked.

"Not really," said Gus. "It may be a version of Arabic more ancient than Demotic, or it may be a completely different dialect. You'll have to submit this to someone fluent in ancient languages." Then he snapped his fingers. "Tell you what—I could take this to Columbus with me. I have a conference there next week. I know a guy from Ohio State who is sharp on these old languages, and he'll be there. I'll have him look at it. He should be able to translate it, or at least give you some idea of what it says."

"That would be great," said Dave. "But we'd appreciate it if you keep this kind of hush-hush. My friend is afraid of starting a land rush of people looking for buried treasure or artifacts."

"Don't worry, I'll be sure to keep your friend's secret safe," Gus smirked. He didn't believe a word of Dave's story. Dave grinned back at Gus. "Thanks."

The three sat around for a several hours, lunching and avoiding discussion of the find. Gus finally said goodbye and departed.

Dave turned to Eden. "What do you think?"

"I think Bimelar might have an idea about the origin of the stone and its inscription. And I think he didn't buy one word of your bullshit cover story."

"Eden, you know West Virginia is full of such tales. Recently, a guy claimed to have translated some petroglyphs in ogham, an Old Irish language, and some other guy says they're in Basque. These people are full of shit."

"Well, it may be my recurring paranoia, but I suspect that Gus learned more than we want him to know."

"Gus Bimelar is a good guy and I think we can trust him. I doubt if he believed my 'friend in West Virginia' story either, but he'll help us if he can," Dave assured him.

A week passed. Quinn invited himself to a Saturday breakfast, so Eden made a mental note to burn the pancakes this time. It wasn't that he didn't like Dave's companionship, but Eden didn't want to be his cook whenever he wanted a free breakfast.

Dave arrived with that homemade briefcase. They chatted over breakfast, and then took their coffee to the sofa. Dave seemed to avoid mentioning the reason for his visit, and Eden took this to mean no good news from Bimelar. His impression was accurate.

Dave took a sip of coffee and announced, "Gus struck out. He showed the photos to his friend. He was unable to identify or read the work, so he scanned the photos and e-mailed them to several ancient language experts who are in a loose-knit Internet group. Some are linguists, some archaeologists, and some biblical scholars. Their consensus was what we already guessed: some form of ancient Arabic, or perhaps a dialect or offshoot of Demotic."

Eden sighed, disappointed.

"If it isn't any recognizable language, it will have to be treated like any other encrypted message: find a way to decrypt it. Eden— we've tried keeping this to ourselves, but I think we've exhausted the cursory-look phase of this. If we go farther, we'll have to reveal more. With those pictures e-mailed who-knows-where, this could get out of hand very quickly."

"I think it's already out of our control."

"I say let's go pull up that slab and see what's there. After that, we can call in whomever we like."

"If you think we can do it in one day, let's go tomorrow. I'm ready to get this over with."

CHAPTER TWENTY-NINE

HILL CUMORAH II?

Dawn broke as they commenced their Sunday morning dig. A heavy mist hung over the terrain, with the low mound standing just above the fog line. Eden felt like a tomb robber in one of those murky tales of the Scottish moors. Dave emerged from the mist carrying a huge steel pry-bar, and Eden followed like his Igor, carrying a shovel. A camera hung from his neck. This excavation would be documented.

The pair moved through the mist toward the top of the rise and the waiting sarcophagus. They removed the sprouting grass and dirt from around the edge of the cover. Dave tried to work his pry-bar under the stone.

"Take it easy," Eden cautioned. "We don't want to chip or crack it."

"I'm being careful," Dave grumbled. "Get that fulcrum rock in there, so I can get some leverage."

Working together, they finally scooted the edge over far enough to get their fingers under it and flipped it carefully to expose what was underneath. The "sarcophagus," as Eden called it, wasn't much more than some flat, native fieldstone that lined a rectangular hole. He couldn't judge its depth because it had filled with fine, dusty silt. He took a picture of the undisturbed soil inside. Then, using a small trowel, he began to scoop out the dirt.

Dave sat on the large rock that had hidden the coverstone. "I'll sit guard," he joked.

Eden had removed a foot of soil when the trowel hit something.

185

Using his hand, he carefully scraped and brushed away the silt. I should have brought a paintbrush to sweep the soil away, like archeologists do, he thought.

"Hey Dave, I hit something. I need to brush away the dirt around it. Grab me a handful of that broom sage, will you?"

Dave complied, and Eden devised a witch's broom, bundling the plants and binding them with twisted broom sage strands. He swept with the brush and flipped soil with the trowel until he revealed all edges of what appeared to be a flat stone that had been polished by streamwater. It was less than an inch thick, with all edges rounded, like landscaping stone—a river rock.

He uncovered the tops—or were they bottoms?—of seven stones, clearing away the debris. "Dave, take a picture. Maybe their position is significant."

Then Eden carefully removed each stone, placing it on the new grass at the edge of the hole, and continued to dig. Within another inch, the trowel clanked against a hard surface. After several minutes of scratching and digging to find the edges of the surface, he realized it was part of the lining the sidewall stones were sitting on. He had reached the bottom of the sarcophagus.

"Come on Dave, help me clean out the rest of this dirt. I think I hit bottom."

Eden turned his attention to the seven river rocks. There was nothing at all remarkable about the exposed side. They looked like any rocks in a streambed, unusual only because they were several miles from any stream large enough to have smoothed them.

Dave finished removing debris from the sarcophagus and joined Eden. "So what have we here?"

Eden picked up one of the river rocks and turned it over. "More writing."

"Hmm, yeah, except this time it isn't Demotic. Or Demotic-looking," Eden said.

"Or Demonic-looking," Dave cracked.

The characters cut into the rock resembled those on the Grave Creek Stone, except there were more of them, in a pattern. They looked like cuneiform tablets he had seen in history books. The characters were made of little wedges cut into the stone, like the ones pressed into clay tablets by the Mesopotamians.

"Yeah," said Dave, "this looks like Sumerian cuneiform."

The fact that both of them thought of cuneiform seemed more than coincidental.

"Can you make out any of it?" Eden asked.

"Oh, sure. It says, for a good time, call Peggy at 1-800... c'mon, Eden! You think I'm an ancient petroglyphologistician? Of course I can't make it out! It just reminds me of ancient chicken-tracks you see in history books, that's all."

At least both of them had paid attention during World History in high school. Aside from that, they were as clueless about the river rock inscriptions as they were about the coverstone.

"Okay, let's look at the bottom of the hole." But within moments, it was clear that the bottom of the hole was a flat stone, similar to the one that covered the sarcophagus. They took pictures and began to disassemble the sarcophagus. Eden thought they should turn it over to experts at this point, but they both were too curious about what might lie beneath the floor of the stone-lined coffin.

They removed all the lining stones and dug around the bottom, defining the edges of the floor. Finally, they were able to pry up the floorstone. And underneath it was—soil. The underside of the floorstone displayed the same sort of Demotic-looking stuff that was on the coverstone. The language may have been the same, but the message was different. Aside from that, the coverstone and floorstone were twins. The same granite, the same neatly dressed sides, the same size, although the floorstone was a bit thicker.

For the next hour, they took turns digging in the soil in the bottom of the hole, excavating another four feet.

"To hell with this," muttered Dave. "Whoever built this didn't bury anything under it."

"Yeah, to heck with it," Eden agreed. "Let's backfill it."

After backfilling, they built a cairn marker over the whole thing with fieldstones, like a grave. Then they loaded the river rocks, coverstone, and floorstone into Eden's truck.

Dave said thoughtfully, "I'll call Gus and talk this over with him. He'll give me hell for digging up the site, but to hell with him."

"Oh, you can bet the professor-types will pitch a bitch about how we carelessly dug up this stuff," Eden said. "But it's your property, I guess. See what Gus has to say. I'll send him the pictures."

So Dave called Gustav Bimelar and Eden emailed the pictures. After a few days, Bimelar called. He would like to see the stones. And could he bring along his colleague from Ohio State?

Eden was feeling leery about the whole thing. He resolved to let the experts examine to their hearts content, while he faded into the background. He didn't want to get any deeper into the mess.

Several days passed. Dave called.

The Deputy tried to sound disinterested. "'Wa'sup?" Eden asked.

Dave sounded disgusted. "They think the whole thing is a wild goose chase. They took a bunch more pictures and the Ohio State guy—whatsisname—Dr. McDonald—Roger McDonald—took rubbings of the coverstone and floorstone. I think he just wants something cool to hang on his office door.

"Anyway, they said their first impression is that someone back in the 1800s was working hard to jerk someone off. They think the whole thing is a hoax."

"A hoax." Eden said flatly. He made no attempt to hide his disappointment.

"McDonald says it might have been someone playing around

with the Solomon Spaulding story—trying to recreate it."

"Yeah," Eden said gloomily, someone too cheap to use gold plates.

"Eden, it does make sense, if you think about it. The site is awfully close to where Spaulding lived out his last days. And Gus thinks someone may have wanted to mess with the Mormons' minds. Hell, it might have been Spaulding himself."

"You said they took more pictures. Do you think they'll give you any more information?" Eden asked hopefully.

"Roger says he'll run a computer program on the coverstone characters. He says it doesn't appear to be a language as such, but it might contain an encrypted message. Probably about a bunch of Swedish monks lost at sea and making it to the Americas—"

"That would be about right, and the cuneiform river stones are, no doubt, the Ten Commandments from the lost tribes of Israel, except three are missing."

"Sounds about like it to me," said Dave, gloomily. "At least now we know we aren't going to get rich. This could be a big controversy for years: Is it a message left by ancient mariners? Or Spaulding's attempt to stimulate interest in his novel? Or a cache of information passed down by ancient astronauts? I can hardly wait until the *National Enquirer* shows up."

"Well, we can always hope it turns out to be a real ancient find," Eden said. "Who knows, who could tell?"

"Start holding your breath," Dave grumped.

"Well, even if it is a hoax, it's still a pretty amazing piece of history. And being from the 1800s, it might even have value to people who collect that sort of stuff," Eden encouraged.

"Look, Eden, I've poked around this long enough to know something: any legitimate archeologist is going to treat this find like the plague. So much controversy has been stirred up over the Ohio Valley aborigines—the earthworks and all—that it's politically incorrect to even speculate on it. Prestigious scientists have had their careers toasted on the Hopewells and the Adenas. This whole area of research got mucked up in the late 1800s and early 1900s. Now, Eden, let's mix in some angry LDS folks... oh, I can just imagine!

He continued, "Here... let me read you some of what Gus and his colleague translated:

"The family name I sustain is Fabius, being descended from the illustrious General of that name. I was born at Rome and received my education under the tuition of a very learned Master. At the time that Constantine arrived at that city and had overcome his enemies and was firmly seated on the throne of the Roman Empire, I was introduced to him as a young Gentleman—

The vessel laden with provisions for the army— (unreadable)—boundless Ocean. Soon the whole crew became lost and bewildered—

On the fifth day after this we came in sight of land, we entered a spacious River and continued sailing up the same many leagues until we came in view of a town. Every heart now palpitated with— (unreadable)—distance from shore. Immediately the natives ran with apparent signs of surprise and astonishment, to the bank of the River..."

"Any of that sound familiar?" Dave asked.

"It wouldn't have before we got into all this. But I've read some of Spaulding's stuff. I'd say it's Spaulding, word-for-word."

"Bingo!" exclaimed Dave. "It looks like we found a plant by the Great One—Solomon Spaulding himself—or a plant by someone who wanted to jerk off the experts with a faux Spauldingesque find. Either way, it makes our discovery just a curiosity."

"Well, it'll make a great display for the George County Museum in Rainelle, unless we can find a collector with cash," Eden smirked.

"Humph. If you want to peddle the stuff, I'll take my cut," Dave said. "But I've pretty much lost interest."

So far, the Deputy's success at treasure hunting matched his success at sleuthing. Peddling their find had no appeal.

And then a little bulb flickered in his brain... maybe the Mormons would be willing to finance a project to discredit the Spaulding story for all time!

CHAPTER THIRTY

LOOK WHO'S BACK

Real spring weather arrived in a hot, humid way that was foreign to southwestern Pennsylvania. The sometime Chief Investigator spent his spring days cruising the back roads, stopping occasionally to wet bait in George County's many streams that wander through the newly greened countryside. Fish weren't the reason for baiting a hook; all went free before glimpsing a frying pan. Eden was preoccupied.

Shele continued to send long e-mails, and Eden felt guilty for not returning long answers. Writing was a joy for her, but a chore for him. In one long, rambling message, she mentioned a job opening at Rainelle College. He should have been excited, but deep down he felt it wasn't in the cards. He was sure she mentioned it just to tease the Dudley part of him.

Eden was examining a fence atop the hill behind his house when he noticed an unfamiliar car in the distance. He thought little of it until it turned up his drive. A Ford Taurus, it had rental written all over it. He trudged down the long hillside, readying himself to be really pissed at some insurance or siding salesman.

The car stopped in the drive, just short of the house, and a woman wearing a scarf and sunglasses got out, adjusted the waistband of her skirt, and looked at herself in the car window. She leaned down for a closer look in the outside mirror.

Eden rounded the side of the house just as she raised up from the mirror. The smile was unmistakable. "I got the job!" Shele announced.

"Abba, uh—uh—duh," he exclaimed.

"Articulate as ever," she smiled broadly, stepping into his arms. Her hands went to his face and held him there for one of the longest, wettest kisses he could remember.

"Just couldn't stay away?" he chided.

"No, I couldn't. I knew you needed someone to look after you. And I couldn't stand for you to work those murder cases without me here to help." She took his hand and they walked toward the front porch and the door beyond.

The following morning, after a soliloquy about how hard it was to put herself back together with only a man's toiletries to work with, she made breakfast, and they began to plan a future together.

Shele was no woman to be argued with. Given their experiences together last summer, they knew each other all too well. He had no idea how he came to invite her to become a permanent part of a two-person investigative team, but she made him believe that at some point he had asked her. He could only hope it would be a long engagement before he would have to face the altar. For the life of him, he didn't remember proposing—but if Shele said he did—who was he to question her?

Eden went back to an office that seemed stuck in a time before the murders and slipped quietly into his typical routine. But, Myra, Elizabeth, June, and yes, Amara McClure were always in the back of his mind, and the case was never put into the cold file. Now with Shele to help once again, perhaps they would get the long overdue break they needed.

CHAPTER THIRTY-ONE

LOOSE LIPS

Eden found out about it second-hand. It was they-say comments, small-town chatter, barber-&-beauty shop gossip, breakfast-at-Mickey-D's rumors. Most of it would be denied.

Andy, Randy, Ted, Pauly. Who'd o' thought it?

First, Andy Walbridge, Director of Walbridge's Funeral Home, was the last person you would expect to be involved. Eden believed that Andy got sucked into it because funeral directors have a tough time socially—liked and valued, but constant reminders of our mortality, so in some circles they are avoided.

Second, Randy Winter had been CEO of Farmer's Bank for twenty-odd years. There was a drinking problem people whispered about, and if anything is whispered about in Rainelle, it contains a germ of truth. Randy wasn't married, and in Rainelle, that was almost as bad as the hint of alcoholism. The rumor was of a gay affair back in college. Gay or not, Randy was just too effeminate for rural George County tastes. He could swim with the big fish in business, but he couldn't make it with the coon-dog-and-pickup set. Moreover, the ultimate sin besmirched his record: Randy hated NASCAR.

Alternative lifestyles are still frowned upon in George County. Every parent has a gut fear of raising a gay kid. No one would directly bash a gay person, but that was as far as it went. It just wasn't acceptable in George County, and the Andy/Randy rumor had floated around for years, the rhyming names helping to keep it alive.

Third, and even a greater shock, was Ted Dunlow, proprietor of Dunlow's Restaurant and Bar. Like Andy, he was another last person you might expect to be part of it. Churchwomen never cared for Ted, but everyone else thought he was a great guy. Some people held a very high opinion of anyone who owned a bar and could draw a free one from his tap, so they considered Ted to be a great guy.

Eden researched Ted's past. He was from some little town on the Elk River in West Virginia. Down there you see a church every hundred yards. Some are very fundamental—snake-handling, lye-drinking. Once Eden discovered that Ted was a member of the Lighthouse True Gospel Church, with its lighthouse atop the spire and cross over the door, it was no surprise that Ted was involved. A call to the Sheriff down there disclosed "that church is fundamentalist, radical fundamentalist. If they was some o' them Mooslims, I'd be worried about 'em."

Fourth and final, Pauly Loughman wasn't on the same plane with the other three—which isn't to say that Andy, Randy, or Ted were rocket scientists. But Pauly must have gone along with them simply because he was dumb.

"Under a spreading chestnut tree, the village idiot sat—" that was Pauly Loughman in a chestnut shell. Not retarded, just unsophisticated and gullible—the sort of guy you could take snipe hunting—twice, or send him to get change for a penny. He wasn't as smart or old as the other three. He was the kid you never chose for the team, so they must have kept him around for shits and giggles.

If they'd only kept Pauly Loughman out of it, the whole thing might have gone undetected for years. But they didn't, and Pauly was their weakest link.

So that's how the whole thing started to unravel. Pauly started out at Ted Dunlow's place one afternoon, and as the evening wore on, he moved on to Lin Kelley's saloon.

The sign out front announced "Kelley's Wagon Wheel Saloon," but everyone called it Lin's place because she manned the bar herself, and as she observed, "the owner works cheap." Lin was one fixture in Rainelle you could depend on. Maybe you couldn't find a doctor, policeman, or lawyer, but you were always sure to find Lin—and many believed she held the most important post in town. She literally lived at the Wagon Wheel, in the apartment above.

If one person could be counted on to spread news, it was Lin Kelley. Tell her anything, and soon everyone knew, from the pompous, sour-faced Pastor Norman up at First Presby, to Shelia Leibeck on the south side of town. If not for her, the Deputy might not have learned the details.

Shelia Leibeck passed for Rainelle's lady of the evening. Everyone, including the priest up at Saint Agnes, called her "She-will-lay-back." They used to pick her up for soliciting, but since she aged a few decades, the law now leaves her alone. Buckey and Eden figured it was better than social security, which she couldn't get, or welfare, which she could. To them it was one more person off the dole and earning her own way.

So Pauly was pretty loaded when he got to Lin's, because when he left Ted Dunlow's place, he stopped by the liquor store and absorbed a pint of Everclear.

Like those times when the stars align just right, things sort of came together that night at the Wagon Wheel. Pauly was disposed to talk, and Lin was there to listen and pull the tap. The bar was empty, the lights low, the air hazy from Lin's Camels, and the aroma of spilled beer mixed with the robust fragrance of urine and disinfectant that drifted from the restrooms. The TV flickered and droned garbled dialogue, better at blaring treble than bass. Its woofer had woofed its last long before the first *American Idol* was idolized. *Raiders of the Lost Ark* was on, not surprising as it lives somewhere on cable 24/7, like *The Beastmaster* or *Dirty Dancing*.

As circumstance would have it, Pauly ordered his Iron City just as John Rhys-Davies was lowering Harrison Ford into the map room at an archeological site somewhere in Egypt. It was a coincidence that Indy Jones was discernable amidst the snow, vertical roll, speaker rattle, and hum.

As Harrison/Indy lifted the crystal from the staff of Ra to catch the light of a very convenient sunbeam, as it flashed across the entire chamber where one exact ray fell on the location of the Well of Souls —

"Hey," mumbled Pauly, "that's jus' like what the grand poohbah-whatsis up at the lodge said happened back in Hamul when the Tihu located where the Araca would be found."

"What the f—?" Lin asked incredulously. "What in the pluperfect hell are you gibbering about, Pauly? You don't belong to them Masons, do you? I know they're big into that Egyptian bullshit flapdoodle — but just what the hell are you talkin' about?"

"Naw, ain't none o' that there 'gyptian stuff. That was discredited years ago. Never was in Egypt — nor Asia neither. Came right over through Ethiopia, through South 'merica — maybe Mexico. That Well o' Souls is jus' a bunch of Hollywood hooey anyway. We got the real goods. Dug up the story just like old Joe Smith done," Pauly slurred. "Never found it though — they never did find it."

Lin frowned. "Never found what, Pauly? You better take it easy on the gulpin' down all that Iron City, Pauly. Let me get you a cuppa mud to clear your head up some."

Normally, Lin wouldn't have pursued Pauly's drunken ramblings. But she was a sucker for anything occult, especially Egyptian, a genuine freakazoid for anything Tut-like. The only thing that might distract her was a daily number or Power Ball announcement.

Lin's coffee was known to revive the dead. Its jolt was similar to those heart-starting machines in airports. After two cups — and just about the time the evil Nazi, Ron Lacey, was melting in the Ark movie — Pauly was sobered enough to become more cautious about what he was saying.

"So it wasn't Egypt, it was Mexico?" asked Lin. She wasn't particularly interested in his mumbling at this point. She needed to keep Pauly around long enough to pay his tab and sober up enough to be legal driving home.

"Who said anything about Egypt and Mexico?"

"You did. You said it wasn't Egypt, it came over through Mexico, whatever it is. That's what you said. I stood right here and heard you say it."

"It could have been South America," Pauly said tentatively. "I ain't supposed to talk about it. Randy says we ain't to talk to anyone about it."

Pauly sounded like a combination of John Malkovich and Lon Chaney, Jr. playing Lenny in *Of Mice and Men*.

Now Lin's curiosity was really aroused, because if there was anything that could get her going, it was when someone said they knew something that they couldn't tell her.

"You ain't supposed to talk about what?" she screamed. "I get it, you can't trust ole' Lin. You can come in here for a freebie once in a while, shoot the bull with me, but you don't trust me."

"Aw, don't be mad at me," begged Pauly. "It's just that Andy and Randy will get pissed off if I tell about the family."

"I don't give a shit about your family. You were talking about the Araca or something like that. What's an Araca? Buried treasure or something?"

"I dunno very much about it," Pauly mumbled. "They don't talk about the Araca now, so much as they talk about how the stones were discovered."

That did it for Lin. First, it was Andrew Walbridge's secret little clique, "The Family"; then the "Araca"; and now, the stones. This was really getting interesting. Pauly knew something juicy and had been told to keep his big mouth shut. Lin could spend the rest of the night on this!

As it turned out, Pauly didn't know very much about the Araca. But he did tell Lin that the family, which he interchangeably called the lodge, was some fraternal organization or cult that developed in the mid-1800s. It was organized after some stones were discovered that bore obscure writing. Pauly rambled on about a man named Rigdon who started the sect long ago. Pauly was getting into it, trying to impress Lin with his secret knowledge of the family.

Then, a few days later, the beans began to spill when Lin let it slip to Eden that Pauly had blabbing about some sort of mysterious cult that was operating in the George County.

Over the years, Eden had learned that Lin, if approached the right way—like threatening to lift her liquor license—could be trusted to keep her mouth shut. She had been very, very helpful with recent drug busts involving some not-so-nice biker types. With that in mind, he decided to enlist her aid in pumping Pauly for more information.

"Lin, I need you to help me out here. I think what Pauly knows might be helpful to an investigation—"

"Hey, none of that," she interrupted. "I don't wanna get involved. You know me. I don't like messing with investigations. That's not my business."

"Oh, I know you Lin. You don't have to tell me that. But I also know you love to help someone when you can—especially if that someone might have to fill out a report to the state Liquor Control Board about underage drinking here in the county," he reminded her.

A few days later, the Deputy got a call from Lin Kelley. "Pauly don't know a whole hell of a lot more than what I already told you," she reported. "But of course you knew that already. Anyway, here's what I found out: Andy, Randy, Ted, and Pauly belong to some sort of bullshit quasi-religious sect that was started sometime around 1848 or 1849 by this Walter Rigdon character. I'm saying it was kinda like a religion, because it was like a lot of other lodges that were popular back then; lots of symbols, incantations, hoodoo, that sort of thing. I think it's more like a good-old-boy clique than anything else.

"Anyway, back then Rigdon convinced a bunch of people that he had discovered runes—that's what he called 'em, runes—that contained messages that only he could decipher because he was a Chosen One. He said the messages were from some lost tribes that moved into America that got here by way of Asia. They came from God-knows-where and set up housekeeping out west in New Mexico or some damn place. Pauly says they were taught that the messages were revealed by a Kachina or something, by name of Makya or something, who will come again to help others and bring peace to the world. He wasn't too clear on how the messages got on the stones and into Rigdon's hands.

When Eden the Investigator heard her say "stones with messages" and connected them with the name Rigdon, a chill run down his spine and he could feel his knees weaken.

"Rigdon also said Makya was a guide, or channel, through the spirit world who would reveal to the faithful followers the location of the Araca. And all the faithful would follow and take orders from Rigdon the Revealer, who is the representative of Makya on earth. He threw in a lot of Great Spirit talk too.

"I think if you could get this load in a spreader, you'd have enough manure to fertilize all of George County," she concluded.

"Anything else you can think of?"

"Like I said, Pauly ain't the sort you give sharp scissors to. Come on now, Eden, level with me. This is some bunch of Peyote-button munchers you're trying to bust, right?"

"You're too smart for me, Lin," he replied, leaving her hanging.

"I'da believed you if you'd denied it. Now you're trying to bullshit the bartender," she said, peevishly. "Thanks for nothing."

"Anyway," he asked, "does he have a clue what an Araca is?"

"He says it's some kind of gadget that focuses the energy of the gods, kinda' like the Ark of the Covenant, I'm figurin'. He don't know what it looks like, but he thinks Rigdon, or someone in the early days—that's what they call anything before the twentieth century—tried to make one. According to Pauly, it was destroyed by some sort of angry beings or was lost. He didn't seem very clear about it, or a whole lot of anything else, for that matter. He said the location of the original Araca hasn't been revealed, and won't be until the end-time—whatever that is. I figure it's like the Book of Revelation story, ya know?

"So Eden, that's it. When you pick Pauly Loughman's brain, the pickings are slim. I think the lodge just let him come along so they would have someone to clean up after them."

Eden chuckled. "You got that right. Thanks for all the help. I'll remember, and if you need anything, you just let me know."

"Oh, there's one other thing."

"What's that, Lin?"

"Pauly said something about not being initiated yet. He didn't seem to be looking forward to it either. You got any idea what that might be all about?"

"Nope," Eden replied, "you know more about it than I do."

He had the same feeling after talking with Lin that he had after his conversation with Colleen: all very interesting but not very useful. There was a lot of weird shit going on in and around George County and Rainelle, but it didn't seem to be connected to the dead women.

Eden did fantasize a scenario in which the three young women wind up in a satanic rite and are sacrificed to Makya at Andy

Walbridge's Funeral Home in a ritual to free up the location of the genuine Araca. In the fantasy, Amara commits suicide to become the spiritual bride of Makya in a ceremony conducted by the resurrected Walt Rigdon. But Eden didn't share his fantasy with anyone, for fear of having to repeat it to Weird Herman Harold McMurchy's shrink.

All fantasies aside... no matter how obscure or indirect... something connected this whole mess together... somehow...

Spring was quickly becoming summer. Shele moved back into Amara's rented house that had stood empty, awaiting her return. Eden told her it was rent money wasted and invited her to stay with him. But she wouldn't hear of it: "People will talk, and after all, I am a librarian at a Presbyterian school."

Well, he didn't need the distraction anyway. If Shele lived with him, he'd get little done—not that there was much to his job now. Later, he heard that Shele had continually rented the old house since Amara died. Rumor was that the owner wanted someone to rent it with option to buy.

Eden's half-hearted request to Buckey for time to work on the girls' murder case was turned down cold—the Sheriff wouldn't hear of it. There was no new evidence, and the case looked like it was headed for the freezer. Most people thought some itinerants killed the girls, and everyone who lacked an imagination—meaning nearly all of George County—thought Amara McClure committed suicide. Any break probably would take the form of some drunk bragging in a bar about their crime.

He prepared to go home when his phone gave off its distinctive ring. "Eden," said the low voice on the other end of the phone, "this is Andy Walbridge over at the funeral home. We've gotta talk."

CHAPTER THIRTY-TWO

WE'VE GOTTA TALK

Andy wouldn't elaborate, but he sounded secretive, insisting that they meet at the truck stop on the Interstate. That venue signaled confidentiality. Locals didn't go there often.

When Eden arrived, Andy sat dejectedly in a booth at the rear, just outside the trucker's noisy bullpen, with coffee and a donut. His trench coat looked slept in, his collar was open, his tie drooped like a dog's tongue, and with a three-day growth of beard, he looked nothing like the dapper undertaker everyone knew in Rainelle. He barely looked up. "Have a seat, Eden."

Andy was no glad-hander, but he normally was as gregarious as an embalmer could be. Eden had never seen him so serious, nervous, or worried.

"What is it, Andy?" the Deputy asked with concern.

Andy made a few stuttering attempts to speak, then sort of broke down. Honest to God, it seemed he was going to cry.

"Oh shit, Eden," he began, "I know Pauly's been talking all over town about my involvement in the lodge, and now you know about it too—"

"The lodge?" Eden said innocently, leaving an opening.

"Dammit, Eden, don't play dumb. You know about the lodge and all that stuff about the Araca, and all—we never should have let Pauly in on any of it—he isn't even an initiated member—he only knows enough to make him dangerous—that was Randy's idea—letting him get in with us. All the decades without a problem—"

"Whoa! Whoa-ho," Eden said. "Take it easy. Just start where you want, say what you want, take it one step at a time."

Andy sat staring at his coffee, not looking up.

"Tell you what," Eden said, "just begin as if I know nothing at all." Which is the truth, Eden thought. I don't know a damn thing.

Andy gave a big sigh and stirred his coffee. He took out a wrinkled pack of Lucky Strikes and a beat-up Zippo and laid them beside the saucer with his partially eaten powdered donut.

"Promise me this won't go any farther than you."

"If it involves criminal activity, I can't promise anything, you know that."

"No, nothing criminal," Andy said. "Plenty of embarrassment, broken confidences, violated oaths, and secret lodge stuff, but no laws broken. I just want you to know what's going on so you don't think I—uh—we have been involved in anything criminal. I'm telling you for my own protection. And I want you to know up front that I didn't have any part in what anyone else might have done— anything I don't know about."

"Andy, maybe you should have an attorney—"

"No!" he said emphatically. "No lawyers. I don't need any more people involved in this. I know what's incriminating, and I'm not going to go there. Basically, there's nothing criminal. It's the career-ruining, scandal-type stuff that concerns me. I want to protect my business and myself from slander, that's all. That's the only reason I'm here."

This was sounding like Andy wanted to tell the investigator enough truth to make anything he said more believable, and to give himself an out if the going got sticky. Eden's bullshit detector was shrieking red-alert. He knew Andy, but only casually. They were acquainted professionally because Eden picked up the results of fatal accidents, and he relied on Andy for accident report information. Eden supposed they could have talked heart-to-heart, but the gay rumors and Andy's ghoulish profession didn't make for amigos simpáticos.

"If all my cautions to you are understood," Eden said, "go ahead, start at the beginning—and take it easy."

"Really, it's all quite innocent. It just seems weird if you haven't been there. You just won't understand."

"Try me," the Deputy urged.

"It's all between consenting adults anyway—"

Good Lord, what are we getting into here? Consenting adults, my ass, Eden thought.

But he reassured Andy: "Okay, okay, it's all right. Just go ahead."

"Well, I met Randy Winter at the bank years ago, when I first applied for a small business loan. We got to be good friends, and he would invite me to his place from time to time, so we got to know one another pretty well. Eventually, Randy invited me to become an inductee into his lodge, Lodge of the Runes he called it. I didn't know much about that sort of thing and, being a funeral director and all, it's pretty hard to get invited into anything socially, so I accepted. I figured it would be a good business move, what with Randy being with the bank and all. I thought then and I still think he's a stand-up guy."

"I've always considered both of you to be solid citizens," Eden said, hoping he didn't roll his eyes.

"I appreciate that Eden. But I'm not going to identify any of the other people who are in the lodge, for reasons I'll get to. You already know about Pauly, and now you know about Randy Winter. And that," he said, "is as far as I'm going with identifying anyone."

He went on to tell Eden how the lodge began, most of which Eden already had learned from Lin Kelley. He continued as Eden expected until he got to the initiation part—that was when he dropped the bomb. Well, not really a bomb, but for George County, it was at least a hand grenade. In South Beach or Key West, it would have been a ladyfinger firecracker. In San Francisco, it would have been a small fart. But here—

For Randy and Andy, it must have been a mere dalliance. But for Pauly, it was a major obstacle to full membership, and it explained a lot. Come to think of it, the hand grenade analogy was apt: he could see fragments spreading out and damaging anyone they touched.

"This isn't to go any further than you and me, you got that Eden? I hope I can trust you. It's embarrassing for most of the members, and if it were to get out... you know what folks are like around here—"

Eden reassured Andy he was fully aware of what folks were like in George County.

He told him Pauly was still a novitiate, because he constantly avoided going through the rites required to become a full member. If it was like initiations into most clandestine societies, the ceremonies and requirements are designed to establish power over the members and to assure that the business and activities of the group stay secret. In this case, the idea must have been to make the induction ritual so ego-threatening that it would ensure continuing secrecy.

"Only the Venerated Ehecacoatl and High Priest Topiltzin are present," he continued. "I suppose they are the only ones who know what happens for sure. Anyway, they are sworn to secrecy, so who knows what really goes on with anyone else. The members are left to assume the rites are the same for everyone in the lodge, but no one knows for sure. Sure, we all know what happened to us as individuals, but that's all we know—we aren't to talk about it, under pain of death."

"Yeah," Eden said, "every secret society that ever existed has a pain-of-death clause in the contract, but I've never heard of a Mason showing up with his skull smote off and his brains exposed

to the scorching rays of the sun. They say that's part of their oath."
Or that was part of an oath he remembered seeing on an Internet
site.

Andy went on, "To tell you the honest truth, sometimes I wish
we had the old days of the lodge back. Back then, a rat like Pauly—"
Andy caught himself and said no more. "Anyway, back then, the
lodge had more going for its members to keep mum. That's all I'm
going to say about that."

He described how the initiation began in front of the entire
membership in a ceremonial chamber they called the Great Kiva.
He told Eden more than he ever wanted or needed to know
about the ceremony. With names floating around like Ehecacoatl
and Great Kiva, it all seemed a natural extension of the Neo-
Tenochitlan theme.

The Kiva rites consisted of incantations and ceremonies to
impress the faithful. And then, at a propitious moment, the
initiation moved into the backroom for what would be the kinkier
and even more secretive stuff. According to Andy, the liturgy
was essentially a metaphorical marriage to the society that all
members—both male and female—must eventually undergo if they
are to become fully fledged family members. The backroom was the
scene where the symbolic marriage was consummated, witnessed by
Topiltzin, whoever that might be.

Andy said they all wore costumes that looked like leftovers from
The Kings of the Sun, and they wore masks so he couldn't identify
the bridegroom Ehecacoatl nor the witness Topiltzin. He couldn't
even tell if they were male or female—at first. Of course, Andy
wouldn't have told Eden even if he knew.

Eden was convinced that Andy and Randy didn't find the
wedding festivities as painful as some others, but since Pauly was
a reluctant bride, Eden decided he didn't swing the same way
they did. It seemed that this lodge was no different than any other

commune, cult, quasi-religious sect, or even established religion. They used the control of sex or celibacy to exercise power over the group.

Andy said that initiates were given something to eat, "like a host." Eden figured it was some sort of intoxicant or hallucinogen — something to get them in the mood. It was difficult to imagine all of them lining up for such an initiation without a little attitude adjustment first.

"I'll always believe that Kate Ryan slipped old Sean that rat poison because he made her go through the initiation rites," claimed Andy. "You can call that talking about a crime if you want, but there's no proof and no way to get any. Both of them are dead now, so it doesn't matter. But I know for a fact they were both inducted shortly before Sean's funeral."

"I don't get it Andy. Why, all of a sudden, do you feel compelled to tell me all this?"

Andy just sat there, stirring the puddle of coffee at the bottom of his cup and nervously rearranging the Zippo and cigarette pack beside it. He looked at the Deputy with a dead-on intensity that Eden didn't think was in him. "Eden, I might be just a hick-town undertaker, but I can tell when the law is closing in on something."

"What are we closing in on, Andy?"

"No, not you," he said. "I'm talking to you right now because you aren't the law in the strictest sense. You guys serve papers, haul prisoners, and do a bit of investigating. Now I'm not belittling what you do, but that's the way it is in this state."

"Thanks for the vote of confidence."

"You know what I mean," Andy protested. "I just feel I can talk to you like a friend. Maybe I'm wrong, but I get the feeling the investigation into those missing girls and the Amara McClure thing is warming up again. That librarian up at the college who was helping out last summer is back—" he paused.

At first Eden thought about assuring him that Shele had come back for the job at the college and to be with him, but then decided to let him squirm a bit to see where it might lead.

"Any other reason you think the investigation has moved to the front burner?" He asked.

"I don't know," Andy began, "with her being back and you running around asking questions and with Pauly opening his big yap—it just seems like you might start poking around again."

"So you think some of the lodge members could have been involved in the girls' deaths, is that it?"

The investigator in him was making a focused effort to be as matter-of-fact as he could, and he was resolved not to sound overly determined.

"No, I didn't mean to infer any thing of that sort," he said quietly. "I just want to be sure that if you start digging into the deeper nooks and crannies of the lodge, you don't start dredging up stuff about me that I would rather didn't get out, that's all."

It was then that Eden decided to let Andy stew a bit. "Andy, you're very perceptive. I don't know too many people who could have figured it. I hope you can keep quiet about all of this and don't go running off and telling Randy or Pauly about our conversation here. I'll keep quiet about this if you can."

Of course, Eden knew he would be on his cell phone talking with Randolph Winter as soon as he got to his car. And both of them would be having a heart-to-heart talk with Pauly Loughman before the sun had a chance to set. Pauly should thank his lucky stars that these weren't the good old days.

Throughout the conversation, Andy never mentioned Ted Dunlow, who he was sure Andy suspected was a thinly disguised Venerated Ehecacoatl. And, Eden suspected that Andy knew a whole lot more than he would ever share with him.

Deputy Eden Whitloe left Andy sitting alone, staring into his now-empty cup; his Zippo was in one hand and a crushed empty pack of Luckies in the other. Feeling more confused and now a bit depressed, Eden headed out to Random Creek, where he could think.

CHAPTER THIRTY-THREE

NOT YOUR TYPICAL IRISH ANGEL

It was a warm May, as warm as anyone could remember. The late afternoon sun broke through a tepid spring drizzle that added to Eden's gray mood. The sun warmed the retreat of his back porch, everything taking on a ruddy glow as he read the paper. Soon the light faded into twilight, and unable to stay awake, Eden made his way to the bedroom and fell into bed.

When the phone rattled him from a deep sleep, he thought it was a workday. Sunday just didn't compute for a while. It was Shele. Did he remember the picnic they planned?

He had taken it upon himself to provide some of the food, a fact he had forgotten completely.

"Oh, yes," he lied, "I'm all set on my end. I thought fried chicken and coleslaw would be good. I'll bring it if you'll be responsible for the dessert."

"Why don't you just pick up some of that shortcake while you are at the Colonel's? I know where the chicken and slaw are coming from—don't try to tell me how you slaved over a hot stove all day."

They drove around awhile, seeking a picnic table, and wound up at the state park in the western end of the county. Shele spread the table cover while Eden rummaged in the picnic basket for plastic knives and forks. They had fried chicken wings—original recipe— slaw, what passed for baked beans, and of course the shortcake. It dawned on Eden that Shele, the cook, had brought nothing but herself to the picnic. The thought that he should be munching on her tender bits for dessert went through his mind. He was sure it would be far tastier than the glop they were eating out of little plastic cups.

She looked up and began to wipe a bit of strawberry topping from her lips and said, "Yeah?"

"Oh yeah," he said, leaned over, and kissed the topping away.

"You glad I'm back?"

"You know it," he replied. "I really missed you."

Eden was saving his announcement for just this sort of "relaxed" occasion, because he didn't know how she might react. He paused and then told her he was renewing the effort to find whoever was responsible for the college girls' deaths.

She seemed thrilled at the prospect. "It'll be just like old times," she said. "Just like last summer—I hope."

"Well, I hope we have better results in finding the killers."

"You know what I mean."

"Yeah," he said, with an evil leer, "I'm hoping for more frequent success there as well."

He spent the rest of the picnic filling her in on events since she left. She seemed particularly interested in Andy Walbridge's tale about the lodge and asked many questions about what Eden had come to call the "Grave Creek Connections." She thought Walbridge's group wasn't so much a lodge as a cult, and that lodge members might somehow have been involved in the girls' deaths. That connection was tenuous at best, but secrecy and sex are a potent mixture where murder is concerned.

Shele said, "Cliques of that sort are secretive, and beyond the initiation I'll bet there are things designed to ensure secrecy. If they are involved in the murders, no one will speak out of fear for their lives."

"I've thought a lot about that," Eden said. "It was a fluke that Andy Walbridge came forward. I suspect that if any members are involved, they haven't let Andy in on anything. He never would have contacted me.

"If I had the resources, I'd plant a mole inside the group—but that's wishful thinking. Buckey, nor anyone else, would authorize the money and risk required. If it were drug-related, that would be different. I could get personnel and money dumped all over me."

"How do you know it isn't drug-related?" Shele asked.

"No evidence. Every civilian thinks all crimes are drug-related. Most street crime is, about seventy percent. But this sort of thing—well, I don't think there's a chance in hell that hard drugs are involved. This is something else, something altogether different."

"If it's only a matter of an investigator's salary, how about this," she said. "I know a couple of women who are off during the summer. I'm sure one of them would be dying to play detective during their summer vacation."

"That's the problem," he said, smiling.

"What do you mean? What would be the problem?" Shele asked.

"The dying part. Look Shele, this isn't one of those Nancy Drew–type murder mysteries. If this goes as deeply into Andy Walbridge's group as I think it might, it could get really dicey for anyone caught in the middle."

"I can see you don't know Aingeal Farrell." Shele spelled her first name and continued. "She isn't anything at all like an angel. You know, I think there is a librarian mold somewhere and every time the need arises, someone goes to that mold and pops one out. Aingeal looks every bit like what you would expect a librarian to look like, and more."

"Uh—what do you mean—and more?"

"She never tried to put any moves on me, and I can't say how she swings for sure, but if you can imagine a truck driver/lumberjack/librarian—that's Aingeal. Big, burly, redhead. No, not hair like mine, like Carrot Top, bright orange-red—with lots of freckles. Picture a red plaid flannel shirt, corduroy pants, and hiking boots, with a face like Abe Lincoln, mole and all. That's Aingeal. She could handle anything old Andy's lodge could throw at her, and she would handle it before breakfast."

"Sounds like your typical Irish lass."

Shele gave him a hard punch on the arm. "And just what do you mean by that?"

"Are you Irish?" he asked innocently. "I had no idea."

With that, she grabbed his head in her hands and planted a kiss full on his lips.

"Now that's Irish!" she exclaimed. And, in her best brogue, she added, "Now, dain'tcha go a-forgettin' it. Help me a-pickin' up aftar we go!"

On the trip back, Eden asked if she thought Aingeal would be interested in helping this summer. Shele said it would be harder to convince her not to get involved, and seemed genuinely excited at the prospect of having her friend join them.

"There's only one thing," Shele cautioned.

"What's that?" he asked.

"She's really a very sweet person, so if you make any comments about her personality, gender, or appearance, I'm going to be really, really pissed at you. You got that straight—Mountie boy?"

"Yes-um, I promise to be on my best behavior."

He added, "But make sure she understands that she'll be strictly on her own. It'll be like *Mission Impossible*. I'll deny everything if any of this gets out, or anything happens to her. On the other hand, if it turns out well, I'll move heaven and earth to make her efforts worthwhile."

"And of course you'll take the credit if it works out."

"You betcha."

The plan was for Aingeal to show up, looking for a place in Rainelle to spend a summer hiatus. She was to distance herself from both Shele and Eden, secretly contacting Shele only when absolutely necessary. She was never to contact the Deputy directly.

After a few weeks, she was to work her way into a relationship with a lodge member, and then try to become a member herself. Eden believed that Randy Winter would be the best target. Andy Walbridge was too cautious, and Pauly Loughman was too damned dumb. Ted Dunlow was younger and better-looking, so Eden suspected he wouldn't be attracted to Aingeal's feminine charms—if she had any. At this point, other lodge members were unknown.

Another major unknown was what Aingeal might do after she gained membership and acceptance by the members. A concern Eden didn't share with Shele was what Aingeal might have to do to gain the complete trust of the lodge.

Eden had a lot of reservations about involving one of Shele's friends in the case, but he was getting desperate and, well—Shele could be pretty darned persuasive.

Shele made the arrangements, and in late May the rumor mill started to crank. The word on the street was that a dyke from upstate had settled in out at the VanBurean place. Kevin Blackwood told Ted Dunlow he rented it to her because the old place wasn't being used by hunters during the summer, and he needed the rent money to keep up the place.

Carl Dulaney seemed to know more about it than anyone else in Rainelle, so the Deputy dropped in to Carl's hardware store for a new pair of water pump pliers.

"Ya hear about the gal that moved into the VanBurean place?" asked Carl, as he put the pliers into a brown paper bag with blue printing on the outside.

"Not really," Eden said, hoping Carl would volunteer some more information. "I just heard a rumor someone was there."

"Great big woman—not fat, just big—big-boned," he offered. "Came in the other day for a broom and cleaning supplies. It's none of my business, understand, but from the look of her, she might be expecting a girlfriend to move in with her soon—if you know what I mean."

"Mannish-looking, huh?"

"You could say that, I didn't. Seemed nice enough. And if you don't mind big and not too pretty, she—well—she was kind of attractive—in a way. Did you know they say Abe Lincoln was queer?"

Eden ignored the question. "Why Carl, I didn't know that sort of woman turned you on," he joked. Carl actually blushed. Hmm, maybe I struck a nerve, Eden thought.

Then Carl admitted he wouldn't mind going out to the VanBurean place to make deliveries. Eden was beginning to have hope that Aingeal Farrell might have an outside chance at getting her foot in the door at the lodge.

"Did you get her name?" Eden asked.

"Angel," Carl replied, "Angel something-or-other. Sure didn't look like one though. I got a different imagination when it comes to angels. She ain't all that bad, but I figger angels to be a bit on the lighter side. They got a lotta flyin' to do—without a broom," he chuckled.

"I see."

"Now don't go running around telling people I got the hots for her. I just think she's a nice gal, that's all," Carl said, as he handed Eden his change and extended the bag toward him.

The Deputy made sure he was headed out the door when he left Carl with "I assure you, your secret fantasies are safe with me." With that, he shot out the door, too fast to hear Carl's rejoinder.

The work day finished, he headed back home. Aingeal, my angel, you might just be able to pull it off, he thought hopefully.

May drifted on toward June. Shele and Eden managed to see each other every weekend. There was little they could accomplish on the murder cases, since most of the ground had been plowed and sifted multiple times. They reinterviewed some people, but it seemed hopeless. By June, all their hope was pinned on the red-headed Irish woman that Eden had not even met.

Shele met Eden's inquiries with, "You'll know something as soon as I do. Relax, this will take time."

Soon it was almost as if Aingeal Farrell didn't exist. The Chief Investigator had tried too hard to put her out of his mind, and it was working. If thoughts of her arose, he squashed them. Better no thoughts at all than face a murky crystal ball.

His hopes rose when he ran into Lin Kelley at the courthouse one day. She seemed surprised when Eden asked her about the new gal over at the VanBurean place.

"Why would I know anything about her?" she asked. Lin knew that Eden knew that Lin should know.

"Come on, Lin, you know everything that goes on in the county."

"It'll take some telling," she said. "You got time for catty gossip?"

They walked to the Greene Door, a local watering hole and lunch counter, where they took a booth in the back. Lin told him all about Aingeal Farrell—more than he wanted to know, and some things that Shele probably didn't even know. Lin must have sources he hadn't even dreamed of.

Finally, she got around to telling him that Aingeal had taken up with Randy Winters "on the side," as she put it.

"I thought Randy Winters was—uh—how shall I put it—" he began.

"A homo?" interjected Lin abruptly. "Maybe so, but if you've ever seen Farrell—well, she's a pretty either/or case herself, if you ask me. I guess you could say ol' Randy's having his cake and eating it—ah—uh—well, you know what I mean."

"Gosh, Lin, I didn't know you were a punster."

"What the hell does that mean?"

"Never mind," he said. "So tell me all about Randy and his angel."

It turned out that Lin had a lot of detail about the "romance" that the Deputy could never have known. But unfortunately, it also turned out that none of it was very useful. He learned that the two had become very tight, renewing his hope that Aingeal might gain access to the lodge.

At that point, he couldn't help thinking about what the initiation might be like for a big Irish lass. He had a feeling it might be the same one reserved for big Irish lads. For most folks, it would be a rite that would assure a lifetime of secrecy. If it involved some sort of felony, a human sacrifice or some such ritual, it could spell doom for his efforts. He might never be able to use the testimony of a convicted felon. Furthermore, he had no idea how far his angel would be willing to go to penetrate Randy's cult. He winced at that word penetrate. Speaking of puns...

CHAPTER THIRTY-FOUR

PIEZOELECTRONICS?

Eden received a call from Dave Quinn. He small-talked about the porch swing, then said there had been no further progress with the river rocks. And then he got around to why he called.

He and Colleen had been reviewing the "mysteries of the region," and he wanted to bounce their thoughts off Eden.

"I don't know if any of this will interest you, but I'd like your opinion anyway," Dave said.

"I don't know—"

Quinn continued quickly to tell him that Colleen had created a database, organizing information they collected from the Internet, the county and Pittsburgh libraries, and anecdotes from local sources. She began to play with the data, adding stuff that seemed relevant and some stuff that didn't. She had spent a lot of time sifting through it, looking for patterns or trends.

Eden remarked, "That's interesting. Colleen doesn't seem the type to use scientific data analysis."

"I've gone through this stuff over and over and I have ideas that I need to bounce off someone to see if any of it gels," Dave said. "I can't sleep with all this crap going through my head."

Dave said he and Colleen were trying to draw connections between what had happened and what Eden and Shele had learned.

"Can you come out so we can talk and look over some of what we've come up with?" Dave asked.

"It's awfully late—"

"Hey, all you got to do is sleep right now, and you can do that

219

any time," he implored.

"Okay, get the coffee ready. But keep the conversation lively, or I swear I'll fall asleep on you."

Eden thought, Groan. Not another evening of mystical bullshit session. But to keep the peace, I'll go. When he arrived, Dave had set up one of those slick boards you draw on with felt-tip markers. There was a disheveled pile of notepaper on the designer coffee table and a grubby, much-used yellow legal pad. It looked like a long evening. Dave had been living alone far too long and had been thinking about the infinite way too much.

"Something to drink?" Dave offered. "There's coffee, and soda in the fridge. I'm afraid to drink caffeine—I don't need any more stimulation. I feel like I'm on speed."

"Okay, well begin," Eden said. "Sharing will relax you."

"All right. One of the hardest things I have to sort out is what Sidney Rigdon really believed, and what was pure bullshit, or what he may have been duped into believing. You remember Rigdon was the one who supposedly stole the Spaulding novel? Anyway, add to that dilemma how much of all this is hoax and how much is real, how much is psychic and how much is scientifically provable, and you can see the—"

Eden scowled and interrupted, "I think you can put most of it in the hoax-and-bullshit category."

"Let's try to keep an open mind on this, shall we?"

Dave forged ahead. Colleen theorized that Rigdon was part believer, part charlatan, and partly taken in by hoaxes that were floating around at the time. He figured Rigdon might have really believed the whole lost tribes story and stole Spaulding's novel, believing it to be New World gospel.

"Who knows," he said, "I have suspicions and pretty good indications that Rigdon and Joseph Smith arranged to have it "revealed" to the world. I don't have hard evidence, but I think

Rigdon, Spaulding, and Smith had some sort of falling out and Rigdon went his merry way and tried to create his own church, or at least a cult based on the *Manuscript Found* revelations. Spaulding wound up in the Amity cemetery, Smith founded the Church of Latter Day Saints, and Rigdon—well, who knows? The word is that another Rigdon—Walter Rigdon—was involved somehow, but it might be that he inherited the group from Sidney."

Eden picked up on the word "cult," but he did not mention the Andy/Randy group. It would only muddy the already murky waters.

Dave went to the sink and drew a glass of water. He held it up to the light and examined it, apparently for sediment. Eden figured he would use it to make a point, but instead he drank without comment.

"I have no reason either to believe or to doubt any of it," Eden said. "If that's what you brought me out here for—to assure you that you're not crazy and you're on the right track—"

"No," Dave said abruptly. "That's not why I called you. There's a lot more, and it's more bizarre."

"Dave, Maybe I should get my hat now. If you're going to start on the mystical, supernatural 'realm,' as you call it, I'm not interested. Nothing against you or your theories. I'm a law-enforcement officer. I have no way to deal with that stuff."

Dave sighed. "Everything Colleen and I examined is in the 'realm' all right, but the 'realm' of the possible. No mysticism, spiritualism, nothing transcendental. It might sound like '50s science fiction to you, but it won't be science fantasy."

"Now, seriously: you remember we talked about the Germans and Russians and their experiments in psychic phenomena? Well, you know what else the Russians were into at that time? Piezoelectrics."

"Pizza who?" Eden said blankly. Oh boy, here comes another whacked-out theory. So much for Dave's promise of science, not fantasy.

"Piezoelectrics. Put pressure on rocks and minerals, and they generate a little bit of electricity. Like the igniter in a barbecue grill! Anyway, this is where Colleen really got interested in the psychic aspects of our "Grave Creek connections"—ley lines, earth movements, geomancy, and earth forces.

"And I got into it when I read about the geology of earth forces—earthquakes, tectonics, fault zones, and such. The piezoelectric connection makes real sense. I'm convinced—although honestly, Colleen has reservations—that electrical forces created by the natural breaking and movement of rocks in the earth explain a hell of a lot more about ley lines than the hocus-pocus mumbo-jumbo of telepathic-telekinetic abracadabra. When I punch that igniter button on my barbecue grill and see the spark—well, I have a hell of a lot more faith in that, which I can see, than I do in whatever else is out there."

"Hmm." That was the best Eden could do. A listening noise. Although, Dave was making sense, sort-of…

"Piezoelectrics," Dave continued, as if the science of generating sparks to roast meat would prove whatever he had dreamed up. "Start out in New Mexico at Chaco Canyon, somewhere around Pueblo Benito—you might even be able to trace it by sighting through a slit in one of the kivas out there—and follow it right across the Great Road—the Hopewell Road—on through to the Ohio Valley to the Grave Creek Mound, and beyond. A ley line has to be some kind of conductor of piezoelectric energy—think of a ley line as a heavy metal bus bar, like they use in power plants, only running underground for thousands of miles.

"Eden, if you don't like this down-to-earth explanation—if you'd rather call them transcendental forces—go ahead. Colleen doesn't buy this piezo-theory entirely, but she and I are convinced that the Grave Creek mound is the terminus on an ancient pathway that conducts, amplifies, and creates new energy from a source in the Southwest. Is Chaco Canyon the ultimate source? I suspect it is only a major terminal, and the ultimate energy source is in South America, probably in the Nazca Plain. The Peruvian pyramids likely are factors, because as we all know, pyramids concentrate celestial proto-energy."

Eden was starting to glaze over, like he used to do in high school when the English teacher interpreted the hermeneutic humanistics of existentialist poetry.

But Dave had really warmed to his subject and was on a roll, perspiration beading his brow. "Now, that same energy radiates—actually, re-radiates—from the Grave Creek Mound, and much of it is focused somewhere around Amity! And at that point, it disappears—or is absorbed—by something," he added mysteriously.

Then he added, conspiratorially, "Eden, I'll bet you anything: on the Amity node of that line, there is an anode or cathode—in other words, a big-ass battery, or a huge capacitor of some sort. Probably induction coils too, to tune the entire network. Anyway, there has to be some sort of collector near there, because energy like that doesn't just up and quit!

Speaking of up-and-quitting, Eden thought.

"But wherever it is, I think no one even knows it exists. Even if someone does, I doubt they have any idea what it is. And the beauty of not having a logical explanation for any phenomenon is that—guess what—the phenomenon can become venerated as a mystical spirit, god, or—a demon."

The fact-bound, physical-evidence-craving investigator in Eden was struck when Dave put the idea in those terms. And the irony that he might have sent an Aingeal in to oppose a demon wasn't lost on him.

"Listen, Eden—it explains a lot of things," he went on. "All the mysterious stuff that goes on in this area, Indians avoiding the Ohio River Valley because it's haunted, the Grave Creek Mound, the weird vibes emanating from the prison—the Germans, the Russians—an elaborate Hindu temple thousands of miles from India, in what is pretty fundamental Christian country, and in—of all places—West Virginia? And on to Amity, and the lost-and-found stones and plates? Those stones and plates may have led to the establishment of a yet another religion, Mormonism? Is this all just coincidence?"

"Dave, maybe you've been at this too long," Eden said quietly. "Now, don't get your dander up, but I'm really not convinced. It's just too far-fetched. You know I'm a skeptic by nature... and I know you've spent a lot of time on this... but maybe that's the problem... you may be too close to it—"

"Okay, okay," Dave broke in. "I'm not a hundred-percent on the piezo-stuff, but I am convinced there is much more to all we are seeing than just random, unrelated, strange occurrences. Eden: If you can stand atop Grave Creek Mound and feel nothing, or you can stare down into the Moundsville prison yard and not feel it, or you don't get powerful vibes at New Vrindavan, or you can't feel the psychic tide in Amity Cemetery—then you can tell me I'm a nut case, and I'll give up."

The Deputy stared at the impassioned Dave for many seconds. Then he slowly dropped his eyes, focusing on Dave's coffee cup on the table. There was nothing he could do but sit in awkward silence.

After several minutes, Eden announced, "Well, it's getting awfully late. You have put a lot of good, hard work into this, Dave. Why don't we sleep on it?"

Eden shuffled off to his truck and headed east to Random Creek. Out there on the western sky, just below the handle of the Big Dipper, a brilliant flash left a long, luminous trail behind it, heading toward the horizon. Go, go, he thought. Go home to Chaco Canyon.

CHAPTER THIRTY-FIVE

IT'S STARTING ALL OVER AGAIN

That night Eden was so exhausted that he fell asleep fully clothed across the bed, sleeping so soundly that the alarm failed to rouse him. Later, when the phone rang, he groggily reached for the snooze button. When that didn't stop the ringing, he tried the phone.

Sleepily, he said, "Mmm... 'ullo..."

"Ullo, your ass!" fired a thoroughly pissed Buckey.

"Oh—what time is it?" Eden mumbled.

"I ain't your fucking alarm clock!" Buckey said angrily. "Buy a watch. Get your ass down here on the double. This shit is starting all over again."

Eden's adrenaline injectors were blasting quarts of the hormone into his bloodstream. The Sheriff explained that yet another woman's body had been found, at one of the ponds on the state gamelands. His demeanor quickly changed from anger to anguish.

"Aw hell, Eden, what tha—what do I do now? A couple of boys found her, just like they found the others, shot in the back of the head and all. A replay of the same old nightmare—déjà vu yet another time. I feel like I'm livin' that damned Groundhog Day movie."

"Sorry, Buckey. I was working late and didn't get to bed—I'm on my way."

Eden Whitloe drove the 20 minutes to the office with the murders replaying through his head, adrenaline high. He relived images of a girl's body at the base of a dam, of the girls in the morgue, of all of them lined up at the foot of the dam. In this context, last night seemed sophomoric and silly, an exercise in fantasy.

As he approached the office, he realized that this new killing actually could be the break they hoped for. Another murder was also an opportunity to find new evidence that could break open the case, and maybe the rest of the murders would fall into place and solve themselves. Please, please, just give me one shred of hard evidence, he thought.

As he parked, another thought struck him hard. Only now did it occur to him that the body of Aingeal Farrell could be resting in one of Dr. Vinnie's cold, sterile drawers. He felt chagrined that this hadn't been his first thought. Now, fear and dread gripped his soul, and he could feel its icy claws grabbing the pit of his stomach as he opened the pickup door, stepped onto the pavement, and steeled himself to visit the victim of a demon that he had somehow helped to unleash.

Buckey was rummaging through a file drawer as Eden entered the office. The Sheriff found the folder he sought and looked up as his Deputy took a seat on the other side of his desk.

"Got a name yet?" Eden asked, his heart pounding.

"Nope."

"Let me guess: a red head—big girl."

"Where in the hell do you come up with this shit, Sherlock? With a master sleuth like you on the job, I might be able to sleep in too," Buckey leered sarcastically.

"Just a guess."

"No, it ain't no redhead, and she ain't anything near what you would call big."

Eden felt a wave of relief flooding him, and the knot in his stomach began to untie. Both Aingeal and Shele were eliminated.

"Looks a whole lot like the others," he said. "In fact, I think you could take 'em all to the family reunion and pass 'em off as sisters. We checked the college, but no luck. She's the right age, so I've got calls in to every school within a hundred miles. If any girls are missing, we'll be first to know."

"What about evidence?" Eden asked hopefully.

"We may have a break on this one. It's right up your alley, 'cause you're the one always looking for shell casings, tire tracks, and semen. Well, two out of three ain't bad. We have a semen swab, a tire cast, and no shell casings, but we know it's the same caliber weapon—a .38."

Buckey explained that the girl was discovered by a couple of college students who were hiking. They found the body just like the others, at the foot of a dam on the gamelands. The young woman had apparently been shot execution style—from the same low angle—and pushed over the breast of the dam. Except for evidence they now had that was missing in the other cases, everything was exactly the same.

"Eden, if we crack this one, we might find out who murdered the others. We finally have something solid to go on." Buckey said this with more enthusiasm than anyone had seen in him for some time.

Eden was hopeful as well. Hopeful that they could catch the murderer, and hopeful that he could get Shele's friend out of whatever she was into at this point. He worked to push Aingeal back into the dustier corners of his mind.

He theorized that the murderer was a pervert who raped the girl and dumped her body. The other girls weren't raped, but it could be that the killer had attempted something that got out of hand. When one was killed, the others were snuffed to keep them quiet. That could explain why the murders looked like professional hits. Killing someone who might talk is a lot different than dragging a kicking and screaming victim to their death.

Not the cleanest scenario, but it was better than ley lines, keyholes, and a cult of latter-day Rigdonites. Now he had to tell Shele.

He slipped out of the office and drove to her house.

"Shele, there's been another murder, very similar. This time with real evidence—semen and a tire track."

"Oh, how awful!" she put her hands to her mouth, suddenly looking fearful. Then she quickly turned thoughtful. "In light of this, I think we should tell Aingeal. I don't want her to get too involved if she'll be pulling out."

Eden frowned. "Well, let's not move too fast…"

"Eden," she was deadly serious. "I know Aingeal. She will do anything to deliver on this case. Would you put her through their stupid, humiliating initiation rite for nothing? Who knows what they might want her to do?"

"Yeah, but I want to be more certain before we yank her out of there," he said. Just tell her there are some new developments. She can figure out what they are; she's a bright gal. Tell her to hold her position and not move forward until she hears from you. Is that good enough?"

"I guess. But I want her out of this as soon as you have a decent suspect. You got that?"

"Shele, I don't like being responsible for her any more than you do. I want her out as much as you."

New developments did not mean that a suspect would be found soon. But Eden knew that if they didn't come up with something fast, the trail would chill—and they would be back to séances with Dave Quinn and Colleen McKay.

Eden walked the streets and parking lots of Rainelle, looking for tire treads that matched the cast from the murder scene, burned into his memory. It was pretty futile, but it was doing something. If they got a break, the tire cast could be strong evidence; as a standalone lead, it was pitiful.

Shele and Eden spent the next Saturday listing the maybes. Using a profile they had developed of the killer, they considered residents of Rainelle and nearby communities. If the individual were indeed a rapist-murderer, he most likely would be 20–40 years old. Since Rainelle was a retirement refuge, eliminating the Social Security crowd narrowed the list quite a bit. A geezer could be involved, but Shele convinced Eden to eliminate the Viagra set. A teenager also was possible, but they lacked time and resources to scan everyone. So they concentrated their efforts on the most likely.

Eden approached the task with his usual logic. "Let's see now... start with 5,000 residents, eliminate the women, and we have about 2,400. Eliminate the bluehairs and we have somewhere around 1,000. Eliminate the rest of those outside our age range... and I think we're down to 300 or 400. There's another of the 40 or 50 usual suspects we don't have to consider because we'll throw those out and let Buckey deal with them. So I figure we have about 350 possibilities. So we shouldn't be at this for more than a decade or two." The Deputy looked mournfully at his partner, who studied last year's *Rainelle College Raindear*. Honestly, that's what they call their yearbook.

They sat on the sofa, yearbook-pondering and bemoaning how little progress they were making, when the phone rang.

"It's Buckey," Shele whispered, handing Eden the phone.

Eden immediately sensed Buckey was not in his usual mood. In fact, he seemed almost exuberant.

CHAPTER THIRTY-SIX

THESE AIN'T NO BRUNO MAGLIS

"Got something for you, Sherlock," Buckey began. "An honest-to-Pete sharp, detailed footprint. I sent Junior out to make a cast as soon as they found it. He really done himself proud this time! I guess those CSI classes I sent him to did some good after all. You know there hasn't been much rain since we found the body, so that sucker is sharp as a tack. You can even see where the heel is worn down a little on the outside," he added joyfully.

"And these ain't no Bruno Maglis," he said, referring to O. J. Simpson's loafers, "but they're not Keds either. If I see anyone with a pair on, I'll know them and I'll bust his ass on the spot. Eden, now we got something to go on."

Eden knew it wasn't likely the killer would be found strutting the streets of Rainelle in the shoes he wore to a murder, but they sure had a lot more information now than a few minutes ago. They now had shoe size, weight, an idea of height, and one more thing to match up with a suspect—if one was ever found. He could imagine going door-to-door in Rainelle with a shoe-sizing stick like those used in shoe stores.

"Do you know what kind they are?"

"No, but they are pretty darned different," Buckey replied. "Got a funny slice cut out of the toe and, get this: size seven-and-a-half. This guy has to be pretty small—if he's not a kid."

And we threw out the teenagers, Eden thought to himself.

Buckey asked his Deputy to stop by for a complete report on the shoe cast, and to give him their suspect list.

"And oh, yeah," the Sheriff said, almost as an afterthought. "We found out who the girl is, or maybe I should say was. Turns out she's from over around Youngstown, Ohio somewhere—name's Pamela Brookover. Don't have much detail yet, but I'll fill you in when I give you the full report."

For the second time in several months, the lawmen felt hopeful they would solve the case. During the next two weeks, Eden and Shele and, for all they knew, half of George County's law officers were appraising feet and tires.

CHAPTER THIRTY-SEVEN

EAVESDROPPING AT THE BARBERSHOP

Eden always looked forward to his monthly barbershop visit—not for the haircut, but for the useful gossip on the lower floor of the old Downey House Hotel. The hotel was long ago remodeled into professional offices, the restaurant into an antique shop, the lobby into a pawnshop. The only thing unchanged in 85 years was the barbershop. Its old chairs might have been reupholstered once, and a shoeshine stand still stood, for which a collector would give his eyeteeth. No one had shined shoes on the massive marble, oak, and brass edifice for 50 years.

Harry Rishoff had been everything you would imagine a small-town barber to be, but he retired, replaced by Harry Woodyard. Eden wondered if "Harry" was a common barber's name.

Harry Woodyard was every bit of 30, in Eden's mind too young to barber. Folks expect experience in such professions. But Harry was the only remaining barber within 30 miles. What he lacked in age was balanced by his ability to talk the talk. Eden didn't like him much, and his haircuts were at best tolerable, but like most barbers, Harry was a fine source of information.

"Three in front of you," Harry announced as Eden took a seat. But only two others were waiting. To his questioning look, Harry added, "Joey Dulaney called for an appointment a while ago."

"Oh," Eden said, picking up a battered, coverless December 1999 *Field and Stream.*

"I'll save you a place in line now if you want."

"Naw, I'll wait," Eden replied. He was, after all, there for gossip.

The two other waiters were quiet, one buried in a *Readers' Digest* and the other fiddling with a PDA.

Harry chattered nonstop. "Think it'll rain out the Steelers game today? That cold front's comin' and I 'spect it'll be pourin' on us by gametime, but you know them Steelers is oh-and-four on the season and I think they made a terrible mistake when they traded that quarterback for that what-his-name from Denver, 'cause he can't get off a pass for crap, and look who they're playing this afternoon — Miami, who is five-and-oh, so whuddayou think? I don't think — "

Sitting in the chair, a silent victim of Harry's verbal flood, was none other than Pauly Loughman. He looked helplessly at the Deputy. "Hi, Eeed." He closed his eyes as Harry trimmed his brows.

Eden hopefully examined Pauly's feet, propped on the filigreed footrest. But his huge work boots immediately scratched Pauly from Eden's mental list of possible suspects. Pauly had passed what Eden was beginning to think of as the "Cinderella test."

For Eden's purpose, the chattering barber and semiconscious customers were a waste of time. And then, without warning, Harry shifted gears and directed his attention toward the Deputy Sheriff.

"Makin' any headway on the latest George County murder?"

Eden braced for the brutal teasing that was about to follow.

"Let's see," Harry continued. "The count is up to — um, what is it, four now, isn't it? If you count that old lady, it's five, I think. It's kinda' hard to keep track. Five women in a little over a year. The county is getting to be a great place to kill someone, don't ya think? If this keeps up, we'll outdo Pittsburgh pretty soon. And they got, what, a half a' million people up there? I'll bet that on a per capita basis, we're way ahead of them already. Pretty soon we'll be a stop for those tourist buses that go up and down the Interstate. Somebody might put up a museum and charge admission — "

"We're still at it," Eden interrupted dryly.

"Well, maybe this last one heard about the others and figured George County provides the best chance of not getting caught. Maybe the killer was some guy from Detroit, heard about the easygoing lawmen down here, and came down to make his hit. Word gets around, ya know?"

"We got some new leads on this one," Eden said evenly, controlling his irritation at the mouthy barber.

"Oh, yeah?" Harry's curiosity was aroused. "What kinda leads?"

"Well now, Harry, you know I can't say anything about that. One reason I came over here was to check you out—to see if you match up with any of our new evidence." Eden pretended to size him the barber. "We're trying to whittle down the list of usual suspects."

Harry looked sort-of shocked. He recovered and added, "Eden, I think you're just tying to—"

"Don't worry, Harry—well, don't worry too much. I think I might have to take you off the list—but maybe I'll just have to wait to see how my haircut turns out," he grinned.

Harry gave the Deputy a big fuck-you smile and refocused on Pauly's sideburns.

Through the exchange, Eden closely watched Pauly and the waiters for a reaction. Nothing. Pauly pretended to be napping and the other two didn't react at all.

Abruptly, Harry reached around Pauly and pulled the barber's cape from his reclining form. He snapped the cape in the air to rid it of hair, and in the same motion kicked the chair release, bringing Pauly abruptly upright, giving him a hand mirror.

"That suit ya?" Harry asked.

"Okay," Pauly replied noncommittally, handing back the mirror. He knew that if he complained, Harry would just do some air-scissor snipping and rush him out.

"Next!" announced Harry.

The guy with the PDA started to get up, but settled back as Joey Dulaney, the call-ahead, stepped into the shop. "Little Joe," who most now called Joey, was maybe 22 and not little anymore, and it occurred to Eden that he was a potential.

Joey wore a cutoff sweatshirt, baggy cargo-type shorts, and a brand new pair of funky-looking shoes, those things rock climbers wear. The shoes got Eden's attention, but the feet did it. The size was right, and if he was the guy, he could have ditched the older shoes.

"Hi, Eden," Joey greeted. "How's the investigation?"

Eden hoped Joey hadn't caught him looking him over. "Oh, I was going over some of the finer points with Harry, just before you came in. It's going great, Joey. How's your dad?"

Joey settled back in the chair as Harry covered him with the cape.

"Just like he always is, crabby as hell."

The conversation paused as Harry snapped the cape's fastener to his neck and looked woefully at the massive mop of bleached blond hair before him, arranged in a wild mousse-spiked array.

"Take it all off," said Joey. "Make like an Army barber and gimme one of those army-recruit buzz cuts. I'll be cool all summer—in more ways than one."

Eden thought Harry found particular delight in running his humming clippers down the middle of Joey's mop. Joey screeched as the clippers snagged in a mess of mousse and a thatch of hair was pulled out by the roots. A mop of yellow hair peeled off and landed beside the chair.

"Hey," screeched Joey, "a guy could get sued for trying to scalp a feller. Take it easy."

The barber finished the quick clipper job almost before he began. One had the feeling that Harry would have paid Joey for the fun he had. Joey paid his seven-fifty and glanced in the mirror. "Great, feels cooler already."

Eden took his turn in the chair. This time Harry babbled about county politics, how the upcoming election was rigged, how secret groups met in smoke-filled rooms to control the government.

It soon was over. As Eden stood and pretended to fumble for change, he dropped a quarter beside the chair. He bent to pick it up, palming a gob of Joey Dulaney's yellow hair, roots and all. He put the quarter and the hair in his pocket, paid Harry, and left.

He felt a bit silly with Joey's hair in his pocket. Little feet and new shoes weren't much to go on. But he would find Joey's Plymouth minivan and have a look at the tires. It was a long shot by a desperate investigator, now grasping for anything resembling a clue. He wanted to haul in Joey's vehicle and check his place for shoes that matched the cast, but there wasn't enough to even ask for a warrant. And asking Buckey to authorize a DNA test on the hair would have brought billows of laughter.

So Eden drove to the Wagon Wheel and told Lin Kelley that he had a problem with the registration on Joey's van.

"That sneaky little freak rip it off?" she asked

"No, it's not stolen. I think it's a rebuild or a repo—something's funny with the title. I just need to examine it and see the VIN number. Let me know when he's in the next time, and you can keep him busy while I take a look, okay?" Lin loved to be a part of these little conspiracies.

The very next evening Lin called. "I think Joey'll be here for a while. I'll keep him busy. I'll call your cell if he starts to leave."

When Eden arrived, he smiled to himself. The van was parked around beside the bar where he could take his time uninterrupted— perfect.

The rear rubber was different than the tires on the front; a different brand and the tread was dissimilar. And the pattern on the rear set was a picture-perfect match. The rear tire on the driver's side perfectly matched the photo Eden brought along, down to the two small pebbles wedged in one groove on the tread. His heart leaped when he saw the two stones. At that moment, the cop in him—the cop that knew the power of real physical evidence—knew they finally had made their killer.

He phoned Lin. His investigation of the van was complete, so she need not detain Joey further.

He wanted to call Shele, but hesitated, afraid she might want to pull Aingeal out of her undercover situation. It was too soon. He needed Buckey's approval to get warrants. There was the paperwork and red tape before they could move on the suspect. And his political-PR sensor said that Buckey might have someone at the State Police whose butt needed bussed. Buckey would want to tell the TV stations when an arrest was imminent. He would handpick the officer who would cuff Joey Dulaney on camera. Plenty of TV news face time lay ahead for Buckey and lucky officer he selected.

This was getting the sled ahead of the dogs. He had to run the hair sample, get a warrant to impound Joey's vehicle, and get a search warrant to examine his home and the room where Joey attended tech school in Pittsburgh. Eden the Investigator really wanted those shoes.

If he got a DNA match on the hair, all the rest would fall into place, and the arrest warrant would be a piece of cake. With DNA evidence alone, it would be an airtight case... but he kept thinking about O. J.'s shoes and the "airtight" case against him.

As Eden expected, Buckey wanted to take over and pursue the case against Dulaney. But soon the George County District Attorney and the State Police got involved. Their PR people spun it like they had done all the footwork, and the county lawmen were just helping the big boys wrap up loose ends on their investigation.

So, no one was more shocked than Eden when Trooper Dan

Brackenridge called. Would Eden be willing to talk with Joey Dulaney? Joey would talk only with Eden about a plea bargain.

Dan groused, "I don't know why he wants to talk to you. We got him six ways from Sunday. Hopefully, he wants to spill his guts about the other murders."

"Exactly what I'm hoping for," Eden said. "Nothing would make me happier than closing these cases. I just hope no one else is involved. I'd hate to see this thing get any messier. Who's his attorney?"

CHAPTER THIRTY-EIGHT

HI-HO SILVA

"Joey's attorney is Albert Silva," answered Brackenridge. "He's from Pittsburgh. Word around the campfire is that he's one of those left-wing sob-sister types. He takes on a lot of pro bono cases, and has a pretty good record of getting certified killers off. You might have read about the last one. He got the wife of a doctor off, after she was caught standing over the body with a smoking gun. It wasn't a real insanity plea either. It was even better. He got her off by pleading some sort of temporary psycho condition. She did a little time in the wacko ward before walking free. No prison time at all. Not as clean as O.J., but she got away with murder, just like him."

"What do you think they want in a plea bargain?" Eden asked.

"Of course Joey wants to walk off scott-free, but I think Silva knows that's a rough go," Brackenridge said. "Personally, I think we've got an easy murder-one conviction, so the most I would give away is 100 years to life. I might go to life with hope for parole after some healthy time, but that's it."

"The last time I heard someone say they had a sure-fire case, it was Marsha Clark. And now O. J. is playing golf in Florida. How is the D.A. on all of this?" Eden asked.

"I think she's on it, but you never know what that bunch might do. You know what I think of lawyers... look, Eden, don't screw this up. This ain't California, and Joey Dulaney sure as hell ain't no O. J. I might give up something to clear these cases, but I wouldn't give away the farm. If the D.A. is willing to stand Dulaney up before a jury in George County, he'll be convicted and get a capital sentence. You can take that to the bank."

Eden scowled. "Don't worry, Dan. I'm not vengeful enough to sacrifice everything to see him toasted, and I'm frugal enough to make sure the taxpayers don't have to pay for a long trial. I'd like to see him cop, but on my terms. I'll tell you right now—Joey Dulaney will get nothing less than life with a chance for parole somctime down the line—even if he knows who killed Jimmy Hoffa. You can tell him that. I'll meet with him if he still wants to."

But days passed into weeks, with nothing from attorney Silva. So, against his better judgment, Eden told Shele about the whole thing—including Joey's attempt at a plea bargain. Well, that did it.

"Enough!" she exclaimed. "I'm telling Aingeal to get her ass out of town right now. I've heard enough. I think we've found the killer, not only of Pam Brookover, but of the other three girls, so there's no use in exposing Aingeal to further risk. Joey Dulaney is a sick-o who preys on young women. I think he's responsible for the deaths of Pam, Myra, June, and Elizabeth. With Myra's, I'm guessing they had maybe a first or second date when he demanded sex—and she freaked, and he did her in. Attempted rape that turned much worse."

Shele didn't say how all this might have happened without leaving evidence of a struggle, other than that bullet in the back of the head. Her ideas concerning the deaths of June and Elizabeth seemed more plausible: Joey had abducted them, or maybe he talked them into going to the gamelands, easy because Joey was known to be an amateur photographer, and maybe he proposed some innocent, fully clothed modeling.

However he got them there, then he could have said, "Look out there while I take your picture." It would have been the last words they would ever hear.

"So how does your Aunt Amara fit into all of this?" Eden asked.

"She doesn't," Shele snapped matter-of-factly. "Simple suicide, cut and dried. Her only involvement was when she tried to con you and Buckey into believing she could help. There is no evidence of anything else—nothing!"

"Then why?" he asked. "Why did she kill herself?"

"Hell, how should I know? Personally, I thought all of that psychic crap was so much horse feathers from the beginning. It was an interesting sideshow, but no one is going to kill somebody because of some "earth forces" or Roswell otherworld stuff. You can go ahead and believe she delved into something that rose up and bit her in the ass if you want, but I'll pass. The reason for most suicides is unknown. Most of the time, I doubt if the victim even knows."

"Anyway, I'm going to contact Aingeal."

Eden had no good counter-argument. She was probably right about Joey Dulaney. He felt sure that Joey would come clean about the other murders. "But I still feel uneasy about your aunt's suicide—it was just too coincidental," he said.

Shele sighed. "I feel the same way, but sometimes you just have to let go."

"Okay then, let me ask you a pointed question: Shele, if you are so damned set on the idea that Joey Dulaney is responsible for all the murders—maybe even more—why are you so determined to get Aingeal out of the Randy/Andy thing?"

"All right, Mr. Fife," she condescended. "I'll explain it so even you can understand! I don't think Aingeal is anywhere near to getting inducted into whatever that demented-ass cult is they have going out there—the Rigdonites, as you call them—but I think it's something Aingeal would like to avoid. To put it bluntly, I don't think Aingeal is into anything like that, so she would appreciate avoiding a probe, especially from these bozos. There, now, understand?"

In a far calmer tone than he felt, Eden nodded. "You made your point. Tell her to leave as quickly as she can. But—I don't want her raising suspicions and making the members nervous. I need to learn more about Mr. Andy, Mr. Randy, and the Rigdonites."

The following day, the law office of Silva & Smith called. Could they arrange an appointment at a time of mutual convenience? Eden agreed to meet Attorney Silva Friday at noon at the George County Jail.

By the time Friday arrived, Eden was resolved: the easiest plea he would accept would be life without parole. Of course, the D.A. would have the final say, but the Deputy was taking a stand. To get that much leniency, Joey would have to confess to the Pamela Brookover killing, for which they had physical evidence. But before Eden would grant that much, he wanted Joey to also implicate himself in the killings of Myra Kinchloe, June Talbot, and Elizabeth Mayow. If he directly confessed to those, Eden would consider life with a chance of parole after 30 years. He was beginning to believe as Shele did about her aunt's suicide, but he was going to bring it up nonetheless.

Silva arrived promptly at noon. Eden was genuinely surprised at his promptness and demeanor. He wasn't at all the weasel Eden had expected. In fact, Silva turned out to be quite likeable, a component of a personality that he cultivated for plea negotiations, one might suppose. He introduced himself, handed the Deputy his card, and took a seat across from Eden's desk.

Joey Dulaney, in handcuffs with a chain leading to ankle restraints, was delivered moments later. He shuffled into the room, led by Junior Slaughter, and was seated beside his attorney.

Eden and Buckey had placed two plaster casts conspicuously on the desk. One was from the tire track at the Brookover murder scene, and the other was from the matching tire on Joey Dulaney's van. Eden wanted it to seem like they were a typical part of the investigation in progress.

"Would you like to begin, Mr. Silva?"

"Do you mind if I look at those?" he asked. "I assume they are the tire evidence. I haven't seen anything but photographs until now."

"Go right ahead," Eden said. "The DNA report is there, and the shoe cast is around here somewhere." He knew full well the shoe cast was in a short bookcase beside his desk, but made a show of finding it. He didn't have a matching shoe, so the evidence was not relevant at this point. He assumed that Joey got rid of the shoes, because nothing turned up in a search of his house or his rental at college.

Silva examined the casts, glanced at the DNA report, and barely acknowledged the shoe cast.

"Well, Deputy Whitloe—"

"Eden, please. Let's keep it informal. I've known Joey here for quite a while, haven't I, Joey?"

Joey nodded silently.

"Okay, Eden," Silva said. "We all know why we're here, so let's get on with it. You have built a pretty convincing case, so let's get right down to what we might do to mitigate the—uh—the unfortunate consequences of a lengthy jury trial."

"What do you have in mind?"

"I'm offering a guilty plea in exchange for as brief a prison sentence as possible. My client might be willing to admit the alleged victim died as a result of a reaction to a self-administered drug that—"

"—that accidentally blew out the back of her head," Eden finished.

"Let me finish, Mr. Whitloe."

Mr. Whitloe noticed Silva wasn't calling him Eden.

"—died as a reaction to a self-administered drug. Since my client was alone with Miss Brookover at the time, he panicked when she went into a coma, believing she was dead. He then tried to cover up her death."

"That's going to be your case!?" The Deputy asked incredulously. "He thought she died while she was with him, so to be sure, he popped a cap on her? That's it?"

"Not quite," Silva said gently. "I think the jury will be sympathetic to a very young man who was confronted with the possibility of being held responsible for a drug-related death. He was in a panic and confused after he had legal, consensual sex with her, and he knew it would appear to be a rape, so he tried to cover it up. Now that is surely criminal, it may well be manslaughter, or some sort of accidental homicide, but it's sure not murder-one. At the most, we are looking at 5 to 10."

Eden knew he was bluffing and fully aware that Silva knew it too. He also knew the Deputy wasn't a member of some feel-good jury that was looking for reasonable doubt that would let his client walk.

"Counselor, I can't comment on what the D.A.'s position might be in this. But let me tell you what I would do. First of all, I would find enough evidence that your client is a little whack-off pervert. And that your depraved, degenerate client first stalked, then lured Pamela Brookover into a situation in which he had an opportunity to dope her and then rape her. He then killed her to keep her from talking about it. I think I know juries around here better than you. As you are aware, this is a motherhood-and-apple-pie county. A jury here might be tempted to enjoy hanging someone for leaving under God out of the pledge to the flag, so I don't think they'll buy your accidental death story for a second. Furthermore, I don't think you have a chance in hell of getting a change of venue. Joey Dulaney will be tried by a jury of his peers right over there in that courthouse — and a couple of the members of the jury may want to give him life without parole, at best, but I wouldn't stake my life on it."

Eden wanted to stay on the good side of Joey, so he turned to him and said, "I'm sorry if I sound harsh. But that's exactly what's going to happen if you use that defense—and your attorney has to know that."

Silva thought a moment. "We are willing to take under consideration a guilty plea for manslaughter, if you can get the D.A. to ask for—"

Eden interrupted him, "I wouldn't even go there. Unless Joey is willing to talk about helping to clear some other similar cases, the D.A. and I are going to press the murder-one rap and believe me, she will seek the death penalty—"

At this point, Silva tried to interrupt, but Eden went right ahead. "Mr. Silva, you know your client is on thin ice here. If he wants a deal, he has to bring more to the table than you've offered. I can see you'll need some time to think about this, so let's call it a day." Eden began to shuffle papers on his desk to let Silva know the meeting was concluded.

Junior came in and collected Joey while Albert Silva collected his hat. After Joey was out of the room and shuffling down the hall, Silva turned to Eden and said, "I'll talk with him about it, but I'm pretty sure that we'll be seeing each other again in court."

He started calling the Deputy Eden again as they exchanged pleasantries. He gathered his briefcase, snapped it shut, and headed for the door. He walked with a bit more of a slouch now that they had their little talk, and Chief Investigator/Deputy Sheriff Eden Whitloe liked that, a lot.

More weeks passed with no further word from Silva. It began to look like he was going to take his chances on a jury trial. Joey Dulaney—Eden really didn't feel much sympathy for him—but if his attorney laid him out before a George County jury, the D.A. would have a field day. Pennsylvania might never get around to putting a needle in his arm, but he would live a life of pure hell on death row.

CHAPTER THIRTY-NINE

JOEY DULANEY WANTS TO TALK

Evidently, Silva had a lot more patience than Joey Dulaney. Within a few days, Eden got word that Joey was asking to see him again—this time without his attorney. Oh boy, he thought. If I met Joey without his lawyer, there will be pure hell to pay. So he phoned Silva.

"Do whatever you think is prudent," said the attorney. "Joey really thinks he can cut some kind of deal with you and get a reduced sentence. He seems to think you are some kind of buddy who will be sympathetic, and you'll help him get a lighter sentence."

Silva sighed. "Eden, I told Joey that you are just playing good buddy cop with him, and if he sees you, I'm off the case. Nevertheless, he persists. I've advised him of the consequences of a meeting, and that anything he says will be used against him. But the young man is determined. As far as I'm concerned, he's all yours. I have a letter that the court has appointed legal aid counsel for him."

"I guess I'll see what I can do," Eden said. "I assure you that I won't do anything that's not in Joey's best interest."

"I know that. Eden, I think you are a decent sort and you won't take advantage of this situation. But I told Joey that I think you are a hard-nosed cop who will make sure Joey spends his life in jail, if he's not executed."

"I appreciate you telling me that. If he killed that girl—and at this point, I have no reason to suspect he didn't—I would like nothing better than what you just described. I don't think I'm all that hard-assed, but when I think about that poor kid left out there

247

in the game lands with her brains blown out—"

"I understand. I know you will do the right thing. Take care." said Silva as he hung up.

Joey insisted on seeing the Deputy alone. To make sure he was 100 percent legal, Eden asked the D.A.'s office to arrange the meeting with Joey.

After some bitching and finagling with Joey's court-appointed attorney, the meeting was arranged—after Eden agreed that any settlement would have to be approved by the defendant's attorney and the D.A.

Eden didn't want to have one of those jailhouse meetings in a room with one-way mirrors and everything on tape, so he asked if the meeting could take place in the Sheriff's conference room. He wasn't much concerned with Joey's welfare. His main concern was to get as much from Joey as he could, and to keep him off the street.

Junior brought the orange-suited Dulaney into the Sheriff's office and led him to the conference room. He seated him at the bare table where Eden waited. The room was empty otherwise, with one barred window. The only thing adorning the wall was a switch that controlled a recessed lighting fixture. There was no escaping this room.

Joey flashed an engaging smile as he said, "Hi, Eden."

"Hello, Joey. How's it going?" he asked gently, making conversation. He really hoped it wasn't going at all well with him.

Joey shrugged, which Eden took to mean as well as could be expected. Using his elbows, he lifted himself on the arms of the chair and settled into it.

"Hey, Junior, Joey here isn't going anywhere—you can take off the cuffs before you leave," Eden said, in an effort to put Joey at ease and to let Junior know he should leave them.

"You sure?"

"Joey and I are old friends, aren't we, Joey?"

Joey nodded and Junior unlocked the shackles, gathered them, and took his leave.

Joey asked if they could talk "theoretical-like." Eden took this to mean that the defendant wanted to offer some possibilities of confession without actually incriminating himself.

"Anything we say is between us. This isn't recorded, no cameras or microphones. You got my word on it. Even if it was recorded, it couldn't be used against you, because I just said it wasn't being recorded." That wasn't entirely true, but in any event, no recording was going on.

"I'll take your word for it, Eden. You're the only one I trust now anyway. That damned lawyer, Silva, was going to piss around and get me a death sentence. I figure I'm rotting in jail right now, so what's to lose? It's not his ass in a sling. He doesn't give a shit about me," Joey said.

So Joey began to talk. According to him, he met Pamela Brookover in a class at tech school. One thing led to another, and they went on a date. Evidently, Brookover didn't think Joey was her type and she tried to break it off. He didn't put it that way, but that was the gist of it.

"I was fine with that, but I didn't think I got a real chance," he said. "I was just looking for—well—she didn't give me a chance."

Eden asked him if he had followed her around or bugged her for another date. He didn't say yes in so many words. But as it turned out, he stalked her for some time. Of course, he didn't see it as stalking. He described it as "only being persistent."

When he told of Brookover's rebuff, it was as if Eden were talking with a latter-day Captain Queeg. As he described their relationship, he would become agitated, then angry, and then quickly recognize he had gone over the line and would become quite calm and rational.

His story was that he got her to go to the gamelands with him for what he called a photo shoot. He explained the shoot was for a class project, and that it could lead to the photos being picked up by an agency and actually used in a magazine advertisement.

"Nothing nude or kinky, strictly legit. All she had to do was stand there with a straw in her hand, with the wind blowing through her hair, and look beautiful," he explained.

There's little doubt that she saw it as some sort of opportunity for a modeling career. After all, she went with him willingly, and there was no evidence of him using force. Likewise, there is no doubt that Joey saw it as an opportunity to try some moves on her.

He claimed she was more than willing to go along, and he didn't use drugs or anything to convince her.

"She might have taken something to put her in the mood, I don't know. While I was standing over her, setting up the shot, she tried to unzip my fly. If she took something, maybe it made her horny or something, I didn't have to beg her," he claimed. "She wanted it. She wanted it real bad. When we finished the shoot, she told me I was going to have to do her before we left. She was, honest to God, begging for it. So—well—uh—so I did it. You sure can't blame me for that, can you?"

"I suppose not," Eden responded, only to encourage him to be open and keep talking.

Joey described how they had cleaned up, and while she was pulling up her pants, she began to tease him. He said she told him he was really, really pitiful and that she had done thirteen-year-olds that were a lot better. As he continued to dress, she continued to goad him. He said while he was putting his camera away, he came across a gun he kept in the camera case.

"My dad bought it for my mom," he explained. "It was one of those Featherlite .38s, not a hammerless, my mom couldn't get off a shot with one of those—too hard to pull. I kept it in the camera bag for protection. These days, you never can tell when a gun is going to come in handy. Anyway, I pulled it out just to scare her, but she kept it up. She said that little old gun didn't scare her.

"Then I got really pissed. Just to frighten her, I took her by the arm and led her to the breast of the dam. I put the gun to the back of her head, and told her about those women they found last summer, and how she could wind up just like they did.

"She pushed back, trying to get away from the edge, and that's when the damned thing went off. I was as surprised as she was—"

Eden could sense he was reliving the moment, even if it didn't happen the way he said. He was seeing the gun go off, the hair blown away from the muzzle blast as bits of brain and blood were sprayed into the air.

Now he was sobbing, "I didn't mean to do it, Eden, I didn't mean to do it. As God is my judge, I didn't want that gun to go off—it—it just did."

"If you only wanted to scare her, why did you cock the weapon?" Eden asked.

"I don't even know I did," he replied. "I don't see how it could have gone off like that—un-cocked—but I don't remember. Maybe it was put away cocked. Maybe I cocked it for effect, to see what she would do when she heard the click. I don't know—I can't remember."

Eden didn't buy the whole story, but decided not to share that at that point. He told Joey there was no reason to doubt his story, but he still didn't think any jury would buy it.

"Let me tell you what the jurors are going to think, and then you tell me what you want to do," Eden said. "The jury will be convinced from the get-go that you lured the girl out there for the sole purpose of raping her, and that's what you really did. You raped her, and then killed her to keep her quiet."

"Oh, no, no, no," Joey interrupted. "It wasn't like that! It wasn't like that at all —

Eden held up his hand. "Joey, some of the sob sisters may believe the part about the shooting being unintentional, but they aren't going to let that stop them from coming up with a premeditated murder conviction.

"And they sure as hell aren't even going to blink when they hand you the death penalty. Some young teenager, they might let slide and give them life. But Joey, you're older and they are going to want a piece of your ass."

Joey was trembling. "It doesn't matter what anyone believes. What can you do to get me out of this jam?" Joey asked.

"There is no way you're going to get out of it. The best you can hope for is to get the charges or the sentence reduced.

"First of all, you can forget about an insanity plea, temporary or otherwise. No jury is buying that shit anymore. If you come clean and tell me everything, I'll see what I can do," Eden said. "The more you admit to doing, the more you confess, the better off you are, as far as I'm concerned. That said, don't go too far and admit to anything you didn't do. It will only make matters worse."

"Let me think about it," Joey said. "I need some time to think — this is all happening too fast."

"How long do you need?" Eden asked.

"Let me sleep on it."

"Okay, 11:30 a.m., sharp. Well, guess I don't have to worry about you being on time, Junior will make sure of that."

CHAPTER FORTY

DULANEY COMES CLEAN

When Eden walked into work the next day, a Buckey greeted him, smiling and waving a paper in the air.

"Your 11:30 appointment with Mr. Dulaney is off," he announced.

"Why, what's up?"

Buckey grinned ear-to-ear and held up the paper. "Got his confession—right here. He wrote it out last night and delivered it this morning."

Eden knew that any protest would fall on deaf ears, but he protested nonetheless: "But I thought I was to be involved with any plea bargain. What did they give up for the confession? What kind of deal did they come up with?"

"Eden, Eden. That's the beauty of it! There was no plea bargain! Dulaney just asked for paper and a pen, wrote out what he claimed he did, then dated it and signed it. He even had a sort of disclaimer about how it was given by his own free will and without duress of any kind."

"So his attorney wasn't involved?"

"Nope. It might not hold up as a genuine, legal confession, but it sure as hell will do the job if we can get it admitted as evidence."

Eden frowned. "Without his attorney present, I'll bet that paper isn't much better than the stuff hanging on rollers back in the toilets. Did he say anything about the other murders?"

"Nope, just Pamela Brookover. But I have a suspicion about the others. I think they'll fit right in there somewhere. Here, take a look at it." The Sheriff handed the document to Eden.

The confession reflected the chronology that Joey had told the Deputy, but there the similarity ended. Joey claimed he had dated Brookover twice and had been unsuccessful in getting her to have sex with him. He said that on the second date, he tried to be a bit more forceful, but she rejected him and said she didn't want to see him again. He said he spent hours and hours thinking about how he would get even with her. After a few weeks, he called and asked her to help him on a class project. She was reluctant, but he promised it could lead to a modeling career and that he would pay her $500 for an afternoon photo session.

I knew what I was doing. It was premeditated. I planned to give her some dope, then to take her out to the gamelands where those other girls were murdered. I wanted to get what she wouldn't give me, then kill her, and leave the body there. I would do her, just like the other girls had been killed, leave her there and drive off.

The handwriting continued into a ramble about how he felt justified and she deserved it, then he went into a digression of legal jargon that he must have felt would make the document look more authentic. At the bottom, it was signed, dated, and witnessed by Junior Slaughter.

Buckey was schmoozing with the receptionist when Eden walked over and slapped the confession back into his hand.

"Okay, Buckey," Eden said. "Why do you suppose he openly admitted to killing her? I was sure he would either cop or try to get by on the accidental shooting story, like he told me last night."

"Damned if I know," the Sheriff shrugged. "I'm just damned glad we have an open-and-shut case. I don't give a shit if he fries."

"I think I know why—" Eden began.

"Know why he confessed?"

"The little bastard is building an insanity defense," Eden said. "If he can convince a jury he's insane, he could get life—until he proves he's not insane any more, then he'll walk. At least, that's what I think he thinks. He will—"

The deafening clangor of an alarm bell suddenly shattered the conversation. People started running to the back of the building, toward the holding cells.

"Is Dulaney back there?" Eden shouted, as they ran toward the cells.

"We kept him overnight so he'd be here for your meeting this morning! Now what the—"

They were both thinking the same thing—escape attempt—as they ran for the holding cells. However, that wasn't what Joey had in mind. He lay on the floor, twitching and thrashing around, his eyes rolled back in his head.

"Careful!" ordered Buckey to two deputies who were opening the cell door. "Junior! Keep your baton ready while Jason takes a look."

Jason entered the cell while Joey continued to quiver, twitching from time to time, but making no threatening moves at all.

"Let him twitch. Just make sure he doesn't bang into something." Buckey had seen dozens of seizures in his time. "When he's done, call the doc in to have a look-see and write a report. You guys, note the time and enter this into the log. Keep our asses covered. If this breaks open, the news vultures and the TV trucks will be back here faster than flies on fresh shit."

Buckey and Eden turned and walked back to their offices in the front of the building. The Sheriff put one big paw on Eden's shoulder as they continued down the hallway. "You know, Eden, I think that crystal ball of yours might just have something. Or maybe those fluorescents did a number on him."

By the time Dr. Vinnie arrived, the seizure had abated and Joey was rational once again. The doctor ordered a further neurological workup.

"Further workup, hell!" exclaimed Buckey. "I want a complete wig-pick on that boy."

As Eden expected, Joey Dulaney had his share of psychological issues in the past. He had been treated for anxiety disorder, depression, and diagnosed bipolar. He admitted to smoking marijuana and messing around with LSD, mescaline, and "shrooms." The seizure might have been a bit of theater, given his history of mental problems, but it may have been unnecessary. No one who witnessed it could be sure whether it was a performance or not.

Because Eden also was the investigator for the three previous murders, he was invited to sit in when Joey announced that he would provide "some further information" concerning them. The Deputy's crystal ball was pretty clear on most of it, but Joey was holding back something that Eden never could have guessed.

Joey began with the death of the first one, Myra Kinchloe. It had all the appearance of a Leopold and Loeb kill-for-thrill murder—without the kidnapping element. Joey claimed he lured Myra to the dam that evening, knowing he was going to kill her. He said he used the same photo-shoot story to get her to accompany him.

But now Joey claimed he was being directed by voices from satellites. The voices directed that Myra be killed. He claimed she was selected because she was "so straight, so snotty, and so Presbyterian." Strangely, he accused her of being a "homophobe." Eden rolled his eyes at that one, figuring it was a politically correct college-crowd epithet thrown around these days, and passed on it.

"So, the satellite voices agreed she would be a good choice. It was real simple," Joey said, "no dramatics, it was so easy. I really didn't get much out of it."

He had taken her to the edge of the dam, posed her, and told her to give him an "expressionless" look off to the swamp beyond. While she arranged her sweater, he slipped the gun behind her and fired up into the back of her head. He said she had fallen like a pile of rags, to the bottom of the dam, and without looking back, he got into his van and drove away.

"I expected to feel something—something like a tingle—or—I don't know—some kind of thrill when I did it, but I just sort of felt empty. No thrill, or anything like that, just kinda dull. I didn't get much out of it," he said, sounding disappointed, seemingly oblivious to the impact of such a statement.

Before Dulaney could continue, the D.A. called for a lunch break and had him taken back to the holding cell. She and the public defender conferred in whispers—to be sure, the Deputy couldn't hear—and then announced the proceedings would resume at 1:00 p.m. sharp.

They resumed at 1:00 and made small talk until the D.A. arrived. They agreed that Dulaney sounded convincing thus far. They also agreed that they hadn't heard anything unexpected.

At that point, Junior shuffled Joey back into the room and shackled him to his chair.

"I suppose you are wondering about June—" Joey began.

"For the record, you mean Miss June Talbot?" asked the D.A.

"Yes," Joey responded. And then he proceeded to tell what none of them expected. He said he hadn't heard anything from the satellite voices for a long time, and thought they were satisfied. But when he heard from one of his friends, he thought maybe the voices were now speaking through his friend.

"When my buddy told me he knew all about Myra Kinchloe and how she died, I was sure the voice was talking to me again—through him."

"Who is the friend?" asked the D.A. "Can you tell us his name?"

CHAPTER FORTY-ONE

TARP THE CARP

"Oh, sure," Dulaney said. "I meant to tell you at first. His name is Tarp. Well, that's what everyone calls him, Tarp the Carp. His real name is Hiram Tarpley, but they call him Carp because— well—uh—they call him The Carp because he sucks."

The D.A. broke in at that point and asked if Joey had an intimate relationship with Hiram Tarpley. Dulaney protested that he wasn't gay, but he had let Tarpley perform orally on him.

"That don't make me gay, I didn't do anything, I just let him do it, that was all. I didn't do anything but stand there."

The D.A. interrupted, "Joey, we're not making any judgments here. We just want to know the facts, that's all. Please continue."

"I don't know how June found out about Myra, or even if she did find out. But Tarp knew, and the only thing I could think of was the satellite voices told him. Anyway, I figured Tarp would keep his mouth shut because I had as much on him as he did on me. I told him I'd tell the whole town he was queer, but I knew something would have to be done to shut June up."

He turned and looked directly into the eyes of the D.A.

"By now you think my head is really screwed up. Well, I'm here to tell you I'm a choir boy compared to Hi Tarpley," he said. "That little queer is into all kinds of that Goth shit. He tortures animals and plays with their dead bodies and everything. He showed me pictures of little kids too. I'll bet if you leave him alone for a few more years, he'll make Jeffrey Dahmer seem like a Sunday school teacher. There's no chance in hell any girl would have sex with him.

258

There's all kinds of stories about bestiality and that sort of stuff. Anyway…"

Joey's attorney interrupted. "Uh—Joey, I think we have a good idea concerning your feelings about Mr. Tarpley. Take a moment to calm down."

After a moment, Joey began to lay out a story about how he had talked Tarpley into helping him kill June Talbot with the promise that he could "play" with her body for a time. Since Talbot's body showed no evidence of rape, Eden wondered what Tarpley might have done, if anything.

Joey said he followed the same pattern and invited Talbot out for a photo shoot. But since her friend had disappeared, she was having none of it. Finally, he convinced Tarpley to slip "one of those date rape drugs" in her drink to knock her out for the trip to the gamelands.

"Hey, the Carp was weird. He had all kinds of drugs, potions, and stuff. I don't have a clue what he used, but it sure worked."

He claimed they had wrapped her in plastic, so after that he couldn't be sure if she was still alive when they got there. But he had made sure she was "snuffed" when they laid her out on the dam. He said he had tried to get Tarp to pull the trigger but he wouldn't.

"I gave him the gun, lined him up and everything, but he wouldn't even cock the damned thing. I don't think guys like that are up to it," he said, indicating he found a certain satisfaction in being able to do it himself. "Finally, I cocked the gun for him and he closed his eyes and fired off the round. Hell, I even had to hold his hand to keep the gun steady."

It was a different pond but it was the same layout. They had laid her out on the dam with her head dangling over the edge. Tarpley or Dulaney fired into the back of her head at about the same angle as Myra. They then unceremoniously dumped her over the edge.

"I felt something with this one," he said. "Tarp went down the slope and did something with her, but I couldn't tell exactly what. He lay down beside her and put his head on her breast. For some reason, this one gave me a bit of a thrill in my stomach."

Joey's attorney whispered something and the D.A. responded with "oh."

The Deputy watched Joey's attorney and the D.A. writing on their yellow legal pads and imagined they both were scrawling "Sick-O." Buckey, who had been sitting in a dark corner of the room, came up and tapped Eden's shoulder. He whispered, "I'm sending a couple of guys out to pick up Hi Tarpley for questioning right now. I'm going to put Dulaney back in the jail to make room in the holding cell for Tarpley."

All agreed they had heard enough for today, and wanted to resume in the morning. However, Dulaney was on a roll and protested that he wanted to continue.

"Hey, I want you to remember, Tarp killed June, but I want to tell you about Beth Mayow—"

The public defender patted him on the shoulder and told him to save it until Monday. "The weekend's at hand, so you think about it the next couple of days. There's plenty of time," she assured him.

The next day, Shele spent the afternoon with Eden. It was a lovely Saturday, and they acted like a middle-aged couple, him puttering around the yard, her cooking dinner and reading a mystery novel. They lunched on small sandwiches and packed in the pasta at dinnertime.

Eden briefed her on the Dulaney confession, eager for her take on how the case was evolving. She was skeptical at first, as he had been, but as they discussed the confession, they grew more comfortable with Dulaney's story. In fact, she became so convinced that she eventually convinced him.

Both doubted the completeness of Dulaney's tale because of

his attempt to paint Hiram Tarpley as a gunman. Eden accepted Tarpley's involvement, but he couldn't see him as a triggerman. He still believed Joey was trying to offset the blame by making Tarpley an equal accomplice.

Shele snorted. "Humph! After we spent all that time on my aunt's psychic crap! It all seems pretty silly now—"

Eden interrupted her. "Speaking of that, whatever became of Aingeal?" He suddenly felt chagrined that he hadn't even thought of her until now.

"Oh, we met at our regular place. I told her what you said—that she should back out. So until yesterday, I thought she had gone back to her job. But then I saw her in the park.

"So I called to ask why she was still around. She was excited, telling me she had gotten her toe in the door of a meeting, so she saw what was going down. She thinks there might be a book in it, or at least a novel! Aingeal has always been the curious type—"

"—and we know what curiosity did to the cat," Eden completed. "Shit! I guess there's nothing we can do. She's a big girl. But I wish she would leave now."

"Eden, you can't say anything that I haven't already. But Aingeal is Aingeal, and she's on a mission, determined to get the story. Like you said, she's a big girl."

Then she added with a note of concern, "You really don't think this Rigdon coven, or cult, whatever the hell they are, is up to anything criminal, do you?"

"I suppose not, but they're a pretty kinky outfit. When you have a weird-ass initiation rite like that, it creates a strong hold on people. And in this town, people will do anything to avoid a scandal. So it leads to a code of silence and cover-up."

"Shele, I haven't talked with Tarpley yet. I want to see his reaction when we confront him with Dulaney's confession."

On Sunday, Eden stopped by the office. Buckey told him they

had picked up "The Carp." Tarpley was more than surprised, and claimed to have no idea why he was being arrested. When deputies explained he was only being brought in for questioning, he said he knew nothing.

"But he really got freaky when we put him in a cell," Buckey said. "I told him it was protective custody, but he wasn't having any of that. He demanded an attorney and his phone call. Of course, I told him he didn't have that right, because he wasn't being arrested or charged, just held for his own protection.

"I wanted to see how he would take to Dulaney's story without having a damn attorney hanging around. Of course, none of what he said would be admissible in a trial, but I thought we might get more to go on.

"Well, he denied the whole thing. But if he had no involvement, I don't think he would have reacted the way he did. He started sobbing and saying things like, 'Oh shit, my mom and dad will die, they'll just die. This can't happen to me, I can't let something like this happen.'

"Then he asked me what he could do to get out of jail—or what he could do to get out of the whole mess. After that he refused to say anything, except he wanted to make a phone call.

"So we'll let him sit and stew," Buckey said. "Tomorrow, I'll let his folks know what's happened, and they can take it from there. Maybe by tomorrow, he'll confess to the whole thing. Or we can play him and Joey off each other until we get the whole story out of them."

Unfortunately, or maybe fortunately for his parents, tomorrow never came for Hiram Tarpley. When his cell was checked around 3:30 a.m., the guard on duty found him dead, hanging by his underwear. He had made a loop and tied it to a grill in the cell wall.

Dead as a carp, Eden thought grimly. If Tarpley had, in fact, pulled the trigger on Joey Dulaney's gun, Eden could feel no remorse for him. Regardless, the Carp's life was over, and his possible testimony with it.

Meanwhile, Joey suffered another seizure and was given some sort of medication.

On Monday, when Joey was brought back to resume the hearing, all agreed not to mention Tarpley's suicide. As far as Joey was concerned, it was simply a continuation of the previous session.

CHAPTER FORTY-TWO

DULANEY COPS

"I'll bet you put me in the back to make room for Tarp, didn't you?" Dulaney asked, as he was seated and his shackles checked. No one responded.

After some small talk to put Joey at ease, the D.A. asked him to continue his story about Elizabeth Mayow.

There were to be no further surprises nor accomplices. Joey's description of the Elizabeth Mayow murder was a carbon copy of the Kinchloe killing, with one exception, perhaps added for effect. Joey announced, "I think I was getting into it by this time. I got an erection."

The Deputy stole a glance at Joey's young court-appointed attorney. Not only had she turned pale, but her complexion was suddenly tinted a bit green.

The D.A. spoke. "All right, I think that is all we need. We might want to ask for clarification later." With that, Junior led Joey shuffling down the hallway.

The D.A. summed things up. "If anyone has anything to add, feel free to jump in, but here's my scorecard," she said, ticking off each death on a finger:

"Myra Kinchloe—motive: rejection revenge and kill for thrill. Perpetrator: Joey Dulaney.

"June Talbot—motive: she somehow knew something about the first killing, so she had to be disposed of. Perpetrators: Joey Dulaney and Hiram Tarpley. I'm not sure what to do with Tarpley's involvement, but it may not matter much.

"Elizabeth Mayow—motive and perpetrator: you can just refer to the Kinchloe murder for that.

"Pamela Brookover—ditto.

"This may be premature, but I'm pretty well satisfied we have the person responsible for all four murders. Of course, we'll renew our investigation of each death. But as far as I'm concerned, the only loose end is Tarpley's participation. And after last night, that is moot. It does raise questions about the Talbot case, but with the others, Dulaney won't walk."

Eden played one more card. "Do you think there is any possibility these guys had anything to do with Amara McClure's death?" Eden held out hope that Dulaney could be implicated somehow.

"Not unless you know something we don't," answered the D.A. "As far as I'm concerned, that one was open-and-shut suicide. It's only of interest because it happened around the time of the murders—coincidental, that's all. I don't see any linkage, none at all.

"So, this whole thing is pretty well settled," the D.A. continued. "Dulaney will enter a plea of not guilty by reason of insanity. That's pretty obvious, I think. Eden, if you want to try to talk him into a guilty plea on the same grounds, I'll move for life with treatment in a mental facility, but that's all I'm willing to go for. He's either a good actor or a complete nut case. Right now I'll vote for the latter."

Months later, Eden sat at his desk, staring at his steaming coffee. This is the way the world ends, not with a bang but a whimper, he mused. After the endless hearings and interminable legal wrangling, there was no verdict. Joey Dulaney was shipped to the regional mental facility at Mayfield, and not death row. The Court sent him away until he could be judged sane enough to stand trial. That might take years, if ever. No one would care, unless he came up for parole or release. And that wasn't likely, because if he ever were judged sane, he faced four murder raps.

Amara McClure's death still haunted Eden. But he came to accept that what the papers had been calling "The Pretty Maidens Murder Case" would be put into the "case closed" files, once they got through all the procedural stuff.

In the meantime, Eden refocused his concern on the welfare of Aingeal Farrell. The notion that some middle-class, middle-aged folks from Nowhere, Pennsylvania were involved in murder now seemed far-fetched and silly. Aingeal needed to spread her wings and fly away.

CHAPTER FORTY-THREE

ON AINGEAL'S WINGS

Eden asked Shele to invite Aingeal to his place for dinner on the following Saturday. There was less chance of anyone seeing them together at Random Creek than at Shele's house.

Aingeal wasn't at all what Eden expected. Oh, she fit Shele's description of "hardy Irish lass" all right, but he expected someone much less feminine. She had a certain Abe Lincoln-in-drag look, but the body of a superhero gal, which came off kind of sexy—in a heavy sort of way. He would not have spent much time pursuing anything with her... but he wondered what might happen if she tried some moves on him.

His Xena–Wonder Woman fantasy was suddenly interrupted.

"So you are the famous Eden Whitloe," Aingeal said, not sultry, but somehow delicate considering the source.

"Sounds like Shele has been treating you to some of her blarney," he replied.

"She makes a good PR officer."

They batted small talk about for several minutes as Shele prepared the table for dinner.

The meal went pleasantly and they were in the full-tummy coffee/desert stage.

Shele offered, "So Aingeal, how about bringing us up-to-date on your studies with the Rigdonubians, or whatever the heck they are."

Aingeal smiled broadly. "Snooping, isn't that what you mean? Well, you guys suspected they might somehow be involved in killing those girls. Now, with the confession of that Dulaney character, that turns out not to be the case. But, you never know what else might turn up."

Eden eyed her closely. "What do you mean, what else might turn up?"

"Well, several things. First, there is the sex cult angle. So far as we know, they're all consenting adults, so there's nothing illegal unless minors are involved. There's no reason to suspect that. I think they're smart enough to keep minors away.

"I've also considered the drug aspect. I'm betting there's a drug element. I've heard they give people something for the initiation rites that has a bitter taste. Given the Southwestern mysticism, my bet is peyote. Peyote, mushrooms, maybe even marijuana with an additive—some kind of hallucinogen—natural stuff, not synthetic chemicals. Someone must have a connection to buy it or the knowledge to grow it.

"I've thought of an organized crime connection, but that's really far-fetched. If you're looking for something unlawful, drugs is most likely, not dealing, just using. And I doubt a judge would take it on, with such upstanding citizens involved.

"So not much there, but it's a lot more fun than rummaging through dusty books. I'm having a great time playing snoop. If I uncover something nefarious, you'll be first to know, and you two can be the heroes."

Eden asked for a chronology of her activities thus far. So Aingeal told how she met Randolph Winter, the Farmer's Bank single, effeminate CEO.

It was one of those 1940s boy-meets-girl stories, only with an age gap. Randy was late 40s/early 50s, and Aingeal was 35. But she, like Lincoln, looked older than her years, plus she adapted her makeup and clothing to age herself.

She chose Randy because he was single, not too awful-looking, had money, a car, and a job. "No tattoos or piercings that I know of—yet," she joked. "He's not a frog that will ever turn into a prince, but he's not a real toad either. I'll watch for the mark of the beast. He's not macho and I sort-of like that. I suspect he might be bi, but not gay—he wouldn't be interested in me at all, if he only swings that way. So far we've gotten along pretty well, been on a few sexless dates, and he's still interested, so that's an accomplishment."

Randy invited her home for dinner several times and he suggested they attend church together. "Randy belongs to one of those holiness churches. He attends a tabernacle out in the western end, somewhere around Brightbrook."

After awhile, at one of the dinners at his home, Randy introduced Aingeal to funeral director Andy Walbridge and his wife. They got along well, as Aingeal continued to gain acceptance into Randy's circle. Eventually, she worked her way into a group of his associates and later into a clique she began to call "the inner circle." This coterie consisted of Andy Walbridge, Ted Dunlow and—to Eden's surprise—barber Harry Woodyard.

Aingeal mentioned a couple of other names Eden didn't recognize, people from the next county. And it was doubtless a coincidence, but one name she mentioned was Russian: Mikail Pavlock, a Ukrainian who had immigrated shortly after the Soviet Union breakup.

Aingeal continued, "I haven't heard anything about the Rigdon group itself. But I'm sure these guys are part of it. I'm also quite sure the wives of Walbridge, Dunlow, and Woodyard are involved. I assume the other wives are in it as well. I'm not sure about whether the Ukrainian is married. If he is, I feel for his wife—he seems like the kind of sweetheart who would enjoy being a prison guard."

Aingeal claimed to be on the verge of being invited to join the group, and seemed genuinely excited about the prospect.

"It's a once-in-a-lifetime chance," she elated. "Think about it: an inside look at one of the oldest undiscovered secret societies in America. It has the smell of dissertation all over it. If not that, then a novel, or at least a National Enquirer piece." She already had requested a sabbatical so she could continue her effort to penetrate the group.

"Umm, since you brought it up—" began Shele.

"Brought what up?" Aingeal asked.

"Penetration. I explained it all to you when this whole thing started. You know what we think the initiation rite may be like—"

Aingeal bellowed a huge laugh. "Ha! I'm a big girl! That's the least of my worries. What I can't avoid, I'll enjoy. Listen, there is little virgin territory left on this body. I did my experimenting in college, and not much of it in a laboratory. My only concern is stumbling onto something that someone doesn't want exposed. Some of these wonderful citizens might even kill to keep their little band's secrets from exposure."

"Okay," Eden said, "just don't come crying to me when something happens. I only want you to know that you're not getting into something on our behalf. If you want to assume the risk—"

She didn't let Eden finish. "Who was assuming the risk when I went into this in the first place? If I thought I needed you for backup, I would have stayed home. Don't worry, no one is going to blame you if something goes wrong."

Eden might have protested her lack of confidence in his abilities, but by now he was washing dishes and the apron did little for his argument or his image.

Aingeal felt that Randy would reveal something important to her soon; he had been hinting. She just hoped it wasn't a marriage proposal.

"If he does that," she said, "then I'll run for my life!"

CHAPTER FORTY-FOUR

A BRIEF REST AND ANOTHER SHOOTING

So Eden spent the summer hauling Joey Dulaney back and forth to hearings, mopping up paperwork on the cases, and surviving some dicey meetings with Pamela Brookover's parents. Adding to the burden, Carl Dulaney had taken Eden's participation in his son's case personally. Carl held Eden responsible for the entire situation, including his insanity defense. It was useless to explain that Joey devised that defense all on his own.

And Eden still wasn't convinced that Dulaney was the schizo he portrayed himself to be. He would always have lingering doubts about how it all came about, but was firmly convinced Joey was the killer and that he alone pulled the trigger in one or more of the murders.

The search of the Tarpley residence revealed absolutely nothing that tied "The Carp" to the case. No shoes with a cut sole and, outside of some Dungeons & Dragons stuff, no weird computer files or books. Schoolmates called Tarpley a loner with that out-of-step, isolated outlook, like the "Trenchcoat Mafia" who perpetrated the Columbine High School massacre. Eden saw a sad, lonely kid who dabbled in Goth stuff to gain attention, but when all was said and done, Tarpley seemed pretty benign. Apparently he had some kind of homosexual affair with Dulaney, and he might have felt it was worth dying to keep it from his parents. Who knows what goes through a kid's mind? After finding him hanging in the George County Sheriff's Office holding cell, everything else was guesswork.

The hot summer of stifling courtroom sessions, tracking down bicycle thieves, and keeping homeless wackos away from the Palace ticket booth finally passed. The summer faded into a haze of ragweed pollen drifting across open fields of dry broom sage set against sunsets that came sooner and sooner each night. The gamelands turned red, orange, and brown, and geese drifted in and out as cattail seeds fluffed their parasols and hung from them, wafted on a breeze that grew a little chillier each day.

The plastic tape that marked the spot where Pamela Brookover was found now was tattered, becoming mixed with pollen and cattail fur as the cool zephyrs of the coming winter slowly erased it.

Like the yellow bits of crime-scene tape, the Dulaney hearings began to wither into memory. Long before the first snow would fall, Joey would be in his new residence up in Mayfield, where he would no doubt remain until his hair was touched with the hoarfrost of the winter of his life.

Out on Random Creek, things became routine once more. There was a little talk of a June wedding. June was now as far away as spring and no one could even imagine spring at this time of year. Shele came more often and stayed longer. She became less a sometime lover and more a taken-for-granted housewife. During Eden's off-duty hours, the pair was inseparable. Traveling to nearby shopping centers, she recommended what he would eat and selected what he would wear. He no longer protested when she returned his selected Hawaiian shirts to the rack and chose a more sedate print. He deferred to her fashion judgment—which always seemed impeccable.

Shele stayed in touch with Aingeal who by now had worked her way into the heart of Randolph Winter. She fended off his interest in marriage, but finally was invited to membership in what he called his "real religion." She told Shele that it seemed an innocuous organization, steeped in the usual symbolism and mystical trappings of a secret society.

"I get the feeling they're all play-acting," Aingeal reported. "They're acting out a liturgy and delivering incantations that might have been meaningful years ago, but now are just trappings of ancient dogma."

"Sort of like Catholics, Presbyterians, or Episcopalians?" smirked Eden.

"You know, I hadn't thought of it that way, but—exactly like that," Aingeal added mirthlessly. "They are very, very serious about it all, and they must deeply believe, but the original zeal of the religion has faded into rote."

Then Shele suggested that the Rigdonites were undoubtedly much like today's students and employees: irresponsible and in need of disciplinary oversight.

"I suppose every organization needs the heavy hand of authority to keep it in line," she said.

Eden recalled the words of Andy Walbridge and how he longed for the "good old days" of the sect, but he let it pass.

It was before the Thanksgiving snow that Joe Bill Tusten was shot. No, it wasn't another gamelands murder. This time it was a gamelands hunting accident—if you could call what happened to Joe Bill an accident. He was taking a nap on a log and someone mistook him for a squirrel. It might sound far-fetched that someone could mistake a grown man for a squirrel, but that's exactly what the hunter from up at Cranberry claimed. As it turned out, it was Joe Bill's head he mistook for the furry critter and when he fired at it, he missed and took off Joe Bill's toe, which was sticking up in the air downrange from his head. In most instances, you could say getting a toe removed was better than a bullet in the head. But in Joe Bill's case... .

Anyway, that's why Eden was out that way, to investigate the shooting. On the way back, he noticed lights and chimney smoke at Dave Quinn's shop, so he decided to say hello.

Dave was busily working on a cocktail table for one of his city clients, but happy to share coffee with his friend. Consumed by the murder cases, Eden had forgotten about their find, but Dave brought it up.

"Hey, I've got news on the stuff we found when we dug up that old stump. Gus Bimelar called. He remembered at a conference a few years back that he ran across a woman who was researching nineteenth-century hoaxes. She was particularly interested in the Rigdon-Spaulding controversy and how it might have been related to the founding of the Mormon Church.

"Well, he didn't pay much attention to this woman back then, because there are so many loonies who have theories about lost tribes and the Mormon Church," Dave explained. "But Gus now believes it's very probable that our find is one of three or four other plants that were made by one of Sidney Rigdon's relatives—Walter Rigdon.

"According to what the woman could find out—she did a lot of genealogical research on the Rigdon family—Walter Rigdon went around the countryside, setting up artifacts that could be discovered, so he could begin his own version of a lost-tribes religion. Maybe he wanted to start a Latter-Latter Day Saints religion of his own?" he chuckled.

"Did you get the name of the woman?" Eden asked.

"You noticed I didn't tell you right away?" Dave teased. "It's a mysterious person you're already aware of."

Eden thought, Colleen McKay—Aingeal Farrell—or even Shele—no—

"Mara," Dave announced.

"Myra Kinchloe? She'd be too young to—"

"No, no, Mara—Amara McClure. Who'da thunk it? She, sure as hell, never said anything to me about her research. Maybe she planned to write a book, and was keeping it a secret."

Eden suddenly had an image of Amara McClure lying on her bed, a .38 slug in her temple. With it came a queasy sensation in his stomach and the instant rebirth of his hunch that her death was not a suicide.

Dave said, "I remember when you were investigating her shooting. I figured she found something she shouldn't have been messing with. Remember that?"

Eden nodded. He remembered all too well their discussions surrounding how Amara killed herself.

"Wow," Eden said. This is quite a surprise. I need a little time to digest this news. This revelation alone might make us reinvestigate Amara's death."

Shaken, Eden said his thanks and departed. As he drove, his mind raced in speculation...

If Amara McClure killed herself... could it have been because she stumbled onto something about the Rigdonite cult? His suspicions emerged from the world of a personal fantasy into a full-blown vision of possibility. Maybe she uncovered something a cult member wanted kept secret. Maybe she tried to blackmail one of them. Maybe she had become involved with them, creating a reason for her to kill herself—drugs—a bad trip—occult dabblings—his mind raced on a trip of its own.

Then Dave Quinn's words from over a year ago came rushing back.

Did you ever wake up in the middle of the night, terrified beyond all reason? If you can divide the infinite into regions, there must be a fairly large one dedicated to mayhem, suicide, and murder. I think most suicides are a result of someone breaking through and finding something over there in a drawer that should have remained closed. I figure Mara was meditating, cogitating, ruminating, or whatever, on this stuff, and had some sort of breakthrough she couldn't deal with. Popped open one of those drawers that's supposed to stay shut.

He didn't say it out loud, but he thought it. Just like Tarp.

And in the middle of that autumn night, several hours later, he did wake up—terrified beyond all reason, for no cause he could imagine. He thought of Aingeal Farrell involved in only God knows what and then went back to sleep and dreamed of Shele and her "hardy Irish" friend. They were trapped, and strangely he was trapped with them, but somehow he wasn't with them. They traveled an endless circuitous route, searching along a curved wall pierced by slits with blades of light coming through them. The wall never ended, never arrived where the journey began, and never repeated itself. It was as Dave Quinn said in a low, echoing, bass voice from deep within the unseen middle of the curved room—

"Infinite."

CHAPTER FORTY-FIVE

FINDING DIAMONDS

Shele, ever the cool head, didn't seem surprised that her aunt was digging into the Rigdon matter, knowing more than anyone imagined.

This exasperated Eden a bit. "But don't you find it odd that she never said anything about it? And that we didn't find any references to her research? Or any of her notes?"

"Yeah, it's a little strange. You'd think we find something. What are you suggesting?"

"Hell, I don't know. It's odd, that's all. Maybe someone got in her house and cleaned it out?"

It was Shele's turn to be exasperated. "Good grief, you never give up, do you?" she exclaimed. "One of the Rigdonites killed Aunt Amara to keep her from finding them out and revealing their cult to the world, and then they went through all her things to be sure no evidence was left behind, is that it?"

"There's no point in continuing this. There's nothing to go on. So let's just drop it, okay?"

"Excellent idea," Shele snapped. "Look, Eden. If you stay at this long enough and get too involved, you're going to go nuts and make yourself sick. It's over—get over it!"

Then she softened, not meaning to hurt him. "Listen, to satisfy yourself, would you like to go back to my place and take another look around, just to be sure?"

"If you wouldn't mind, I think I would like that," he said, a bit too quickly.

He could tell she was more exasperated than angry. Like her little unruly boy, she was patronizing him.

"Tell you what, Eden. I'm going shopping tomorrow afternoon. You can go over and spend the whole day if you like. Play detective, look it over from top to bottom. Maybe you can find some secret passages or a treasure box or maybe—a—uh—an occult library in the attic—or—maybe a dungeon in the basement."

He tolerated her sarcasm, but seriously wanted to take a new look. He wanted to see what his old eyes, which knew less, might have missed.

Then Shele, with her knack for doing the best thing at the right time, suddenly hugged him, wiggling sensually against him. "Only one thing," she teased. "If you find any treasure, it's all mine. And don't get any kinky ideas if you find a dungeon."

The following day he drove to Amara's old Victorian. He had the place to himself until Shele returned at 5:00. He let himself in with the key she gave him, a typical modern key, not a skeleton key as one might expect for a house that age. It was a modern key because the locks had been replaced with modern locks. In fact, the whole door had been replaced with a modern steel Victorian-style door, faux finished to imitate oak. The place was essentially the same as it had been since his first trip there with Buckey. Except for the missing cats and their associated smells and some new feminine touches, he would have expected Amara to appear at any moment, turban and all, except she was somewhere in a jar.

Where to begin? Bottom-up, he decided: start with the dungeon in the basement, then finish with the occult library in the attic.

As he reached the basement door, just off the kitchen, he looked around, trying to imagine what he might have overlooked the first time around. The basement stairs were steeper than normal, typical of houses of the time. No light switch, so he flicked on his flashlight. At the bottom, he had to duck beneath a beam. Over the years, someone had rigged a clothesline around the basement, and now rotted cotton rope hung neck-high at some points.

In the center of the "dungeon" was a naked bulb with a pull chain. He tried the chain, tapped the bulb, and gave up. His flashlight would do.

In a far corner was an old side-arm water heater, disconnected. A modern water heater stood near a fairly modern gas furnace. The furnace connected to ancient ductwork that apparently once had mated to an old coal-fired monstrosity. Asbestos tape hung in shreds from the old ductwork. Webs of some hopeful spiders were rigged between the floor joists.

In one corner, someone had built a room of rough boards and lined it with shelving. On the shelves were mostly empty jars, but some contained dark stuff with whitish mold growing on it. A thick layer of dust covered everything in the basement, and it appeared that no one had entered it in years. He assumed this little rough-board room had been someone's 1940s fruit cellar, perhaps an attempt to augment war-rationed food.

Typical basement junk adorned the walls and was neatly arranged around the outside of the room. He shone his flashlight along the perimeter of the main room until he came full circle back to the old water heater in the corner. It was then he noticed some scratches on the floor where it had been moved, but there was no way to tell how fresh the scratches were. He shone his light behind the water heater and saw the edge of an old door someone had stored. As he brought the light around toward the front, he could see its lock—one of those old-fashioned keyholes Amara seemed so fond of. Closer examination revealed the door to be fairly sturdy— and not just leaning there, but fitted into the wall. Being covered with decades of grime and the water heater in front of it, no one would have noticed the door. And it appeared not to have been opened recently.

He tried the knob but it wouldn't budge. He jiggled it, but it was locked. He tried a knife in the jamb and a screwdriver blade in the lock, without success. Determined to see what was behind that door, so he made his way back upstairs to the kitchen. Every kitchen has a junk drawer, and it took him only a few tries to find it. It contained the usual small tools, an old latchhook for rug making, crochet hooks, batteries, odd hardware, a small Swiss Army knife and—the prize he sought—a skeleton key.

He took the key downstairs to the locked door. Surprised that the key turned so easily in the ancient lock, he turned the knob, and the door opened. The only problem was that it opened outward, so the water heater blocked the way. Eden edged behind the water heater and pushed it away from the door. He then opened the door as far as he could and shone the flashlight into a very small, dark room.

Surprising rays of sunlight seemed to come through a small window, slicing through the darkness to reveal a floor covered with small bits of what looked like coal… and realized that he was in the coal bin, where they used to stash a winter's supply for the former furnace. He turned his flashlight on the source of the sunshine and found the hatch to the coal chute, through which they once loaded coal from the outside.

Until after World War II, George County homes were heated by coal, cheap and abundant. Later, clean natural gas became plentiful, so furnaces were converted to gas and old coal bins were abandoned. Normally, the opening to the coal chute would have been bricked over or sealed. But the door to this chute, open slightly at the bottom, had never been sealed or even fastened shut. This wasn't unheard of; after gas was installed, some homeowners simply forgot about the old bin and chute.

So what?

Well, finding a coal bin in an old home normally would be of little interest, but in this case, he had found a possible entry into the house, and a hidden one at that. The fact that all the doors were locked when they found Amara's body was now meaningless. Maybe no one came in through the coal bin and made their way to Amara's room... but it could have happened that way. There were no signs of entry, but anyone who discovered that the chute opening was unfastened, and had a skeleton key for the door, could have entered easily and left, without anyone knowing.

With bits of coal crunching under his feet, Eden carefully backed out of the small room, locked the door, and shoved the old water heater back in place. The room looked exactly as it had when he arrived. He found an old piece of rug to wipe his feet on, then made his way back upstairs.

The main floor of the house had been taken over by Shele, so he gave it only a cursory examination. The second floor was also unremarkable. He looked through the closets for access panels someone might have missed, but found none. At one point, He pulled the plumbing access panel from behind the upstairs tub, but the space was empty save for plaster dust, cobwebs, and mold from sweating metal pipes.

He figured the best chance of finding anything new was the attic. The police had gone through it, but he doubted they paid much attention since it was a routine suicide investigation.

The attic wasn't at all what he expected. In the center were several new corrugated cardboard boxes along with a few plastic containers with lids. All were taped shut and labeled. Evidently, this was where Shele had stored all of Amara's belongings. And the attic looked as if it had been cleaned by the world's most fastidious housecleaner. He guessed that was one Shele Ocevan.

He began to inspect the containers. He found one labeled NOTES and peeled the tape from the top. There was the loose-leaf notebook containing references to Russians and Moundsville that

Shele had shown him earlier. There were some old yellowed tablets
he hadn't seen before. They weren't informative, and didn't reveal
anything Rigdon-related. They seemed to be notes taken during her
client sessions. They had escaped one of her flash-paper fires.

It struck him that, since he hadn't been able to find anything,
perhaps he should instead look for nothing—in other words,
something removed, something missing, something noticeable by
its absence. He picked up the loose-leaf notebook and thumbed
through it, wondering if any pages had been removed.

He turned to a familiar page where was scrawled:

- GN Dulnev—*Parapsychology and Psychophysics*

- VP Zolokazov & VA Zagriadsky, *Experiments on Levitation &
Telekinesis*

- LM Porvin & SV Speransky—*Study of the Man-Animal Bond*

The next page seemed to continue Amara's ramblings, but a
couple of pages later, at the bottom, he spotted an incomplete
sentence:

"He had been a member of the Mahoning Baptist Association
from 1820 to 1822; thus, he was returning to Baptist Congregations
which appreciated both his preaching ability and his support
of Campbell's doctrines. The Mahoning Association sheltered
Campbell's reformers until it was dissolved in 1830, when most of
the members joined the newly-formed Disciples of..."

He turned the page expecting to see "Christ" or some reference
to Campbell or Campbellites. Instead, he found another interrupted
sentence that obviously did not connect to the previous page:

"...the ravages of time, that I could not read the inscription. With
the assistance of a leaver I raised the stone."

Hmm. It appeared that an entire wad of material had been
removed. Eden later would affirm his suspicion that this was a line
from the introduction to Solomon Spaulding's *Manuscript Found*,
which begins:

"Near the west bank of the Coneaught River there are the remains of an ancient fort. As I was walking and forming various conjectures respecting the character, situation, & numbers of those people who far exceeded the present Indians in works of art and ingenuity, I happened to tread on a flat stone. This was at a small distance from the fort, & it lay on the top of a small mound of Earth exactly horizontal. The face of it had a singular appearance. I discovered a number of characters which appeared to me to be letters, but so much effaced by the ravages of time..."

For whatever reason, someone—perhaps McClure herself—had removed a sizable number of pages from the notebook.

Well, it proved that Amara McClure had been dabbling in either the works of Spaulding, or more likely, Rigdon. It confirmed Dave Quinn's information that she had been involved in Spaulding-Rigdon research. But unless someone could make a case that her research had gotten her into trouble with modern-day Rigdonites, it was of no help.

He poked around her notes and the house for the rest of the afternoon until Shele arrived. He helped her bring in shopping bags, dumping them onto the kitchen table.

"Got you a new shirt," she announced, proudly. "You'll have to get rid of that old plaid one that makes you look like some kind of hick."

"Thanks a bunch," he said. Then after he thought a couple of seconds, added, "uh—uh—for the new shirt."

She didn't appear to notice and continued. "So, did you turn up anything interesting? Any treasure or ancient books on witchcraft?"

"Nothing much," he said. It wasn't a complete falsehood. Where the notebook was concerned, he could truthfully say he hadn't found a thing.

"Shele, do you know anything about the heating system this

place had before the gas furnace was installed?"

"Only that it must have been coal-fired," she said. "All these places used coal up to the late '20s or early '30s. Some didn't convert until way up in the '50s. Why?"

"I just wondered if you knew anything about a coal bin in the basement, that's all."

For whatever reason, Shele paused. "I've never seen it, but then I never poked around down there. Did you find one?"

"Yeah. It just had some coal chunks that we could convert into diamonds if we had enough money. That's as close to a treasure as I came."

CHAPTER FORTY-SIX

AINGEAL RETURNS

They returned from dinner to find Shele's answering machine blinking a welcome. Eden turned on the comedy channel while she retrieved the call. He was so engrossed in one monologue that he didn't notice time passing. Suddenly Shele appeared in the archway between the dining room and the parlor.

"Aingeal left a message to call, so we've been talking the past 20 minutes. Lord knows how much longer she might have talked, but Randy came in, so she had to shut up. I'm meeting Aingeal tomorrow in Morgantown. She has something important on the Rigdonites. She's afraid someone might see us, so we're meeting at the Morgantown Mall."

Eden offered to shadow them, out of sight.

Shele thought that was silly. "I'll be fine, Eden. She probably wants to tell me about her induction into the group. She just wants to remain incognito. I didn't sense fear."

Eden wasn't all that assured. But he agreed to be a good boy and headed home.

At his office the next day, Eden expected to hear from Shele by afternoon. When she didn't call, he felt uneasy, yet there was nothing unusual about her not calling during the day. She avoided calling him at work. So, no news was very good news.

But when she didn't call that evening, he began to—not really worry—but wonder what was up. By 10:00, he had enough and dialed her number. He got her answering machine, so figuring she was screening calls, he asked her to pick up. She didn't, so he left a message for her to call ASAP.

The next day, Shele called shortly before noon to invite herself to lunch. She didn't mention last night's message. Had she checked the machine? Well, she got home after midnight, hadn't thought to check messages, and forgot to check this morning. She promised interesting news over lunch.

"Aingeal is getting it on with Randy," she began abruptly, eyeing Eden sideways. Eden thought she said it to see how he would react. He decided to be matter-of-fact.

"Well, not totally unexpected. She's on her own out there. If she gets the hots for someone, why not? No crime in that."

Shele expressed the opinion that Aingeal wasn't just horny or interested in a romantic relationship with Randy—she was leading him on. And Aingeal wasn't above getting some gratification in the process.

To this, Eden simply responded, "Whatever."

Shele seemed a little annoyed that he reacted so neutrally to her opening volley, so she fired again. "And—" She waited to see if he would ask her to continue.

"And—what?" He was sucked in.

"And—she's been inducted into the Lodge of the Runes. That's the name of the bunch—or at least one name they use. Anyway, she was inducted and went through the initiation rites night before last. Have you ever heard of Ehecacoatl or Topiltzin?"

"Yes. Ehecacoatl is an Aztec name for the wind or a tornado. It roughly translates to wind snake. And Topiltzin is a high priest who is supposed to be Quetzalcoatl, the feathered serpent, in human form."

"Hmm, you're up on this stuff," she said. "Well, the initiation was all set up beforehand with Andy playing Topiltzin and Randy filling in for Ehecacoatl."

"So, you're saying that when they went for the backroom rites, old Randy was plowing ground he'd had his plow in before," Eden smirked.

"Whenever I'm at a loss for words, remind me to call you. You have such a way with them—Mr. Sensitivity," she scolded.

Shele added more. "Topiltzin is the human form of Quetzalcoatl, and he is the one who left the Americas on a raft of snakes with a promise to return. Scholars have suggested that the myth of Quetzalcoatl, as a priest, is based on pre-Columbian contact between the Old World and the New world.

"I looked some of this up in the library. The early western explorers of Mexico saw parallels between the pious nature of the High Priest Topiltzin and early Christianity. Many Mexican historians of that period, such as Garcia, Becerra Tanco, and Siguenzay Gongora, believed that the Apostle St. Thomas was the original Topiltzin.

"So, talk about your pre-Columbian lost tribes! You have one group dealing with North America and another hung up south of the border. Pretty ironic," she said. "Randolph Winter, the one true, white-skinned god, come to save the afflicted—"

"—and initiate the Irish," Eden added with a chuckle. "And don't forget Andy Walbridge, the big blowhard wind god—now that's irony for you."

Shele explained that Aingeal wanted to meet with both of them, to plan her next move. She felt the door was open, but was uncertain how to proceed.

"Do you have any ideas?" she asked.

"No, but I see a problem, from my viewpoint in law enforcement. Listen, Shele. All we have here is a curious cookie who has wormed her way into a group that probably has constitutional, religious freedom protection. Beyond that, the Lodge of the Runes members have individual rights to privacy. I can foresee a lawsuit if we continue to meddle and snoop—to say nothing of bad relations between these people and the Sheriff's Department.

"I don't have probable cause, so there's no reason to intrude on folks who aren't committing a crime. I'm curious as hell about this whole thing, but remember what happened to the cat. And above all, I don't want to involve my department in this."

"No balls, huh?" teased Shele. And it worked, of course. That's how she got him to come along and meet with Aingeal.

No, they didn't ask for details concerning her initiation. It wasn't because Eden wasn't curious, but he didn't want Shele to slug him.

Aingeal now knew the Great Kiva was located west of Amity, just north of the George County line—right on the ley line aligned with the Palace of Gold and the Grave Creek Mound.

They studied a map. The location was a mile off the main highway. Aingeal said it just looked like an old barn from the outside, but inside it was fairly elaborate. The exterior was typical vertical board batten siding, so it appeared to be just another dilapidated barn, in a little better shape than most that dot the countryside.

At one point, as they poured over the map, Aingeal got pencil and paper and began to sketch. When she finished, they had a good idea of what the barn looked like. It was rectangular, sitting on an embankment, supported on the lower end by a wall of cut stone. On the far end stood the remains of a cut stone silo, which was significant. Few barns with silos existed any more; a stone silo was a real rarity; and even more unusual were what looked like ventilation slits that ran vertically at random intervals around it. They appeared decorative, but Aingeal said they were "symbolically functional."

"What do you mean, symbolically functional?" Eden asked.

"I haven't seen it yet, but Randy told me that at special times of the year, the slits line up with celestial features, and ceremonies and festivals are coordinated with their appearance through the slits. Of course, the summer and winter solstices are of particular interest, but there is another crucial alignment that will occur only three times in the next 100 years. He told me the three times will be in September 2040, July 2060, and November 2100," Aingeal explained.

"Sort of like Stonehenge?" asked Eden.

"Exactly. Each night this past year, three major planets formed nearly a straight line in the west—Jupiter, Mars, Saturn. By April, four planets were all bunched together like one bright star—Mercury, Venus, Mars, Saturn.

"Anyway, according to Randy and Andy, on the featured night—around St. Patrick's Day—the alignment appeared through the slit and passed through to a niche on the other side of the Great Kiva. The alignment must have been some heavy-duty event, because they wouldn't explain much about it. They said I had to advance through several levels of enlightenment before I could understand it."

After Aingeal's initiation, the members gave her their version of how the Lodge of the Runes was founded. There were gaps between the group's version and what Eden and friends had learned about the actual history. The whole Spaulding-Rigdon-Smith mess was steeped in controversy, and no one was sure who was planting misleading evidence.

Walter Rigdon, founder of the sect, had little connection to Sidney Rigdon. Some claimed Walter was a cousin, some an uncle, and others said Walter wasn't related and wasn't even a Rigdon. According to one story from those who doubtless were considered heretics, Walter Rigdon was in fact Doctor Philastus Hurlbut, who was excommunicated from the Mormon Church for participating in the Spaulding heresy.

Whoever Walter was, he had—much like Joseph Smith or the guy in the Spaulding novel—found a stone buried in the ground and used a lever to pry it up. This revelation did a great deal to confirm Eden's suspicion that old Walt, or Hurlbut, or whoever he was, had planted his own stones, perhaps including the ones Dave and Eden had found.

More and more, it appeared that Rigdon—whoever he was—had planned his discovery as a competition to Smith and the Mormons. It was his way of getting even for excommunication—forming his own version of a religion based on the lost tribes and lost gospels. After the finding, Rigdon had the opportunity to write his own gospel and to create his own version of a New World religion. He probably added the south-of-the-border twist so it wouldn't appear to be just a Spaulding or Smith rip-off.

It was suspected that, sometime during the Great Depression in the 1930s, the Rigdonites grew obsessed with the Ark of the Covenant. At that time, renewed interest in the paranormal flourished, and Celtic-Germanic cultism ran rampant. With their proximity to Moundsville, they could have come in contact with Nazi mystics who were working there. The interest in the Ark no doubt reinforced the cult's belief that they were among the truly chosen.

So, it was easy for Rigdon to retrofit the Ark into the original schema of their religious dogma. Tracing it from the Americas, back through Chaco, and from there to Mexico, to Ethiopia, to Egypt, and then to the Holy Land, was a simple matter for the simple-minded. Since they were so secretive, small, and didn't have the resources to build a magnificent temple, a reproduction of the Ark would have made a fine anchor point for the newly formed Rigdon cult.

"Take a look at this," Aingeal said. She laid out the tablet she had been using. On the page was the beginning of a drawing of the old barn's floor plan.

"The actual Great Kiva is the part of the silo that's at floor level.

It wasn't a lot different than pictures I've seen of smaller kivas from Pueblo Benito at Chaco Canyon—except this one is higher. I think there is another chamber below, because the floor is wood and has a hollow ring when you walk on it."

She began to sketch again, drawing a room off to the right of the silo.

"This is where initiations take place. It's a lot different than the silo area, which is just cut, unfinished stone. The initiation room is paneled and decorated in a sort of mid-1800s classic revival style. Other than a large initiation altar, the most striking feature is a door here on the north end," she said, as she drew a symbol for a doorway.

"I have no idea where it leads or what's behind it. When I asked, they said only those who held the highest rank—Venerated Elders—were permitted to enter. It looked quite heavy, and it is decorated with a gilded sun disk, rising from a sort of notch. Below that is a golden dagger being thrust into a spiral."

"Hmm... those symbols are consistent with Chacoan solstice features," Eden added.

Aingeal nodded. She explained that the main part of the building—the main floor of the barn—was their meeting room, like a church sanctuary except the seating area was smaller. There was a section of pews, but the floor space in front was more like a dance floor you would see in a bar. She imagined it was used for processions. In the rear was a small anteroom, which she supposed was a cloakroom.

There was no altar, as such, in the sanctuary. She believed that any ceremony requiring an altar would have been held in the room where her initiation took place.

She and Shele planned to go for a closer look sometime soon, when no one was around. They planned to spook out the place on the outside for a burglar alarm, and then see if they could get inside.

Once in, Aingeal wanted to find out what was behind the door with the Chacoan symbols.

Eden was thinking about curiosity and cats again. "You do whatever floats your boat," he said. "But leave me out of it, okay? Oh, I'll be around if you find anything criminal. But if you get busted for breaking and entering, don't look for me to bail you out. I'll tell everyone I never heard of you two."

"Don't worry," said Shele. "You can stay home and keep your skirts clean. We'll go out and do the real investigating."

CHAPTER FORTY-SEVEN

AINGEAL AND SHELE REPORT

The pair operated much faster than Eden could have imagined. By the very next weekend, Shele called. They had made good on their threat to snoop out the Rigdonite barn.

She promised a Rigdon Report when she came out for the weekend at his place. By now she was so accustomed to Eden's Random Creek estate that there was no need for Eden's help, or interference, in the kitchen, where she busily prepared breakfast for them.

"Well, it's creepy," she said. "You go out the main road, then turn off on a little lane that crosses railroad tracks, and just beyond the tracks is the barn. Yes, it creeped me out—both the railroad tracks and the barn.

"Anyway, it's a pretty far-out place. You would expect more security, but they just locked the door. Once we got by that, it was smooth sailing. They don't even have a basic alarm system. I suppose after all the years of calm, they became complacent."

"The only problem out there would be juvenile vandals," Eden said. "But tell me, how the heck did you get through the door? Did you jimmy it or pick the lock?"

"It was really tough," Shele grinned. "Aingeal has a key. She filched it from Randy's pocket when he left his clothes on a living room chair one day. She took it to Carl Dulaney's hardware and made a copy. Leave it to Aingeal to find the easy way. You see, Mr. Inspector Whitloe, women don't have to resort to complicated ways to getting things accomplished."

"Why, thank you, Ms. Steinem. I'm sure Bella Abzug would be proud of you both," he said unctuously.

Shele characterized the barn's interior much as Aingeal had. The sanctuary must have been a notch or two up from the interior, since it was paneled with a drop ceiling. The Great Kiva itself was nothing more than a cut stone cylinder. Other than the small slots that pierced it, it was unadorned and unremarkable. According to Shele's account, they had plugs that could be installed in the slits to keep the weather out. However, some were not in place when she was there.

She went on to describe the "initiation stone." It was a strange affair that consisted of a padded kneeling area that was raised from the floor by about seven inches. From the side, it looked like a kneeling ram, but it wasn't any kind of sheep anyone would recognize. The initiate knelt, facing the mysterious door that Aingeal spoke of earlier, then leaned forward into a sort of bench affair. At the top of the incline, there was a padded chin rest that would have been the top of the ram's head, with a forged iron handle on each side of it—like ram's horns. Resting on one's knees, leaning forward with the posterior raised and hands on the grips, it was perfectly positioned for an approach from the rear. Aingeal told Shele it had been covered with a red satin sheet with a comfortable pad under it when she was initiated. It was quite comfortable and the whole initiation experience might not have been too bad, if Andy Walbridge hadn't been right there watching.

"Sounds like something we might want to try sometime," Eden offered.

Shele smirked.

"Anyway, we were surprised to find the door at the front of the room was unlocked. In fact, it didn't even have a lock. It was held shut by a big wrought iron bolt and looked like something from the Spanish Inquisition. Come to think of it, that's what the initiation bench looked like too. I'll bet with all the kiva, Aztec, Anasazai motif, you would think we found peyote in there, wouldn't you?"

Eden couldn't figure why an image of Myra Kinchloe, laid out in the morgue, flashed through his mind. Then he remembered that Dr. Vinnie had said something like, "had some mescaline, we think." I wonder if Joey Dulaney knows the Rigdonite's dealer? He made a mental note to follow-up on that.

"Well, we sure did," Shele exclaimed.

"Sure did what?" Eden snapped back from his thoughts.

"We found peyote, Eden. How would you think this group of tired old middle-aged hippies could get it up for any of the ceremonies? I'm sure Andy, Randy, and the bunch needed more than just a little buzz to get into the mood. And I think Aingeal needed more than Jim Beam or Bud Lite to get her head into shape for getting onto that thing in front of Andy and Randy."

As an aside, Eden told her, "I don't think Buckey would want a drug rap against them. We might get them for a possession misdemeanor, but they would make some cockamamie religious freedom defense, get a slap on the wrist, and that would be that. If they have the right judge, he might even throw out the case on grounds of religious persecution."

Shele said the interior of the altar room was plain, but there was a curved stairwell toward the back that led down under the floor level of the main room to a chamber below the silo. It was really the foundation of the silo, and except for the fact there was only one opening in the outside wall, it was a continuation of what was above.

"But get this, Eden. In front of the opening in the wall was this—well, I think it was probably Rigdon's or someone's attempt to reproduce the Ark of the Covenant. If it hadn't been for poor craftsmanship, it would have been spookier than it was. It was okay as folk art, but no masterpiece."

From her description, it sounded like what was shown in *Raiders of the Lost Ark*. Or, according to the Exodus description, it was an ark or chest of setim (acacia) wood, two and one-half cubits long, and one and one-half cubits high (5 feet by 3 by 3) overlaid with gold, with a crown of gold extending around the chest upon the top edge. Four rings of pure gold were set in the four corners, two on one side and two on the other, through which were passed the wooden handles overlaid with gold, used in carrying the sacred chest.

"The thing had angels on top," she said. "One was kneeling, with forehead down to where it touched the top of the box. The second angel was kneeling, but the body was upright. The first angel's wings were swept back, and the other's were extended. It was arranged so someone could recline on the first angel and lie back with their outstretched arms on the second. One could even grip the extended thumbs of the second angel while reclining in this position. If they did take that position, the angel's nose would be right against the top of their neck. The thumbs were sort of worn so it looked like someone had been holding onto them, perhaps at several different times.

"The damned thing looked like a sacrificial altar—almost like the one in the other room, only here the person would be lying face-up. Hey, maybe they do one of those sacrifices where they cut your still-beating heart out with a flint knife," she laughed. Then, dropping her smile, "I'm only kidding. There wasn't a trace of blood anywhere."

She continued, "It was all pretty freaky. I had Aingeal help me up on the angel wings, to see if it would work as a sacrificial altar. You know, it was reasonably comfortable, except for two things. The forward angel's nose pushed into the base of my skull and there was some pointy thing coming up from the other angel's hair that just about went up my ass. With my clothes off,

I'd have experienced one of those probes the guys who have close encounters describe."

Shele explained that she and Aingeal were curious about the weight and tried to lift the handles on the box. They found the rings weren't solid gold, but gold-leafed—probably made of copper or bronze. They were surprised that the handles weren't attached to the box, just to its lid. When they lifted the handles, the lid came loose, and they could see the interior.

"Since there was no place to set the lid down, we rotated it so we could see inside. We expected the Ten Commandments, Aaron's Rod, or a pot of manna. But the only thing inside was a large blue glass cylinder or pot. Its bottom and sides were covered with more gold leaf—more like foil. The only part not covered was the top edge, so we could tell it was cobalt glass.

"And there was a copper strap that stood up from inside the cylinder and flared out at the top, like a spring. It looked like it would contact the lid when closed. It was polished on the flared end to make good contact with the lid, or on through to one of the angels on its top. On the end was another strap, only it was connected to the outside of the cylinder."

"Damn, Shele, that sounds like a Leyden jar! Scientists way back used those to store electricity. Ben Franklin stored the lightning discharge from his kite in a Leyden jar. It's essentially a large capacitor that holds an electrical charge. Once it was charged up, a Leyden jar could deliver quite a jolt if you touched it. Now, that explains the angel's nose and the pointy thing that poked your butt—those were contact points for a good electrical zappola! I'll bet Walter Rigdon built his Ark with this primitive electrical system that would zap the fear of God into anyone who fooled with it. Between his runes and his Ark, he must have been Da Magic Man. No wonder he developed a following. Walter Rigdon must have been a damned clever fellow."

Eden wondered how ol' Walt might have charged up his Leyden jar. Later that night, Wikipedia explained it. At the time the group was founded, experimenters were using an electrophorus, an apparatus for generating static electricity, consisting of a hard rubber disk that is given a negative charge by friction, and a metal plate given a positive charge by induction when in contact with the disk. Another website gave directions for making one from plastic and an aluminum cookie sheet.

Eden continued, "I can just imagine Rigdon luring one of the faithful onto the device, then zapping the living shit out of him just to prove he was The Man.

"Did you find any books or records showing how the thing was used?"

"No. But if Randy has anything like that lying around, it won't take Aingeal long to come up with it," she grinned. "We think the Ark is a leftover from the first days when Rigdon got his congregation running. But it hasn't just been sitting. Someone polishes and maintains it. There wasn't a speck of dust on it, and it appeared to have been used fairly recently. We thought is might be another version of the initiation stone, but there's really no way for someone to stay up there with another person on top of them."

CHAPTER FORTY-EIGHT

CATCHING THE LAST TRAIN

Maybe she had made a sudden connection or remembered something she could not wait to check out. Patience wasn't Shele Ocevan's strong points. They would never know. But for whatever reason, She revisited the old barn, home to the Lodge of the Runes—in the wee hours past midnight, alone.

On that night, a cold front bulldozed across George County, generating intense lightening and rolling thunder. All the better for Shele, as the thunder masked any noise she might make and the lightening coverd the beam of her flashlight.

As Shele left the barn, her heart quickened as she approached the railroad crossing by the barn. The rural crossing was similar to the one her parents had encountered on that fateful evening. It had no gate or lighting, just a warning sign that glowed in her headlights through the downpour. She had remarked to Aingeal about the crossing when they first visited the barn. "These rural rail crossings really creep me out. There may not be a train in sight, but that doesn't matter to me. I fly over them whenever I get the chance."

Tonight was different. As she approached the crossing, she suddenly heard a train's horn, loudly cutting through the pounding rain and thunder. Instantly trembling, her face then bleached white in the eerie light from the oncoming locomotive's huge headlight. The double-diesel coal hauler hurtled toward the crossing at full speed, filled with George County's black gold, heading for the power plants that would devour it.

The locomotive's blinding light rapidly neared the crossing, its horn sounding a frantic warning—clearly, the engineer had seen Shele's headlights. She stopped well back from the crossing, put the shifter in park, and waited, eyes shut tightly, hands over her ears. She could feel the rumble of the approaching evil giant. She hyperventilated, fought the queasiness in her stomach, clenched her fists so hard that her nails cut into palms, and gritted her teeth to the breaking point. Soon it would be over.

Then she felt a disconcerting bump. Puzzled, she looked to the rearview mirror. She gasped to see a large black pickup truck, its dark windows concealing the driver, almost touching her car. Again, more insistently, the big truck bumped the rear of her little compact, which began to move forward. Shele jammed both feet on the brake and struggled to put the shifter in reverse, but the truck relentlessly pushed, forcing her car toward the crossing, now only feet away, as the locomotive's blinding headlight came within a house-length, and the train's horn blasted continuously. The train's wheels shrieked as the engineer helplessly attempted to brake the demon's forward motion. Behind her, the truck's engine screamed and tires spun, spewing blue smoke, forcing her onto the tracks.

She started to scream, but the shrieking, smoking tires and screaming train brakes drowned any sound she could make. In an instant, 30 million pounds collided against her 2,500-pound compact, screeching metal on metal as the engine of her destruction carried her down the tracks from the crossing. It was a full quarter-mile before the train's crew finally stopped it, and the remains of Shele's car peeled from the front of the engine and rolled to rest beside a small stream.

The engineer and brakeman leaped from the cab, running toward what was left of the vehicle. The crumpled car embraced a crumpled Shele, who was still conscious, just barely. The trainmen could see anything they might do would be futile. They frantically tried to reassure her. "We called an ambulance! Don't worry miss, you'll be okay!"

Shele knew better and tried to speak. "The Araca... the kee... kiva... key... holy... Eden...you don't know... Eden... run... away..."

Then there was only darkness. The kind of darkness that ends all worldly pain, a place "whence no traveler can return."

CHAPTER FORTY-NINE

THERE'S NO WAY TO SOFTEN THIS

When the phone rang just as Eden was fixing breakfast, he fully expected to hear Shele's voice. However, it was Buckey.

"S'up, Buckey?"

"You need to get in here right away."

"Why? Is something wrong?"

"I'll tell you when you get here."

Driving in, he tried calling Shele but got her answering machine. He grew worried. He broke his own protocol and phoned Aingeal.

"I haven't heard from her," Aingeal said. "Why, is something wrong?"

"No," Eden answered. "I just thought maybe she was with you."

When Eden got to the office, Buckey opened the door for him—completely out of character for the Sheriff. "Sit down, Eden," he said gently.

Buckey cleared his throat. "Eden, there's no way to soften this. Shele Ocevan…"

"What about her?" Eden interjected, his heart instantly pounding, sensing the worst.

"Shele was on a back road up north of the county line early this morning. Her car was hit by a train at a crossing."

Eden turned white as he buried his face in his hands.

"She's dead, Eden. We talked with the engineer. He saw her car, blew the horn, tried to stop, but it was too late."

"Oh, God! Her car was stalled on the tracks?"

The Sheriff looked at the floor. "No, Eden. A truck pushed

her onto the tracks. The train crew saw it all. The son of a bitch deliberately pushed her into the path of that train."

Eden sat stunned, speechless, his mind racing.

"It happened around 4:15 this morning. An hour later, we found the truck a few miles away, burning. No plates. It's still too hot to read the VIN. But I'm sure it was stolen."

It was all too sudden, like being hit by a meteor in broad daylight. Eden felt shattered and numb. No feeling for taking revenge, no room for hate. Nothing...

"Eden, I know neither of you have any family... if there is anything I can do... I'm really—uh—very sorry. Ah shit Eden," Buckey sobbed.

The next few days for Eden were that foggy blur that we numbly march through following the death of a loved one. Buckey helped with arrangements. The memorial service included Shele's colleagues from Rainelle College, Eden's friends, and every law enforcement officer in the county. Shele had wished to be cremated, so now Eden had the ashes of both Shele and Amara McClure to remind him of the past year.

Despite his workaholic style, Eden began to neglect his job. That happened when Annie died, too, and Buckey had supported him until he got back on his feet. But this was nothing like that. Shele's death was somehow not palpable and his grief was different. Compared to losing Annie, he wasn't grieving at all, and that worried him.

Their June wedding... somehow he knew it really wasn't in the cards. They had made plans, but it never seemed real. Maybe it was denial; maybe subconsciously he felt a new marriage would betray Annie's memory. Eden felt inferior to Shele. They kidded a lot about his competence as a law officer, but in fact he was just a Deputy in a one-horse town. He never was fully convinced that the highly intelligent, exquisitely beautiful Shele Ocevan really wanted to spend her life with the person he knew himself to be.

Now he was the closest thing she had to a relative, so he became appointed to dispose of her belongings. She had no will, so anything of value would be auctioned, with the proceeds going to the state. He asked Aingeal to take care of Shele's personal stuff; he couldn't bear going through that experience again.

Aingeal agreed and added, "You know, Eden, I've had enough of Randy Winter and his Rune Goons and their wacky bullshit lodge. I'm returning to my old job in New York. With Shele gone, it's not the same—"

"Aingeal, you don't have to tell me it's not the same without Shele. I don't think anything will ever be the same. Aingeal, before you leave... could we talk about some things? Could we meet for lunch?"

Two days later, Aingeal called, packed and preparing to leave. They agreed to meet at the Interstate truck stop.

As he headed out the door, the phone rang again.

"Eden! Scotty McMillan!" Scotty ran a towing service, body shop, and junkyard. "Dan Brackenridge told me to call you—"

Eden scowled. "Hey Scotty, if it's another junker out in the west end, call Junior—"

"It ain't no car, Eden. I got a box of things from the trunk of that librarian's car. You know, the one that got hit by that train? Well, I got her stuff here, if you want to pick it up."

"Oh. Thanks, Scotty, I appreciate that. I'll be right out."

On his way to lunch with Aingeal, he stopped by Scotty's junkyard.

"It's over there," Scotty said, pointing with his cutting torch to what was left of her car. "It's in that'n—in the trunk—lid's popped." He adjusted his torch and resumed cutting.

Inside the squashed trunk was one of those plastic boxes with two lids that fold together to close over the top. The box was distorted from the impact. He forced up the lids. Sure enough, there was a shoebox with Shele's handwriting that announced the shoes were "MUDDERS."

Just like Shele to keep spare shoes in the car, he mused. There was a flashlight, a few books, a notebook, some magazines, and other papers buried beneath. He put the box under the cover of the pickup and headed for the Interstate.

When he arrived at the truck stop, Aingeal was already in a booth in the back.

They chatted awhile about not much of anything. And then the conversation turned to what little she knew of Shele and how they had met. For Eden, this was way too painful and he wanted to avoid it. Sensing that, she shifted to her experience with Randy Winter.

"Randy was really kind of sweet, not that I wanted anything long-term with him. On one level he was okay; on another, he left me cold. I got the feeling he cared a great deal more for me than I felt for him, but so it goes. Don't get me wrong—I'm not a heartless bitch, I let him down easy. I told him I had to get back to New York, and he should see other people. I didn't say it that way, but you know what I mean."

"Yeah, I've heard that one."

Then she talked about the Rigdonites. To anyone that learned of their existence, they called it Lodge of the Runes. But to the members, it was the Rigdon Tabernacle. As it turned out, they actually did call themselves Rigdonites.

Aingeal believed that Philastus Hurlbut was the mysterious Walter Rigdon, and he was the legitimate founder of the group—if there was anything legitimate in the whole thing. The group insisted that Hurlbut was related—by some spiritual relationship—to Sidney Rigdon.

Philastus Hurlbut, or Walter Rigdon, or whoever the hell he was, had rigged a site near a fort where someone would "discover" the runes. That done, he was on his way to forming a New World/Lost Tribes religion. Eden figured that's why he took on the Walter Rigdon persona, to align himself in people's minds with Sidney. With a little knowledge of electricity and basic physics, he was a notch above the average southwestern Pennsylvania bumpkin of the nineteenth century and was able, like a modern televangelist, to flimflam the faithful. The only trouble was that the faithful lacked wealth. They were dirt farmers and small-town merchants so the "church" was doomed to similar poverty.

Aingeal went on, "The Rigdonites are a hodgepodge of Pre-Columbian Indian stuff, Aztec, Inca, Anazai, Adena, Hopewell — along with a liberal sprinkling of Mormonism. In the '60s or '70s — probably to boost membership — someone threw in Carlos Castaneda and some of his bullshit. The Mormon part is why I believe the Hurlbut heresy theory," she said.

"I'm sorry I wasn't able to come up with more than occasional use of peyote, Eden. In all, they seem to be a pretty benign bunch. A bit kinky, but just a gathering of late-blooming flower children. I think you'll find a similar population in any remote area. Harmless to a fault."

Eden thought otherwise, but said nothing.

She learned from Andy that the group met sporadically to perform ceremonies of "the Ancients." They also would observe celestial phenomena through the year, nibble some peyote buttons, have visions, and dabble in the paranormal and occult.

"When those silo slits aligned with celestial objects, they performed ceremonies and made offerings — and no, I couldn't find evidence of hearts being removed or animal sacrifice. I think Randy would shit himself if he saw a drop of blood. He was a real pansy when it came to that. And, on the topic of pansy, I never figured out if he was bi or not, but I suspect he was.

"There is one thing though," she said thoughtfully.

"What's that?"

"Remember that alignment of planets we talked about, the one that will only happen three times in the next century? Evidently that is a big deal with them. No one, and I mean no one, would talk about it. Believe me, I tried to pry it out of Randy at really opportune moments, when his defenses were down."

So there it was. The Rigdonites seemed like just another bunch of nut bars who would get together for fun, fellowship, hocus-pocus, voodoo, or whatever their shtick was. Getting into the group's inner circle was kinkier than some clubs, but considering the backwater they came from, what else did they have for entertainment?

"Oh, and I just remembered—there may be others."

"Others?"

"Other Rigdonite groups, other members somewhere else, I'm not sure. All I know is that one time when Randy and Ted were together, Ted mentioned something about others in upstate New York. I got the impression some drifted up to the Rochester area in the early 1900s. But when I asked, they shrugged it off and seemed get a little agitated, so I didn't pursue it. But who knows—maybe I'll write a book."

Then they talked about Shele, sharing their admiration for her, and noting the frustration over her murder—no leads thus far—the truck indeed was stolen and no other evidence was found at the scene. When Eden and Aingeal parted, Eden couldn't know it would be the last time he would see her.

In a funk, Eden went home, pulled into the garage, removed the plastic box from the back of his pickup, and placed it on a shelf at the rear of the garage. Later he would be unable to recall doing that. He immediately went to the bedroom and lay down on the bed and went into a sound, dreamless sleep.

CHAPTER FIFTY

A LARGE PLASTIC BOX

June came, then July. The late July rains for which Rainelle was famous arrived and lingered to steam up an August that ended with cool breezes foretelling early fall. Months had passed since Shele departed, but a cloying emptiness remained, an emptiness he never felt after Annie's passing. It hung on, a loneliness hadn't felt before, lingering through the fall and chilly winter.

March's lion-like winds roared down from Canada and cut into Eden's bones before his depression lifted. It must have been the anniversary of the Myra Kinchloe's disappearance that brought it all back into focus.

A vague feeling had been haunting him—a feeling that Joey Dulaney was responsible only for the death of Pamela Brookover, and that Shele's Aunt did not commit suicide. He still felt that Joey admitted to the other three girls' killings to enhance his psychotic scheme to escape a death sentence.

He remembered having a dream that included someone knocking at the back door. He awakened and still half-asleep, at 3:30 a.m., he stumbled for the door and found the swing that Dave Quinn had made moving in the March wind and tapping the side of the house. He suddenly remembered that he didn't put the damned thing away for the winter. Now, he would have to refinish the swing before using it this coming summer.

Thinking of the garage struck another chord. It was at that moment that he was consumed by a need to touch something that had been Shele's. When he put her box of things in the garage, he knew he would not do anything with her belongings. It was a form of denial. He didn't want the memories, the pain of touching things that reminded him of her. But all of that suddenly changed, and he felt a powerful need to connect with what little he had that remained of her.

Still in a T-shirt and pajama bottoms, he slipped on old loafers and ran to the garage, the brisk March wind blowing in his face. The plastic box was where he left it. He grabbed it up and raced the weather for the house. He placed it on an end table near the sofa and quickly cleared the coffee table so he could lay out its contents.

For some strange reason he had difficulty bringing himself to open the lid. For some time, he sat, staring at the box as though it were a Pandoran container. However, once opened, he couldn't wait to get at the contents. He set the shoebox aside and lifted out a round cookie tin. Next were some magazines, and under them a book. It was an early stained, weathered copy of *Manuscript Found.* There also were copies of *The Old Straight Track*, and *Journey to Ixtlan*, and the entire text of *The Teachings of Don Juan: a Yaqui Way of Knowledge.* Down under that was a newspaper with headlines that read, "Third Co-Ed Found in Gamelands." He found a fat, hefty legal envelope with a tie of ribbons around it. A peek inside revealed 200 to 300 pages of lined notepaper, filled with the unmistakable, diminutive handwriting of Amara McClure.

After adjusting the lamp, he laid the envelope on the table beside the sofa. He settled back into a sofa cushion, took a deep breath, and began to read. And the first thing he read was, "This document to be placed in my deposit box and read only in the event of my demise."

An instant chill struck Eden, an ominous foreboding, a tightening in his stomach. Jesus, he thought. Was the note instructions to her attorney, or someone else? And how did it come to be in Shele Ocevan's car? He began to read.

"This is an attempt to explain my demise, which is imminent. That being said, let me make clear that life is not so dear to me. I am nearing old age and have lived what I experienced to the full. I have nothing to leave, I have no living relatives, so there is no need for a will."

Odd, your niece Shele is a living relative, even if you didn't see her often, Eden thought. The oversight must have been a lapse on Amara's part.

If that wasn't jarring enough, the next page began with, "My Involvement in Rigdonism." For the next several pages, Amara explained how she had been recruited in her thirties. Oddly, or perhaps not so oddly, she did not mention her initiation or the rites.

A lengthy history of the founding of the Rigdonites followed. It agreed with what Eden, Shele, and Aingeal had figured out, and added some apocryphal embellishments as it went. Even after her death, Amara planned to make the whole thing sound a lot better than it was. She devoted several pages to some "ancient astronauts" nonsense, trying to establish a link between them, the Anazai, and the lost tribes.

Eden disciplined himself to keep reading thoroughly, even as his mind raced ahead, impatient to get to the part in which Amara felt endangered. And it was a good thing he kept reading diligently, for he might have missed the introduction to that section. It began with blather about the alignment that must have happened around St. Patrick's Day.

"The time of the celestial alignment was drawing near and a suitable suppliant had not been found. If the ritual were to have efficacy, the subject would have to be "true of heart," and young, not past the age of 25."

She used at least a full page to deride modern society and its morals—along with the inability of the group to find a suitably chaste suppliant.

"I know from personal and direct knowledge that Theodore Dunlow said for us not to worry, if push came to shove and we couldn't find anyone, he would arrange for one of the co-eds he knew to be a stand-in. Let it be known if there is anyone who is blameworthy in all of this, it is Mr. Dunlow."

Next, she went on to explain the importance of the celestial alignment rites. Apparently no one really knew the origin of this liturgy, but the idea was that there would be one last occasion during the lifetimes of the group's members when the alignment would occur. Therefore, there was a great immediacy. Amara wrote that she did not know if Dunlow had panicked, or if it was his plan all along. Nonetheless, at the appropriate time, he produced the goods.

"I saw Mr. Dunlow, Mr. Winter, and Mr. Walbridge bring a young woman who was in some sort of stuporous state to the meeting that was held that momentous night. Although I have no direct knowledge of them placing the woman on the Ark, I do know they took her to the room for that purpose.

"According to our teachings, any woman who was without sin, who is placed on the Ark during the alignment, would be physically transmogrified into Makya, the princess of peace who would rule the earth for the next 100 years. We were so instructed by the Glorious Teacher, Reverend Rigdon, and there was no doubt that this would happen, since he has predicted all other world events with great accuracy. This is not an item to be taken lightly, and it is not something to be taken on faith alone. It is a very real occurrence.

"This would be the final repudiation of all other false religions and philosophies and the establishment of the Rigdon Tabernacle as the true followers of the Great Spirit. Makya would be his representative on earth until 100 years passed and the next alignment ensued.

"We are also reminded that if a suppliant who has committed the sin of adultery is placed on the Ark she would be terribly punished, and if this were to happen at the time of the alignment, the punishment could be death."

Unfortunately, it didn't quite work out the way they planned. Evidently, Ted Dunlow had slipped Myra Kinchloe a drug—probably mescaline and who knows what else. Then he and his buddies, Andy and Randy, had taken her to the barn and plopped her on the Ark. What happened next is unclear, because Amara didn't see it, but it's not hard to imagine.

"The next time I saw Miss Kinchloe, she was being carried, nude and lifeless, through the sanctuary to a room at the rear. There was the smell of burning hair and there seemed to be smoke rising from the back of her head."

It was apparent, at least to Eden, they put her on the Ark and contact was made between the nose of the forward angel, one of the terminals connected to the Leyden jar, and to an earth ground, the other terminal, which was the function of the second angel. She was placed between the contacts—with one of them well implanted—of the Leyden jar and at some point was electrocuted when it arced over. Now, whether any of this was due to the alignment, the line that ran from the barn to Chaco, piezoelectric energy from tectonic plates, or some sort of other charge they stored in the Leyden jar, no one would ever know. But Eden suspected psychic energy or paranormal forces had little to do with it.

Of course, there is no way to know if Myra was dead when she was taken from the Ark. She may have been rendered unconscious in much the same way a stun gun knocks out a would-be attacker. She may have been in a coma for a short time and died later. No one would ever know.

"I know that Mr. Dunlow and others conferred and I heard them say they would have to consult with the Venerated Masters. The

Masters are among the older members of a group located at one of the Tabernacles somewhere in Upstate New York.

"I have no direct evidence, but from what I could learn, it was decided that although the incident was accidental, the implications for the group were considered so dire that it would have to be managed by the Elders. According to rumors, two or three people from New York came down to dispose of the body. I remember the name Stroheim."

At that point, Eden felt an electrical charge that would have rivaled the Ark at full tilt. He remembered Amara's "friends," Erich and Norma. From one standpoint it was unbelievable, but from another, it made perfect sense. Amara's Stroheim had to be Eric Strohman.

The Masters, or their agents, had put Myra back into her clothes, took her body out to the gamelands pond and blew out the back of her skull out to cover the electrical contact that led to her death. So, Joey Dulaney probably had nothing to do with Myra's death. She was murdered by some of Rainelle's finest citizens through their zany pseudo-religious nonsense club. And the second and third murders may have been to cover the first.

By now, Eden was convinced she had written these pages as a suicide letter. It was part apologia, part justification, and part final attempt at redemption—her legacy. Amara had made a determined effort to mislead them in their early attempts to find Myra. She was an accessory to what had happened, but she was dead now, far from the reach of the law.

And why were Amara's notes in the trunk of Shele's car? Had she removed them from the loose-leaf binder to cover her aunt Amara's activities? He recalled that Shele had invited him to search her house—but of course, not her car.

313

CHAPTER FIFTY-ONE

VICTORIAN DIAMONDS

Eden pondered how to present this case to Buckey. He could just imagine telling the Sheriff about a secret cult that had existed under his big nose for all his life. The case had the ambiance of *Invaders from Mars*, and Eden had the feeling of being on his own—like the child who knows the town has been invaded by martians and only he knows there are aliens among the everyday folks. He doesn't know who they are and no one will believe his story.

Eden could imagine telling the Sheriff how a cult had accidentally killed Brad Kinchloe's daughter and covered up her death by making it appear to be a murder. Worse yet, he would have to convince the D.A. that she should prosecute several upstanding voters of Rainelle and then dig up the Joey Dulaney murders all over again. He would have to present a case that would, at best, lead to an accidental manslaughter conviction for several of the town's professional people. And after that he would have to convince her to involve another state to find two people who probably had disappeared into an underground religious cult by now. And all of this in an election year. Worst of all, Eden would have to convince Buckey and everyone else that all this really happened and that he wasn't some kind of conspiracy nut.

His head reeled, overwhelmed by paranoia. Who knows, maybe Aingeal wasn't a helpful angel but a demon sent by lodge elders to divert the investigation. Wasn't she from Upstate New York? But that couldn't be, she was a friend of Shele's.

Suddenly, his mind returned to Shele. Going through the rest of her effects, he found clippings about the murders and the Dulaney hearings. He found magazines, a peyote button, and a tin container with crochet hooks, bobbie pins, and interestingly, a single skeleton key. He found an old, stained *New Yorker* magazine that didn't have anything to do with anything.

Finally, his eye was drawn to the shoebox on which Shele had written, "MUDDERS." He didn't think he particularly wanted to see an item that was so personally Shele's, but nevertheless, he somewhat reluctantly opened the box. Inside were some well-worn sneakers, no doubt her second—emergency—pair. Overcome with grief he had not been able to release, he picked them up and held them to his breast as a child would hug a precious doll. Weeping, Eden Whitloe held them there, staring into space and remembering the summer day she returned to Random Creek. It was the day she came running to him after she had been away so long. Tears were now streaming down his cheeks.

For whatever reason, he happened to look down to where he had been holding the shoes against him. Had he hugged them too tightly, could a bruise have formed on his arm so quickly? Of course not. It was only tears mixed with the dirt from the bottoms of the shoes—coal dust.

Daniel I. Morris is a retired college professor, newspaper publisher, artist, and writer. He lives with his wife Barbara in Southwestern Pennsylvania and they winter in central Florida.